THE WILL OF GOD!

Paul J. Walkowski

Branden Publishing Company

Library of Congress Cataloging in Publication Data

Walkowski; Paul Joseph, 1945 —
    The Will of God.

    I Title.
    PF35730.A42548W55 1988   813'.54   87-32578
    ISBN 0-8283-1917-0

Branden Publishing Co.
17 Station Street
Box 843 Brookline Village
Boston, MA 02147

For My Parents

Acknowledgements

There are several people I want to thank for the time and effort they invested in making this, my first novel, a reality. Thanks to Darlene, Anita, Jo and Don for reading the manuscript, proofing and commenting honestly on its contents. Thanks to J.C. Productions for their patience and kind attention to detail, and for caring about me and my work. Thanks to Florence for helping in the editing. Thanks to Mary, Don and Tom, for believing in me and for their contributions. Thanks to my publisher, Adolpho Caso, for having the confidence in this new author, and for making his offices available to me on request. And a very special thanks to my nephew, Tommy, whose fertile imagination, ideas, patience and encouraging comments at every step along the way made this book a reality.

Preface

Although this work is fiction I have taken the care and liberty of including certain factual places, people and events in the plot to heighten suspense and add an air of realism to the story. For instance: The drug war occurring in Boston in 1985 is factual. Its connection to the fictional character Carlos Ortega is not.

The town of Tingo Maria in Peru is an actual town noted for its drug trade. *The Fortress in the Forest*, however, is fictional. Most of what is said throughout the book regarding the drug trade and the drug kings is factual, based upon weekly newsmagazine reports researched during the writing of this book. The massacre at Huallaga Valley in Peru is factual, although Carmen's parents, being fictional characters, were not actually murdered in that raid.

Events such as the assassination of Colombian Justice Minister Bonilla, the bombing of the American Embassy in Bogota, and the wild gun fight in Guadalajara, Mexico between police and drug runners are true events.

As for the leftist groups, the *Shining Path*, *Red Fatherland* and *M19*, these groups are real, and although not involved in any of the events leading to the murder of Carlos Ortega, are as dangerous and active in the revolutionary struggle in South America as I say they are. As for their involvement in the drug trade, it is clear their influence is growing.

Juan Ramon Matta Ballesterous is a real person, and his involvement in the murder of Drug Enforcement Agent Enrique Salazar is a matter of record. His two associates, Quintero and Carillo are real people, although their involvement in *The Will of God* conspiracy is purely fictional.

Pablo Escobar Gaviria is a real person, and his connection to the drug trade is factual. He does, indeed, control a drug army estimated to be 2,000 strong.

Drug King Roberto Suarez Gomez is also a real person, and he is known to hire Libyan hit squads and assassins to protect his vital interests.

To the best of my knowledge there is no society or group known as *The Will Of God*. And any connection to additional characters created in this novel from that group, or any additional characters created to heighten suspense, are purely fictional, and any resemblance they may have to any individuals living or dead is purely coincidental.

Foreward

Tingo Maria, Peru, 1910

The murder of Colonel Garcia Lopez on a quiet Friday morning, June 27, 1910, was brutal and ruthlessly executed.

Garcia's death is pertinent to everything which follows, since it marks the ascendancy to promience of one of the most sinister organized crime societies in all of South America, the *Voluntad de Dios*, and the rise to power of one of the most influential and ruthless Mafiosos bosses of all time, Simon Gabriel de San Martin. As much as anyone, this is his story also.

On the morning of his death, Colonel Garcia sat serenely at a sidewalk cafe in the heart of the small town of Tingo Maria. He was sipping a cup of coffee, waiting patiently for his monthly *remittance* from the local merchants — a payoff actually. A just desert, he figured, for the *protection* afforded the peasants of this poor farming town.

The protection money was to be delivered by a courier hired by local merchants. The routine was well established, and proceeded this way without incident, except once, every week for the past three years. Garcia would arrive at the cafe with his men, they would sip coffee while sitting at a table closest the street, and wait.

The men exuded confidence, and a certain arrogance born of unbridled power. They didn't mind being observed. Indeed, they wanted the townspeople to take notice of their arrival.

Garcia and his men were well known to the people of the region — and universally disliked. They took women when it suited them, intimidated men, fondled children — girls especially — and were a menace to the public safety. They were also members of the local security force assigned to protect the region.

And they were punctual — especially when it came to collecting their debts.

Their predictability would be their downfall.

With his feet stretched leisurely in front, and body turned sideways, right elbow resting on the table, Garcia leaned back in his chair, tilting his head slightly to catch the early morning rays of the sun. His two companions were equally relaxed. Although bodyguards, they acted bored and disinterested in what little activity existed in the town at this early morning hour. One shuffled lazily through a deck of cards; the other sat with his arms folded in front, hat pulled down over his brow as if to shield his eyes from the glare of the sun's rays, his head bobbing slightly as he fought to ward off the sleepiness overcoming him.

It was nine twenty-eight. At exactly nine thirty a boy would arrive, bow respectfully from the waist, and wish Colonel Garcia a good morning. He would place a small cloth sack on the table, step back, and wait anxiously, not taking his leave until dismissed, until the money was weighed.

For his part, Garcia would always sneer at the courrier, for he held the people of this small farming community in utter contempt, and he enjoyed intimidating them — even their children. Only when he was satisfied the merchants had given all that was expected of them would he allow the messenger to depart.

Once, when he only *thought* he was being cheated, he shot a merchant point blank in the face. He did it so casually, it terrified the people for months, and the incident lived in their minds for years afterward. Farmers are no match for armed soldiers.

On the day of that shooting the courrier had delivered the money as instructed. Garcia lifted the bag in the palm of his hand, mentally weighing its contents, as was his usual practice. He jiggled the bag once, then twice, then three times. And his brow arched. The bag was light — he thought.

"Where is the rest?" Garcia growled, his eyes betraying the evil inside.

"I know nothing Señor. I am only the courrier," the youth said, his voice trembling as he spoke.

"Did you spend it?" Garcia taunted menacingly.

"Oh, no, Señor Garcia, I would not do that," the boy answered anxiously.

"Did you buy yourself a young girl? Heh?" Garcia said as he reached for the boy's groin. The guards thought this amusing and held the boy by the elbows, preventing him from backing away.

"Señor, please. I did not take your money," the boy said, jumping back, clutching at his crotch.

"Then you know some of it is missing?" Garcia was no longer smiling.

"The merchants, señor, their business has not been good, please," the boy pleaded.

Garcia ordered the boy closer, signalling that he wanted to whisper something in his ear. When the boy's head lowered, Garcia whispered, "Fetch me the owner of this slop house."

The boy bowed nervously, then did as he was told. Moments later the owner of the Cafe approached the table apprehensively, his hands outstretched, "Señor Garcia, I. . ."

A shot exploded abruptly, terminating the explanation in midsentence. The owner fell dead where he stood. "Let this be a lesson," Garcia said to the horrified witnesses as he placed his revolver casually back in its holster and turned to walk away. "If you do not pay for protection," he said instructively,"how can you expect to receive protection?"

It served as a frightening lesson — for a while.

After three years, the people of Tingo Maria were tired. Garcia and his men would not go away. Indeed, as time passed, the abuses seemed to multiply. Garcia could not be pacified nor paid off. He could not be reasoned with nor appealed to. Always he wanted protection money. Always those who disagreed with Garcia would disappear, or their wives and daughters would be raped. And always Garcia would arrive a day or two later to lecture the people of the small town about the need for protection from such ruthless bandits. But everyone knew who the real bandits were. And they feared them.

After weeks of heated discussion and debate, the merchants decided to call upon a local outlaw known only as Ramon. Word of his daring raids on government outposts, and of his valiant struggle to free his people from the terror of the hated security forces inspired peasants of the region. It also blinded them to the rumors of his own savagery and brutal suppression of opponents.

The message from the merchants of Tingo Maria implored Ramon to visit Tingo Maria, to rid the town of the vermin Garcia. It was a simple and straight-forward message, more or less. The townspeople wanted Ramon to kill Garcia and his guards, and to dispose of the bodys far outside the town's limits. Then, they wanted Ramon to leave them in peace.

Ramon received the message, and accepted the offer. But planned his own place and method of execution.

On the morning of Garcia's death Ramon rode leisurely into town with his son Simon Gabriel by his side. They tethered their horses to a hitch across the street from where Garcia and his men sat. Their arrival drew barely a glance from the unsuspecting soldiers, but gasps of horror from local merchants who hid inside when word of Ramon's arrival was made known to them.

Ramon drew a deep breath as he patted his son's shoulder. "Shall we do business before or after breakfast?" he said as he casually adjusted his pants and gazed in the direction of the morning sun.

Simon Gabriel glanced carefully around the small town. "We are being watched, father," he remarked casually.

"I know," his father whispered, as he wiped a bead of sweat from his brow. "Those are the soldiers over there," he said, nodding over his shoulder at the resting men.

With his back toward Garcia, Simon Gabriel reached under his cloth shirt and removed a silver revolver from inside his pants. "There are other people there, father," he said, nodding discreetly toward several residents sitting near the front entrance to the cafe. "What should we do with them?"

"They are of no concern to us," Ramon said. "Unless they interfere."

Simon Gabriel nodded.

"I think we should do it now," Ramon said, matter-of-factly.

Garcia was sunning his face. His eyes were closed. The bodyguard facing the street had his hat drawn over his eyes and his head was bobbing, his eyes were also closed. The third man sat with his back to the street. He was flipping nonchalantly through a deck of cards. The heat of the sun beating down on his back caused him to remove his hat, allowing it to hang temptingly, like a large bullseye, covering the exact point where the bandoleers strapped over his shoulders intersected. That's where the first bullet found its mark. The bullet hit with such impact that it passed through his spinal cord and heart, out his chest, and through the center of the table before falling into the dirt. The motion of the projectile caused the first guard to lunge violently forward and fall over the surface of the table, his arms spread-eagled across its surface.

Women screamed and children wept in horror. And terrified merchants stepped nervously outside their stores, driven by curiousity to witness the gruesome execution they hoped would not occur in their town.

The second guard jumped from his chair and stumbled backward erratically, knocking the table forward as he stood. His movements were awkward and confused. Another loud crack from Simon's gun signalled the death of the second guard who was tossed back across a second table when the .45 slug shattered his chest bone, exploding his heart, killing him instantly.

Garcia, who was leaning back in his chair when the first thunderous explosion ripped through the inside of his first bodyguard, fell fully backward when the second slug entered the chest of the remaining guard. Garcia was flat on his back, feet sticking up over the edges of the chair, unable and afraid to move.

"Señor. . .," he pleaded as he tried to look into the face of the outlaw Ramon. Garcia raised his hand to shield the sun from his eyes. "What is this about? Do you know who I am?" he said as he wiggled nervously to free himself from his exposed position. "You will pay with your life for this insolence," he threatened, hoping to intimidate his assailant.

Ramon smiled, raised his gun, and without a word shot Colonel Garcia in the wrist. "Ayeee. . ." Garcia screamed in pain as blood spurted uncontrollably from the severed artery. His movements were more frantic now as he kicked the chair forward and struggled to stand.

Again, witnesses cried in horror as they huddled in a small cluster away from the shooting, fully expecting they would be the next to die.

Blood mixed with yellow dirt in front of the Cafe as the final moments of Garcia's life played out for all to see.

His wounded hand dangled grotesquely against his chest, soiling his dirty brown shirt with fresh blood.

Garcia was now on his feet, weak and dizzy from the loss of blood. "You shall pay for this. . ." he snarled arrogantly, not knowing who he was addressing. "You shall pay for this," he cried, as he moved toward Ramon.

"And you can go to hell," Ramon said coldly.

Another shot. And Garcia was knocked backward and off his feet again. It was a belly wound — fatal, painful and bloody. Garcia was alive but motionless. His eyes wide, he watched in shock and disbelief as his intestines pushed against the hole in his belly, oozing inch by inch through the opening which tore sideways and across his stomach.

Ramon stood silently and watched his victim die.

"You will say nothing," Simon Gabriel instructed one of the terrified witnesses as he pressed a sharp knife into the man's ribs. "When you are questioned by the security forces tomorrow, you will tell them you made a mistake," he said as he gazed toward the crowd, his eyes wild, face flushed. "You will tell them you were confused," he said excitedly. "And when they ask you how Garcia died. . ." he said, pausing, "you will shrug your shoulders and tell them you don't remember."

"But Señor, they know I saw your father shoot Garcia," the man said. The *they* he was referring to were the other villagers who would surely shift the burden of responsibility onto *his* shoulders, hoping they might escape the wrath of the security forces which was sure to follow. "I saw this with my own eyes — and the government will know this. They will send me to jail, or worse if I don't cooperate." Wiping a bead of sweat from his brow he pleaded for understanding — but received none. "Señor, please. What am I to say when they ask me how Garcia died? Am I to say it was simply . . . *The Will of God?*"

Simon Gabriel thought for a moment and smiled. "That is exactly what you are to tell them if you want to see your wife and daughters again. All of you," he shouted as he turned, and waving his gun at the growing crowd of onlookers, addressed the townspeople and their families, menacingly. "When you are questioned by the security forces about how Garcia died, you will tell them Garcia died because it was *The Will of God*, and nothing more. Do you understand?" he repeated. "He died because it was *The Will of God!*"

1
The Parting

Friday, May 17 1985

BOSTON, 4:50 A.M. This was going to be an important day in the life of Carlos Ortega. Perhaps the most important day in his life. Two weeks after learning that a contract had been issued for his life, Carlos Ortega was going to confess his sins. And they were many.

This confession, however, would be like no other. For today Carlos Ortega would make a very special deal with his God. In return for eternal salvation, Carlos Ortega would tell his friend — his bishop, everything he knew of the *Voluntad de Dios*, and of the unthinkable sin about to be committed by an organized crime society with the sinisterly disarming name, the society of *The Will of God*!

Yes, Carlos Ortega was a religious man. Like most of his countrymen he was a devout catholic. At least he thought of himself as a good catholic. He was also a murderer, a terrorist, a rapist, a drug smuggler — and probably all those things his enemies accused him of — and much more.

But if he was a rapist, he rationalized, the women deserved raping. Indeed, in earlier days, rape was not so much a violent act, or even an act of passion, as much as it was a definitive statement to those who stood in his way. Nothing was sacred where business was involved. Not women. Not children. No one. If you were an enemy of the *society*, you would either be killed or taught a terrible lesson. There was no gray area. And he taught many lessons.

And the men he killed? Well, they probably deserved to die anyway. After all, they would have killed him had they the opportunity.

"This — is justice," he would always remark, pausing momentarily between the words *This* and *justice* before shooting his victims squarely between the eyes. That's how he liked to do it. Face to face. No last cigarette. No chance for mercy. And he believed with his heart and soul that justice prevailed each time a victim's brain exploded inside his head.

And as for the charge that he was the driving force behind *Los Grandes Mafiosos*, the South American equivalent of the American mafia, well, that's not the kind of thing one discussed in public.

This — is justice? he asked of himself as he lay in bed this morning, reflecting on his life, practicing his last confession on what he never guessed would be the last day of his life.

Bless me father for I have sinned, he pleaded to himself with great emotion, eyes tightly closed, squinting, hands folded over his chest, internalizing powerful emotions, pushing his thoughts right through the pearly gates. Past the objections of those he murdered. Past the skeletons and ghosts of innocent people whose lives were lost after they were ruined by his damnable trade.

But God would have to listen to *this* appeal, he reasoned. After all, this confession was going to cost him his life. For the word was given that Carlos Ortega must be dealt with — severely. And for anyone who could bring Carlos back, or prove that his death was a prolonged, brutal and particularly painful one, the reward would be handsome.

It was exactly two weeks ago that Carlos learned of this contract. And he knew his days were numbered just as surely as he knew that his last confession would have to work. *Voluntad de Dios* knew where he was — Boston. Knew what he knew — everything. Knew what damage he could cause if he told what he knew — Irreparable. And knew what they had to do to stop him — Murder him!

From the eastern slopes of the Andes, in what many DEA agents referred to as "A little shit hole of a town" called *The White City* — Tingo Maria, home of the cocaine trade in Peru — and vital link in a much larger chain which spread across Bolivia and Colombia, the word was given that Carlos Ortega *must* be dealt with. And everyone knew what *that* meant. You break the silence, you die! This — is justice!

I have given my life, dear Jesus, he begged. *Grant me forgiveness. Forgive my sins.*

The sound of thunder outside his window caused Carmen to rustle beside him. Carlos gazed at her sleek, smooth body. And all thoughts of confession vanished as he relished the sight of her nakedness beside him. It may have been bitter and damp outside, but the room was warm. And both he and Carmen lay beneath only a sheet, which now half-covered her sleeping form.

Though only sixteen years old Carmen had endeared herself to Carlos as few women he had ever known. She had an innocence about herself; yet she was mature for her youth. And her physical presence aroused in Carlos Ortega a passion surpassing anything he felt for any other woman.

Carmen was also his confident. Not well educated, if you measure education on the basis of formal schooling. But she was wise in the ways of the world: compassionate, warm, sensitive and trusted.

By the end of the day only she and his bishop would know what he knew. And before the end of the weekend only she would be alive to tell the story. Thus, her fate was inexorably linked to his, and the events which were to follow.

But the day was young. And the gentle, smooth, sensuous curves of her olive colored back and firm, round buttocks, sensually highlighted by the intermittent flashes of grayish early morning lightning, caused warm waves of passion to build gradually in Carlos' loins, and fill his mind with only *one* thought as he anticipated making love to her from behind this last day of his life.

Another roll of thunder caused her to stir once again, but this time the hint of a good morning smile passed between them, and Carlos fulfilled his anticipations before they both fell into a deep, satisfying sleep.

By mid-morning, the storm which had been battering New England for three days was at its fury. And the intermittent, muffled rolls of thunder, and dull flashes of lightning which encored their lovemaking earlier, were more ominous now, joined by a blinding rainfall which furiously battered the windows and sides of the boarding house in which they were staying. A portent of things to come, Carlos mused as he rose quietly from the warmth of the bed, careful not to disturb Carmen.

He walked across the room and stood motionless by the window, thinking of nothing in particular, just mesmerized by the rhythm of the storm's incessant pounding. He was naked. A silent flash of lightning startled him. He turned to face Carmen. She looked so peaceful and inviting — and warm. He released a long sigh as he realized that the time had arrived when he must prepare a letter to a friend he hadn't seen in many years. Slipping into a pair of shorts, Carlos sat at a small table by the window and struggled to compose his thoughts. After several moments he began his final communication.

My Dearest Friend Rivero, he began, searching for the right words to tell his story.

I trust and pray this letter finds you safe and in good health. Please forgive the long absence between my correspondence. When you read the diary attached with this letter, however, you will understand why I had to place such distance between us. And why I sent you to America so long ago.

Carlos paused and stared at Carmen, who had turned, and was now sleeping on her back. Her breasts, and smooth firm belly exposed outside the sheets.

A young girl by the name of Carmen Velasco Terry Ortega, my beloved wife, stands before you now. I love her with every ounce of life and spirit which remains in my body. She knows everything about me and can be trusted completely. Indeed, if it were not for Carmen, I would not be alive to write you today.

Carlos paused and gazed at Carmen again. She looked so soft and innocent beneath the covers. How he wished he could have spared her this final ordeal.

Years ago when I was a boy, he wrote, slowly measuring his words, *Simon Gabriel entrusted my life to your caring hands, and you served him well. You and Manuel were my guardian angels. I now ask you to assume the same responsibility for Carmen's care. Look after her my friend. Protect her until she is old enough to fully understand what has happened — and why. Her life in America will not be an easy one. It will be different and difficult. And she will need time to assimilate into the American culture. By my final actions I hope to have bought her that time. I know that under your care she will grow into a fine young lady of wealth and influence.*

Carmen is both an orphan and a widow, he wrote sorrowfully. *Her parents were murdered by the Maoist Shining Path guerrilla movement. They were among those butchered last year in a raid on an American-sponsored cocaine-eradication camp in the Huallaga Valley. I am sure you read about the massacre in your papers. She has no family, Rivero. Soon she will not even have me.* Carlos paused again to clear a thin film of tear from his eyes.

I have provided Carmen with enough money so she will never need for anything. And I have arranged through the regular channels for her fortune to be safe and protected from loss. Her accounts are part of this letter, which I am certain will be my Last Will and Testament. Rivero, I ask that you hold these numbers separately, and on her behalf. And that at the proper time you relinquish to her what I have bequeathed.

I have so much to say, he continued, feeling melancholy and sad, *and so little time to say it. My heart is filled with sorrow, and I am despondent over the events of the past few weeks.* Carlos could not have anticipated the pain he would feel as he wrote this letter. And for the first time, he actually doubted the wisdom of his delay.

Please forgive me for not informing you sooner, he wrote, *but Manuel, your brother, was murdered a month ago by the same treacherous group which killed Carmen's parents.* Carlos paused and sighed. *I cannot begin to tell you of the loss I have suffered as a result of this. He died in my arms and I wept like a baby when he gasped his last breath. Both you and Manuel were like fathers to me — but I need not tell you that.*

Times have changed, Manuel. You must know this by now. It's not like the old days when we conducted business for our own material wealth and physical pleasure. It is no longer the Voluntad de Dios as we knew it. Influence from the Russians and Cubans has spread like cancer throughout the region, and everything is so ideologically motivated now. Greed and lust for power have been replaced with greed and lust for power and intense class hatred. And not just among our own people, but throughout all of South and Central America. And the disease spreads daily. Our economies and people are hopelessly out of control, influenced by the socialist movements which have driven us to the brink — both economically and socially.

It was not The Will of God that events turned out the way they did, Carlos wrote underlying the last point. He knew Rivero would understand. *I fought to prevent it from happening, but could not stop the decay from occurring throughout the country. It was only a matter of time before the thinking of the younger members was influenced. And now they have taken over. Our numbers have diminished of late. Manuel was one of the last of the original founders.* Carlos interrupted his task once again to compose his thoughts. Much of what he was writing was already in the diary. He stood and stretched, staring out the window, then at Carmen. His thoughts racing back through the years. When his mind cleared he sat down again and continued. *I am sorry for rambling and burdening you with the sad details of our demise. But you and I are the last of the original group — and soon I will be gone.*

Your services are needed in another important matter. As I write this letter Enrique's life is in mortal danger. When I discovered what the Shining Path planned I was shocked, as you can well imagine, since they know nothing of my connection with this holy man. As you read the diary you will see why I decided to leave Peru and travel to America with Carmen. Why I must go to Enrique and tell him personally and ask his forgiveness. Why I must cleanse myself of this treacherous sin about to be committed by my own creation, and why I must ask God for his forgiveness also.

Whether I am successful or not, he wrote, *you must deliver the diary to Mr. Walter Pendleton, head of the United States Drug Enforcement Agency. You must also see to it that the FBI and CIA are also contacted and informed of the switch. The diary contains the names of every contact we have in the United States. It also contains the most current list of every minister, judge, foreign dignitary, diplomat, military official, politician and bureaucrat in the countries of our region who are on the payroll of our organization. I have also provided direct and conclusive proof of Soviet involvement in this most evil scheme. Evidence so strong not even the most disbelieving politician in America will be able to refute the documentation.*

Finally, my friend, I have taken measures to ensure that The Will of God as I see it is carried out. I have managed to deal with over fifty tons of refined cocaine heading for the United States. Carmen does not know of this, and I trust she will never know it was done by my hand.

Carlos then described the *measures* he had taken and what options and actions he left with Rivero in that regard.

Only an event as tragic as this, he concluded, drained of energy, angry, frustrated and saddened that his life would end like this, *will prevent it from ever happening again. Only by such a national tragedy will the American people wake up to the danger they face from groups such as ours. The price they pay for taking Manuel's life and trying to take Enrique's is a small price to pay, as I judge it.*

Carlos leaned back and smiled a melancholy smile, concluding his task with these words: *Who would have thought that I, Carlos Ortega, son of Simon Gabriel de San Martin, would actually bring it all to an end? Times have changed, my friend. They have changed so much.*

I must take leave now. The rest lies with you and Carmen. She has read the diary and has sworn on her parent's grave not to open this letter, but to stand before you as you read it. Look at her Rivero, and see me. I love her so much. Please protect her as you did me. I shall miss you both dearly.

Carlos signed the letter, *Most sincerely, and with my warmest regards and deepest love. Carlos.*

With the completion of that task, Carlos turned his thoughts to other matters. It was a dark and dismal day. The kind of day that makes you want to roll over under the warmth and security of your covers. But it was getting late, and Carlos knew that his bishop's agreement to meet with him briefly at noon must be met promptly — for it would take the better part of the afternoon to say what had to be said. He sealed the letter and noted "personal" on the fold, placing it in the front of the diary he would ask Carmen to deliver on his behalf.

"You are worried," Carmen said softly as she embraced his pillow and looked across the room but not directly at him. She had watched in silence as Carlos wrote his letter.

"Not for myself," Carlos assured her as he turned and looked lovingly in her direction. And Carmen understood.

"Carmen," he said slowly and tenderly, "If anything happens to me you must deliver this diary to only one man. You have his name, his number, his address."

"You must tell no one else of the book," he said with great feeling and emotion, emphasizing that it was only her perceived lack of knowledge of what was in the book which would protect her if she were questioned by those who were sent to eliminate him.

"I understand," she whispered. A tear trickled down her cheek as she propped herself against the pillows and backboard. Her breasts, bare except for a slightly visible path of clear liquid running from one of her eyes down her silky neck to rest on the tip of her left nipple.

As Carlos moved toward her, he was once again struck by the depth of his emotions and love for this simple girl who had accompanied him on the most perilous journey of both their lives. Carmen shared the same emotions and was filled with a sense of wanting as her eyes caressed his slim, firm body moving toward her.

"It is not fair that a girl of your age should have such a responsibility," Carlos said solemnly as he sat beside her. He leaned forward and kissed her gently along the nape of her neck. Carmen moaned slightly and moved her hand along his thigh until she touched him intimately. "Carmen," and there was a long pause as both drew strength from their renewed passion. "If I should die. . ." And his words trailed off as Carmen pulled his head gently toward her.

"I understand," she assured him lovingly. And the storm raging outside was matched by the fury and passion which raged within their small rented room.

They exchanged few other words that morning, except for a brief, sorrowful good bye. Their plans and paths would never cross again. She was to vanish into the community. For she was an illegal alien, and her life would not be an easy one, at least for the time being. But the Latin community in Boston, as it was in other parts of the country, was a close community which formed a protective net around any Latin who sought anonymity within it. And if Carmen learned nothing else during her brief time with Carlos Ortega, it was that anonymity was a virtue.

In time she would be one of the richest women in America. She would appear on the cover of every national magazine, be granted a personal audience with the Pope, lunch with the President of the United States, and fall in love for the second time in her life with a man who would bring her closer to death than she ever wanted to be.

But today, Carmen was a frightened, young girl. Alone, and filled with a terrible sense of foreboding. She wept — and for good reason.

2
The Meeting

The headline in the morning Herald told the story: "COKE HIT SQUAD STALKS DRUG BARON RUMORED TO BE IN BOSTON. Quoting a "highly placed source" the paper reported that at least three cocaine hit teams were believed to be in the city searching for a reputed Peruvian cocaine dealer named Carlos Ortega. The paper couldn't quite make the connection though. Why Boston? Why Ortega? What was the motive? All the "highly placed source" would say is that they were here. He was here. And when they found him, he would be dead. Period!

Very interesting, Carlos thought as he casually sipped a cup of coffee at a local donut shop. It didn't appear to surprise or bother him that his location was so quickly discovered. He knew he was a marked man from the day his plans to defect were known. Anything that followed was simply theater. And then there was Carmen. He knew he would never see her again, even though he assured her otherwise when they parted earlier. Reminiscing, Carlos ran his tongue along the surface of his lips, tasting the sweet traces of Carmen's full lips. He would miss her.

According to the newspaper, the hit squads were rumored to have orders to capture or "torture and kill" their victim. The reward if they succeeded in bringing him in alive was said to be an astronomical $2 million. It was that clincher which piqued the interest of the DEA and touched off a bloody bounty hunt among the city's toughs who hoped to collect on the reward themselves.

With this incentive, bodies were piling up faster than police could count them in the Grove Hall section of the Roxbury, a predominantly black conclave of the city, and the Dudley street area, a barrio which abutted the black area and housed ninety percent of the illegal Spanish-speaking aliens in Boston.

Worse, the indiscriminate killing was flowing over onto the streets. If you were addicted to the stuff, $2 million could buy eternal bliss. All you had to do to collect was kill enough people. One of them was certain to be Carlos Ortega.

Carlos squirmed uncomfortably in his chair. The picture used by the paper was not a flattering one, he thought, as he perused the story for additional information which might be useful. It was a telephoto shot made, no doubt, by one of those "highly placed sources." Fuzzy. Lacking in detail. But it was him all right.

To the brain damaged addicts who smoked, chewed, injected and sniffed the precious white powder, it was Pulitzer quality photo. Enough to kill anyone who even resembled Carlos Ortega.

"Pretty bad stuff, huh?" the waitress said as she poured another cup of coffee.

Carlos was startled slightly by her intrusion. Involved in his own speculation, he thought she was referring to the coffee. He lifted his cup as if to question, then realized.

"All the killing," she said, nodding at the paper.

"Oh, yes," he said nonchalantly. The waitress was an elderly woman with a friendly face. "Quite bad," he added.

His eyes glazed over as he studied the picture of himself. There he was, standing right beside a smiling, very well paid off General Louis Roberto Riza, at one of the cocaine refining stations situated deep in the forest of the Chapare region of Bolivia. The roots of the *Voluntad de Dios* went deep and wide, controlling production in every drug producing country in the hemisphere. Still, Carlos wondered how the hell they ever got that picture.

Carlos leaned forward, propping his elbows on the table. He cradled his head in the palms of his hands, took a deep breath, and resolved to clear his mind of the evil past. It all seemed so irrelevant now, he reasoned. Today there would be a reconciliation between two old friends. Between a man and his God.

Carlos sat upright and stared out the window into the torrential rain. In forty-five minutes he would meet with a boyhood friend who was today an important bishop in the Catholic church. A popular American bishop with connections and influence all the way to the Vatican.

As Carlos thought of Enrique, he was touched by the genuine emotion he felt for his lifelong friend. And his blank stare produced a small tear as he recalled how he and Enrique played, prayed, dreamed, fought, wept and went their separate ways so long, long ago.

It's ironic how their lives evolved, Carlos thought. Times were different in 1954. People were different. Tingo Maria was a poorer town them, its people surviving mostly on barter and what little trade existed: farming, logging and some animal breeding. Not much has improved in thirty-one years, he thought. In those days his country's main export products were cotton, sugar, coffee, milled rice and wild rubber. There was the cocaine trade then as there is today. But it was different in those days. A different type of trade.

Carlos sipped his coffee, almost hypnotized by his own recollections and fond memories of less complicated days. Carlos was twelve years old in 1954. And at that age he didn't completely understand the fascination he *campesinos* had for this leafy substance. But it made him laugh to see adults stagger, fall and act carefree from the high they received when they chewed or smoked it.

At twelve, Carlos was a frail boy — thin, tall and quiet. He was a studious boy, naive, trusted and liked by those who knew him. In a village where jobs were scarce and poverty rampart, Carlos was honored to be a message carrier for the powerful provincial boss, Simon Gabriel de San Martin. "You are my favorite campesino," Simon Gabriel would often say to him upon the completion of one of his journeys. "And you will learn this business well, because you are willing to listen."

"You will be my eyes and ears in the village," he would say to Carlos, solemnly, holding the boy gently by the shoulders, studying his eyes for traces of character and trustworthiness an heir would need. "And you will protect our business from those who would try to hurt us. Is that not right my little friend?" And Carlos would nod, listen and say nothing, for he was in awe of this man who trusted him with such responsibility.

Those were turbulent times, Carlos remembered, and Simon Gabriel de San Martin, being a cautious man, would not jeopardize his business operations by hiring people, even children, with loose lips. For the *messages* Carlos would deliver were important messages. So important, in fact, they were always carried in small, carefully wrapped pouches, sometimes a dozen at a time, all in a knapsack which looked very much like a school bag, and was quite heavy at times.

Those business operations being managed on the eastern slopes of the Andes, involved more than farming, as Carlos would soon learn.

And Simon Gabriel de San Martin was more than a likeable, grandfatherly old businessman. For the better part of sixty years, Simon Gabriel controlled every day life in the province. He was, for all practical purposes, the *Godfather* of the region — respected, feared, admired and honored. Governments came and went, political leaders were assassinated and replaced; the rains fell; forests grew; and one generation of poor followed the other. But the business operations of Simon Gabriel de San Martin, just as they were passed on from his father, Ramon, always remained and flourished. This was *The Will of God*!

It was while delivering a knapsack full of *messages* for the business one day, that Carlos met José Enrique Michelsen, a farm, boy ten years older than himself.

Three times a week, Carlos would journey from his home in Tingo Maria, and head west to a large camp situated three miles within the thick forest which sat between his village and the other side of the highway. Although the forest was eight miles wide at its widest point, by travelling straight through on foot, horse, or small wagon, one could cut almost sixteen miles off the trip along the dirt road which circled the forest cluster and served as a highway for larger vehicles.

Carlos was known by most of the local toughs, who knew whom he worked for, and knew better than to interfere with his business trips. On this day, however, three members of the outlawed American Popular Revolutionary Alliance, a leftist group which enjoyed little local support, but was successful in intimidating the farmers of the region, mistook Carlos for just another peasant boy ripe for recruitment.

As he rounded a densely covered bend in the dirt path, Carlos was confronted by two of the older youths who stood before him. Maybe nineteen years of age. Scruffy. Worn uniforms. Definitely trouble he thought, as he stepped back cautiously, hoping to run rather than invite a confrontation.

A third youth jumped Carlos from behind and grabbed him around his neck with such force that Carlos' feet were actually lifted from the ground.

"Well what do we have here?" the leader taunted as Carlos squirmed to untangle himself from the grasp of the biggest of the boys who took obvious pleasure in jerking his arm tighter around Carlos' throat.

Carlos cried in pain and gasped for precious air as he struggled to free himself from his captor.

"A real fighter," laughed the other of the two youths standing in front of him. "Hold him steady!" he ordered the boy holding Carlos. And the choke hold was drawn even tighter.

Carlos' face turned maroon as he continued his desperate attempt to breathe.

As one of the youths approached, Carlos kicked outward, landing his bare foot on the jaw of his assailant.

"You little bastard," the youth growled angrily as he fell backward, landing on his rear end. "I'll teach you a lesson you won't soon forget," he said as he leaped toward Carlos and let loose a volley of punches, jabs and kicks which drew blood and cries of pain from Carlos.

"Wait!" the leader ordered as he opened the pouch containing the *messages* from Simon Gabriel. And he produced a plastic bag of powder which he held up for his companions to see. "Bring him in the bush," he said ominously, more intent on finding out where Carlos came from, where he was going, and where he got such precious goods.

The mood changed swiftly from troublesome to outright danger-ous once inside the bush. After a fierce struggle in which Carlos was punched repeatedly, the biggest of the boys succeeded in pinning his victim to the ground.

"I have little patience, my friend, for little worms like you. And will ask you once," the leader snarled menacingly into Carlos' face, stressing the word, 'once'. "Where did you get this?" he said as he waved one of the bags of cocaine in front of Carlos.

Carlos said nothing.

"Miguel!" the leader called to his partner. "Show this little worm we mean business. Cut off his fucking cock!"

With that, Carlos screamed for the first time. He was stripped of his pants and shirt by two of the boys, while being held to the ground by the other. Carlos was bloody, sweaty and dirty, having fought furious-ly to free himself from the suffocating grasp of the biggest of the youths. And terrified beyond anything he ever felt before. He was only twelve years old.

Miguel withdrew his knife from its sheath, obviously enjoying the drama. And kneeling over his victim, began to cut Carlos slowly from his neck to his navel. Carlos refused to cry again. He would say nothing. He would not betray the trust of Simon Gabriel. Tears streamed from his eyes as the knife began to slice through the top layer of skin from his chest downward.

Growing more impatient and frustrated with his victim's silence, the leader produced a dirty handkerchief from his pocket, and stuffed into Carlos' mouth to ensure that his certain screams would not be heard by passersby. This alone was enough to cause Carlos to gag, since the handkerchief was soiled with mucus and bore the putrid scent of sweat.

This obviously amused the leader who, standing over Carlos, ordered that the boy be stretched. He made a gesture to his companions to pull as hard as they could on Carlos' hands and feet. Having done that, he began to urinate on his kicking, fighting, bucking prey.

Carlos' heart was pounding so hard he thought it would burst through his heaving chest. Tears, blood, dirt and sweat caused his vision to blur. He felt he would soon pass out. He almost welcomed it. And the midday sun glimmering through the tree tops grew dim as Carlos began to lose consciousness when the rancid yellow liquid splashed against his face and onto his open wounds.

Almost thirty-one years had passed since that confrontation in the forest, and Carlos still clenched his fists and felt uneasy with the humiliation he suffered at the hands of those three thugs on that hot day in June, 1954.

He eyes were shut tightly, as was his mouth and nostrils. The stinking hot liquid poured over his entire body and face. And his captors laughed so hard they began to cry.

It was difficult to recall exactly what happened next, except that Carlos opened his eyes just long enough to see a goat jumping over his chest. Goats all over the place as a matter-of-fact. There was a moment of confusion before Carlos realized that someone, perhaps a local farmer walking his herd through the path, came running to his rescue.

Too weak and frightened to move, Carlos was in awe of the young man who came to his assistance. And for as long as he lived he would never forget the sight of José Enrique Michelsen flailing away at the toughs, who although his own size were no match for his furious surprise attack from the bushes.

Goats, sticks, rocks, all came from the bush at once, creating enough confusion and wild activity to convince the ruffians that the entire Peruvian Army, goats and all, had descended on their young asses. It was enough to send them running in all direction. But not enough to prevent the leader from grabbing the bag with Simon Gabriel's prized 'messages' in it — an action he would live to regret.

Enrique was twenty-one years old. A handsome young man with clear, golden skin, strong hands and the bearing of a refined gentleman. Yet, he was farmer. Poor. Honest. Hard-working. Carlos observed that he was also quite strong since he managed to lift the biggest of the attackers from the ground as if he were no more than a bag of rice, and throw him into the thicket with virtually no effort. When the leader lunged at Enrique, he was met with a right cross which must have surely broken half-a-dozen teeth. As for the one named, Miguel, Enrique kicked the knife from his hand and followed that with a series of pushes, jabs, kicks and punches, leaving Miguel a bloody pulp — and all in a matter of seconds. An Angel of God, Carlos thought, as he lie there bleeding, mesmerized by the almost ballet-like precision assault of his rescuer.

Once the young ruffians were dispersed, Enrique turned his attention to Carlos. "My friend," Enrique asked compassionately as he knelt beside Carlos, propped the boys head gently against his knee, and cleaned the mud, blood and urine from his face with a dry, clean cloth. "What could you have done to deserve this?"

Carlos could not speak. He was in shock. He looked at Enrique and sobbed.

No more was said until they arrived in the village. There, friends and neighbors welcomed the boys, tended Carlos' wounds, and offered warm words of thanks and encouragement to the young man from the other side of the forest who Divine Providence surely sent on a journey of trade that day.

Carlos slept for days, and dreamt of the family he never had, having lost his father to war and his mother to sickness when he was still very young. He never understood just how she died two years ago. Just that one day he returned from school to find his neighbors gathered at his home — weeping, sorrowful and solicitous of his attention. But Carlos understood the loss. And part of him died with his beloved mother. The villagers were his only family now. Of course, there was Simon Gabriel. But Carlos would never presume himself to be worthy of adoption by such a grand man as this.

Two days passed before Carlos recovered from the shock and infection caused by his brutal encounter. When he did awaken on the third day, he saw his friend, Enrique, sitting beside him, praying.

"Tell me I am not dead," Carlos said weakly as he reached out and touched Enrique's hand.

"Carlos, you had us all worried," Enrique said with a smile as he embraced the outstretched hand.

"I. . . I don't know your name," Carlos said drowsily.

Enrique smiled. "I am José Enrique Michelsen."

Carlos returned the smile, then closed his eyes and slept some more, comforted by the knowledge that his friend was there to watch over and protect him.

3
The Present

Carlos sipped his coffee, leaned back in his booth by the window, took a deep breath and smiled. Memories of his friendship with Enrique comforted him enormously. It was 11:15 A.M.

It's funny how the mind works, Carlos mused to himself. Thirty-one years had passed since the day he first met Enrique, and he remembered it just as if it were yesterday. Every little detail was clear. The room he was in. The morning sun shining through the window. His comfort when he woke and saw his friend sitting beside him actually praying.

When Carlos woke again, it was to the sound of voices outside his room. Carlos stretched, exuded a leisurely yawn, blinked a few times and rubbed his eyes. The grogginess soon subsided, and after steadying himself against the side of the bed, he stood and walked slowly toward the familiar voices. He slowly opened the door leading from his room and observed two heavily armed men talking amiably with Enrique. He recognized his friends.

"Carlos," one of the men cried with joy, obviously happy to see him on his feet, and well enough to walk. "Simon Gabriel sent us to inquire about your health," he said excitedly. "He has asked to see you as soon as you are well enough to travel." And with that he and the other man rushed to where Carlos was standing and embraced him warmly.

Enrique was intrigued by this juxtaposition and familiarity. He was also pleased to see his small friend so obviously in the close companionship and care of these two able bodyguards.

"Simon Gabriel has instructed that we are not to leave your side under any conditions," the one named Manuel said sternly.

"We are your guardian angels," smiled the one named Rivero, who gently embraced Carlos.

"Have you met my friend Enrique?" Carlos asked child-like, oblivious to the importance of what was being said to him. "He saved my life and prayed for me for. . ." And he looked at Enrique quizzically.

"For one week," Enrique said respectfully.

Carlos walked over to where Enrique was standing and embraced him as a brother. "Can Enrique stay with me? Can he be my friend."

"I must be going, Carlos." Enrique said as he lifted his small bundle of clothing from the floor. "But I am sure we will meet again," he said optimistically. "Your friends have paid me well for my livestock," he said, gesturing to Manuel and Rivero, "and have promised that if I make the trip once a week to bring new produce and cattle to the village, they will guarantee a buyer each time."

"That is good," Carlos said, nodding his head and smiling broadly. "I will see you then at least once a week on the path which cuts the forest. We can walk to the village together."

"Carlos," Manuel interrupted, "We must leave soon. Simon Gabriel anxiously awaits your arrival."

Carlos and Enrique exchanged a brief farewell, making arrangements to meet at a designated location every Wednesday on the path which cut the forest between one village and the other.

When Enrique departed, the man named Manuel looked at Carlos solemnly and said: "Simon Gabriel has present for you, Carlos."

"What is it?" Carlos asked curiously — innocently.

"Not what Carlos, Who," Rivero said. "Simon Gabriel also asks that we pack what belongings you have. You have a new family now Carlos," he said calmly and softly. "A new father who has heard of your stoic and brave silence in the face of such physical and mental abuse."

And Carlos smiled, knowing this would be the best present he ever received.

4
The Test

Simon Gabriel greeted Carlos with open arms and tears. For Carlos still carried the scars and bruises of his encounter with the three rebels in the bush. And this humbled even a powerful man such as Simon Gabriel, who knew of his young friend's suffering and silence in the face of cruel torture.

The camp which Carlos would now call home was not your typical forest camp. Indeed, the *Campamento en el Bosque*, the *Fortress in the Forest* as it was called, was comprised of over fifteen buildings of various sizes and shapes stretched out over an area three miles long and one and a half miles wide. The main villa situated at the center of the compound consisted of six acres of beautifully landscaped property with a swimming pool, a putting and shooting range, small theater, helicopter pad and tennis courts. Surrounding most of the complex was a well-concealed chain link fence seven feet high at its highest point, capped with electrically charged barbed wire. The remainder of the perimeter was protected by a well-maintained concrete wall with guard towers set at intervals along its length.

The entrance to the *Fortress in the Forest* consisted of a two, twelve foot, steel-reinforced, wooden doors, three inches thick, secured firmly to concrete walls over two feet thick. In one word the *Fortress* was virtually impenetrable: protected by fence, steel, and concrete, inhabited by over two hundred and fifty employees and their families. This was the heart of the empire over which Simon Gabriel de San Martin was absolute ruler. Inherited from his father, it was his private country within a country, the command center of a ruthless drug syndicate with tentacles in every nation of South and Central America. Soon it would all belong to Carlos.

On his first day at the camp, Carlos was welcomed and given caring medical attention. Rest was the order of the day. With Manuel and Rivero standing watch in twelve hour shifts over their young ward, Carlos was encouraged to ask questions and to familiarize himself with his new home.

"We will talk tomorrow, Carlos," Simon Gabriel said when they met earlier, patting Carlos gently on the shoulder as he spoke. "Today, you will be shown your new home." He spoke slowly, softly, fatherly. "Learn it well, Carlos. Trust Manuel and Rivero. They will stay with you and give you whatever you ask for."

Carlos looked at the two men standing off to the side and smiled, then looked at Simon Gabriel and asked, "My new home?"

Simon returned the smile and nodded. "I have business to attend to today, Carlos," he said. "I regret," he continued, his breath coming in increasingly shorter gasps, "that I cannot. . . personally. . . show you around. . ." Simon Gabriel was obviously having difficulty controlling his breathing. And this frightened the boy. "Yes, Carlos, this. . . will be. . . your new home. . .. We," he said as he pointed to Manuel and Rivero, "will be. . . your new family." As he completed those words he began to cough uncontrollably. He clutched one hand to his chest as he coughed, and with the other removed a handkerchief from his pants pocket to cover his mouth. His face was wretched in pain.

Simon Gabriel's physical distress confused Carlos who didn't understand the cancer eating at the old man's lungs.

Manuel and Rivero rushed instinctively to where Simon was standing and offered their assistance, although it was obvious to Carlos they didn't quite know how to help. They were helpless and awkward in the face of Simon's discomfort.

"No, no, not me," Simon Gabriel said, waving his trusted aides away. He straightened, drew a deep breath, holding it momentarily, releasing it slowly through his mouth. "The boy," he said, nodding at Carlos. "The boy." His breath was short and his voice was rasping and weak. He coughed once again, clearing the mucus from his lungs, and when satisfied the attack had passed, reached out and touched both Manuel and Rivero on their shoulders, directing them to Carlos' side. "From this day," he said, "let nothing distract you from the boy. Is that clear?"

Manuel and Rivero nodded obediently.

"Please excuse me, Carlos, but I must go for my treatment now," he said as he turned and walked toward the door. "We will talk tomorrow."

Carlos stood motionless as Simon Gabriel left the room. His throat felt constrained and tight, and he wanted to cry when his heart told him Simon Gabriel was dying.

"Come," Manuel said softly, placing an arm around Carlos' shoulders, "there is much for you to see, Carlos, much for you to learn."

As hard as he tried, Carlos could not erase the vivid image of the old man leaving his room earlier, stooped over, wheezing, having great difficulty breathing. Nor could he fully explain the hurt he felt inside when he thought of Simon Gabriel's suffering. The bond between the two was cast. A bond Carlos would come to understand better the following day when Simon and he talked again.

Later that first night as Carlos lie awake in his room, his mind filled with anticipation, curiosity, excitement and, yes, doubt — this was, after all, so new to him, so sudden, and he didn't fully understand why 'he' was so honored — before he drifted off to sleep, Carlos prayed that he would not awaken and find it had all been a dream. That would be so cruel, he said to himself as he yawned, closed his eyes and dreamt of his mother.

Carlos woke early the next day filled with anticipation. After clearing his mind, he studied his room — it was beautiful. He pounced lightly on the bed. Real mattress. Real feathered pillows. Luxurious. It was not a dream after all. Although he visited the camp many times over the past two years, he was never treated to such a grand reception. Yes, Carlos knew where he was. He didn't yet know why. And this. All this luxury. Certainly Simon Gabriel was a generous man — but this generous?

Carols rose quietly from his bed and walked silently across the room to examine his private bathroom. Still in a daze he stopped by the window next to his bed. He looked out the window past the sprawling compound and marvelled at the view. It was more beautiful than he had ever imagined. From this perspective it was as if he were in another world. Like being in America, he thought. There was such order, and what appeared to be organized activity.

A warm breeze caused the sheer white curtains to lift gently. And Carlos tilted his head back to breathe in the refreshing, moist morning air. A shrill human scream emanating from the distant jungle piqued his curiosity momentarily. Then, there was silence. And Carlos thought no more of it as he went about the business of casually investigating his new surroundings. Although he knew was awake, he moved about as if he were still in a dream.

A knock on the door interrupted Carlos' investigation. It was Manuel. "Carlos, this is Manuel. Are you up and about yet?"

"Yes," Carlos answered, not certain what would follow.

The door opened slowly and Manuel and Rivero stood smiling. "Simon Gabriel asks that you join him for breakfast. And that we bring you to him — when you are ready," Manuel said, respectfully.

Carlos was famished and he needed no additional prompting. He removed his pajama bottoms, then paused in confusion, wondering where his clothes were.

"Over there," Rivero laughed, anticipating Carlos' next question.

"These?" Carlos asked as he walked over to the chair and lifted a clean set of clothes from the seat. They were the finest fabric available. There was not so much as a soiled spot or tear. Not even a worn knee. Carlos was excited — and impressed. He may have only been a child, but Carlos knew expensive clothing when he saw it.

"This is beautiful," Carlos said as he stepped into his pants. He lifted the silk shirt to his face and inhaled its freshness. He turned and faced Manuel and Rivero, an expression of confusion on his face. "I don't understand."

"Come," Manuel said as he extended his arm toward Carlos. "It will all be clearer to you later."

"You mean this is mine?" Carlos asked innocently.

"It will all be yours someday, Carlos," Rivero smiled as he lead Carlos from the bedroom.

Breakfast with Simon Gabriel was pleasant enough. Indeed, in latter years Carlos would often reflect back on that morning and remember it as magic.

They greeted one another cordially when Carlos arrived and assumed his position at the table. Manuel and Rivero stood off to one side and said nothing.

"Did you sleep well, Carlos?" Simon asked sincerely.

Carlos nodded.

"Was your room comfortable?" Simon inquired. "Are you satisfied with your clothes?"

Carlos sat with his hands by his side as he studied the gentle man across the table from him. He nodded respectfully after each question.

For as long as he lived Carlos would not forget that morning. The sun shone bright yellow in a perfectly clear, blue sky. The birds chirping contentedly in the carefully landscaped trees situated around the patio of red brick. Colorful potted plants of every description and hue placed neatly on the floor and hanging from custom-built stands gave the impression one were sitting in the midst of a flowing, living, all embracing rainbow. If it were not a dream, Carlos thought, it was as close as one could get to such a place. Indeed, the private estate of Simon Gabriel was the embodiment of perfect order and tranquility. It was certainly not the Peru Carlos knew. And Simon Gabriel, refined and fatherly, a man of great wealth, power and violence, was also shown that day to be a man of equally great warmth and gentleness.

"Please," Simon motioned with his hand, pointing to the food on the table, "Eat. Enjoy."

As Carlos ate, Simon Gabriel talked quietly. No need to rush and explain everything today. "Carlos, ever since I lost my wife and son two years ago," Simon said, "I have felt..." he spoke slowly, "...an emptiness within." He studied Carlos' swollen face. Did the boy understand?

"My mother died two years ago," Carlos said innocently. But Simon already knew.

"Our paths crossed then, Carlos," Simon said, leaning back in his chair, resting his elbows on the arm rests. "But you were too young to know what our meeting meant to me then." Simon explained how the two funerals were held on the same day. And how Simon in his grief and Carlos in his exchanged glances at the ceremonies, each with tears in their eyes. "I looked at you, Carlos, and I could see that you had integrity and character. That you were a brave and proud young man. I could tell all this from your bearing."

"But how...?"

Simon raised his hand and smiled. He could read the confusion written on Carlos' face. "Do not wonder how I can do these things, Carlos," he said. "I can do them," he said, emphasizing the word can. "After the burials, I questioned people in the village about you and your mother. And they told me what a fine young son you had been to your mother." Simon paused, his head nodding slightly, eyes fixed intently on Carlos, who had stopped eating and was returning the same pensive stare, "I knew from that day, Carlos, that I would never remarry. Never have another son." Simon paused, took a deep breath through his nose, then released a long sigh through pursed lips. The sorrow he felt in his heart was expressed in his face, "I was an old man even then," he said, with a trace of a smile.

"These things are difficult emotions to put into words, Carlos," he said as he reached across the table and patted the side of Carlos' face. "We will have much time to talk of them later." Simon paused again, to wipe a tear from his eye. He leaned into the table and with hands outstretched, gently clasped Carlos' fingers. "I want you to be my son,

Carlos," he said humbly. "I would be honored if you would accept me to be your father."

Carlos was stunned. The moment was special. He nodded yes.

Simon smiled, then leaned back and said: "It is The Will of God, Carlos that we have been brought together in tragedy and in trust."

Two more screams pierced the morning quiet. "Why is that man screaming?" Carlos asked, concern reflected on his face. "I heard a scream just like it this morning."

Simon patted his lips with a clean cloth, and stared into the forest. "It is the Voluntad de Dios," he said almost hypnotically. "It is the reality of life you must learn while you are here, Carlos." Simon rose slowly, and glancing at Rivero and Manuel, said: "When you finish your breakfast, Carlos, Manuel and Rivero will show you your new home. They will stay by your side at all times."

"Are you leaving?" Carlos said disappointedly.

"I must leave on a short trip," he said, promising that when he returned they would talk more. "We will talk of your future Carlos. Your position within the business. You see, I am a sick old man. That is why I must leave this beautiful home regularly." He rubbed his chest and said: "My lungs are not as strong as they once were." And with that , he walked to where Carlos was sitting,   leaned over , and kissed the boy gently on the forehead.

Manuel and Rivero understood from that gesture that the offer had been made and accepted. And that from that day forward, Carlos Ortega was a member of the family. Indeed, as soon as Carlos could assume the responsibility, he would head the business. But first he had to pass a test in the forest with the screams.

5
Revenge

Carlos looked at his watch. The time was drawing near when he would have to leave for a meeting with his bishop.

He ordered one more cup of coffee, then went over to the phone and called for a taxi. It's amazing how calm he felt. Where would he go after today? What would he do? These were questions he could not answer. It made little difference, he thought, since he was financially comfortable. Rich, as a matter-of-fact.

He sat down once again, mesmerized by the steady cadence of the rain, wind and inclement weather outside. His thoughts were filled with reminiscences of days long gone bye. But of one day in particular he was now a captive of his thoughts. The day of revenge.

It was the latter part of June, 1954. Raining like today, Carlos recalled. His trip to the forest that morning would signal his initiation into a select circle of businessmen whose rule and power exceeded even that of the governments of the countries in which they operated.

For one week Carlos had been indoctrinated in the business of the *Fortress in the Forest*. Each employee was introduced and told that Carlos Ortega was the son of Simon Gabriel de San Martin. Manuel and Rivero made it perfectly clear that Carlos was to be given the respect of the father. And that his decisions concerning the business, the employees, and any other matter which came before him was binding.

During this period, Carlos observed a different respect paid Manuel and Rivero. To Carlos, they were his protective friends. His guardian angels. To the people of the region, Manuel and Rivero were feared and respected. Their words were not to be taken lightly. Indeed, Carlos saw that when they spoke they commanded the undivided attention of their audience. And their words were carried by all who could hear to those who could not. Ignorance of the law was no excuse for disobedience, Carlos was told. And Manuel and Rivero were the law to the people of Tingo Maria and surrounding areas.

The day of revenge occurred at the end of his first week at the camp. It began early with Manuel knocking lightly on Carlos' door. "Carlos, are you awake, my friend?"

"Yes," Carlos said with anticipation, having been told the previous evening that he would once again have to confront the three who had humiliated him in the bush.

Carlos dressed quickly, then walked quietly beside Manuel and Rivero as they escorted him down the clean, dry halls of his home, out past the garden where earlier he and Simon Gabriel sat and chatted, and down a dirt path toward the small road which looped around the estate.

"The time has arrived when you will be expected to collect the present your father left for you," Rivero said with a tinge of pride as he escorted Carlos to the small covered wagon which sat waiting. The deed would be done before breakfast.

Although the rain was falling heavily, Manuel and Rivero refused to sit inside with Carlos, opting to walk instead, ever vigilant of everything which occurred around them. The rain didn't seem to bother them either. And this intrigued Carlos who was just beginning to understand how loyal his guardian angels were, and to what degree they would endure hardships and discomfort on his behalf.

Manuel in front, guiding the horse. Rivero slightly to the rear, glancing from side to side and behind to ensure their privacy. The driving rain was so fierce it almost obscured his presence, but Carlos knew Rivero was there.

The wagon stopped less than a mile from the gate at the front of the compound. As Carlos waited, preparing himself emotionally for the events which were to follow, Rivero approached the rear of the wagon, and from under a cover, withdrew a large revolver, a knife, a machete and some towels.

"Carlos, my friend, I am afraid you will have to get a little wet from this point on," Manuel said apologetically as he opened the side door, motioning for Carlos to join him outside.

Carlos' heart began to thump wildly. He could feel the adrenaline rushing through his veins as he stepped from the dryness of the wagon into the torrential downpour. An explosion of thunder caused Carlos to withdraw one step and pause where he stood.

"Do not be afraid, Carlos," Manuel said. He held out his hand for Carlos to grasp. "Today, justice will be administered. And you will be the judge."

"I'm not afraid," Carlos said as he stepped into the rain. Carlos looked around and surveyed the area, a trait he acquired from Manuel and Rivero who had to be two of the most cautious men he ever observed. "I want to meet them again," he said dryly and without emotion as he traced the purple scar running from his neck down his chest. "I, too, have a score to settle, remember."

The men nodded, then turned toward the thick forest, and with Carlos between them walked toward the clearing ahead.

In a matter of seconds, Carlos, like Manuel and Rivero was drenched. All three were oblivious to the conditions around them, though, except one: the groans coming from the forest in front of them. Carlos learned from his talk with Manuel and Rivero of the night before what was expected of him today. Today, he would seal his commitment to the *Voluntad de Dios* with the blood of those who violated him. And this would serve as a lesson and reminder to all others in the region that Carlos Ortega, son of Simon Gabriel de San Martin, had come to manhood. And that his authority and control over all matters — even life and death — was plenary.

As they approached the clearing in the bush, Carlos noticed a dozen well armed men standing in a half-circle around what could only be described as three of the most pathetic, bloodied bodies he had ever seen. But Carlos showed no emotion or revulsion. He walked to the center of the gathering and stared coldly into the bloated, battered faces of the three rebels who a few weeks ago had almost taken his life, who would have surely taken his life had Enrique not interferred.

The storm was growing worse. The thunder seemed so much louder in the forest, he thought. Maybe it's because there's no place to hide in the forest. And the wind and driving rain, pounding and tearing leaves makes you feel so vulnerable. Yet, the deed was to be his. And he alone, not nature, would hold the balance between life and death this day.

An eerie silence settled over the clearing as Manuel strutted to the forefront of the men.

"Simon Gabriel de San Martin," Manuel began, his voice strong and strangely cold, "has ordered that this trash be turned over to his son." His entire body seemed to swell, and his face contorted in anger and contempt as he paraded before the three prisoners who were bound, gagged and tied in a kneeling position before the assembled men. The trial had begun with no introduction, no jury, no defense. "They have not only stolen what belongs to us," he said as he addressed those gathered to witness the executions, "but they have committed acts of unspeakable violence against one of our own. And this will never be tolerated." He stood directly in front of the three.

"Carlos!" He motioned for Carlos to step forward. A flash of lightning accompanied by a slow roll of muffled thunder set an ungodly stage for the gruesome events which were to follow. "It is not necessary that you know the names of these pigs. Do not even look upon them as human beings," Manuel said as he turned and faced Carlos. "Be brave, my friend," he whispered. His eyes were cold and dark, and his face was resolute and stern. As he said it, he reached forward and cupped Carlos' chin gently with the tips of his fingers. "It is only necessary that they know who you are," he said assuringly.

Although Carlos smiled confidetly, he struggled to conceal the fact that his insides were quivering like jelly.

Rivero, meanwhile, stepped quietly from the rear of the gathering. Tucked in his belt were the revolver and machete. He held the long knife in his hands.

"Look up at me, you bastards," Manuel growled as he swirled around and faced the moaning captives. Rain splashed against their faces as their eyes squinted through swollen membrane. "This is Carlos Ortega, son of Simon Gabriel de San Martin. Do you recognize him?" he asked before kicking one of the prisoners squarely in the face, breaking the swollen, tender skin, causing blood to gush from the raw wound.

"You have begged for your lives for an entire week," he said with disgust and scorn. "Now, I want you to tell me in the presence of Carlos Ortega. Do you want to end it now?" Except for their incoherent wailings and please, and cries of anguish and pleadings, they stubbornly, and very foolishly, withheld any request for a quick death. Manuel nodded and smiled. He would enjoy this test.

Manuel reached down to the one named Miguel, and lifted his face. "You are the one with the knife," he said as he pulled Miguel's hair back, forcing his chin to rise, and rain bounce off his forehead. "You are the one who was in the cutting business a few weeks ago, eh?" Manuel spat, growing more angry with each passing moment. "Now you will feel the knife." His voice was menacing.

"Rivero!" he shouted.

Rivero rushed forward, and before anyone knew what was happening, knelt face to face with the prisoner named Miguel, reached into the man's pants and cut off his manhood which he pulled out and threw on the ground. The screaming was almost unbearable. "Kill me!

Kill me!" Miguel begged, dropping from the waist, squirming in pain. "Please. I beg you. No more. No more. Kill me. Please."

Although Manuel purposely blocked a direct view when the deed was done, he did step aside as Miguel begged. The sight was horrible, and it caused Carlos to shudder. Yet, Carlos knew this would have been his fate had the one named Miguel had his way a week earlier.

"Carlos!" Manuel said coldly and with a strange calm, ignoring the cries of the dying man. "This man has asked that he be put to death. What is your pleasure?"

Carlos stepped forward, his eyes locked on his victim. He hesitated, then stared upward at the rhythmic movement of the trees. Think of nothing, he told himself. He closed his eyes and his mind to the human misery he saw before him. This was business! When he looked down again, his face was expressionless. "I grant him his wish," he said quietly. And Rivero withdrew the revolver from his belt and handed it to Carlos.

Carlos moved closer to Miguel, and without so much as a flinch, ordered the dying man to look him in his eyes. "This," Carlos said as he paused and looked around at each of the men gathered around him, "... is justice." And he squeezed the trigger of the revolver, sending Miguel's head reeling backward then forward. And it was all over for Miguel.

By this time the other two were delirious. Begging, squirming, pleading, weeping. Manuel then moved to the biggest of the remaining two. "And you are the one who likes to stretch people by the neck," he said, his eyes filled with contempt and hatred for the remaining two. And the storm within his heart grew even more violent than the storm outside. "A little boy is all you can handle?" he taunted.

"Perhaps your arms are too long," he mimicked. "Perhaps you should not be so big." Manuel was clearly intending to be done quickly with this one, who was reduced to such babbling and terror that he was barely understandable. "What do you wish," Manuel shouted violently into the man's face. But before an answer could be given, Rivero pulled his machete and hacked off an arm. Clean.

"You fucking scum," Manuel hollered at his victim, once again stepping in front of Carlos, blocking the boys view of the actual act. "Be quiet and answer me. I asked you a question," he shouted over the cries of the mortally wounded man. "What do you wish?"

Somewhere between the screams and begging, Carlos heard a plea for a fast death. "Carlos!" Manuel said respectfully, his chest heaving slightly, betraying the fact that even he was affected by the events of that day. "This man has asked that he be put to death. What is your pleasure?"

By this time, Carlos was stunned, incapable of feeling any emotion. "I, I grant him his wish," he said hypnotically, remembering the jerking, stranglehold placed around his own neck. He could still feel himself gagging and choking and crying, as he stepped around Manuel and stood before the biggest of the three. He raised the gun slowly. "Look at me!" Carlos ordered, coldly. placing the barrel against the man's forehead. "This," Carlos said as he once again stared into the faces of those gathered, "...is justice." And a loud explosion sent another victim's head kicking wildly backward and forward. And it was over for this man.

"Mother of Jesus," the leader pleaded. "I beg you for my life. I am sorry. I am sorry. I am fucking sorry." He kept repeating those words. But to no avail — and he knew it.

"And you are the one who shouts orders for his friends to follow," Manuel chided angrily. "You are the donkey's ass who takes pleasure in another's suffering." Manuel's temper was near uncontrollable. "You are the fucking pig who dared interfere with our business?" And Manuel slapped the leader's face, causing blood to spill from an open wound.

"I am fucking sorry. I am fucking sorry. I am fucking sorry." He kept repeating those words.

Manuel was glaring now. "You are the one who likes to fill one's mouth with urine and dirt and rags and human mucus?" Manuel was shouting now, almost in hysterics. Another clap of thunder and bright flash of lightning filled the forest air.

Manuel did not wait for Rivero this time. He withdrew his own knife and sliced both sides of the leader's mouth, drawing blood, gargles and inhuman shrieks. The leader was choking on his own blood, spitting between gasps for air, trying desperately to keep his wind pipe open and clear. "Now that your mouth is bigger," Rivero taunted as he stepped forward, "perhaps you will hold this for me." And as Manuel looked on, again blocking direct view from Carlos, Rivero stuffed the severed member into the leader's mouth.

Vomit, blood, human parts — everything burst from the man's mouth all at once. And in his eyes, Manuel could see a plea for a quick death.

"Carlos!" Manuel said calmly and slowly as he stared into the man's swollen, weeping eyes. "This man asks that he be put to death. What is your pleasure?"

Carlos' answer stunned everyone. He walked casually up to the leader who was stooped over and weeping, lifted him by his hair, forcing him to acknowledge his presence, and said: "This — is justice." And with that, ordered that the man be left to die on his own.

Manuel and Rivero looked at each other in surprise, then smiled, as they offered Carlos towels to wipe himself.

Rivero wiped his machete clean while staring menacingly at those gathered. He threw the towel into the mud, adjusted his revolver in his belt and strutted casually to the center of the dozen witnesses. His tone was grave and threatening. "Let there be no doubt in anyone's mind," he said above the fury of the storm, "that justice was served here today." He walked around the half-circle, studying the eyes of each man as he passed. "Let there be no doubt that Carlos Ortega has earned his place among us and that he has served his father well. He has earned the right to be one with us. It is the Will of God," he admonished sternly. "If there is any doubt — or objection," he intoned, placing his hand against his revolver just in case there was any objection, "let it be spoken now, here, today."

There was silence.

Rivero, paused, then nodded his approval of the unanimous consent.

From that day forward, Carlos Ortega would be feared and respected. Not because of who he was — although that was certainly a significant factor in much of the respect shown him — but rather because of what he was capable of doing. And this, more than anything else, made him a man to be reckoned with — even though he was only twelve years old.

6
The Confession

"Check, sir?" It was 11:45 A.M.

Carlos glanced up and nodded yes, noticing that the taxi had arrived and the driver was waiting impatiently outside. Carlos rose from the table, folded his morning paper, arranged his raincoat and hat, and paid the bill.

"Sir, I don't think I can make change for this," the waitress said nervously as she pondered what to do with the crisp one-hundred dollar bill.

Carlos smiled. "Keep the change," he said nonchalantly. It was all so irrelevant now, he thought, as he walked to the front door.

As Carlos stepped from the entrance, he glanced cautiously to the left and right. It always paid to be certain you were not being followed. He noted the traffic was light, due no doubt to the foul weather. Since the driving rain and high winds made it difficult to look straight ahead, Carlos just hunched his shoulders, drew himself into the dryness of his coat, and walked toward the waiting vehicle.

"Where to buddy?" the driver asked impatiently, not even waiting for Carlos to fully enter the cab before demanding a destination.

Carlos scowled. "The Roman Catholic Chancellery," Carlos responded, a little irritated by the rush.

"That's only up the street," the driver complained, greatly annoyed that he gave up his position on the call line to travel less than two miles with a fare. "I can't fucking believe this," he mumbled to himself, but loud enough for his passenger to hear.

In other days, Carlos would have slit this guy's throat for such a remark. But now? This was America, he reasoned to himself, and things were different here. More decadent. Carlos smiled at the thought, for it was this decadence which made him a billionaire. "Fuck you, Americans," Carlos mumbled, but loud enough to cause the driver to glare through the rear view mirror.

The ride was short. "There's a minimum charge, buddy. You owe me five bucks." The driver spoke contemptuously as he pulled alongside the curb near the main entrance to the Catholic center.

Carlos slipped the man a twenty dollar bill and told him to keep the change. Arguing with this guy was not worth the effort, he figured. Besides, a meeting with Bishop José Enrique Michelsen was something which should be done with the proper attitude. He wasn't about to let a creep interfere with this joyous reunion.

As he stepped from the vehicle, Carlos adjusted the collar on his raincoat and pulled his hat snug on his head. He glanced around cautiously as the car sped away, surveying the area for suspicious movements. He froze momentarily, having sighted something which seemed out of the ordinary. A car parked across and slightly down the street. Its headlights were on and wipers moving. Just waiting. But waiting for what? There were no traffic lights on the street, nor any vehicles passing nearby. Neither was there any pedestrian activity. So why was the car just sitting there? Its passengers immobile in the front seat. Staring straight ahead. At him.

Although the men in the car could not be identified, Carlos felt uncertain enough as to the reason for their being there that he decided to walk away from the Chancellery, toward a store — hopefully one with a rear entrance.

Carlos moved; the car moved. He stopped and crossed the street; the car paused in the middle of the street, waiting for Carlos to make the next move. Anticipating danger, Carlos ducked quickly into a small grocery store where he browsed along shelves filled with canned goods and boxes, newspapers and magazines.

After a few moments he glanced outside, hoping his suspicions were just the result of an overactive imagination. What he observed sent a chill down his spine. The car had stopped across the street. Its lights and wipers were still on. But the passengers were no longer in the front seat. They were approaching the store, glaring through the window, looking directly at him. Instinct told Carlos to move quickly. To make his final confession. To tell his bishop everything.

Still shaking the rain from his coat, Carlos moved quickly toward the telephone booth at the rear of the near-empty store. He placed a dime in the receiver and dialed the operator.

"What city please?" the voice prompted.

"Operator, connect me to the Roman Catholic Chancellery please," Carlos said, his breathing quickening as the sense of danger grew.

"What city please," the nasely operator prompted.

Carlos grunted. "Boston, goddamnit. The Chancellery. Please operator this is a matter of life and death."

"You'll have to dial that number yourself sir," the operator said, wasting what few precious moments he had left to live.

It seemed an eternity before the number was given. Damn! he thought, as he dialed, How could they have located me this quickly? His mind raced as he listened impatiently to the phone ringing on the other end. Had they discovered Carmen's whereabouts also? he wondered. The phone kept ringing. Damn, Why is it taking so long to answer?

"This is the Chancellery. May I help you?" The voice was that of a man. A familiar voice to Carlos. Should I say something? he thought to himself. Then decided against it.

"Yes, please," Carlos was deeply concerned now. The men had entered the store and were searching the aisles. "I must speak with the bishop. Please tell him. . ."

"I'm sorry sir," the voice interrupted, "but His Eminence cannot be disturbed at this time. He is expecting a visitor momentarily. And after that he will be leaving for the weekend. May I take a message?"

There was no time for niceties. "Tell the bishop this is Carlos. Carlos Ortega," he said as he glanced down the aisles, noticing the men were heading straight for the phone booth. Hoping that he wasn't noticed, Carlos turned and faced the rear of the booth. "Please. This is a matter of life and death. Just tell the bishop that Carlos must talk with him. Now! He'll understand. He'll come to the phone. I'm the one he's supposed to be meeting with."

There was a long pause on the other end, and Carlos understood why. Then, "One moment please."

Another brief pause.

"Carlos?" It was Enrique.

The first man to approach the booth slapped his hand hard against the glass door to get Carlos' attention.

"Enrique, please do not ask any questions," Carlos said hurriedly as he leaned against the glass frame, hoping to buy himself an extra moment. "My life is almost over. And yours is in jeopardy. Forgive my sins my friend. It is *The Will of God*. It is *The Will of God*. They will try to kill you. . ."

Enrique did not understand the commotion he heard, almost as if there was a struggle occurring on the other end of the line. "Carlos, I know you are in great danger. I saw this morning's paper."

"Please do not ask any questions, my friend," Carlos pleaded desperately.

"Where are you, my son? Let me have Brother Dominic meet you somewhere."

"Enrique, trust no one..." Carlos said, his breathing heavy as he pushed against the door. Then there was the sound of breaking glass.

"Carlos! I will give you shelter at the Chancellery. You must tell me what is going on?"

"Please, Enrique. Listen. Your life is in grave danger," he said. "They will attempt to..."

The struggle grew more furious.

"I am listening Carlos. I am listening. Please..." May the almighty father bless you, Enrique thought as he pressed the phone to his ear and prayed for Carlos' safety.

"Enrique!" Carlos was in pain.

"Carlos!"

"You must trust no one but Riv..."

"Carlos?" Enrique's face reflected enormous strain and pain. "Carlos!" he shouted into the phone. His hands were trembling now. And he had an awful, empty, nervous feeling in the pit of his stomach.

"Who is this?" the voice on the other end demanded abruptly.

"This is Bishop Michelsen at the Chancellery. Please, is Carlos Ortega there? Is he all right?"

The phone went dead.

"Your Eminence," Brother Dominic said as he saw his bishop sway back and forth. He rushed to Enrique's side to offer support. "What is it Your Eminence? You look as if you are about to pass out. What was that phone call about, Your Eminence? Please, it's very important that you talk about it," Brother Dominic said, his face mirroring the same concern as Enrique's. And he, too, felt that terrible uneasiness within the pit of his stomach.

Enrique steadied himself against Brother Dominic's strong arm and walked slowly across the spacious room, dazed. Feeling terribly sad, Enrique knelt before the crucifix hanging on the wall. It was the same crucifix Carlos had given him as a farewell present when he left for America so long ago.

Enrique sighed, then bending at the waist, placed his hands over his face and spoke softly. "Please forgive his sins, father. Please forgive his sins."

"Your Eminence?" Brother Dominic said as he offered Enrique a fresh glass of spring water. "Please take this, Your Eminence," he said, speaking reverently, slowly, softly. He knelt beside his friend and pressed for answers. "What is happening? Is there anything I can do?" he asked, desperately wanting to know so much more.

Enrique took the water and sipped from the glass, composing his thoughts. He looked at Brother Dominic in silence, then took a deep breath and said: "I believe something terrible is going to happen." His voice was filled with sadness and emotion. "But I don't understand to whom. Or when."

With Brother Dominic's assistance, Enrique stood and walked to his desk. He sat and slumped in his chair. His mind racing. Should I call the police? he thought. Then ruled that option out since Carlos was wanted by the police. And besides, what would he tell them?

"Brother Dominic," Enrique inquired patiently, calmly. "Did the man on the other end of the phone give any indication where he was calling from?"

"He said nothing, Your Eminence. I was hoping he might have mentioned that to you," Brother Dominic said disappointedly.

Enrique's face again mirrored concern and great pain with that answer.

He leaned back in his chair, placed an elbow on the armrest, and with his fingers began to stroke his chin. Almost a full minute passed in uncomfortable silence. The two men just faced one another. Staring.

Although he knew Enrique was in deep concentration, Brother Dominic pressed for additional answers. "Your Eminence. Please."

"Brother Dominic," Enrique began slowly. "You must tell no one of this phone call. Not until I say I am ready to explain what has happened. Do you understand?"

Brother Dominic was a trusted aide - - and friend who respected the wishes of his bishop. He would remain silent, if that was his bishop's wish.

"What about your trip to Vermont, Your Eminence? Should I cancel it?"

Enrique wanted very much to cancel his trip and remain at the Chancellery today. Indeed, for the entire weekend, if necessary, to await a return call from Carlos.

"I'm afraid that that will be impossible, Brother Dominic," Enrique said, his concentration on Carlos being broken momentarily. "I have already spoken with Bishop Connolly, and he is on his way to the retreat as we speak." Bishop Connolly and Enrique were members of

the Catholic Bishops' Conference Steering Committee on International Affairs. They were scheduled to meet and spend a quiet weekend in
Vermont camping, fishing and mapping out procedural matters and
recommendations they would offer the Holy Father when they met
with him in Rome on Thursday, the twenty-third.

"Oh my God," Enrique moaned. It was only a passing thought, but
could Carlos' call have had something to do with that trip? Could
Carlos have been trying to tell him something about that when he
said, Trust no one?

"Your Eminence," Brother Dominic pleaded. "I cannot stand the
suspense. What is it you are thinking. What is bothering you? Why are
you so worried? Perhaps, if you talked about it, I could help you."

Sensing Brother Dominic's frustration and concern, Enrique asked
his personal aide to be seated. He would explain who Carlos Ortega
was, he said, and why his call this morning was so disturbing. He owed
Brother Dominic that much, he figured.

For one hour and forty-five minutes Brother Dominic was captivated by Enrique's account of his life. He was, more to the point,
strangely fascinated, almost as if he were reliving his own boyhood
experiences, by the story of two boys who walked and talked every
Wednesday for three years. But how Carlos was secretive about his
dealings in the forest camp where he lived.

Enrique explained how after meeting Carlos, his livestock business
grew and prospered. "For many months I could not understand why
my life changed — or what I was doing differently than before, that I
should be such a successful trader," Enrique mused. "Then I learned
that Carlos was responsible for my new-found wealth."

By 1957, Enrique explained, he was twenty-five years old. Carlos
was fifteen. But much more mature than other boys his age. "It was
then that I confided my wishes to enter the services of our Father in
Heaven to my friend," Enrique said with a melancholy voice. "I remember the surprise on Carlos' face when I told him," Enrique smiled
with fond remembrances. "He couldn't believe it. He was so happy for
me."

Enrique paused and gazed at Brother Dominic. How many years
had Dominic been his aide? And how infrequently had they sat and
talked like this? "But I am surely boring you, Dominic," Enrique said
with genuine feeling.

"On the contrary, Your Eminence, I couldn't be more interested.
Please continue," Brother Dominic said, sensing his bishop's need to
talk about such things. To express his feelings openly, assured that
what he said would be held in the strictest confidence. "I have often

wished that I might once again see the country of my birth," Brother Dominic said, his eyes swollen and red also.

Enrique sighed. Everything was so confusing. What did Carlos mean when he said "trust no one." And the identity of the one person he did tell Enrique to trust was cut short. And when Carlos said, it was "*The Will of God...*" What was he referring to?

"Your Eminence?" Brother Dominic prompted, gently. "Please, continue."

"Oh... yes," Enrique said. "Our lives in Peru were different then, Brother Dominic. We were desperately poor people. And our people needed so much. Not just physically, but in the spiritual sense as well." Enrique paused momentarily, rose and turned to face the window behind his desk. Leaning on the window's edge, he stared into the raging storm outside, sighed, turned again and continued. "Between the wars, revolutions and bloody political struggles which sparked the most inhuman violence in my country, there remained the dignity and nobility of my people. The farmers. The peasants. The working people. Oh yes, there were many good people in all walks of life. Their lives — our lives — were in such turmoil, though."

Enrique walked from behind his desk and paced casually to the painting of Jesus hanging on his wall. "Each person had to find his own way of dealing with the despair and confusion brought on by our unstable political climate. I found my peace through Jesus," he said as he stared lovingly into the eyes of Christ. Turning to face Brother Dominic, he continued. "At the age of twenty-five," he said retrospectively, "perhaps for the first time in my life, I understood what my vocation would be. And just how much I could give to my countrymen through the loving heart of Jesus Christ."

Enrique, paused, stared at the painting, then walked back to his desk, sat, sighed and said with affection: "Carlos helped me in fashioning my life — although I don't think he ever suspected that I knew that it was through his generosity that my continued education and eventual enrollment in the Catholic University at Lima was made possible."

"Carlos must have been a very special young man," Brother Dominic said. "I feel very close to him myself."

Enrique smiled and sighed once again. But this time the sigh was one of fond remembrance. "Rich, Brother Dominic?" Enrique said somberly. "I accepted Carlos' generosity so I could serve Our Lord. But I understood that even as a young boy Carlos was changed by his experience the day I saved his life. Something about his eyes..." Enrique paused, took another deep breath, and wiped a tear from his eyes. "May God forgive me, but I could never bring myself to criticize him. Or question what he did. Although I suspected many times what 'business' he was really engaged in." Enrique rose and walked slowly toward the crucifix. He reached up and smoothed his hand over the body of Christ as he spoke. "I truly loved the boy," his voice cracking with emotion, now. "And would pray myself to sleep each evening asking God to understand and forgive his human weaknesses, and to accept my penance as retribution for Carlos' sins."

"In 1961, while I was still at the University, Carlos came to visit me," he continued, facing Brother Dominic again. "I was astounded by the sight of the young man who came before me." For the first time Enrique smiled broadly. "Carlos drove up to the front gate of the University in this enormous Cadillac. He had an entourage consisting of four other automobiles behind him. And what appeared to be body guards in each car. I knew none of the men expect the two who were his closest friends — a man named Manuel, and one who I saw less often, named. . ." Enrique paused, to refresh his memory. It was so long ago. "Yes, " he said, having remembered. "His name was Rivero."

Brother Dominic smiled.

"I must tell you, Brother Dominic, that if ever there was a doubt in my mind that the souls of my countrymen needed saving, these two gentlemen reinforced my faith in both my mission and my Lord. They were good men, Brother Dominic. Caring men. But like the land from which they came, they were capable of such extremes. I often wondered how good and evil could exist so closely in one body haven't you?"

"Many times, Your Eminence."

"Yet, who are we to judge? I often wondered what power my friend Carlos exerted to command such respect — and fear. I met Manuel and Rivero only twice in my life," he said. "Once when I saved Carlos' life, and once when he visited me at the University. Yet I know they were always near him, even though I couldn't see them. They were so loyal to him."

A light knock on the door startled both Enrique and Brother Dominic. "Your Eminence?" It was Sister Margaret. "You asked that I remind you of the time. It is now 2:30 p.m.."

Enrique glanced at his watch. "I am sorry, Dominic. I fear I have wasted your time. Thank You Sister," Enrique said as he stood, adjusted his clothing, the papers on his desk, and then dismissed them both.

"Brother Dominic?"

"Yes, Your Eminence?"

"Thank you."

When he was alone in his study he sat and cried once again over the loss of his dear friend. Carlos was in trouble, and there was nothing *he* could do to help him.

During the remainder of the afternoon, Enrique was obsessed with Carlos' words. What did he mean when warned that *his* life was in danger? If the scheduled trip to Vermont were not so important, he would have cancelled immediately, and sent someone else in his place. But that was impossible.

As he finished packing later that day, checking one last time to be certain he had the map and directions to the cabin, Enrique had a frightening premonition. He shuddered. And a cold sweat formed lightly on his brow. Am I going to die before the end of this week end? he asked himself as he gazed upward toward his God. Then, just as quickly, he dismissed all such thoughts, attributing them to the gloominess he felt for Carlos.

It was 3:30, Friday afternoon. He should have heeded his premonitions.

7
Quite Weekends

Saturday, May 18 -

WOODSTOCK VERMONT: 8:30 A.M. Dawson Page enjoyed his occasional weekend trips to Vermont. As he lie in his tent that morning, warm and comfortable under the covers of his sleeping bag, he casually reviewed his plans for the weekend. If the weather held, he would do some hiking, shopping and leisurely travelling along the back roads. Other than that, nothing out of the ordinary. Just a quiet, peaceful day.

As for the storm which had been battering the coast for the past few days, it continued to whip stubbornly off shore to the north. It hadn't made its way far enough westward to threaten his plans. Today's forecast, however, anticipated a spiral southwesterly movement inland, and some violent weather for the central Vermont region when this occurred. In spite of the threat of bad weather, though, there was something about the mountains which drew him back year after year — regardless of conditions. So, Dawson was determined to enjoy the weekend and hunker down come what may.

Boston's skyline was beautiful, he thought, as he drew the downy covers around his shoulders, still groggy and too comfortable to move outside just yet. And he loved the city, having been born and raised there. But Vermont was — different. Quaint. Majestic. Independent. Here, a man could clear his mind and just think, relax and reflect on his life.

That's why Page visited Vermont whenever he could find the time. In the quiet hills surrounding Woodstock Page could escape the blaring of horns, the rush hour traffic jams, trucks double parked

along city streets, endless construction and digging projects, conges-
tion — and the interminable noise of urban living. In sharp contrast to
life in the city of Boston, Vermont was, well, peaceful — even in the
blinding rain.

Page arrived in Woodstock on Friday the 17th. He pitched camp
outside the town's limits, and relaxed for the remainder of the day,
just as he planned. He ventured into town only once to purchase a
magazine and a cup of coffee, then headed back to camp, satisfied that
even if the weather didn't cooperate he'd find enough to occupy
himself to make the trip worthwhile. Friday afternoon was restful and
uneventful.

Friday evening Page went for a leisurely walk along the stream
which flowed lazily past the entrance to his tent, emptying into a
basin a quarter of a mile to the south. Page knew this terrain intimately and chose his campsight well. He had been coming to this same
location now, for almost a decade. That's why he walked confidently
in the woods, and thought nothing after spending an evening in town
of strolling alone along the forest trail which ended at the rocky
clearing along the water's edge. He never once worried about getting
lost. Indeed, the kerosene lamp he kept burning dimly outside his tent
served as a reassuring marker. It was all he ever needed to locate his
position. He had good night vision anyway. Night vision was something Page developed into an accurate science while in Vietnam. The
flicker of a match, the moon reflecting off an unsheathed bayonette,
even the whites of one's eyes, given the proper conditions, were
enough to give one's position away. And death would stalk silently to
find that target just as surely as day followed night. The very thought
sent a shiver down his spine.

By ten Friday evening Page was relaxing in the security and quiet of
his tent. More to the point he was stretched out comfortably warm
inside his sleeping bag, listening to the radio. With the soft orange
glow of his kerosene lamp as illumination Page read until he felt
groggy. And nature did the rest. Life was beautiful and uneventful, he
thought as he dimmed the light and drew the covers above his shoulders, and fell asleep.

And then came Saturady. A day he would never forget.

Page woke slowly, allowing his mind and body to adjust to the
damp, cold conditions outside. Although it hadn't started to rain, Page
knew it was bound to get worse. He also knew that any procrastina-
tion he indulged now, like asking himself if he *really* wanted to get up
at that early hour, would surely catch up with him later, but only then
it would probably be raining. So, with calculated determination, Page

slipped out of his warm sleeping bag and snuggled into his pants and shoes before the early morning chill lowed his still warm body temperature. Having completed the most difficult part, first — accepting the inhospitable chill in the air — he stepped bravely outside, rubbed his hands together, blew a few short breaths, massaged his biceps, adjusted his clothing, stretched his arms outwardly and inhaled deeply. Good morning, Saturday, he chided himself. Where's the sun?

The sun, as he quickly observed was nowhere to be found, and the weather was definitely going to get worse. And sooner than the weathermen predicted.

Given the deteriorating conditions Page decided to strike camp early, jog into town, and do some browsing before heading on. Time would pass quickly.

With the tent secured in the trunk of his car, and his body fully awake, he headed for the main road. I'll jog into town, then walk back, he thought, anticipating a healthy breakfast at the Woodstock Inn, and the benefit of a brisk walk afterward. As Page hiked from the woods, stopping regularly to admire the powerful contours of the mountains and rugged terrain of the valley, he remembered how once, about four years ago, while walking out of these very woods, he crossed path with what looked like a giant grizzly bear.

"There aren't any grizzly's in those woods," a doubtful store owner told him when he recounted the events of that close encounter four years ago.

"But it was a bear," Page insisted quietly, "And it was big. I was walking along the water's edge up by Courtesy ridge, when this dark brown bear came out of the bushes and crossed my path. I guess we were both a little groggy and surprised by each others presence. He stopped and stared. I could see his nose sniffing wildly, trying to identify my scent."

"And I suppose you were shitting your pants," the storekeeper smiled as he leaned over the counter and motioned for his assistant, who Page suspected was the store owner's son, to step over and hear his incredible story.

"Just about," Page said coolly, not giving an inch to doubt. "I knew that if I ran away he would probably give chase and eat a little earlier than me."

This drew a chuckle from the two behind the counter.

"So?" the young assistant promoted. "What happened then?"

"So I talked to him. Real soft like. Nice bear. Like I was purring at him. So what brings you to the water this early in the morning? And then he growls, showing me his orthodontics," Page said.

"I think this city boy is giving us a line, Jerry," the owner said to the younger boy.

"Swear to God this is the truth," Page said earnestly. "I'm talking; he's growling. And I know I'm dead if he should decide to drop on by for a closer sniff."

"Did you have a gun?" the assistant asked.

"Just my knife," Page said.

"Jeezus."

The store owner frowned in disbelief at the boy's awe.

"Then, he stands on his hind legs and stretches his paws wide, still sniffing. Probably giving me a closer look. I can't run, and I can't attack for obvious reason. This thing is as big as a bus. . ."

"Yeah?"

"So I decide to stroll down to the stream, and act as if he weren't even there."

"Incredible," the boy said.

"Unbelievable," the owner added as if to correct the boy.

"And then the strangest thing of all happens. I bend down to scoop some water up in my hand, not knowing what else to do, I mean I was exposed and all, and there was nowhere to run. And this brown bear drops down on all fours and walks over to where I'm kneeling and begins sniffing at my head."

"Mr. you ought to report that to National Geographic," the store owner said disbelievingly.

"I swear this is true. The bear just sniffed at my head for a few seconds, turns and begins sipping water right beside me. Like I was one of the family."

"And the moral to this story is?" the store owner asked incredulously.

"There is no moral, my friend. Just the truth," Page said with a shrug. "He sensed I was no threat. He might have even enjoyed my company. I can't explain it. But it happened just the way I told you it did."

"Did you ever see the bear again?" the boy asked.

Page shrugged and said no. "I never actually saw him. But once last year, when I was staying up in the woods, I got up one morning and went outside to get dressed. The weather was better than today. I noticed large tracks outside my tent, and saw the ground was matted near the front flap."

"Like he was sleeping outside your tent?" the boy said.

"I guess," Page said.

"Jeez," the boy repeated.

Page smiled to himself as he cleared the woods, recalling that story. To this day when he sees the boy in his father's store, the boy calls him over to reaffirm the truth of his account.

After a few limbering up exercises he was ready to head to town. "Once a marine, always a marine," he chanted as he began jogging along the bank of the winding Quechee River. "Here we go Recon, here we go," he sang in cadence to his steady pace. As Page jogged, he mused how he was not really an outdoorsman. Not in the slightest. He didn't hunt, although he was licensed to carry a gun in Massachusetts. He wasn't really into hiking or even camping, except for these occasional trips. He just liked the mountains and considered it important to be near them from time to time.

As he ran that particular morning, his mind was not on business, or the weather, nor the fact that it was a tad cold and he was hungry. His mind was on Khe Sahns, Vietnam, twenty years ago.

Two things Page loved about Vermont: One was the very New Englandness of the place. You can have the other states, he would often say. Vermont is what New England is all about. Mountainous. Scenic throughout. The other attraction, and he never fully understood the reason for this, was his fascination with the resemblance to Vietnam. Now, there was a beautiful country, he thought, except for the war.

Maybe it was this love/hate relationship which drew him back all these years and caused him to draw the parallel. He loved the mountains; learned to love them, actually, while he was in Vietnam. But he hated the war. War was in the mountains, though. Especially for the Marines in the northern quadrant of Vietnam. And death stalked uncompromisingly in those mountains.

Yet, Page always volunteered to go into the mountains when a forward observer was needed. Maybe that's why he volunteered for reconnaissance duty as often as he did. He blended. Like the way he blended with the bear, twenty years later. Reconnaissance also allowed him to work alone which he preferred. And he loved it and hated it both at the same time. That was 1965.

By 1966, Page was up to his ass in death and destruction amidst the beauty of the one place which brought him his greatest comfort — the mountains around Khe Sahns. What a desolate, beautiful place, he thought.

The marine base at Khe Sahns was actually little more than a runway, situated on a low flat hill, surrounded by much higher mountains and thousands of North Vietnamese regulars. Because of their precarious position, the marines cleared all vegetation from around the air base, giving them a clear line of fire at anyone approaching the perimeter. They called this space the a dead zone, and defended it for dear life against all takers. Even in '65 the marines knew a bloody siege would one day follow. And it did. In those early days, though, the major battles occurring between marine defenders and North Vietnamese regulars occurred in the surrounding mountains, with the marines usually winning, but not without paying dearly for that small piece of real estate. That's where Page killed his first and only civilian. And the nightmare of that experience stayed with him until this day.

She was a young girl. Maybe thirteen. Maybe even younger. Page had just taken up position at his listening post about a mile outside the camp's perimeter, on the western side of the runway. It was beginning to turn dark, when Page thought he heard voices — Vietnamese voices. The rules of war are never clear, especially for those closest to combat. There, the struggle is guttural, and you have to improvise. If you don't improvise, and you delay too long, and you guess wrong, you could end up dead.

The three civilians were walking away from Page's position, actually, when the limb upon which Page was perched snapped. Not a loud snap by cosmic standards, but a crack loud enough to be heard in the quiet forest. It was dusk. The girl turned and glanced back over her shoulder. She and her companions were about seventy-five yards away from his position. What could she possibly have seen?

Page nestled the silencer-equipped sniper rifle into his shoulder and squinted through the sight at the girl's heart. Please go away he prayed earnestly, not wanting to kill her.

She had a quizzical expression on her face as she stood and stared back. Her companions, meanwhile, continued walking, laughing. Were they just civilians out for a stroll? Or Viet Cong reporting to *their* camp?

His finger brushed lightly against the trigger. *Please, little girl. Look somewhere else. Don't say anything. I can't understand you anyway. If I even think you're looking at me, though, I'm going to have to kill you.*

Her companions called her name, and she answered, almost as if she were telling them to go on, that she would be along shortly. They were out of sight now, thirty yards or so in front of her and walking. Obviously they felt she was familiar enough with her surroundings, and were comfortable leaving her behind.

She turned away from Page, and began to follow her friends deeper into the forest, when curiosity overcame her. She paused, turned and stared in his direction. And she died instantly, quietly, cleanly, alone. One shot.

She would never own a doll. Celebrate Christmas. Smile at her mother. Fall in love. Buy a dress. Go to school again. Or. . .

Oblivious to everything else, Page slowed his pace to a brisk walk. His mind racing back over those awful days. It's funny, he thought, how after twenty years his bitterness about the war, and sense of betrayal grew.

It was something Page never discussed with anyone. Not his family. Not even his closest friends, except other veterans. And then, even they wouldn't or couldn't verbalize their feelings for years. It wasn't until Hollywood started making movies about the war, and books were published, and people began looking on the conflict, not so much as a political happening, as a tragic event, that really thinking about it, even to one's self, was possible.

He picked up his pace once again and his pulse quickened — more out of anger, now, than exhaustion.

Oh, he talked about it occasionally when he got home. How can you avoid talking about something as significant in your life as your participation in a war? Yet, he felt betrayed, then, as he was sure other veteran's felt. And he engaged in many angry debates with neighbors, smart-assed college kids and their left-wing professors about such issues as morality. But what the hell did they know of morality? Morality to the protesters was best served when we cut and ran, and abandoned our allies, our friends. The Vietnamese were real people, though. They suffered and died along with us. What a fucking mistake that was, he thought.

Peace with honor is a phrase which cuts to the soul of every Vietnam veteran. It was the rallying call of cowards who saw victory in our defeat. Who saw honor in our humiliation. Who wallowed in their own self-righteousness when we were finally driven from that country. Page could neither forgive nor forget the liberal establish-ment for abandoning those allies. Indeed, as the years passed his thoughts were filled increasingly with guilt and sorrow and remorse as he remembered a thousand times the image of those last American soldiers cowering on the roof of the American Embassy in Saigon, kicking and punching innocent civilians trying desperately to flee with us. Damn, he thought. Every time he remembered it it grew worse. And it was impossible to stop remembering. Impossible!

Page jogged faster, determined not to let the years catch up with him. Once a marine, he chanted as he ran, always a marine. Forty years old, he took great pride in his ability to endure these challenges. Yet, his mind would not retire his thoughts.

As much as he tried to concentrate on other things, he couldn't stop thinking about betrayal. His mind raced uncontrollably over those last few months in Vietnam. So long ago. What did the protesters know about betrayal? When you see your friends die miserable deaths, when you see people look up to you, and actually believe you won't let them down, not desert them as the French did, when you experience these feelings and understand these emotions, then — maybe — you will understand betrayal.

"We ain't the French you dinky-dow mutherfuckers. We're Marines. And we kick ass. We won't desert you. We won't run away. Trust us!" How many times did he yell that in the face of a cynical, frightened South Vietnamese soldier or civilian?

No it certainly wasn't easy to forget. Maybe that's why Page came to the mountains each year. So that he would never forget. Never lose sight of man's — of his own fallibility.

The Woodstock Inn was just down the street. He'd stop there long enough to have a cup of coffee, read the paper, and if the weather held, head for a walk in the hills. If the rain came as predicted, he'd pack his gear and drive north to Sharon, through Pomfret. It was a lesser-travelled road than the interstate which ran parallel to it, but more scenic, especially to one who appreciated the absolute splendor of the area.

Mercifully, the ghosts of history past vanished as he approached the center of town.

It was a cool morning, and Page noticed upon completion of his run, that he barely worked up a sweat. He felt relaxed and content with himself, having completed his exercise routine with enough reserve stamina to go the extra mile if he had to. After pausing momentarily on the outskirts to rest, he strolled leisurely along the oblong-shaped median strip which divided the highway and served as a small pedestrian park in the center of town. Page sat for a few moments on one of the benches, closed his eyes and took a few deep breaths. You could actually breathe the heavy mist which clung to the base of the mountains and enveloped the length of the town.

Leaning back, with his legs stretched out in front, he massaged his face and smoothed his hands through his hair. Maybe I'll give the paper a call, and check on the week's distribution, he thought as he rose and walked leisurely across the street, admiring the landscaping at the front of the Inn.

Page strolled leisurely to the entrance of the Inn, and paused momentarily before entering to view the Inn's landscaping and scenic mountain setting. Beautiful, he thought. Absolutely beautiful.

He entered the Inn, heading immediately for the pay phone in the lobby. One call and then I'll eat, he thought, as he dialed his Boston office.

"Hi Janet," he said cheerfully, as the receiver on the other end was lifted.

"Dawson, is that you?" she asked, surprised to hear from him this early.

"In the living flesh," he answered.

"Dawson, you have to be the craziest person in the world going camping on a weekend like this. Is it raining up there yet?"

"No, not yet, Janet," he answered.

"When are you coming back to Boston, Dawson?"

"It's nice to talk with you also, Janet," he said mockingly, adding, "If the weather gets any worse, I'll pack up early and just go sightseeing in the mountains. Sorry honey," he teased, "you know I am about plans. I hate to break them once I make them."

"You mean you're stubborn," she insisted.

"Any messages?" he asked, ignoring her taunt.

"Ah, let me look. . ." And there was a long pause as his secretary shuffled through a mound of paperwork on her desk.

"Janet," Page said, needling her some more, "this phone call is costing me a hundred dollars. And I haven't even had breakfast yet."

"Well hold on, I'm looking," she shot back. "Oh yes, you have a phone call from Brother Dominic at the Chancellery. He said he wanted to talk with you about the interview. I think he wants to cancel it."

"Cancel it? For what?" Page asked.

"I don't know. He didn't say. He didn't say he actually wanted to cancel it, Dawson, he only said he wanted to talk with you about it. But I think he wants to cancel."

Dawson thought for a moment. Brother Dominic was an aide to Bishop Michelsen. "Janet, if he calls back let him know I'll be returning to Boston Sunday afternoon. I'll call him them."

"Dawson?" Janet pleaded one more time but to no avail. "I wish you would head home today. I just have this funny feeling. Maybe it's the weather or something. It can't be getting any better where you are either. There was a terrible car accident on the Interstate last night. Dawson, why don't you head home today."

"You miss me don't you honey. Admit it. You have the hots for your boss. It's my animal magnetism. Come on, say it. You miss me terribly don't you."

"Yeah," she shot back, "so does my husband."

Dawson laughed, and told Janet to take the rest of the day off. Nothing ever happened on weekends, he said.

8
The Sighting

The cup of coffee which Page planned for breakfast became a thick Vermont cheese omelette with extra cheese, pancakes, a side order of bacon, large orange juice and three cups of coffee. So much for roughing it, Page mused to himself as he finished his meal and perused the morning paper in the cozy warmth of the largest of the Inn's three dining rooms.

Friday's news was the usual. Car accident here. Robbery there. Hijackings, muggings and assaults. By Page six he began to wonder why he even wanted to read the paper. Shit, mud and corruption everywhere you looked, and this was supposed to be a vacation, of sorts.

There was this one interesting story, however, on page eight about an abduction at Mich's Variety store in Boston. Page knew the location. MAN ABDUCTED IN BROAD DAYLIGHT! STUNNED OWNER SAYS TWO MEN HELD KNIFE TO VICTIM'S THROAT.

"Boston police are trying to piece together the events leading up to the violent abduction of a man who stopped to place a phone call at Mich's variety store yesterday afternoon," the story began. "According to witnesses," it continued, "two Hispanic males, approximately twenty-five years of age, casually walked into the variety store at about 11:50 A.M., apparently looking for a specific person. 'All hell broke loose when they found him,' one of the witnesses said. 'There was blood coming from everywhere as they dragged this poor guy from the phone booth. It was horrible.'"

"Police have been unable to attach a motive to the abduction," the story concluded. "But according to police spokesman, Lieutenant Robert O'Neil, 'drugs are suspected to be involved.'"

Page didn't dwell on the news item, except to reflect on his own commitment to speak out on the problem whenever he could. His own paper, the News Tribune, although a small publication, did have influence at city hall, and was a respected journal in its own right.

In any event, Page was determined not to let any local news interfere with his weekend escape, which he observed from looking out the window, was already in jeopardy from some ominous looking clouds swirling in from the northeast.

It didn't take long for the weather to deteriorate either. That's how it was up north, Page thought. Yesterday wasn't such a great day. Today would be worse. So what else is new?

Because of the certainty of bad weather, Page decided to forego his walk along the town's perimeter, Instead, he would take a leisurely drive north and do some additional sightseeing along the way. At least that's what he planned.

By 11:45 A.M. Page had completed his agenda in Woodstock: shopping, sightseeing and relaxation. When satisfied that the weather would not cooperate for a longer stay, he packed his camping gear, secured his equipment in the trunk of his automobile, and prepared to head north. Not surprisingly, the weather grew nasty faster than anyone anticipated. The weathermen were still reporting the possibility of heavy rain and wind for the region at the very time heavy rain and wind were sweeping over the mountains.

Page headed north, anyway, through Pomfret, a sleepy community consisting mostly of small rolling hills, wide shallow valleys and scarce population. It was very scenic in the hills around Woodstock any time of the year, and even more so in inclement weather.

As he recounted the details of events which were to follow to the police later that day, he was unable to give an exact location where the sighting actually occurred. He did agree, however, to personally accompany the police to the soft shoulder where he thought he last parked his car.

As best he could remember, the time was 12:30 P.M.. The rain and wind were fierce. Worse than Page or the weather bureau anticipated. Driving became almost impossible. And any travelling which could be done was done slowly and with great care.

There were very few cars on the road, Page recalled. And the cold rain actually turned to sleet for a short period, freezing on the front window faster than his wipers could clear it from his view. In spite of the hazardous conditions, he remembered, he didn't feel the least uneasy. As a matter-of-fact he relished the inclement weather. Enjoyed the warm, cozy feeling inside his car. Soft music. Great stereo system, he thought, as he sludged along at twenty-five miles an hour, careful not to slip off the road. Mighty damp and cold out there, he said to himself, never thinking he would be near-buried in the muddy terrain shortly.

"There's a heavy rain and freezing advisory in effect," the radio announcer said, "for the central Vermont region. Drivers are advised to be cautious of slippery road conditions, especially in the upper elevations. . ." Page turned his radio up to hear more details. ". . .and, motorists are being asked to stay off the roads until the front moves on through later this afternoon. . ."

Not wanting to take any chances, Page was particularly observant of conditions all around: front, rear, sides. The rain and wind was so heavy, and temperatures so varied, that a temperature inversion caused a heavy blanket of fog to rise from the valley. Ghostly apparitions, Page thought as he slowed still more, not wanting to slide off the side of the road and end up stuck in a mud hole — or worse.

"Shit!"

Instinctively Page swerved to avoid the raccoon which decided to cross the road at the precise moment his car passed. His attention was instantaneously brought back to his immediate front. Heart pounding, Page slowed and checked his rear view mirror briefly to assure himself that he hadn't left a raccoon hat lying on the road in place of a living creature. He shook his head and smiled when he noticed nothing there. But he was unnerved momentarily by the incident, and his senses — and respect — for the deceptive beauty and potential treachery of the region were aroused to an even greater height by that momentary diversion.

The rhythmic, almost frantic motion of the wiper blades clearing the pounding, driving rain from the windshield, the heavy wind rocking the car with gusts which threatened to take control and blow it off the road, the claps of ear-shattering thunder and frequent bright flashes of lightning which occasionally struck as blinding bolts, and the rising fog, all caused Page to doubt for the first time the wisdom of travelling this seldom used road. Maybe Janet was right after all, he thought, as he focused his vision on the road in front.

Nice going, Page, he ridiculed himself. Great decision, heading into the mountains, into the storm. Solid judgement on your behalf.

Then he came to that spot on the road to which he would later bring the police. It caught his attention for only an instant. But something definitely flickered brightly, about one-hundred yards ahead and below — in the belly of the clearing beneath. Perhaps it was a flashlight, or the beam from a car's headlights.

Page slowed his vehicle almost to a stall. It was difficult to identify the object from his location on the road. And the rain, wind and fog made it near impossible to see clearly without binoculars. But there was something there. Was it a set of headlights? An accident? he wondered.

Page pulled over slowly to the side of the road. It made little sense to sound his horn, he figured. Naturally, he would offer his assistance, if any was even needed. After all, it could be just a couple of hunters or campers packing their gear as he did earlier. No need to create additional confusion by making a fuss. He would observe for now. See if there was any trouble first.

When the car was safely stopped, Page reached to the back seat and pulled a set of binoculars from his gear gag. Then, grabbing the raincoat beside him, drew it over his head and stepped out into the driving wind and rain.

As soon as he could he steady himself against the force of the wind, he placed the binoculars to his eyes and squinted to sharpen his vision, hoping to identify the forms below. At first it was difficult. Then. . .

"Holy shit," he mumbled, as he crouched low against the fender. He removed the binoculars from his eyes. Wishing he had a dry cloth, he wiped his eyes in disbelief. By now his body was drenched and he was shivering from the raw cold. Were his eyes deceiving him? Was a body actually being buried? He wiped the rain from his eyes again, then lifted the glasses in an attempt to get a better look. But it was impossible to see clearly from that distance.

Page moved instinctively to turn off the headlights of his car. Then, after a moment's reflection he moved even more quickly to the trunk to remove the .357 magnum pistol he carried there. Hoping he wouldn't need it, he removed it from its case nonetheless. "Where the hell are the state police when you need them," he whispered to himself as he leaned under the rear hood and loaded six rounds into the chamber.

More curious now than anything else, still secure in the belief he was a distant observer, Page eased the trunk closed, then moved quickly for cover behind a tree, about twenty feet off the road. Leaning against the wet bark, Page strained to get a better look at the events unfolding below. He lifted the binoculars to his face again and inched around the craggy surface. Everything was shadowy, though. The fog didn't help matters either. But he could see — something. The body being buried. Something about it. Damn, he thought. They're placing it in a shallow hole in the ground. But why?

Again, he was forced to interrupt his own observations to wipe the rain from his face. The hair. That's it. The hair. Blowing wildly about. Distinctive. A lot of white hair, and a hand hanging limply, eerily.

Page's mind raced as he weighed the options available to him. Should he go for the police? No, that wouldn't be wise since he didn't know exactly where he was. Wait for a passing motorist? Maybe. But he didn't want to create a scene by bringing attention to himself. And even then, what was the likelihood of a motorist stopping for a stranger in this type of weather? He smiled to himself as he thought about that last question, for he stopped. No, there was only one option — wait. Wait for whoever was down there to leave, then go down and take a closer look. A brief look just to confirm what he saw. He dreaded the thought. But he couldn't just walk away. Someone was probably murdered — and being buried before his very eyes. Even for Pomfret, this was not your normal burial procedure. No, indeed. He would take a quick look, then report the entire incident to the police. But first he had to confirm what he observed.

He turned and crouched behind the tree. He was wet and uncomfortable — and yes, frightened. It was the same type of high he experienced when he was in force recon, but he was twenty years old then. And that was in time of war.

Just when he thought matters couldn't get any worse, they did. A loud crash of thunder, followed by an enormous cracking sound and blinding white light caused him to jump away from the tree — and none too soon. Every hair on his body stood straight out as the electrically charged bolt raced instantly down the tree which moments before he was propped against.

His breathing quickened, uncontrollable due to the proximity of his own death. His conditioning paid off, though. As quickly as the series of events unfurled, he realized the need to control his actions. Relax, Page, he said to himself. Take it easy. Slow down. Just hold on. Steady yourself.

Then it occurred to him. On no, I'm not kneeling any longer. I'm not crouched behind the tree. I'm standing straight up. Exposed. I didn't give my position away, the lightning striking the tree exposed me. It created a diversion for the two below, causing me to drop my guard momentarily. Now, they were looking upward, straining to see the form standing atop the hill. His form. Damn! he thought, as he gazed down only to see them straining to see his form.

When the two men sensed their grizzly deed was observed, they halted their work abruptly, and ran toward what appeared to Page to be a waiting car parked on the small dirt road on the other side of the bush. Page was thankful for their departure, but confused. It was all too easy. Why would they go through all the trouble of burying a body, only to run when observed by a stranger? Unless, they intended to come back soon.

Page held the .357 by his side as he made his way cautiously down the side of the slippery, steep hill. As he approached the bottom of the incline, he paused and glanced around. The car had sped away, leaving him alone with the corpse.

Ankle deep in mud, now, Page walked carefully through the soupy surface. As he moved closer to the scene of the burial, he noticed that a dirt road did indeed run along the side of the clearing. And where it ended, he didn't care. All he wanted to do was confirm the existence of the body and leave.

It was midday. Dark and foul. The wind swirled around him as he walked guardedly toward the partially covered body. The rain battered his face every time he gazed straight ahead, so he walked with his head and eyes down. Toward the center of the small clearing there was situated a dead tree trunk. To his rear was the steep hill leading back up to the road. The semi-circle of forest which surrounded this site was thick with trees — and the dirt path over which the two men apparently made their getaway.

Very slowly, Page approached the protruding hand. It was the hand of the man with white hair. Page dropped to one knee, hoping to create less of a silhouette — or target, whatever the case may be. He looked in each direction to ensure his privacy. In this location he felt complete exposed and extremely uncomfortable and concerned for his own safety.

Once satisfied that he was, indeed, alone, he directed his attention to the body which was buried in front of him. God knows he touched enough dead bodies in his lifetime — too many. But that was in time of war, when even the unnatural was a given natural. But this was not war. It was not real. Or was it?

He moved closer, now, and noticed there was something on one of the fingers — a wedding ring? He felt nauseous, but had to touch the outstretched hand to inspect it more closely. It might be the only clue he could report to the police later. The only identification of the body in the mud. Gently, he lifted the well manicured finger with the back of his own index finger, careful not to disturb anything. He noticed the ring was an ornate, beautifully sculptured piece of jewelry. Because it was turned around on the finger it only looked like a wedding band. That's probably why the murderers ignored it.

But Page could not ignore it. The ring was inscribed with some type of Latin connotation. Probably a college ring. Obviously worth some money. Clearly, whoever was buried here was not murdered in a failed robbery attempt. Anyone who took the time to bury a body in a place like this, on a day like today, Page thought, was hiding something. Immersed in his thoughts, he was startled by an explosion of thunder. He dropped the hand and fell backward into the mud. "Shit!" he mumbled. Time to get the hell out of this place, he thought.

As he rose to wipe himself of the mud, a twig snapped behind him. Slowly, afraid to make any sudden moves, Page reached into his belt to withdraw his .357. Death was stalking all over this place, he thought as he braced for any unexpected, sudden activity. He knew someone was behind him. He could feel their presence. But how far behind? In one smooth motion Page turned and dropped to the ground, causing rain and mud to splash about his body. The two murderers had returned. That was the clearest thought he had. After that, Dodge City, as the shooting began.

Page was an expert shot, and even though he was scared to death at that moment, he controlled each round, remembering how easy it was in a firefight to unload a chamber prematurely into the woods before a target was even identified. Many good men died in Vietnam after having emptied their M-14's into tree trunks, thinking they were enemy soldiers. He resolved never to follow in their footsteps. Before he would shoot, he would identify the target — then blast the bastard into hell. Period! And that's what he had to do now, because he only had six rounds. He had to be accurate.

Unwisely, the two had not taken the precaution of picking him off from the safety of the woods. Maybe it was all the ground fog and rain. In any event, they were as exposed as he — even more so. And although they fired first, their rounds were misdirected. The first bullet from Page's revolver thumped into the chest of one intruder, sending him reeling backward about five feet before he fell flat on his back, body twitching in death throes, splashing mud and water around himself. It would soon be over for this man.

Somewhere in the volley which followed, a bullet from the other man's revolver struck the ground in front of Page's face, causing water to splash into his eyes. Instinctively, Page moved away from the debris. Unconsciously, he began to stand. And that's when the next bullet creased the top of his head. Page knew he was hit. The bullet dazed him slightly, numbing the entire right side of his face. He dropped his gun and staggered backward awkwardly, seeing white firefly-like apparitions.

"Oh no," he mumbled as he dropped to his knees, blood trickling down his forehead, into his mouth. He could taste his own blood. Everything was growing darker. He fell backward into the mud, on top of the half-buried body. Yet, he was still conscious. Still aware that he was alive. Luckily for Page, his assailant had also run out of ammunition.

Page knew his only chance for survival would be for him to feign death, which given his present predicament, he felt was not that far from the truth. He laid motionless as the blood continued to ooze down his forehead. It's amazing how calm he felt. His survival now was a matter of calculation. If he could feign death he would live. One, plus one equals two. Every time.

He couldn't see his assailant. He could sense him, though. He could hear the man's heavy breathing. He could hear him curse to himself at the sight of two additional dead bodies. Why doesn't he finish me off? Page thought as he lie there, confused, knowing he was being studied for signs of life. Perhaps it was all the blood, which, from the sensations he was experiencing, certainly felt like a major head wound. Maybe his assailant was just confused and as unsettled as he was. Whatever the reason, Page was left for dead, along with the body in the ground. One covered entirely by mud, except for the protrusion of a hand; the other body — his — sinking slowly in the mud, muddy and bloody.

He had to look. Had to glimpse the man who shot him and assuredly killed the unlucky fellow buried beneath. This was one newspaper story he would not leave filled with blanks — or vague references to events which transpired. Indeed, if he live to tell about it, he wanted to know what the man looked like who tried to kill him. Page simply, had to know more. Very slowly, carefully, Page squinted through one eye, praying he would not be observed. Luckily, the man's back was toward him. Not much to go on, Page thought. It seemed that whoever was standing over him was as confused as he was. The man appeared to be heavy set. Large framed with black hair. He wore a long, dark blue raincoat.

Then, the stranger began to walk slowly away. There wasn't enough time for Page to observe detail. He was feeling extremely weak and dizzy. Hold on, he prompted himself. Hold on. Just prior to passing out, his eyes glimpsed something — odd. Something out of place. He blinked rapidly to clear his vision. It was a silver object. A small shiny silver object on the bottom of the man's shoe. A gum wrapper? Nothing made sense. Nothing.

Page was certain he was going to die. Life is a bitch, he though, as the rain fell heavy against his face and drenched his clothing. He thought of his family. Of his ex-wife. It was time to make his last confession — but to whom? Oh my God. . . I am. . . heartily. . . sorry. . ..

9
The Dig

5 P.M. "Mr. Page!" The voice was unfamiliar.

Dawson's eyes adjusted slowly to the white fluorescent glare of the hospital's bright lights. His awareness returning gradually.

"What happened?" he asked as he rubbed his right hand against his forehead, shielding his eyes from the harsh white light. "Where am I?"

"Mr. Page, my name is Lieutenant Dowling," the plain clothes officer said as he crossed the room and stood by one side of the bed. "That's Sergeant Blakey," he said, pointing across the bed at a tall, muscular, uniformed officer standing opposite him. "We're with the Vermont State Police."

Page glanced at both officers then fell back gently against his pillow.

Dowling spoke again. "Sergeant Blakey found you wondering through Pomfret a few hours ago. You're okay now, Mr. Page. You're in the hospital. As for what happened to you, we'd like to know that ourselves."

Page stared at Blakey, then back at Dowling. He propped himself up against the pillow and back board of the hospital bed, and rubbed his eyes once again. "I think I saw a man being murdered. Or at least being buried." Page spoke hesitatingly as he tried to piece it all together. How much did he actually remember? How much did he dream? He continued, slowly. "I parked my car by the side of the road to see what was going on. . ."

"Excuse me Mr. Page," Dowling interrupted as he removed a notebook from his pants pocket and began to take notes, "we didn't find any vehicle parked alongside the road. Nor was there any body to be found." He looked across at Sergeant Blakey who nodded his agreement. "When you parked your car by the side of the road, are you telling me you did this before or after you saw a body being buried?"

Page massaged his hand through his hair, obviously annoyed with his disorientation. "Something . . . something very strange happened this afternoon," he said, a puzzled expression on his face. "Today is still Saturday isn't it?" he asked.

"It's a little after five o'clock in the evening, Mr. Page," Dowling said. He then motioned for Sergeant Blakey to step around the bed and meet him a few feet away. Just out of Page's hearing range. "Excuse us for a moment, Mr. Page," Dowling said glancing back over his shoulder.

"What do you make of it, Jim?" Dowling whispered.

"I wish I knew what to say, Lieutenant," Blakey said with a shrug. "The weather is clearing somewhat. If the hospital gives him a clean bill of health, maybe we ought to drive him out to the area where he says he parked his car — out where I picked him up. . ."

"Lieutenant," Page said, feeling a little stronger as his body recovered from the shock of earlier. He sat up in bed again as he spoke. "I think I can take you to the place where I left my car. Where I saw the man being buried."

Dowling looked at Page, then at Blakey and shrugged. "Maybe."

Page positioned himself on the side of the bed, careful to balance himself since he was still shaken from the events of the afternoon. "I can give you additional details on the way out there if you'd like."

Dowling and Blakey looked at one another again and said nothing. They knew this was the only option open to them, and were thankful that Page suggested it. Witnesses can be real pains in the ass when they want to be, when they choose not to cooperate or get involved. "Mr. Page, would you like to call an attorney or have one present during this period?" Sergeant Blakey asked, more out of reflex than accusation.

Page frowned. "Am I under arrest or something?"

"No sir," Lieutenant Dowling added, quickly, "We just want to be certain that you're in complete control of what you say." Dowling paused, then sighed. "You are correct, Mr. Page. Something strange did happen this afternoon. You were shot. The doctor confirmed that a bullet did crease your skull, and that you are very fortunate it wasn't a pussy hair lower."

Page laughed. "Look Lieutenant, I appreciate your honesty. I'll do everything I can to assist in your investigation. If you'll just get the doctor in here so I can sign myself out, I'll be happy to do whatever I can to help you solve this mystery." As he spoke, he stood slowly from the bed. "I came to Vermont to relax — not get shot in the head and end up in a hospital."

"Fine, Mr. Page," Lieutenant Dowling said, assuring the witness that they appreciated his cooperation. We'll do everything in our power to assist you in locating the person who shot you," he said. "And as for the assertion that a body was buried, we'd be grateful if you would direct us to the location off the road where *that* alleged incident occurred."

Dowling asked Blakey to locate the doctor, and to secure Page's release if he was well enough to travel. Dowling believed Page's story. He sensed that Page was honest about what he witnessed, and that he had no part in a crime — if a crime even occurred. If a murder did occur in Woodstock, Dowling thought — and the murderers were still in the area — the department would have to act quickly to apprehend them. "Mr. Page," Dowling continued as he crossed the room and stood in front of Page, "we don't get many stories like yours around here. Woodstock, Pomfret, this whole area," he said while making a circular motion with his hand, "is pretty quiet. If what you say is true, it'll be absolutely imperative that your information be accurate. And we get started as soon as possible."

"I understand, Lieutenant. I may be a little wobbly on my feet now," he said jokingly as he rubbed the top of his head, "but this bullet wound is no figment of my imagination — although I wish it were."

Sergeant Blakey returned with the admitting doctor. "Well, Mr. Page, how do you feel?" the doctor said as he approached and checked the bandage on Page's head.

"A little shaken," Page answered as he studied the young intern who was busy searching for any additional injury. "And I have a slight headache."

"Hmm hmm," the doctor said.

"Other than that I feel fine — I think. What I'd like to do is get out of here and begin to put my life back together again. This hasn't been one of my most productive days, doc."

"Hmm, hmm."

"Ouch! And your pulling on my scalp doesn't help matters any either."

The doctor continued to examine Page for signs of shock, trauma, bleeding. He was professionally unaffected by his patient's protestations. "Fortunately for you, Mr. Page, your wound is superficial. We have no reason to ask you to remain overnight, unless, of course, you want to. As far as I'm concerned, if you feel steady on your feet, you're free to go whenever you wish."

"I'm as ready as I'll ever be."

"Just be certain to keep an eye on the wound for infection."

Lieutenant Dowling wasted little time in moving his investigation forward. It was getting dark fast, and he wanted to begin his search before what little light remained disappeared behind the mountains. It's dark in the mountains on a clear night. It's near impossible to see anything when the sky is overcast — and there was one hell of an overcast sky this evening.

"Sergeant Blakey, I'll radio ahead for additional men to meet us here. I'll also ask the locals to join us." He looked at his watch. "We had better call ahead to the garage and have a tow truck and some spotlights ready in case we need them. I'll also touch bases with headquarters and ask for permission to have you work with me on this thing. If that's okay with you."

"Fine Lieutenant," Blakey said. He knew the State Police often shared jurisdiction along small state roads with local police departments, and he was seasoned enough to realize that a case such as this involved paperwork, mounds of paperwork, in fact. And he knew the local police wouldn't feel the least slighted if state jurisdiction were invoked.

Page raised his hand to his face and rubbed his eyes, then walked over to the sink and splashed some water on his face. "I'm going to need some clothing," he said, noticing that he was wearing hospital pajamas.

"Your clothes are being held for evidence," Sergeant Blakey said. "When I brought you in you were covered with mud, Mr. Page. We wanted to hold your clothes until we learned more of your condition. When I went for the doctor, I asked one of the orderlies to get you some replacements. The nurse told me they would be ready momentarily."

"I can't believe this actually happened to me," Page said as he washed himself.

"Can you tell us anything about the man you say was being buried?" Dowling asked. "Anything at all. What did he look like? What did the men burying him look like? How many of them were there?" He was pressing.

"Slow down Lieutenant," Page said as he toweled himself, facing the two officers. Blakey was sitting on the edge of the bed taking notes. Dowling was standing in the middle of the room.

Page straightened himself, took a deep breath, then exhaled slowly, relieving the pressure he felt building. "When I arrived at the scene, the burial was already taking place. At first, all I noticed were head-lights from the car. I thought it was an automobile accident. So I pulled over to the side of the road to take a closer look. . ."

"Would you like a cigarette, Mr. Page," Dowling said as he lit one up.

"No thanks, Lieutenant, I don't smoke," Page answered.

"A wise decision," Dowling answered, prompting, "Go on with your story."

"I didn't think anything of it at first. I took my binoculars from the back seat of the car to get a better look. That's when I noticed two men carrying the body. . ."

"Can you describe him? The body of the man being carried, that is."

"I'm sorry Lieutenant. From where I was parked on the road — and with the rain and ground fog, it was difficult to make out any great detail. It was a man. Maybe in his sixties. All I could make out was that he had white hair. A lot of white hair. That was the most identifiable thing about him."

"Let me just go back for a moment to the men carrying the body, Mr. Page. Were there any identifiable characteristics about them. Anything at all?"

Page thought for a moment before answering. "Nothing, Lieuten-ant. They were wearing dark clothes. Maybe raincoats. . ."

An orderly walked into the room with Page's new clothes. The police said nothing while he was there. When he left, Page continued with his story. "I spent the weekend in a small campsite just outside Woodstock. I go there occasionally just to do some thinking. I've used the woods for target shooting from time to time," he added with apprehension.

"You have a gun?"

"Yes," Page answered directly. "I'm licensed."

"Do you hunt, Mr. Page?" Blakey asked.

"Not at all Sergeant. I just like to plink now and then."

Lieutenant Dowling looked at Blakey and shrugged. Vermont's gun laws only required that out-of-staters who carried guns through the state carry them unloaded in the trunk of their automobiles. Page apparently conformed to that requirement, and neither officer pur-sued the matter further — at that point.

When Page finished dressing, Lieutenant Dowling suggested he take them to the scene of the alleged crime. "You can continue the story as we drive out there, Mr. Page," he said as they walked from the room.

It occurred to Page as he walked down the long corridor that the clothes he was given were inmate colors: dark blue denim dungarees and pale blue shirt. He hadn't checked, but wondered if there was a number stenciled on the back. As they walked, he wondered about the man he shot. What would happen when the police learned of that incident? Might as well get it out of the way now, Page thought, as they exited through the emergency ward.

"Lieutenant," he said as they stopped at the carport outside. Page's face reflected the concern he felt inside. "Whoever the people were that I observed, they tried to kill me..."

"I know, Mr Page," Dowling said uncomfortably.

"I'm not certain I know all the details of what happened this afternoon," Page said cautiously, "...or even why. But, I shot one of the men." Page paused, looking at the two officers when he said it, realizing, perhaps, for the first time the seriousness of his own situation."

Lieutenant Dowling's answer was reassuring. "Why don't we just wait until we get there, Mr. Page, before you go any further. Let's see what we come up with."

It was getting darker with each passing moment, and heavy rain clouds hung ominously over the valley, giving the mountains an eerie appearance. Page drove with Lieutenant Dowling. Sergeant Blakey followed in his marked cruiser. Two local cruisers from Woodstock followed, along with a tow truck with emergency lights attached. An ambulance was ordered to stand by in the event a body was, indeed, found.

They drove from the hospital in a slow caravan consisting of flashing blues and reds. During the entire drive a light mist driven by a stiff wind splashed against the windshield of the cars. The weather added an almost surrealistic, unnatural setting to the countryside.

It was during the trip to the sight that Page told Lieutenant Dowling of his newspaper background, and of his close personal friendship with Lieutenant Robert O'Neil from the Boston Police drug unit. "I don't know if I'm going to need a personal reference by the end of this day or not, Lieutenant. But if one is needed, Bob will tell you whatever else about me you may want to know.

"If it's okay with you, Mr. Page, I'd like to place that call now."

"It looks that bad?" Page asked.

Dowling smiled. "Not really, Mr. Page. Not yet. But I would like to get that small detail out of the way first."

They drove in silence for a short while longer as Dowling made the call and confirmed Page's background. Everything checked out as he figured it would. "Mr. Page, I tend to go along with my instincts. And my instincts on this thing tell me that you're telling the truth. I know this is difficult for you. But believe me, we are on your side. If you witnessed a crime this afternoon, we want to know about it. You're doing the right thing by telling us what you saw. We're not going to put any more pressure on you than asking you to be as exact as possible. We'll play it by ear from here on in, okay?"

"Fine with me," Page said.

As the motorcade made its was slowly along the winding road, Page grew more familiar with his surroundings. "Over there, Lieutenant," Page motioned as they approached the spot where he believed his car had been parked. Had been? The car was gone.

The line of motor vehicles followed Lieutenant Dowling's lead car, and cramped tightly onto the small, dirt soft-shoulder which formed an unofficial rest area for tourists.

"It's down there," Page said, almost hypnotically. "That's where the body is buried."

10
The Discovery

The officers trekked their way slowly down the side of the slippery wet hill which emptied into a circular clearing approximately one hundred yards below. Although surrounded by forest, the clearing was obviously accessible by small vehicle as Page said it was. And it was muddy.

"Christ," Blakey said as he sank ankle deep in the mud, intentionally avoiding the deep furrows made by an automobile's tires. The newspaperman's story was gaining credibility each moment that passed. "What side of this clearing should be looking, Page?" he called out.

"Just up ahead by the tree trunk, I think," Page said. "Somewhere near the left-of-center of the flats, that's where I stumbled across the hand."

The men walked carefully through the mud, stopping occasionally to study their location. No protruding hand. No sign of a grave. But there were car tracks — and they were made recently. The heavy rain would surely have washed away any traces of earlier visits to this area.

On the other side of the clearing Lieutenant Dowling searched the area where Page said his attackers stood. He stared into the mud, carefully moving the top layer of dirt from side to side with the bottom of his shoe. His foot touched something. A bluish object. He glided his foot lightly across the muddy surface again and again, hoping his eyes hadn't deceived him. They didn't. He removed a pen from his shirt pocket and knelt, extending the tip of the pen into the trigger housing of the weapon at his feet. "Page, over here," he called out as he lifted what appeared to be a .45 caliber semi-automatic from the soupy surface.

"Everyone else stay where you are," Dowling ordered as the other officers began to move in his direction. "We don't want to walk over evidence which may be buried in this mess. Sergeant Blakey," he continued. "You better call for a photographer and notify headquarters."

"Yes sir," Blakey responded dutifully.

"Everyone else just be careful where you walk."

Page took less than three steps toward Dowling when his foot sank into the mud, resting atop — something. "Lieutenant," he called out, "I think I found the body," he said as he stepped back carefully and moved away from the area he just walked over.

"John, have those spotlights directed down here," Dowling shouted to the truck operator. "Frank," he was calling to one of the local officers from town, "I want this entire area cordoned off. You and Lewis start that project now. And rope off a walkway from the top of the hill to the spot where Mr. Page is standing. I don't want people trampling all over this place burying any further evidence."

It was approximately 6:45 P.M.. The spotlights from the tow truck were turned on, illuminating the atmosphere surrounding the swampy area. This, coupled with the flashing blue and red lights atop the cruisers, added an air of the supernatural to the already ill-omened setting.

Lieutenant Dowling walked carefully to where Page was standing. Neither man said a word. Both knew a body was, indeed, buried here. Only the mud had to be removed to confirm the remainder of the story.

Sergeant Blakey hollered down, asking if additional men would be needed. "We could use some additional cruisers for traffic control, Sergeant," Dowling shouted back, noticing that what little traffic there was on the road was backing up as each driver slowed almost to a stop to observe what was going on below. "Other than that we can handle it from here. And get the county medical examiner on the line also. I think we're about to find a body."

"Well, Mr. Page?"

"Is that a gun you found?" Page asked, pointing to the soiled weapon wrapped in cellophane protruding from the Lieutenant's raincoat.

Dowling nodded, then knelt in the mud. "It looks as if we're going to get a little dirty this evening, Mr. Page."

"Yeah," Page said as he knelt opposite the lieutenant and assisted in carefully parting the mud and water. They were about six inches down when the feel of wet cloth replaced the feel of cold mud. "Go slowly, Mr. Page. Try not to disturb anything," Dowling cautioned.

Carefully, they parted and lifted mud from the corpse, exposing more and more of the body underneath. "It's a lousy business, Mr. Page," Dowling said. "I hope you have a strong stomach."

Twenty-three years on the force hadn't prepared Lieutenant Dowling for what he was about to uncover. "Oh my God," he said softly as he meticulously cleared the area surrounding the man's face. Page grimaced at the sight.

Deep cuts in the skin were filled with mud and water. Dowling gagged, turned away, took a deep breath, then continued slowly — carefully. The neck was not just cut, it was ripped open — torn apart. The lips were missing — cut off. The tip of the nose — gone. "Jesus," Dowling murmured. The tongue was hanging limply, almost as if it were yanked out. The dark black hair. . .

The expression on Page's face turned from shock to disbelief. "Lieutenant," he said abruptly, "this isn't the man I saw them burying." Frantically, Page began to clear the mud from where he supposed the corpses' arm was. Lower and lower, he pushed aside the blanket of mud until he reached the hand. "He's not wearing any ring."

"Huh?" Dowling said.

Page lifted the ring finger. "He's not wearing any ring," he said excitedly, nervously. "The man I saw buried here was wearing a ring. This man has no ring."

"Easy, Mr. Page," Dowling cautioned as he reached out and grabbed a hold of Dawson's arm. "We found the body, didn't we?" He sounded confused. "This has to be the man you saw being buried."

"I'm telling you Lieutenant," Page said emphatically, "this isn't the man I saw them burying." He paused to regain his composure. "Something's very wrong here, Lieutenant. Very wrong." Page tried desperately to reconstruct what he saw, to rationalize the discrepancy in his own mind. Was he absolutely certain the man he saw them burying had white hair? Or did it only appear to be so? He shook his head, then looked across at Lieutenant Dowling and said: "I've never been more certain of anything in my life, Lieutenant. This is not the man I saw them burying."

As they went about their grisly task the clouds opened, and the rain started falling heavily over the entire area again. "Great," Dowling humphed.

Both men knelt in the mud and stared at each other for another moment, assessing the situation before commenting. A crack of thunder startled everyone in the area, and men began to complain why this had to happen on their shift. Dowling looked down at the partially uncovered body once again and said: "If this isn't the man you saw them burying, Who the fuck is he?"

Page could only respond: "I honestly don't know, Lieutenant. I honestly don't know."

The approach of the ambulance interrupted their concentration and conversation momentarily. Dowling slipped back into character. "Don't touch anything, Mr. Page. Let the medical crews do their work from this point on."

Both men stood as the team of EMT's was directed to the site of the gruesome discovery.

"The medical examiner is on his way, Lieutenant," one of the medics said as he approached through the thick mud. "Christ this place is eerie," he said as he glanced around, not paying attention to what lie in the mud. As the EMT's moved closer to the body, one recoiled, and holdind his hand to his mouth said: "Holy shit! What the fuck is that? Is it human?"

"Was," Dowling responded matter-of-factly, adding: "Try not to throw up all over yourself, Dave, we have a guest here from out of state."

"Pleased to meet you," the younger of the two said as he smiled meekly at Dawson.

"He's all yours, boys," Dowling said as he stepped back and gazed around, drawing his raincoat up around his shoulders as he spoke.

"Not ours, Lieutenant. He's property of the county M.E. to be exact."

As the men spoke two additional state police cruisers arrived at the scene. Within a relatively short time the press could also be expected, and then all semblance of order would break down. Dowling glanced skyward, and grunted at the thought that it was going to be a long, uncomfortable evening. It was raining harder now, but the wind had subsided. "We would be thankful for any small favors you could provide us, Lord," Dowling said as he trudged slowly back up the hill with Page.

For the remainder of the evening the police worked scouring the area, looking for additional evidence, for clues which might tell what happened — and why. Dowling asked Page to accompany him to headquarters for additional statements. The state's ballistic squad would have a full report on the weapon ready by Sunday afternoon, he explained. The medical examiner would also prepare a preliminary report on the man they found. That report would be ready by mid-morning also.

"I guess I have no choice in all this do I, Lieutenant."

"Mr. Page, I have no reason not to believe what you've told me. You could have simply told us nothing earlier this evening and left us with our thumbs up our asses." Both men walked toward the ambulance as he spoke. "Mr. Page I need you. I need your testimony. I need your recall. You have to help me fill in the details. Besides," he continued, surveying the abundance of automobiles at the scene, "you have no vehicle, and we'd like to see where that turns up." Dowling interrupted himself. "Mr. Page, if your vehicle was taken at the time of this murder, that means there must have been at least three people at the scene of the crime. Three people in the station wagon you observed."

Page thought about that prospect. He did manage to shoot one of his assailants. The other could not possibly have driven two automobiles away from the scene. He shuddered and nodded his head in agreement. He was, indeed, lucky to be alive. Lucky that whoever it was that stood with his back to him believed he was dead.

It was 9:15 before the body discovered in the mud was removed and the ambulance left the scene. The delay was due to the fact that the M.E. was dining with his wife at White River Junction. When he did arrive, he made a perfunctory examination of the corpse and gave this somewhat abbreviated, unceremonious statement to the police: "He's deader than a doornail, gentlemen. News and story at eleven." And with that he left for the examining room of the morgue where it would be up to him to fill in other details.

The police continued their search of the grounds. Page and Lieutenant Dowling returned to the station where hot coffee and donuts took precedence over other matters.

It was 10:00 P.M. and both men were dirty and hungry.

As they sat at the squadroom conference table, Dowling studied Page's face. He slouched forward, head resting in the palm of his hand, the other hand tapping lightly on the table. His mind raced furiously as he tried to piece it all together. Page had been cooperative, and had given the police what information he could. His story concerning his trip to Woodstock was verified. He was positively identified by the waitress and hotel manager — both lifelong community residents. And his phone call to Boston earlier that day was confirmed by the telephone company. His references were impeccable, as was his personal demeanor. Based upon hours of conversation, it was clear that Page could neither identify the man who shot him, nor positively say what type of station wagon he observed, except that it appeared to be a foreign car.

Tapping his cup lightly, Dowling had to summon years of experience. "Mr. Page. . .,"

"Please, Lieutenant, just Dawson. . ."

Dowling reciprocated the courtesy. "Thanks. The name's Larry. Dawson, I'm going to release you tomorrow after we read the autopsy report and do a ballistics on the gun we found at the scene. We haven't yet found your revolver which you say you dropped when you were shot. And we haven't found any other body at the sight. At least not as of this time we haven't. You did say you owned a .357 magnum?"

"Yes, that's correct," Page responded. His head began to ache again as the strain of the day built.

"When you go back to Boston, stay in contact with your friend, Lieutenant O'Neil. I'll have my office contact him tomorrow or Monday when we have more to go on. You may have to come back up here next week or later — depending."

"I understand," Page said. "I'll do what I can to help, although I don't know much more than I've told you already."

Lieutenant Dowling looked at his watch. It was getting late and they were both tired. "You'll need a room to catch up on some sleep and get cleaned up. The county will pay for it," he added parenthetically. "I'm going to assign one of my men to watch over you this evening while you sleep. He'll be stationed in the lobby. I don't want anything happening to you."

"That's fine, Lieutenant," Page sighed. "Call it quits then?"

"Yeah, I guess so," Dowling said as he rose and extended his hand to Page. "I'm sorry for the delay, Dawson, but I'm sure you understand. We have to be sure everything is okay."

Page rubbed his forehead, careful to avoid the wound just behind the hairline. "I made the understatement of the year this morning to my secretary," Page recalled as the two men walked out of the station house, "I told her to take the weekend off. That nothing ever happened on weekends."

Dowling paused, then smiled. "I guess you were wrong," he said.

11
Final Questions

Sunday, May 19

9:30 A.M. The phone rang several times before Dawson answered it. Although he enjoyed a quiet and restful evening's sleep, he was still groggy and his bones ached.

"Hello," he said as he propped himself against the pillows. His voice sounded tired.

"Dawson, this is Lieutenant Dowling," the voice on the other end said. "I have some good news for you."

"I can use it," Page replied as he squinted in the direction of the morning sun shining through the room's curtains. Deceptive, he thought, since the sun's rays only pierced breaks in the clouds. "What's up, Lieutenant?"

Dowling wasted no time. "The preliminary report from the medical examiner indicates that the body we discovered was dead long before being placed in that grave, probably twenty-four hours prior to our discovery."

Page's spirits were lifted. "How can you tell that?"

"Well, in addition to other medical evidence, there was little or no blood in the mud around the corpse. Freshly killed bodies ooze some liquids." Dowling shuffled additional papers until he found what he was looking for. "But more important, there was no indication of any bullet wounds in the body. Which means the gun found at the scene is not linked with the murder of the man we uncovered."

"Did they locate my gun?" Page asked.

"No! Although, according to the hospital reports, the .45 could have caused the wound on your head. Look, Dawson, I'm heading into

Woodstock this morning anyway. Let's grab a bight to eat at the Inn. I'll go over what additional information we have then."

"Fine," Page said. "I'll be ready in about a half an hour."

"Oh, and one last thing," Dowling added. "Your car was found early this morning, abandoned on 89 South, outside of White River Junction. It was stripped, and most of the paperwork was gone. It's being towed back to the garage where we'll have a few of our people go over it more thoroughly. But that won't be done until late Monday."

"Is that normal procedure for a stolen car?"

"Not as a rule," Dowling answered, "but in this case we want to dust it carefully for fingerprints just in case it was moved by the people you saw bury that body."

"My car was being driven toward Massachusetts?" Page asked. "That means if it was taken by the people who shot me, this could be a contract hit from someone out of state."

"We're not sure of that, Dawson. But it is one possibility. It could also mean the guys you saw burying that body live in state, down by the Junction. The murder could be a local affair. Although I have to tell you that that's one hell of a long shot for a state like Vermont. That kind of thing just doesn't happen in this part of the country. Not that kind of murder."

"What do you mean, 'Not that kind of murder'?"

"It's too gruesome, Dawson. The body we discovered last night wasn't just murdered, it was butchered. And it was a slow death, at least according to the M.E.. In any event," Dowling concluded, "we'll meet for breakfast in half an hour?"

"Right."

"See you then," Dowling said, and hung up the phone.

Dawson sat in his bed for another ten minutes, thinking. Resting. Christ, what a way to spend a weekend, he thought as he finally slipped out of bed and ambled over to the window to gaze outside. His eyes adjusted slowly to the morning brightness as he parted the curtains and gazed out over the hotel's landscaped property. It was such a peaceful setting, he thought. How deceptive. Indeed! As much as he tried to disassociate with the events of the past day, and assure himself everything would work out, he could not take his mind off the body of the man being buried — and of the man he shot. Where the hell was *that* body?

No use worrying about it now, he decided. You can't alter the past. So, Page resolved to play the day by ear, so to speak. Try to look at the positive side of things. Think like a newspaperman, he prompted.

One: neither the medical examiner nor Lieutenant Dowling appeared to have any doubts about his story.

Two: His head no longer ached. And that alone was a big plus.

Three: The body taken from the shallow grave gave no evidence of being shot by a .357 or any other weapon for that matter. This alone cleared Page of any suspicion in that ugly aspect of the crime.

Four: The body the police found was dead at least twenty-four hours prior to Page stumbling upon it. Yes, things were definitely looking up, he thought. His alibis checked out — thank God for honest people. And it looked like his involvement in this entire affair would be drawing to a close shortly.

It was 9:45 A.M.. Page would be meeting with Lieutenant Dowling shortly. Although he showered the previous evening, he showered again this morning. As he dressed, he actually felt relaxed and confident for the first time, taking comfort in the fact that circumstances, at least, were in his favor today.

These thoughts occupied his mind as he walked to the lobby and awaited Lieutenant Dowling's arrival.

He didn't have to wait long. Dowling arrived promptly, with folders containing the latest reports in hand.

Although he liked and trusted Page, Dowling was still a cop on a case. And this case baffled him. He had to know more. He had to tie up all the loose ends. "Good morning, Dawson," he said as they approached each other, extending their hands in friendship. "Is the dining room here okay with you?"

"Fine," Page said, pointing toward the huge fireplace in the center of the lobby, "I don't think they'll cook us a meal here. The other guests might complain."

Dowling laughed as they walked from the lobby. "Dawson, there is one question I overlooked last night. And it's been bothering me ever since. You said the man you saw being buried had white hair. You sounded pretty certain about that detail, even when I pressed you on it."

"I am certain about it," Dawson said.

They both paused in their conversation when the hostess approached and asked if they would like a table near the window. Dowling smiled cordially that he would, and asked if they could have some privacy while they talked. She understood what he meant.

Once seated, Dowling leaned into the table so as not to disturb other guests, and continued his line of questioning. He spoke softly, yet with firmness. "I've got enough questions to ask about this case as it is, Dawson. That aspect really puzzles me. Christ, we've had crews working at the site all night and they haven't come up with any additional bodies. I know we've been over this last night. But is there anything new you can give me. Anything at all, no matter how trivial it may seem."

Page thought carefully before answering. "There was the white hair and the hand with the ring. That's all I can remember, Lieutenant. The man who shot me was wearing a long overcoat — dark blue, I guess. There was just too much ground fog, rain and wind for me too see much more from atop the hill. Believe me, I tried. But I just stumbled upon this thing. I wasn't prepared, either emotionally or physically for what followed."

Dowling said he understood. He rubbed his hands together, ready to call it quits, when Dawson volunteered one last piece of information.

"There was one thing which I observed which — I don't know — It just didn't seem right."

Dowling stared intently without saying a word.

"When the man who shot me turned away, and I glanced in his direction, well, I noticed something shiny on the bottom of his shoe. Maybe it was a gum wrapper or a brace."

"Could it have been a tap?"

"You mean like a tap dancer?"

Dowling chuckled. "No not a dancer. But, you know, how some people wear those things to preserve the heels of their shoes."

"Jesus, Lieutenant, taps went out with engineer boots."

"Yeah, I know. But it's something."

"I don't know, Lieutenant. I just don't know what else to say."

12
Little Lies

Monday, May 20

7:45 A.M. Dawson arrived at his office early Monday morning.

The return trip to Boston yesterday afternoon with his friend, Bob O'Neil, afforded him additional opportunity to unwind, and express his concerns about events of the past few days with someone he could truly trust. O'Neil listened during most of the trip, assuring Dawson along the way that things would work out.

"You need some time off, Dawson. How long has it been since you took a real vacation anyway?"

"I don't know, Bob. You know the work doesn't bother me. It never gets me down."

"Look Dawson," O'Neil said, "by Monday afternoon we should have a positive fingerprint identification on the man they found in that grave. The state police accept your story. They believe you had nothing to do with the murder of that poor bastard. And I don't think you will have any problems from the D.A. either. As for the man you say you shot. No body, no crime."

"I'm really concerned about that aspect, though Bob. I know I shot and killed him. But beyond that I don't know anything."

O'Neil understood his friend's concerns, his stubborn pride. Dawson had been through a great deal of pain in his own lifetime, having separated from his ex-wife, Joyce two years ago. He never did get over the loss of the one woman he loved. "Burn me once shame on me," Dawson would say when asked why he never looked for another woman, or why he never remarried — and there were plenty of willing and wanting candidates. "Burn me twice, shame on me." And then he'd laugh and change the subject, but never go into any greater detail. O'Neil understood the hurt, though, and never prodded him to find someone else. Dawson and he were like brothers. That's why he didn't push him now. Why he wanted to give Page time to work it all out his own mind first — before probing any deeper.

"Go to the office tomorrow, Dawson, put someone else in charge of the paper for a week and take some time off. Besides, Dawson, you should clear up the matter of the missing gun with our own licensing unit before the gun shows up in another crime. See an attorney, just to cover your ass. Nothing traumatic. Just precautionary. And stop over the house Monday evening. I'll have Susan cook up a couple big steaks. Invite that girl you've been dating over. What's her name?"

"Anne?"

"Yeah, that's the one."

"No, I couldn't do that, Bob."

"Why not? Damn she's built like a brick shit house."

Dawson laughed. "Yeah, I know. But she's only interested in sex. She doesn't need to eat."

O'Neil laughed heartily as the conversation drifted to other things besides murder. And it was a welcomed relief for the both of them. As it turned out Dawson did agree to take some time off, having worked three years without a real break. He often thought that's what drove Joyce off. "You have one too many loves in this house, Dawson Page," she would say in the middle of a heated argument, concluding with ". . .and one of these days you're going to have to choose which one stays and which goes." And then she would grow distant.

Dawson arrived at the newspaper office early Monday morning, reflecting on his conversation with Bob yesterday, convinced that he really did owe himself a little rest. He would talk with his assistant Janet when she arrived, and have her manage the business until he returned. Everything else would just have to wait — including his meeting with Bishop Michelsen.

"I'll do that interview when he returns from Rome," Page told Janet later that morning. She was immediately suspicious that Dawson was in some sort of trouble. "Just let the Chancellery know I won't be able to make it, that's all." As for the unexpected time off, he explained that he was involved in a minor automobile accident while in Vermont, and would have to leave the state during the week to pick up his car. He could never tell her the true story. Janet was a worry wart. No use driving both of us crazy by telling her what really happened, he thought.

"Dawson Page," Janet said in her *You are about to be lectured voice*. "It's not like you to walk away from this paper for an entire week."

Here it comes Page told himself, braced for the onslaught. "What about next week's assignments?" she demanded.

"Have Andy make them," he said nonchalantly, as he twirled an elastic band around his fingers. Andy was his assistant editor.

"Oh?" she said, her eyebrows rising. "Have Andy make them, huh? Now listen to me Dawson Page, you are not leaving this office until you tell me the whole story. Something's up and I want to know what it is." She rose as she spoke, positioned herself between him and the door, and threatened to physically restrain him if he tried an end run.

Dawson laughed, and remained seated at his desk.

"You come back here without a car, and with a bandage on your head, and expect me to believe nothing's up? When was the last time you took a vacation?"

Dawson shrugged. "I don't know. I guess I'm overdue."

"Over three years ago." She answered, factually. "Now all of a sudden you tell me you just want to walk away for a week?"

"Yeah," Dawson responded matter-of-factly.

"I wish you would take a vacation, Dawson, believe me you need the rest. You know I can manage the business as well anyone. But what you're telling me here today, I don't believe. Let Andy do it?" she chided, mimicking his voice.

Page laughed. Janet was all of five feet four. Thin, nice legs and firm breasts. He noticed those sort of things even in his secretary. And he cared for her, deeply. That's why he decided at the outset not to tell the truth. "Look, Janet," he explained, "I'm fine." He reached up and removed the bandage. "See, just a small bump."

She folded her arms and tapped her foot lightly. "Well? Do I get an honest answer, or do I stand here all day."

"Go ahead and stand there," Dawson said. "Did you know that when the sun shines through the window I can see right through your dress. Did you know that?"

Her eyes widened and face her flushed.

"It's not the first time, either. Just the first time I told you."

Janet smiled. "I know what you're trying to do, Dawson, and it won't work. Now, do I get an answer or not?"

She wasn't budging. "And don't try to change the subject, either, teasing me with that macho bullshit. I want an answer." The words were tough; her voice wasn't.

"Look, Janet, it's a small cut. I got it while climbing a hill that's all."

She raised her eyebrow and stared in disbelief.

Page tapped his desk lightly. Okay, he said to himself, if she wants the truth lets see if she'll buy this lie. "Okay, okay, for chrissake. If you want to know the truth" — he was really lying now — "You were right. I should have stayed home Friday. I had the flu, but was too stubborn to admit it. I was so sick Saturday afternoon I fell asleep while driving through the mountains. I drove right off the damn road and hit a tree of all things. I was knocked unconscious and taken to the hospital by the state police. The doctors said I had," and he motioned with his hand, "some type of German virus. I'm supposed to rest for the week. Take it easy. I just didn't want to upset you about the accident."

"Ah ha! I knew it," she said triumphantly, thumping her index finger on the desk.

She bought it, he mused to himself as she rushed to where he was seated, and with the wrist of her right hand checked his head for high temperature."

"I have a rectal thermometer in the bathroom if you want it," he joked.

"It's not funny, Dawson. You could have been killed."

Check mate!

"Dawson, you're just like a big baby. Afraid to tell me that you were sick, and that you damaged your car that way. I should tell you that I told you not to drive to Vermont this weekend, but I wont — even though I should." And she smiled as she said it.

Page leaned back in his chair and purred. "Where were you when I needed you a couple years ago?"

Janet leaned over and kissed his forehead gently. "I was walking down the aisle saying *I do* to the other man in my life. You know, the professional wrestler."

"There's no such thing as a *professional* wrestler is there?" he joked. "Don't worry about things here, Dawson," she said, ignoring his jibe, "Go home and rest," she said as he walked back to her desk and shuffled through a mound of papers. "I'll see that everything flows on time, and that we meet deadlines."

"Thanks Janet," Dawson said as he rose, walked across the room and kissed her gently on the forehead. "You know I really can see through your dress when you stand by the window."

"So you want I should wear slacks?"

"Only if they're cellophane."

"You know you really are an asshole, Dawson. I'm the only one who understands you, you know. So be careful you don't blow it."

Dawson laughed. "Thanks Janet," he said as he walked to the door. "I just love it when you talk dirty to me."

A paper ball whizzed by his head when he turned to open the door.

He felt relaxed when he left the office, confident the paper would be printed on time, and that Janet would keep things afloat until he got back next week. As a matter-of-fact, it felt good to talk to someone not associated with the weekend's activities.

Being officially on vacation, Page decided to walk along the beach and relax at the *Island* before heading home.

13
Going Into Hiding

The News Tribune office, located in a store-front on East Broadway in South Boston, is less than a mile from the beach. Quite often on bright sunny days such as today Dawson would take a break from the pressures of the paper and stroll along the well-maintained shoreline, organizing his thoughts while enjoying the scenery of Boston Harbor. It was 10:00 A.M.

South Boston, a working class community consisting of approximately forty-five thousand residents is shaped in the approximate definition of a triangle, with water on three sides, abutted on the north, south and east by the Atlantic Ocean, and on the southeast by the scenic islands of Boston Harbor.

At the tip of the triangle on the ocean point is a revolutionary war fortress called *Castle Island*, or the *Island* to natives. On warm summer evenings the *Island* is crowded with joggers, families out for a stroll, young and old lovers ambling hand-in-hand, and children playing on swings, to name a few activities. It is, perhaps, one of the more popular places for city residents who know the charm the area offers. From the Fort one can sit atop the rolling hill which surrounds it, since it sits atop this hill, and observe planes landing at Logan Airport across the bay, or boats sailing leisurely through the harbor which separates South from East Boston.

This was the waterfront Page loved. It had a charm, history and beauty unmatched anywhere on the East Coast — even with the sometimes frantic activity of boats, planes and people all moving to their own rhythmic schedule. It was home to Page. Secure. Familiar. It was the one place in Boston where Page could go and relax, and take his mind off the events of the weekend. That's why when he left the office earlier he headed for his favorite spot at the *Island.*

He couldn't have heard his phone ringing every fifteen minutes for most of the morning. *Today he would relax.* He couldn't have anticipated what was to follow. *He just wanted to clear his mind.* He had no way of knowing that his best friend, Bob O'Neil, received an urgent phone call from the Vermont State Police earlier, recommending that he be taken into protective custody — at once. *Just a leisurely day at the Island.* Nor did he know that Lieutenant O'Neil was searching the city frantically, in a desperate attempt to locate him before others did. *Not a care in the world.* He just wanted to be lost in the crowd, a nameless face once again.

The brown '79 Chevy screeched to a halt, double parked on the street. A man exited hurriedly, not even bothering to turn off the ignition.

The door to the Tribune office flew open and Bob O'Neil rushed in. "Is he here Janet?" he asked impatiently. "I've got to locate him, and fast," he said in a demanding manner as he peered over her desk, without saying hello, good morning — anything.

Janet looked up, stunned by his abruptness. It isn't like Bob to be this pushy, she thought.

"I presume you mean where is Dawson?" she said, as she glanced past him, and out the window at his car, and the marked cruiser alongside it. "And for chrissake will you calm down, Bob. You nearly scared me to death rushing in here like you did."

"I'm sorry Janet," he said sincerely. He wasn't comfortable with his abruptness either. He adjusted his remarks accordingly, hoping that a different approach would speed the process along. "It's extremely important that I locate Dawson as soon as possible," he said calmly. "I've been trying to reach him all morning, Janet. Do you have any idea where he might be?"

Janet's face turned ashen. "Oh, my God, Bob, does this have something to do with the weekend?" she asked, sensing O'Neil wouldn't be this upset unless Dawson were in serious trouble. "Janet I just need to locate him. Please," he said, waving away further questions, "Just answer my question."

Now she was really worried. "Please, Bob, What's going on? It has to do with the weekend doesn't it," she said, slumping against the backrest of her chair. She raised her hands to her face, hiding her quivering chin; her eyes were fixed on O'Neil.

O'Neil remained stone silent and just returned her stare. "I'm sorry, Janet. I'm really sorry," he said, "but this is police business. The less you know at this time the better. You have to trust me, Janet. If you have any idea where I can find Dawson, tell me now."

Janet's eyes were misty, and her hands trembled as she asked herself where Dawson would go on a beautiful day such as today. "He. . . he left about an hour ago, Bob. I. . . I thought he went home. . ."

"Jesus Christ!" O'Neil moaned as he turned and faced the front door, gravely concerned for Dawson's safety, and angry with himself for not reading Dawson better yesterday. How could I have left him alone last night? he thought to himself as he paced back and forth. "Janet," he said as he swung around and faced her again, "he's not at his house. I've been calling there all morning."

"Well, he was here for a while, Bob. . .," she offered meekly.

"Does he have any other appointments that you're aware of?"

"No. None."

O'Neil took a deep breath, then released it slowly through pursed lips. "Where could he have gone?" he asked.

Janet looked up, her eyes were filled with tears now. She was thoroughly confused and frightened. "The only place I can think of is. . ." And as she began to say it O'Neil repeated the same words, "Castle Island."

"Down the Island," O'Neil shouted to the officer in the marked cruiser as he bolted from the newspaper office and ran to his own car. He jumped behind the wheel, reached for the magnetized blue flasher he kept on the seat beside him, placed it on the roof of his car, and sped off behind the cruiser ahead of him. As he raced up Broadway past City Point, then across Farragut for the Boulevard his mind was preoccupied with only one thought: If whoever it was that killed Carlos Ortega, and dumped his body in a shallow grave in Vermont, could locate *him* so quickly, how much more quickly would they be able to locate Dawson Page, the man who took a bullet in the head when he interfered with their grisly plans. They took Dawson's car for a reason. They had his registration. They have his address. They know where he lives, for chrissake. Whatever it was they were trying to hide up in those hills, whoever they were, they now knew all they had to know about the intruder who might be able to finger them in the future. And that wasn't healthy.

Page stretched leisurely in his beach chair, took a deep breath, exhaled slowly and relaxed as he listened to the sounds of Boston Harbor, unaware as he rested that a burly man was approaching from behind.

"Page!" a voice called from afar, almost drowned out by the roar of a 727 taking off from across the bay. "Dawson!" the voice grew louder as it approached rapidly from the bottom of the small incline.

The burly man peered at the resting figure, then across the grassy hill, at Bob O'Neil, approaching steadily, his hand on the butt of his revolver.

"Mr. Page?" the man said.

"Huh?" Dawson said as he placed his right hand over his eyes to shield the bright glare of the sun. He was startled momentarily by the presence of the large man hovering over him.

"I'm Detective Gomez," he said as he flashed a gold badge. "We've been looking for you all morning."

O'Neil stopped running when he noticed that the man standing over Dawson was a member of the department's drug enforcement unit. O'Neil walked slowly toward Dawson, taking several deep breaths along the way. Sonofabitch, he mumbled to himself, thankful his friend was located.

"Dawson, Old buddy. How 'ya doing?" he said as he walked around the chair, trying to act nonchalant. "I see you've met Sergeant Gomez."

"What's up, Bob?" Page asked suspiciously. "Why the police convention?"

O'Neil waved the question away and rubbed his chin before answering. "It's nothing, Dawson. We had to locate you, that's all," he said as he glanced around carefully. "Look, I'm afraid this thing isn't over." Without going into greater detail, Page knew exactly what thing O'Neil was referring to.

"It's nothing about you, Dawson. It's about the body you found up north." O'Neil looked nervous, concerned. "Gomez, go down below and call in. Let them know we found him. . ."

Gomez nodded.

"But for chrissake, don't let them know where we are."

Page straightened himself in the beach chair as he studied his friend's face.

"Don't bother getting up," O'Neil said as he sat on the grass beside his friend. "Remember when we were kids, Dawson, how we used to come up here and play?"

Dawson smiled and nodded his head, and continued to listen without saying a word.

"Life was sure easier then, buddy." O'Neil paused as he plucked a blade of grass from the ground and rubbed it back and forth between his fingers. "Dawson, the man's name was Carlos Ortega. Does that ring a bell with you?"

"No."

O'Neil grimaced and shook his head. "Dawson, he was one of the top drug dealers in South America. We knew he was in Boston during the past two weeks, but were unable to locate him."

"Until this weekend," Dawson volunteered glumly.

"I'm afraid so," O'Neil said as he tapped his knee. "Something very big is going down, Dawson. You know that, already. You've covered the growing violence in the paper. But this murder signals something big. Dawson, the DEA informed us that a two-million dollar contract has been issued for his life. Christ, you've had to notice the increased drug activity in the city over the past few weeks. We've been hearing rumors that hit teams from Peru, Bolivia and Colombia have been sent to the city to locate this guy."

"Jesus," Dawson said. "I guess that's why they took him up north and killed him — to cover their tracks."

O'Neil shook his head. "I wish it were that easy, Dawson. These people couldn't care less about another dead body being dumped on the streets. We think it's bigger than that. Dawson, we believe that Ortega was ready to spill the proverbial beans on the South American mafia. Do you have any idea how powerful these people are? The damage we could do to their operations if he talked?"

O'Neil stood and brushed the dirt from his pants. Dawson continued to stare in silence. "The DEA office at the Kennedy building is like an armed camp, for chrissake, although you'd never guess it from the outside. But believe me, the FEDS don't like the mood out there one bit. These Latins are crazy bastards, Dawson. They don't subscribe to our way of life, the Bill of Rights and all that shit. It's alien to their culture. They'd just as soon cut your fucking heart out as look at you twice. They're all crazy, Dawson. And I'm sorry to say that whatever secrets they were trying to bury in those hills, they now believe you know. And they aren't about to allow that condition to exist for long."

Dawson rose slowly, placed his hands on his hips, looked across the harbor, and stretched slightly. "How many times did we come up here as kids, Bob?"

"Did you hear what I said, Dawson. They know who you are."

Dawson smiled as he stared into his friends eyes. "They can go fuck themselves, Bob, if they think I'm going into hiding for the rest of my life. You know that that's not my character. You know I won't do it."

"Dawson, it would only be for a short while. Until this thing blows over," O'Neil pleaded.

"It's never going to be over, Bob. You know that. Not until something dramatic happens to dry up the supply — or the demand."

"Dawson, we can't guarantee your safety if you just walk around the streets. What about the newspaper? Janet? The staff? If whoever killed Carlos Ortega wants you dead — and I think they will — they'll take you and the whole crew out just to cover the possibility that you might have talked."

"Bob, we grew up together," Page said, his voiced filled with emotion. "You know I'm not going to give up my home and move to a safe house, just to placate these foreign assholes."

"I know that, Dawson. But you become a liability to everyone around you. Look, I don't want to lose you, Dawson. You stumbled onto something bigger than you, or the entire police department might be able to handle. They have your name," he continued, referring to the murderers. "They know where you live, your phone number. Probably where you work by now. They'll be looking for you."

"I know."

"I want you to be real careful about the way you move around the city from now on, Dawson. Keep a watchful eye wherever you go. Stay out of dark alleys. Know what I mean?"

Dawson nodded his understanding.

"I want you to take a drive with me. I want you to meet someone."

It was a sad moment for the two friends as they stood and looked at one another. They both understood their lives would never be the same again. Dawson was on the hit list from a group of people who had the power and money to hit wherever and whenever they pleased. Something had to give.

14
Rivero

Monday, 10:30 A.M. The time had at last arrived. Carmen spent the weekend in her small rented apartment preparing for her meeting with Rivero. She practiced what she would say, how she would look. She repeated Carlos' words to herself constantly. "You must deliver the book to only one man."

She knew of Rivero, but never met him. Yet, somehow, she trusted him. If Carlos loved him, she said to herself — and *he* made such a sacrifice for Carlos — surely I can trust him. Surely I can place my trust and my life in his hands.

On Saturday afternoon, Carmen shopped and purchased new clothing. During the evening hours she watched American television and practiced her English. For the better part of Sunday, Carmen studied tourist maps of the city and spent hours walking quietly along the near-empty streets, just observing. In this pursuit she strolled down Commonwealth Avenue, past Boston University and through Kenmore Square, heading toward the Public Gardens in the heart of the city. Once there, she familiarized herself with shops, restaurants, hotels, streets, and the movement of people. One thing struck her. No one looked concerned or hungry. Even the few homeless she saw on the streets were, by standards in her country, fat and overweight — meaning well fed. Indeed, Carmen was surprised to observe the large number of Latins on Boston streets, all passing here and there without so much as a nod from other passersby. America, she thought to herself. What a fascinating place.

The tour was necessary, even though tiring on her feet. For it was important that she feel comfortable in the city. It was tough enough being an illegal alien, she thought. She could not chance being stopped or questioned because she looked confused. She must adapt. So adapt she did. Yet, even with her resolve, she felt terribly lonely and empty without Carlos. When most girls her age were concerned with boys and belonging, Carmen was concerned with matters of life and death. That's why she welcomed the dawn of the new day, Monday. Today she would meet Rivero. Her promise to Carlos would be fulfilled.

Carmen ate breakfast and showered immediately afterward. When she was finished, she dried herself slowly with a clean, soft towel. Her mind was elsewhere, though, as she patted the beads of water from her skin.

Carmen was young and firm figured. Her hair was long and soft. Her eyes were clear and provocative, set against flawless skin. Her breasts were round. She was full of life.

She closed her eyes and swayed slowly back and forth, embracing the towel, remembering. Remembering the gentle touch of Carlos' hands, his inviting mouth, their bodies close together. Carmen sighed, as she remembered his firm figure, and recalled how she used to run her hands along his smooth back while he made love to her. How she glided her palms over the hard muscles in his biceps and shoulders as he labored above her, bringing her closer and closer to the ecstasy she craved whenever they made love. Then, she broke her trance, and scolded herself for allowing these thoughts to overcome her — especially at this time. It was not good to remember a man in such a manner, she thought, for the passion was easily ignited, and she trembled when she thought of their lovemaking.

Her eyes were sad, and her heart sorrowful, as she gazed into the mirror. She had lost everyone who ever meant anything to her. And she was completely alone. For this reason, Carmen prayed Rivero would accept and protect her. But then, there was his profession. He would have to protect her, she reassured herself. He was a man who could be trusted with great responsibility.

The day was young and Carmen was eager to begin this final phase of her Americanization. When she completed her chores and was fully dressed, she sat on the side of the bed, reached for the phone, and dialed the private number Carlos had given her. She sat impatiently as the phone rang several times. Then, a man's voice answered. It was a surprisingly soft voice, she thought.

"Rivero?" she said. Her heart was pounding so hard she thought it would jump right out of her chest. She was overcome with apprehension as she spoke his name. Damn, she thought. I spoke *his* name. Carlos said I was to protect his identity — even over the phone. She regretted her impetuosness, yet realized it was too late to retract what she had done. Why am I so nervous? she asked herself.

"Yes," Rivero said — and waited. He was shocked to hear his name mentioned, to hear the name he stopped using so long ago. Who could this be?

"Carlos asked that you see me," she said with trepidation. "He said that you would understand if I told you it was *The Voluntad de Dios*, *The Will of God*. Please Rivero, I have a letter for you, along with something very personal from Carlos — a diary."

Rivero was stunned by her frankness. "You are a young girl?" he asked considerately.

"Yes," she said, shyly. "I am Carmen Velasco Terry Ortega. I am Carlos' wife." She spoke softly, fighting to hold back her emotions. But it was difficult, given the sudden realization of her lonliness. She began to sob as the tension and emotional trauma she felt inside was finally relieved. "He is dead, Rivero. I just know he is dead," she said, her voice quivering. "And I am so frightened and alone." She wept openly and freely, for the loss was just too great to hold in any longer. But when she wept, she wept more out of frustration than sorrow, for she knew she had to be brave — but wasn't. Wiping her eyes, she continued. "I need to see you, Rivero. Please, will you help me?"

Rivero was uncertain and confused. The strain of the past two days had finally peaked — and now this: Carmen's call. He leaned forward in his chair, placed his elbows on his desk, and rested his head in his hands while cupping the phone to his ear. He rubbed his eyebrows and thought for an uncomfortably long moment before answering. "Do not cry, my child. I will see you today if you wish. Do you know where I am? he asked.

"Yes," she said humbly. "I will be there within a half hour if that's okay with you."

"Yes, it is," he answered. "Come quickly, my child. We have much to talk about, and I have so many questions to ask."

Rivero placed the received back on the phone, rose slowly from his desk and walked across the large room toward the window. He wasn't at all comfortable with the events which shaped this weekend. He searched his memory for clues which might explain what he couldn't yet understand.

And then there was Carmen's call. Rivero knew Carlos was in serious trouble. Yet, it was clear Carlos had not intended for 'his' identity to be revealed — except to Carmen. And there had to be a reason for that silence. Indeed, the entire affair was a mystery. Rivero gazed out the window, hands clasped behind his back, and thought.

Why would Carlos keep his marriage to Carmen a secret — even from him? There was only one answer: Carlos must have feared for her safety and wouldn't jeopardize a breach caused by the written word. Carmen would be introduced to Rivero — personally. The reason for the veil of secrecy, he thought, must be contained in the letter and diary she carries. Even with all the doubt, he realized he had few choices but to wait her arrival.

Carlos must have truly loved this girl, Rivero thought, for him to break the silence — a silence Carlos asked that Rivero impose on himself while in America. Even correspondence between the two was channeled through a contact in Miami so as not to arouse suspicion. When a letter arrived addressed to Rivero under his assumed name, he would say, simply, that it was a letter from an uncle in Florida — and no one would suspect anything more.

As he considered his options and weighed what actions he would take, Rivero sensed that time was closing in on him, and that sooner than he cared he would have to confront his past; that once again he would have to live by the gun to settle old wounds. He looked at his watch and grew anxious as he waited for Carmen's visit. His anxiety was soon relieved.

The doorbell rang while he was immersed in his own violent past. The time had at last arrived when Rivero's real identity would be known. He gazed out the window, peering down the long walkway leading to the front gate, and tried to glimpse the figure of the young girl standing outside.

"Yes?" The voice came through a small box mounted by the gate at the entrance to the estate. It was a woman's voice.

Carmen answered in a quiet, respectful manner. "I am here to see Rivero." She erred again, and bit at her lower lip in frustration. How could she accomplish the task at hand when she was so clumsy? she thought. She knew she was not to use his real name, yet she used it twice already. "I mean, I am here to see. . ."

"It is all right, my child. I am here." It was Rivero's voice which interrupted. Carmen felt so embarrassed. "Please come in," he said. His voice was soft and reassuring.

Carmen entered the complex, excited and more than a little intimidated by the surroundings. She walked slowly toward the main building, turning in each direction as she proceeded, awed by the richness and grandeur of Rivero's home. When she was but half way up the walkway, a man appeared at the front door. Even from this distance she could see his smile. He was a tall man. Older than she expected.

He carried himself well though, with military bearing. He looked to be strong. Solid.

Carmen felt completely at ease within these surroundings. The grass was green, and the lawn was perfectly landscaped. And the trees were so full for this time of year. There were even flowers in bloom in the garden along the edge of the mansion. The estate was rich with color, order and life. She felt immediately comforted and soothed, and smiled easily as Rivero approached her. In her heart, a heart which had seen much pain and suffering for its years, Carmen felt like a young girl again.

As they drew closer, Rivero opened his arms, offering her the protection and assurances she so desperately needed. And when they met, they embraced warmly — like father and daughter. And she wept and sobbed and smiled and drew strength from the man Carlos trusted. He *would* protect her, after all.

Rivero glanced at his watch, stepped back slightly, and placed his hands on her shoulders. "You are safe now, my child," he said, searching her eyes. She looked so innocent and vulnerable. Then his attention was drawn to the book in her hands. "I am Rivero, my child. Is that the diary you have for me?"

"Yes," she said as she clutched the book to her breasts. "And I have a letter from Carlos. He asked that I stand before you as you read it." Carmen reached up and wiped the tears from her eyes which were puffy and red from her tears.

River smiled broadly. Carlos always did enjoy drama, he thought. "Then we should waste no time, Carmen. You must come to my study and let me read it. Then, we will talk."

Carmen nodded respectfully, then walked with Rivero as he led her inside, his arm around her shoulders, her arm around his waist. When she entered the mansion, she paused and sighed, overwhelmed by the magnificence of Rivero's home. It was so — rich. "I have never seen anything like this," she said with genuine awe, as she genuflected on one knee and said, humbly: "May the Blessed Virgin and Her Son, my Lord, God, Jesus Christ forgive my sins. I am not worthy to be in this place."

Rivero reached down and patted her head lightly. "Please, Carmen. This is just a house. Come," he said as he reached down and lifted her gently by the arm, "walk with me to my study."

"But it is such a special house," she said as she followed.

Once inside his study, Carmen indulged her girlish impulse to inspect everything. Her curiosity amused Rivero who sat as his desk and just observed. She gazed out the large tripple-panelled windows which faced the front lawn. She inspected the book case built into one of the walls. At the rich paintings hanging on the other. When she was finished with her inspection, she turned and faced Rivero once again. "I am sorry," she said, shyly, raising her shoulders upward like a little girl. "This is all so beautiful."

Rivero smiled. He understood her awe. "Carmen, you have so much energy. I can feel it from across the room. But we must take care of business first. You have a letter and diary from Carlos."

"Oh, yes," she said. She had almost forgotten. She approached his desk, holding the diary against her breasts. She passed the letter first. Although tempted many times, she kept her promise to Carlos and had not read its contents. She stood before Rivero as Carlos asked, and said nothing as he studied the envelope.

He opened the letter carefully, slowly, and began to read what Carlos had written. His expression turned from curious to sad, to troubled. Tears welled in his eyes as he read, *Look at her Rivero — and see me. I love her so much, and want you to protect her and care for her as you did me. I shall miss you both dearly. . .*

"Oh my God," Rivero sighed, glancing at Carmen after he said it. Her face was filled with apprehension. "So many years have passed," he said, speaking softly, looking into her eyes. "Carlos has asked that I look after you. That I be a father to you, as I was to him."

Carmen's face mirrored her concern and doubts.

River spoke solemnly as he placed the letter on his desk and looked directly into her eyes. "You will be my daughter, my child, as Carlos has asked, if you will accept me as your father." And as he spoke these words he rose, feeling suddenly terribly old and saddened by the loss of two old friends — Carlos and Manuel. Yet, when Carmen raced around his desk and embraced him, squeezing him is more appropriate, and looked deeply in his eyes and wept with joy, kissing his cheek, he felt younger and refreshed. Her tears brought back so many memories, so much responsibility. Rivero understood what Carlos was asking, and he found himself surprised and touched and honored that his devotion and friendship to Carlos elicited such special trust.

"We have no time to waste," Carmen sighed, urgency filled her voice. "You must read the diary today. It may not be too late. I am so unfamiliar with these things."

River understood her anxiety. "Do you have a place to stay?" he asked.

"Yes, here. . .," she said, and with a pen wrote her name, address and telephone number on the pad from his desk.

"Carmen," he said as he held her gently by the shoulders again. "You must tell no one of this meeting. You must tell no one of my identity. I spoke with Carlos Friday — but only briefly. . ."

"What did he say?" she interrupted "Did he tell you of me? That I would be calling? Did he ask you to help me? Or say where he was going?"

"Carmen, I could not break my vow of silence, even to Carlos, unless he specifically asked it of me. You must understand, the kind of people you are hiding from. If I passed Carlos on the street, I could not even acknowledge his existence unless he asked it of me. We are dealing with people with many contacts — tentacles like an octopus that reach into every crevice of society. Silence has been our best and only defense. Now, you must share that same burden with me. You understand how important this all is?"

She nodded in silence.

A knock on the door startled both of them. "Yes?" Rivero asked, cautiously.

"Brother Dominic, His Eminence has asked that you visit him in his study."

"I will be there momentarily, Sister Margaret," he said dutifully. He drew a deep breath, held Carmen by the shoulders and smiled broadly again, reassuring her that everything would turn out fine. He kissed her gently on the forehead and called her daughter. "I will read the diary tonight, Carmen," he assured her, adding sternly, "Do not leave your apartment until I call you."

15
The Lesson

Page drove to police headquarters with Lieutenant O'Neil. It was 11:00 A.M.. Gomez followed as a backup. During the entire trip, Page noticed that his friend was especially occupied with surroundings. Vehicles entering from side streets, he'd watch them very carefully. Any unexpected slowing of traffic ahead would cause his head to rise from his shoulders — peering. What's the delay, O'Neil would mumble to himself. One street person made the mistake of stepping in front of the unmarked car while it was stopped at a traffic light. He banged on the hood as he walked by, startling the two passengers. Gomez rushed out of his car, immediately behind O'Neil's, and slammed the man across the passenger fender. The man nearly pissed himself. Meanwhile, O'Neil's hand never left the .38 at his side.

"Stupid shit," O'Neil snarled as he watched through suspicious eyes.

"Jesus, Bobby, he's just a wino," Page said, noticing his friend's jittery reaction.

"He makes one move toward the door," O'Neil said coldly, "you get your head down and don't look up until I give the all clear."

Dawson looked at O'Neil, then slouched in his seat, placing his knees on the dashboard in a relaxed fashion. "Bobby, you're getting crazy in your old age. You read too much of that Mike Hammer shit."

"Maybe," O'Neil answered, looking across at Dawson. "When you're dealing with drugs, Dawson, you can never be too sure. And believe me, buddy, whether you want to admit it or not, someone has name your name and number. And someone like this. . ." he said, pointing to the man being led to the sidewalk by Gomez, ". . .could be a harmless wino, just like he looks, or a druggie, fucked out of his mind, looking for a chance to earn a week's fix. Just trust me, Dawson, you can never be too cautious. Never!"

They arrived at police headquarters by 11:20 A.M.. "Dawson," O'Neil said as he parked the car by the front entrance on Berkeley Street, "we can't hold you under protective custody. And you don't have to go to a safe house, if you don't want. But I'm asking as a friend that you meet with a friend of mine. He's with the DEA. We'll go to lunch and talk, that's all. And maybe you can give us some additional information on what you saw."

"What if I'm not hungry," Dawson said lightly.

"Don't bust my balls, Dawson," O'Neil said, unimpressed with his friend's sense of humor. "The guy's name is John Geary. He's a good agent, Dawson. Maybe he can give you some information on what's been going on from his perspective, and maybe even tie it all into what you saw up north."

"So that's why the ride to town."

"Yes," O'Neil said, continuing. "When I found out this morning from the Vermont State Police who Carlos Ortega was, I decided to give John Geary a call. He'd find out eventually, anyway, and ask me about you when the file was passed to his office. Look, Dawson, we've worked together before on a number of operations which were, shall we say, questionable in terms of their legality — but necessary in terms of information we've been able to gather. He'll tell you what you have to know to stay alive. Oh, and one last thing. Technically, this meeting shouldn't even be taking place, so what we say will have to be off the record. No notes."

"Staying alive? Confidential meetings? Thanks Bob," Page joked, although he knew his friend had *his* best interests at heart. He was also aware enough to know that his witnessing of the burial in Vermont over the weekend put his life in jeopardy — conversations such as the one they were having brought that point into finer focus.

O'Neil turned off the ignition, and the two men stepped out of the car. "We'll head down to Flash's" O'Neil said as he led Dawson across Berkeley, down Stuart Street toward the Greyhound bus terminal. Flash's was a small Greek-owned restaurant located near Park Square. Being around lunch time, O'Neil figured it would be crowded and noisy — a great place to do business.

The weather was sunny, windy and warm, so they walked slowly and did some woman watching along the way. Indeed, it was a perfect day in May — in marked contrast to the weather of a few days ago. "It's funny how things change, Bobby," Page commented as they walked down the street. "Friday, I was involved in nothing more than my day off, and the paper. Today, I may be the most wanted man on some banana republic's hit list."

"Correction, Dawson. . ." O'Neil interrupted as he stopped outside the door of the restaurant, "You're talking about the South American mafia, when you talk Carlos Ortega. These people are light-years ahead of their governments in the way they do business. They're international in scope. And there's nothing bananerish about the way they operate. They're organized, tough, single-minded in their purpose. They're ruthless beyond anything we've experienced in this country, Dawson." O'Neil paused when the expression on Dawson's face told him he was, perhaps, over dramatizing events.

"I'm sorry, Dawson, for giving you this lecture," O'Neil said, realizing he was pressing the point. "I realize I've been giving you a lot of lectures lately. But I'm concerned about this thing. My gut feeling is they won't let it rest, knowing you may have seen something."

Page shrugged his shoulders and acknowledged he was interested in meeting with Geary, who happened to be crossing the street as they talked.

John Geary was a neighborhood guy, born in Boston. He stands about six feet two and has sandy brown hair. Page liked him immediately. He was open and relaxed and had a friendly smile. Not some tight-assed bureaucrat with button down brains.

"Dawson, this is John Geary, a good friend," O'Neil said as he extended his hand to Geary. "John, this is Dawson Page, my best friend."

The men exchanged greetings and shook hands, and talked about the weather as they proceeded inside the restaurant and ordered their lunch.

"So you're the guy in the paper," Geary said as they sat down at a table near the window.

Page and O'Neil looked at each other in surprise. Neither had seen the morning paper. Geary unfolded the Herald which he carried in his rear pocket and showed them the article which described, "a witness who police have cleared of any suspicion in the crime, but who may have evidence which could lead to an arrest."

"Shit!" O'Neil exclaimed in exasperation. "Who the fuck wrote that story?" he asked rhetorically. This is precisely what they didn't need, he thought as he read about the mystery of Carlos Ortega. The article was brief, and when he was done perusing it, he passed it to Dawson who just shrugged it away saying he had seen the original.

"Very funny," O'Neil remarked dryly.

Geary wasted no time. Page liked that. "Dawson, Bob gave me a brief outline of your situation this morning. How much do you know about Ortega, the South American drug trade and the people who run it?"

Page shrugged and said he knew something of the violence occurring in the city, and that he had used the paper in the past to speak out against the proliferation of drugs in the neighborhoods. Beyond a very sketchy outline, he said, he knew nothing. "I hate to admit it, John, but like most people I read about it, being a newspaperman I write about it occasionally — and go about my business. I'm all ears now, though."

The three men proceeded to eat their meals. Geary talked as they began. "Dawson, a couple weeks ago we arrested a man in Cartagena Colombia. His name is Juan Ramon Matta Ballesteros. He's said to be the boss of bosses in the Mexican cocaine industry. A heavy hitter. A very powerful and deadly character. His organization supplies over one-third of all cocaine shipped to the United States. We believe he was behind the murder of one of our agents, Enrique Salazar in Mexico. I'm sure you read about that murder."

Dawson, nodded. The story appeared in most of the major dailies and newsweeklies throughout the country.

"He's scared, Page. Offered the arresting agents almost half-a-million dollars cash if they would let him go. We also have two of his top men in custody, a guy by the name of Quintero and another guy named Carillo. Do either of these people mean anything to you?"

"No."

"I can't say too much beyond that, except one of them is ready to spill the beans for immunity. But he's a tough cookie, and he won't talk unless he gets a whole set of guarantees we just can't offer."

"Why not offer him what he wants, then fuck him?" Page offered.

Geary laughed, "You and Bob ought to get together on that one," he said as he nodded in O'Neil's direction.

"Anyway, what we've been able to piece together is that there is turmoil in the organization, violent and bitter turmoil between the old timers who want to run the cocaine trade as a business, and a newer breed which views the cocaine trade as kind of a tool with which they can usher in world revolution. This latter group is loosely connected with some extremely violent fringe elements known as the Sendero Luminoso, the *Shining Path*, and the Puka Llacta, *Red Fatherland*."

"I smell left wing politics here," Page said.

"It cuts both ways, Dawson. You've got right wing Contras running this shit from the other side also."

"Great."

"Anyway, the two groups we suspect of being connected to this murder happen to be left wing. They've been involved in acts of terrorism against people who oppose their peculiar type of cocaine politics. They're the same groups responsible for the massacre of those civilians in the Hallaga Valley region of Peru back in '85. Nineteen croppers butchered beyond recognition. It served as one hell of a lesson to others in the region, and has kept informers at a premium. And these aren't the only atrocities they've engaged in, either. The point is, Dawson, these groups aren't going away. As a matter-of-fact, their influence is growing daily. We know as a fact that they get aid from Cuba and Nicaragua." Geary stopped long enough to take a few mouthfulls of food before continuing. "Anyway, we suspect that Ballesteros is part of the older group as was Carlos Ortega. They don't want anything to do with the fanatics, but are finding their own organizations being infiltrated with younger, more communist-oriented conqueros, soldiers, who get off on the idea of turning the United States into one giant cesspool."

Geary leaned into the table as he spoke, emphasizing his message by tapping his finger lightly as he spoke, "Something happened to cause Ortega to break with the mafia down there. Something very big. It has everyone here guessing, and the smart one's scared shitless. As we see it, and we're only piecing parts together now, the older group had to strike a compromise with the younger leftist group to prevent a major cocaine war from erupting throughout all South America. The prize is uninterrupted cocaine trade with the United States — hundreds-of-billions of dollars each year."

"Jesus Christ," Dawson said. "You mean they intend to flood this country with cocaine?"

"Exactly!" Geary said. "Our sources say the deal goes down like this: The revolutionaries will not interfere with the traditional drug business if, as an accommodation, the older boys give them a symbolic trade off, some sort of a socio-political hit, for lack of a better word. The leftists want to make a statement on the road to world revolution."

"And what does that mean?" Page asked. "Are they talking about assassinating somebody in the United States? Like the president?"

"Possibly," Geary responded. "The entire Drug Enforcement Agency is at a high level of alert. As is the FBI and a few other intelligence units few people know about. Look, Dawson, they assassinated Colombia's justice minister a couple years ago. They tried to blow up the fucking United States Embassy in Bogata. For chrissake in one battle in

Guadalajara, Mexico, the local cops armed with pistols were slugging it out against cocaine running guerrillas armed with Russian made Ak-47's. No contest, boys."

"Bob?" Page interrupted, "Is it that bad up here?

O'Neil reached for his coffee, to wash down a mouthfull of scrambled eggs and toast. "When John's done, I'll give you a brief rundown on what we're dealing with here."

"Fine," Page said, nodding "John?"

"One drug king by the name of Pablo Escobar Gaviria has a private army of over two thousand men. Who's going to fuck with him? To these people, Dawson, political assassination is a way of life. Violence is an everyday occurrence. Add to that this leftist shit, and you have monufuckingmental problems on the border of the good ole US of A."

Page looked across at O'Neil, then at Geary. He knew the problem of drug abuse was epidemic, but even he didn't see the local problem as part of the bigger picture. "Isn't there anything we can do to stop these guys, John? I mean we are the United States for chrissake."

"We're trying to work with people in the region, but blood is being spilled. And much more than we or they are prepared to admit at this time. Much of what I'm telling you is all a matter of public record, so I'm not telling stories out of school, here. Dawson, the drug trade in this country alone is bigger than most officials care to admit. There isn't one school in this city where drug trade isn't thriving. Just look at the street corners in the neighborhoods. It's down to that level. The kids using this shit are no fucking good, Dawson. They're zombies. Potential murderers."

"But what about the drug bosses in South America, why can't we get to them? What's the problem there?"

"Dawson, in Bolivia there's this drug king known as Roberto Suarez Gomez. He thrives on this shit. We try to get the peasants and farmers to work against him because of what he's doing. We try to educate them on the dangers and drawbacks of the cocaine trade. What does he do? He uses part of the money he makes from selling drugs to send their children to school. He pays their fucking hospital bills when they come to him. How do you fight against that kind of patronage? And he hires Libyan experts to train his security forces, just in case the people forget how magnanimous he is. The point I'm making is this: The guy you saw buried in that grave in Vermont was the leader of this mafia. He found out something about the plans of the leftists, and didn't like it. He tried to change it, but found that in the interest of revolution and business, the compromise would take place over his objection."

"And we have no idea what that accommodation is?" Page asked.

"We're talking about a drug business which nets over one-hundred billion dollars each year. Every day well over five thousand Americans take cocaine — and that number is growing. Countries such as Colombia, Peru, Bolivia, Mexico and Panama are being overrun with the drug trade — and revolution tied into it. With all that," Geary concluded, "no accommodation can be ruled out." He took a deep breath, then added, "Now, if you gentlemen don't mind I'd like to eat some lunch."

"Dawson, do you remember that story a few years ago about the American mafia running an international beauty contest? It made all the papers. It was a front for a drug running operation. At the time, of course, we didn't know anything about it being sponsored by the mafia, or having anything to do with drugs — although we had our suspicions." It was now O'Neil speaking. "Took all the girls down south of the border for a vacation, doped them up and took nude photos of them while they were out, and then stuck cocaine in their vaginas before they brought them back to the United States? One of the girls was an agent of ours. They discovered her identity and broke a bag while it was inside of her. She freaked out and killed herself." O'Neil shook his head in disgust, "I mean, these were only kids, Dawson. Can you see how far they'll go? A beauty pageant..."

Geary interrupted, "Dawson, Ortega is the key. We know he was in Boston. But was he just passing through or was he headed to Vermont? Who was he looking for? What did he find out that made him split with the organization? As it stands right now, you are closest living person we have to unraveling that mystery."

"And I don't know anything," Page replied, feeling a little disappointed with his inability to offer any concrete evidence.

"Dawson, I want to put a tag on you. Sergeant Gomez will head the team. You met him this morning at the 'Island'. If they come after you, I want you to have some protection."

"Sure, Bob," Page said, "If you feel it's necessary. I still want to go about my business, though, without interruption."

"No problem," O'Neil assured him. "You won't even know he's there."

"How did it ever get this bad?" Dawson asked. "Why can't we just round up the pushers, regardless of their age and lock them up?"

Both O'Neil and Geary stared blankly as Dawson prodded. They understood his frustration.

"You guys are the cops, and you're telling me we can't stop it?"

O'Neil offered an explanation which drew a nod of agreement from Geary. "Dawson, with all those eager-beaver third year law students cutting their teeth with legal aid, we'd have lawsuits coming out of our ears if we ever went after everyone we knew was pushing this shit. And parents screaming in our ears about how their little babies were framed. How their little babies would never get involved in such activity. And then you get the ones who tell you to leave their fucking kids alone. One fucking generation of parents with their heads up their asses telling another generation to report any cop who even looks at them suspiciously. I'm telling you, Dawson, you think it's frustrating being a civilian. How would you like to have to listen the shit we have to listen to every day?"

"But Bob. . ."

"I'm telling you, Dawson, it's hopeless. Society is going to shit. The best we can do is try to keep innocent people from being hurt. And we're not terribly successful at that."

"If you don't stop the pushers and the users, who you know god-damned right well will turn into pushers one day, everyone suffers. . ." Dawson paused and gazed around the restaurant, then turning to Geary said, "I'm sorry, John. I don't mean to take it out on you, but when are we ever going to learn?"

The three men exchanged small talk for the rest of the meal. They joked about those things men joke about when together, and tried as best they could to resume a normal conversation after the subject of drugs was exhausted. But it was difficult, given the nature of their previous discussion, to fully relax. O'Neil assured Dawson that Gomez would be with him continuously for the next week or so. Geary suggested that the DEA and Boston Police set up some sort of official communication over the Ortega incident — maybe a task force to monitor the movement of drug traffickers in and out of the city — until someone or something happened which made sense out of the recent rash of killings.

"And for chrissake, don't forget to call the U.S. Attorney's office," Geary said as a reminder to O'Neil, "You know how sensitive they get over these things when they're not informed."

16
The Switch

He practiced for this role for over two years. He endured excruciatingly painful operations and plastic surgery. He made several unlawful
entries into the United States to study his subject. He attended endless
devotion services, and spent hours reviewing pictures of his look-
alike. And those boring tours of the chancellery in Boston. If he were
not so committed to the accomplishment of his mission as he was, he
would have taken a walk a long time ago.

And those endless hours reviewing staff photos.

"This is father so and so."

"This is Sister Margaret."

"This is the fucking chef," he mimicked wickedly.

Jesus, he wanted to kill them all. And then there were those tedious-
ly long lessons in English. They call me a psychopath, he thought. I'm
smarter than all of them. They should all die!

His sons would be well taken care of, though. Attend the finest
universities. His daughter would be escorted everywhere. His entire
family would be protected and cared for, for life. The highest form of
status in his country. As for the days and months of loneliness, he was
supplied with women and girls of every description, and as many as he
wanted, whenever he wanted. And he wanted as many as he could get.
This was going to be a dangerous mission, might as well enjoy myself
while I can, he figured. And as for money, he had lots of it.

All this planning would eventually pay off. It had to, he assured
himself. Once at the final destination he would commit the act, then
seek sanctuary in a friendly country. No detail was overlooked. His
Soviet and Cuban teachers taught him well in the use of self defense,
subversion, murder.

As his training progressed he was actually encouraged to kill a few people to develop his skills. Be disciplined when you kill. Be committed to the act, and have no regrets. Here, take this young girl and do as you wish with her. Kill her if it pleases you, for she is a criminal just like you, an outcast. She won't even be missed.

Indeed, Madrid was an eager student. After two years he actually developed a craving to kill — and an *obsession* with killing one man in particular. Now, his mind was a weapon. Steel-willed. Determined. Obsessed with his mission. A petty criminal when he started — a psychopath named Pablo Escobar Madrid — was now Bishop Jose Enrique Michelsen. Tall. Dignified. Cultured. Deadly. From the top of his head, mantled with healthy   pure white hair, to the tip of his toes, he was a changed man.

As he lay in bed this afternoon, recuperating from the flu, he recalled the events of the weekend, and of the enormous planning the organization devoted to this one task. How stupid and gullible these Americans are, he thought, smugly content with the deception. Everything, from the donation of the archdiocesen retreat in the hills of Barnard Vermont, to the arrangement for two bishops, members of the Catholic Bishops Conference on International Affairs, to meet at the retreat on May 17th. It was perfect. Except for the weather, the plan proceeded without a hitch.

He relived each detail with satisfaction. At 6:00 P.M. Friday afternoon Bishop Connolly received a telephone call at the cabin informing him that his parents' home had burned down and that his mother and father were in critical condition at the Springfield Hospital. Bishop Connolly was so distraught, and visibly shaken, that he suffered a tragic heart attack on the way to the hospital — and died. Too bad, Madrid purred. I wonder if we had anything to do with that, he laughed to himself. He knew they did.

Connolly's friend, Bishop Michelsen, would then be alone in the cabin. A perfect target. Not kidnapped. Not held against his will. It was a planned trip to Vermont, away from the business of the archdiocese, all by himself. Then that traitor shows up. Carlos' call almost screwed up the entire plan. The one thing they didn't plan on was Ortega's bout with his conscience. Loose lips sink ships, Pablo scoffed. Now Carlos has no lips. Or nose, for that matter. This amused Pablo, since it was his idea to give Carlos a lip cut.

The new bishop sipped his tea and reveled in the flawless execution of the plan. Even the unexpected phone call from Carlos set the stage for an improvization. The real Bishop Michelsen would be forced to call the chancellery, tell them the sad story of Bishop

Connolly's parents' death, and inform everyone he was on his way home. Of course, he did this with a gun pointed at the back of his head, not expecting that he would soon be dead. He believed he was going to see his friend Carlos Ortega again. Fat chance!

Madrid was angry that he couldn't attend the actual burial. He was only the driver, not yet a full Bishop. Not until the real one was six feet under.

Imagine that, he said to himself, me, a bishop, a lowly driver.

Then that idiot shows up, Madrid cursed. This Dawson Page, he shoots one of us and thinks he can get away with it? If I were not a bishop I'd cut that mutherfuckers heart out and shove it up his ass, Pablo thought as he wiped a bead of sweat from his brow. Damn flu!

His mind raced: The organization couldn't care less about the American finding Ortega, Pablo thought, as he recounted the day in his mind. But this *shit*, Dawson Page, sees the real bishop going under — so his body had to be removed and buried elsewhere. Too bad the American slob didn't die in the mud. He was gone when they returned to finish him off. I wonder where he went? Pablo asked himself as his mind conjured up several tortures he would inflict on the American with the gun if he had the opportunity.

Anyway, the real Bishop Michelsen was good enough to bring his papers and itinerary with him to the cabin. So Friday evening was not a total waste. Pablo spent the time reading over schedules and plans. After all, this was a *first* trip for both of them.

He laughed to himself. Can you imagine that poor American bastard trying to convince the police that Carlos had white hair? It wouldn't make a difference anyway, he figured, since Page, didn't know who's body was being buried anyway. The plan would work!

Then, there was *this* part. The injection of the flu virus. Madrid hated that part. The very thought of bugs sent chills up his spine. He hated the little crawley, hairy things. Especially the microscopic kind. They were the worst kind, he thought as he pursed his lips and swallowed hard, hoping to forget that he actually injected billions of these little creatures into his system. He remembered how he dealt with the bugs in his jail cell, the hundreds of little crawley things which would climb up your nose when you fell asleep. The secret to winning the war, then, as now, was to make an example out of a few. Build a wall around yourself and punish those who dared climb over it. Inflict cruel punishment on a few, leaving their bodies scattered around for their friends to see. That would show them. See? See, what happens to little fuckers who fuck with me. I hate bugs. I hate people.

Sweet Jesus, they're all over the place. People. Bugs. Kill one, you kill the other.

Yet a compromise, of sorts, had to be made. Before retiring Friday evening, Madrid injected a virus, containing enough bacteria to cause temporary laryngitis and minor discoloration of the skin.

"Oh Bishop Michelsen, you don't look well at all, and you sound just terrible," Sister Margaret said shortly after he arrived at the chancellery Sunday morning.

Of course, Sister, he said to himself, mocking her concern. I am dazed. Of course I don't look like myself. I have the flu. Yes, yes, thank you Sister. Help me to my room. And later I will ask you to help me to the bathroom. Hold my we-wee while I pee. Anything to degrade someone like you. I might even develop an erection while you hold me. That would show you. And then, I'll ask you to take me to the kitchen. Show me all around this place under the pretense that I am not well enough to get around myself. I am disoriented. Oops! Sorry Sister. Was that your breast I touched? And in two days I'll be gone. Off to do my job. And yes, Sister, if I get the chance to shove it in you before I leave, I will. Of course, you'll be dead by that time.

Madrid's hallucinations were interrupted by a light tapping on his door. "Your Eminence, are you feeling better?" It was Brother Dominic. He was genuinely concerned with his Bishop's condition.

"Ah, Brother Dominic," Madrid said weakly. His voice was raspy, hoarse. "Please come in." His voice didn't sound natural at all.

The door opened slowly.

He clutched the rosary beads by his side and spoke slowly, deliberately. "I have recited the rosary three times, Brother Dominic, in remembrance of my good friend, Bishop Connolly." He added a long, sorrowful pause for effect. "I am incapable of expressing my sorrow, My heart is broken over his loss. Surely, our Lord has a reason for taking our brother in Christ — but at such a crucial time." His voice trailed off.

"We are all grieved, Your Eminence. But now you must take care of yourself. You have much to do in preparation for your trip to Rome," Brother Dominic said. He was deeply concerned.

"That's why I called you, Brother Dominic," the imposter said. "I'd like you to prepare my bags for the trip. You know where everything is. I feel so weak — too weak to move about — although I do feel better than last night." He didn't want to overdue it. "Be certain my tickets are taken care of. All my papers are arranged. Clothes are ready to go. What time is my flight, Wednesday? Oh, yes, seven o'clock."

"I'll see to everything, Your Eminence," Brother Dominic said. As he turned to leave, for he could sense that his bishop was growing tired, he paused and turned again, facing his bishop one last time. "Oh, did you hear any more from your friend Carlos Ortega?"

Momentary panic. Know what? "I'm sorry, Brother Dominic. I've been so involved with Bishop Connolly's death, and this flu, it escaped my mind. We spoke Friday. Beyond that. . . I. . . Was there something I should know?" Pablo squirmed uncomfortably beneath his covers. He could feel the urge to kill building once again.

Brother Dominic was surprised with the answer. But his face remained emotionless. "We spoke Friday, Your Eminence. You told me of your close personal ties with Carlos." He paused and looked deep into his bishop's eyes. Something was not right. Something was different, he thought, as he awaited an answer. His mind wondered, then he shook his head and dismissed an absurd passing thought.

You fucking smart-assed swine. I'll cut your fucking heart out. Do you hear my thoughts? You bastard. I want to kill you. I want to kill you. Can you read my eyes? I want to kill everyone in this place. I want to. . . "Of course, Brother Dominic, I understand. I *have* been acting a little strange lately. Maybe it's the trip, the loss of Bishop Connolly so suddenly. Maybe it's just the flu. We will talk about Carlos later." He closed his eyes and sighed. Maybe this will get him out of here.

"As you wish, Your Eminence." Rivero closed the door behind him as he let the room, feeling uneasy and confused. Bishop Michelsen sounded terrible. He didn't even look like himself.

17
Visiting Hours

The phone in Rivero's office rang five times before he lifted the receiver. It was 2:20 P.M. "Chancellery, Brother Dominic. May I help you?"

"Brother Dominic, this is Dawson Page, from the News Tribune." Page was calling from his apartment, having been escorted there earlier by Lieutenant O'Neil, who waited until Gomez arrived before leaving himself.

Page hadn't planned on working today, but decided to call the chancellery for this one interview, hoping to work on it during the week just to keep his mind active.

"Oh, yes, Mr. Page, I have a note on my desk to call your office this afternoon regarding a meeting with Bishop Michelsen," Rivero said distantly as he flipped through his calendar index — noticing from of the corner of his eye the diary sitting at the edge of his desk. I must read that soon, he said to himself. Carlos' letter hinted there were major changes in the organization, and that Rivero should be aware of them for his and Carmen's safety.

"I'm sorry, Mr. Page, but His Eminence is ill, I'm afraid. He's developed a rather nasty case of the flu, and we're trying to keep his schedule as clear as possible. We may just have to cancel that interview. As you know the bishop is scheduled to leave for Rome this week."

"Yes, I understand," Page replied considerately, although somewhat disappointed with the cancellation. "Would it be possible for us to get together this afternoon — only for an hour or so." Silence. So Page pressed. "I realize you're busy Brother Dominic, but I've taken the week off from the paper, and was looking forward to working on this story while I had the time — to give it the attention it deserves. . ."

"I don't know, Mr. Page," Rivero said hesitatingly, not wanting to precipitate unnecessary media interest in what had occurred.

"To be honest with you, Brother Dominic, my last couple days have been anything but normal, and I would really like to have the opportunity to meet with you and do this story. I'll keep it brief."

Although Rivero was preoccupied with other matters — namely, the call from Carlos, and Carmen's unexpected visit — he consented reluctantly to the meeting. "But we must conclude the interview in the allotted time, Mr. Page. I hope you understand."

They agreed to meet at 3:30 P.M..

Having settled that matter Page called the office to inform Janet of his plans, and to let her know he was feeling fine, and that he would be at the chancellery interviewing Brother Dominic if anyone was looking for him.

"I know you're concerned, Janet," he said as she prodded him for additional information. "But you have to believe me when I say I'm in no direct danger. I'm sure you saw the morning paper by now. My name wasn't even mentioned. And I have a police detail assigned to me until this thing clears up. It'll be okay. Honest!"

Janet had her doubts but accepted Dawson's assurance that he was safe.

Meanwhile, Rivero began reading the diary. This was as good a time as any, he thought, as he sat in his study, relaxed in the Victorian chair positioned by the window. He would read by the warmth of the sunlight.

Bishop Michelsen was sleeping. The staff was busy doing their normal chores. Carmen was safe. Carlos was. . .? *That* troubled him, troubled him greatly. But there was nothing he could do about it now. Sister Margaret was instructed to allow no calls through, and to see to it that Bishop Michelsen, acting very strange since his return from Vermont, was not disturbed. As much as could be, everything was normal.

Rivero peered out the window briefly, adjusted himself in the chair, removed a pair of reading glasses from his shirt pocket, placed them gently on his nose, and began reading Carlos' words. Each page of the diary weighed heavily on his broken heart, since he knew these were Carlos' last words to him. Carlos, my friend, why did I ever consent to leave you? he asked as he read slowly — page after difficult page. So this is what it has all come to, he thought, embittered, disconsolate, disillusioned. It was just too much to digest in one sitting. Yet it had to be done. He placed the diary on his lap and gazed out the window, staring blankly at the gentle movement of leaves on the trees, and he remembered fondly how it used to be...

He was twenty-one years old when he first met Carlos. For fourteen years they were like father and son — brothers, friends. They made the business grow and flourish together. Indeed, the lucrative life of crime inherited by Simon Garbriel from his father Ramon, passed down to the adopted son, Carlos Ortega, was refined, modernized and expanded under Carlos' watchful eye. Indeed, it was Carlos who ultimately brought the various crime factions together and argued for unity in the drug trade. Carlos was a visionary.

Rivero smiled as he remembered. That was... 1961? Rivero massaged the bridge of his nose and smiled as he recalled the adventures they shared together. They were magnificent bank robbers, cagey extortionists, ruthless killers when they had to be — and then there was the burgeoning drug trade.

Rivero interrupted his own recollection of days gone by, and fixed his gaze across the room at the crucifix hanging on the far wall. And he thought how times had changed. How he had mellowed. And then he remembered again... how it used to be.

"Millions can be made if we just work the business together," Carlos pleaded, at the specially called meeting of fifteen gang bosses in Puerto Victoria, Peru in '61. "If we can just unite for a common purpose, we can do more together than any one of us could ever hope to accomplish alone."

Yet none would listen to the youthful Carlos. He was only nineteen years old in 1961. And others, more mature and experienced, were not convinced they should relinquish control of their independent operations to this new group which promised greater power and wealth.

"Why should we agree to sign on with you," the bandit Mollendo sneered intransigently. "A boy and two nanny's."

Rivero and Manuel who stood impassively by the door of the tavern stiffened and clenched their jaws at that unflattering reference to their manhood.

Carlos noticed their irritation, raised his head slightly, and with a barely noticeable flick of his finger signalled them to remain where they were. This was not the time, nor the place to argue the point. He leaned forward in his chair and said quietly, "You should listen more closely Mollendo because we are right. Because times are changing.

Because our people are poor. And because we must move into the international arena if we are to survive. Because it is good business."

The others sat quietly, but doubt was written on their faces.

Mollendo was clearly speaking for all as he persisted with his taunts. "And the boy and his nanny's will guarantee us a fair cut of the profits from this new crime empire?" he taunted sarcastically, waving his arms in the air. "You call us together from all over to tell us that we must give up our wealth and combine it with *your* organization for the common good?"

"Not give up your wealth Mollendo," Carlos said evenly, "combine our wealth, for a bigger purpose, a bigger prize. The movement of drugs throughout this hemisphere alone will make us wealthy beyond our wildest dreams."

"I brought twenty strong men with me today," Mollendo interrupted abruptly, jerking his head backward, toward the window, outside where his men slept. "Sanchez, brought fifty. de Sisa brings another nineteen." He clenched his fists as he spoke, contemptfully, "You bring two nanny's and yourself — a boy, with a virgin ass," he laughed as did the others. "And you presume to tell us what is and what is not good for our business?"

Carlos stared resolutely at Mollendo. He hid his inner rage well. "I would not refer to Manuel and Rivero as nanny's again, Mollendo. It shows disrespect."

"Fuck your respect!" Mollendo shouted, pounding the table, pointing insolently at Carlos as he spoke. "You stay out of my area Carlos, and keep your..." and has he spoke the words he nodded across the room, "...your two bodyguards, and your men out of the affairs of my region. For if you interfere with my business, there will be war. Do you understand?"

The room erupted with agreement and acrimony.

Mollendo continued. "I respected your father, Carlos. And out of respect for him I do not leave this room now. I sit here and I listen to a boy. But you are just a boy. You will have to earn my respect, not the other way around."

"I take it you speak for the rest?" Carlos said evenly as he lifted a napkin from the table and patted his lips. He paused and looked around the room calmly. The others said nothing. "Very well, then. It is *The Will of God*." Carlos then stood and looked at his watch. "It is late, gentlemen. The Inn is yours for the evening. I trust you will find the accommodations to your satisfaction. We have provided young girls for each of you. They await you in your rooms. Your men are being similarly serviced in their quarters." He exhaled a gusty breath and summoned all the humility he could muster, given the abrupt ending of what he hoped would be a fruitful meeting. "Tomorrow, we will look at the sunrise together, I hope, as equals, none higher or more important than the other."

Carlos then motioned to his two bodyguards, and Manuel and Rivero stood aside, opening the doors leading from the tavern's private meeting room. Awaiting the guests in the empty tavern were dozens of scantly-clad teenage girls, perfumed and radiant, eager for the abuse they knew awaited them. Such was the power of cocaine. And such was the power of their beauty that not one of the fifteen crime bosses thought clearly enough to consider his own mortality that fateful evening.

It was early the next morning, as the men who slept in the stables began to awaken and drift outside, that the power and brutality of the society of *The Will of God* was evidenced and burned forever into the minds of all who witnessed the gruesome display. Impaled on fifteen poles outside the tavern Victoria were fifteen heads. And beneath those heads, standing as calmly as could be was Carlos, Manuel and Rivero, their clothes soaked with fresh blood and pieces of human body, evidence of their hand in the eerie display.

"Join with us," Carlos prompted as he paraded before the gathering of men who stood in silence and horror. "And we will make millions together. We will share what your bosses hoarded to themselves. Today we will chose new leaders from among you." He emphasized the word you. "Leaders who are not as blind as their predecessors. Leaders who like money, and the power and luxury it can provide." Carlos paused and waved at the bodiless heads behind him and asked: "Which of your leaders speaks ill of us? Which of the bosses objects? And if you are asked later: Did the bosses protest? You can answer that they remained silent. That it was *The Will of God* that they step aside for new leadership."

Indeed!

Little would anyone have expected, then, how quickly the millions would become billions, or how powerful the society called *The Will of God* would one day become. Carlos matured quickly, with Rivero and Manuel constantly by his side to advise and support him, and the organization grew.

Carlos, Rivero and Manuel. They were inseparable. It was *The Will of God*! Until 1968. Carlos knew that Enrique's vocation would carry him far beyond the mountains of his country. Indeed, while still in school Enrique was recognized as one of the more promising young seminary students. Within a year he would be called upon to travel to the United States to further his studies and work with the many Spanish-speaking immigrants flocking to its shores from places such as Cuba, the Dominican Republic and Mexico.

The church hierarchy believed, rightly so, that there was a great need for better understanding between the people of South and North America. Father José Enrique Michelsen with his easy-going manner and gently style was dispatched to fill a spiritual need, and to assist in bridging the cultural shock experienced by so many Spanish immigrants who settled in the land of this powerful neighbor.

Rivero smiled again as he recalled how devastated Carlos was when Enrique told him of his promotion, and of his impending transfer to the United States.

"But there is much work for you to do here, my friend," Carlos pleaded weakly, knowing he could not — would not stand in the way of his friend's good fortune.

"The Lord's work is everywhere, Carlos. I am a soldier for Christ, can't you see? I must go where the need is greatest."

"But. . ." Carlos began.

"My friend," Enrique said as he reached out and touched Carlos' shoulder, "Surely you must understand my duty. My honor."

Carlos nodded dolefully. He understood all too well those words.

On the day Enrique left Peru, Carlos embraced him warmly and said simply, "I will send you a present, my friend. But you will not know what it is. You will just have to trust me that your friend has not forgotten you."

Enrique stared into Carlos eyes and laughed, puzzled by the message. "You always did have a flare for the theater, Carlos. I guess I will just have to wait and see if I can figure it all out for myself."

The two men embraced again, and Enrique studied Carlos' face for the last time. "You will always be special to me, Carlos. No matter what you do, or what people say about you, I will always pray for you. I will pray every day for your soul." And he laughed and shook his head. "You are incorrigible, Carlos. Yet you are my closest friend, and I cannot bring myself to stand in judgement of you — or your business. You have had a difficult life. And who's to say what direction any of our lives would have taken were it not for circumstances." Of course, Enrique was never told the true nature of Carlos' business — and he never pressed. "Thank you Carlos, for everything." Those were the last words he spoke before boarding the plane at Lima.

Rivero wiped a tear from his eye. *He* was the present Carlos would eventually send. He arrived in Boston in 1971, and was assigned to the chancellery by special arrangement as an aide to Monsignor Michelsen. He would remain with Enrique as he remained with Carlos for the remainder of his life, for that was his honor and duty. This was the code he was taught from the time he was a child. Honor, above all else. It is what Simon Gabriel, and then Carlos, instilled in their loyal conqueros. It was this sense of loyalty and dedication which, as he read the diary, he concluded was absent from the new breed.

Rivero continued to read — and learn. Over the past few years there had been dramatic changes in the organization: Infiltration by younger members, enamored with Marxist slogans, loyal to no one but the party, eager for violent confrontations and outright defiance with established leaders. Carlos' words were no longer the *final* words where these men were concerned. To them, Carlos was just another ". . .rich capitalist property owner, out to exploit the labor of the working class."

Jesus, Rivero thought as he read further, things have gotten out of control. The drug trade is out of control. At one time those in positions of power exercised discretion in their use of this stuff. Now, it seemed, every junkie fashioned himself a Grande Mafioso.

The pain in Rivero's eyes vanished and his jaw tightened as he turned the last few pages. The adrenaline pumped through his veins and his blood seemed to boil as the plan became clearer. They intend to do this? he asked of himself. This cannot be! He turned the pages faster, reading in disbelief what the newer breed planned. And he began to understand why Carlos left his homeland so abruptly. Carlos escaped with Carmen when he discovered what the *compromise* was. A deal of necessity was struck between the newer revolutionaries and the older leadership, which was a patriarchal society headed by Carlos.

The *leftists* were demanding total capitulation to their wishes — or else — open warfare. But what they planned was outrageous. They wanted to murder Enrique Michelsen, replace him with a look-alike, and send that man off to Rome to assassinate the Holy Father? How could they bring such dishonor to their people? How could they believe they could pull this deception off?

Yet. . . a meeting was held at the cabin in Vermont. The murder of Bishop Connolly's parents did occur. But did the organization actually succeed in replacing Bishop Michelsen with an imposter known as Pablo Ernesto Madrid? Is the man in Enrique's bed Enrique of someone else? The flu prevented even Rivero from making that determination. Whoever it was that was lying in Enrique's bed, he lost his voice temporarily, and his skin color was terrible. If only there were more time, Rivero thought.

But surely, the real Enrique is here safe! Surely he escaped the fate they planned for him. That's why Carlos came to Boston. To warn Enrique. Besides, Rivero reasoned as his mind raced, I spoke with Enrique earlier. And I haven't heard from Carlos, so I must assume Enrique is safe.

Rivero stood, walked over to his desk, and lifted Carlos' letter. Placing his glasses on the bridge of his nose again, he read Carlos' last words over and over: *If I am successful and able to prevent the switch, you will know this also. For the newspapers will surely carry the story.*

I must read the morning paper he said to himself as he placed the letter in the diary again, and returned the diary to his desk. I must review the events of the weekend once again, before I do anything else. Carlos called Friday... Why didn't I identify myself then? he asked in anger. Enrique returned from Vermont Sunday morning... There was just too little time.

River walked behind his desk and sat, leaning back in his chair, resting unevenly on one elbow. After several moments of intense thought he decided what course of action he would follow. He reached for the bottom draw, opened it, and from the rear quarter panel, removed a silver key taped along its smooth surface. He studied the key for several moments, turning it in his hand as if he were weighing the broader meaning of its use.

Carlos sent him to America to protect Enrique from just such a possibility. The time had arrived when he could no longer afford to be indecisive. He must discover the truth — and act!

River locked the draw and walked from the study, passing the room containing Enrique — or Madrid, he would soon find out just who occupied the bishop's bed. He glanced along the length of the hallway before entering his room. Old habits die slowly.

Not wanting to be disturbed, Rivero locked his door behind him as he stepped into his private quarters, eyeing the room cautiously before entering fully. If the *Voluntad de Dios* wanted to guarantee that their scheme went as planned, they would surely silence those closest to the bishop — or at least neutralize those who might raise a question as to his authenticity. Rivero prayed the new breed was not as meticulous as the older ones.

Once satisfied he was alone in his room, he knelt beside his bed and removed from underneath a foot locker containing *personal* items. He inserted the key and opened the locker slowly. Inside: One .9MM automatic pistol with silencer. One Israeli UZI — automatic, illegal in the United States. A long knife, a present from Carlos.

Rivero studied each weapon carefully, making sure all parts worked and were properly lubricated. He positioned the locker under his bed again and placed the pistol and knife under his robe, nestling the smooth blue steel against his waist, which, he was satisfied to observe, was properly trim for a man his age.

His first thoughts were of Carmen. He reasoned that he had ample time to deal with whomever it was in the bishop's bed. He was not yet certain the man was an imposter, so there was no need for immediate action. Carmen's safety, however, that would have to be assured. It was his honor and duty to look after her.

He hid the UZI, but not so inaccessible that he would have difficulty getting to it if it were needed. The .9MM was accurate and deadly. Good for close-up work, The UZI was simply destructive. A professional killer knew the difference. The knife? Used properly it was as deadly as any weapon.

After several minutes preparing himself emotionally for whatever action was necessary, he walked quietly back down the hallway, past the bishop's quarters. He paused at the bishop's door and glanced inside. The bishop was sleeping. The flu really did incapacitate him. He closed the door.

As he walked to his study, the doorbell, muffled and barely audible from the living quarters on the second floor, signalled the arrival of his guest, Dawson Page. Rivero looked at his watch. Page was right on schedule.

Sister Margaret met Dawson at the entrance and led him upstairs advising him in hushed but firm tones all the way that he was to take no longer than an hour with Brother Dominic. "Visiting hours must be restricted, Mr. Page," she whispered apologetically as she led Dawson down the richly carpeted hallway, past Rivero's, then the bishop's room.

"That's fine Sister. I appreciate the opportunity to even be here today," he said as they approached Brother Dominic's study.

The door to the study opened smoothly and quietly, and Rivero, who heard them approach, greeted his guest with outstretched hands. "It's nice to finally meet you, Mr. Page. I'm sorry for the change in schedule, but I'm sure you understand." He noticed Dawson was holding the morning paper.

"Thank you Brother Dominic," Dawson said as he entered the lavish room. "This room is absolutely beautiful. I've never been in the chancellery before, Brother Dominic. I hope you don't mind my curiosity. The architecture and workmanship. . ." he said as he studied the panels and ceiling, "is impressive — almost inspiring."

"Please feel free to look around, Mr. Page," Rivero said as he pointed toward the front window, "I'm sure you will appreciate the view of the front lawns."

Dawson took the cue and turning toward the window began to move in that direction.

"Oh incidentally, Mr. Page," Rivero said, motioning with his hand for Page to pause, "I notice you have the morning paper. May I borrow it for a moment?" Rivero didn't care how awkward it sounded, he had to see for himself if there was any mention of Carlos.

Page obliged, and after handing the paper to Brother Dominic, ambled to the front of the study. "You are right, Brother Dominic," he said as he gazed outside, "the landscaping is spectacular." He then turned to face his host and noticed two things almost instantaneously: One, the intensity on Brother Dominic's face as he scoured the paper, leaving the distinct impression that what he was searching for was more than of passing interest. The second thing he noticed was the portrait of Bishop Michelsen hanging on the wall. Serene. One hand clutching the crucifix dangling from around his neck. The bishop's ring was exquisite and ornate. His snowy white hair. . .

At the very moment Page realized whose body he observed being placed in the grave, Brother Dominic found what he was looking for. His eyes raced across the article. Frustration and anger filled his heart, as did a deep sense of hurt as he scanned the newspaper account. He glanced up and noticed Page staring trance-like at the portrait.

"The hair. . . The ring. . ." Page mumbled.

"Brother Dominic," Page quizzed. "Where was Bishop Michelsen this weekend?"

"In Vermont," Rivero said as he glanced at the open paper, reading the underlined text, ". . . a witness, who police have cleared of any suspicion in the crime, but who may have evidence which could lead to an arrest." Rivero was in mild shock. "You?" he asked.

"This can't be a coincidence, Brother Dominic," Page said, feeling unsettled and unsure of himself. "I. . . I saw that man being buried this weekend. . . yet. . ." He stared intensively into Brother Dominic's questioning eyes. "Is the bishop alive?" he asked, genuinely confused, and for good reason. Until this very moment he accepted the explanation that his eyes deceived him. That the man they found in the grave was actually the man he saw being buried. So when he asked, "Is he alive?" he was hoping to resolve that mystery once and for all, expecting Brother Dominic to say, "Of course, Mr. Page, he's sleeping in his room." Of course, that's not what happened.

Rivero's face was blank. His stare, empty. His eyes, cold and calculating. "Mr. Page, you just confirmed something of enormous importance to me."

"Then I did see Bishop Michelsen murdered. . ."

Rivero drew back at the words and glared. His expression answered Dawson's question.

"Oh my God," Dawson whispered. "We have to call the police, Brother Dominic. This is incredible," he said as he drew his hands up and massaged his face. "I. . . I can't believe this all happened. Why would anyone want to murder Bishop Michelsen? Yet, I did see that man being buried," he said as he pointed at the portrait. "Brother Dominic, what's this all about? What's. . ."

Rivero rose from his seat and interrupted quietly. "Mr. Page, we do not know one another at all. But for some reason which I don't fully understand we have been brought together at this incredible moment — in this place," he said with a wave of his hand as he approached Dawson. "You must believe me when I tell you that what you discovered is only half the story. And I am just beginning to piece it all together myself."

Page said nothing.

"You must trust me, Mr. Page," Rivero said as he reached out and touched Page's shoulder. "I have someone I want you to see before we do anything else," he said as he reached under his robe, almost as if he were adjusting his belt. He awaited Page's answer. He didn't want to kill an innocent man, but would not hesitate to do what he had to do to protect Carmen. "We cannot go to the police just yet. You must trust me," he pleaded.

Page didn't understand exactly why, but he accepted Brother Dominic's cautionary words — he trusted him. Besides, he knew Sergeant Gomez was not far away. "I trust you, Brother Dominic. But I don't understand."

"I know you don't, Mr. Page. Did you drive here?"

"Yes."

"Good, we will have to use your car." Rivero's mind raced. "Please bear with me for a moment, Mr. Page," he said as he wrestled with his thoughts. It would be illogical to assume that the people who killed Enrique and went through this elaborate scheme of replacing him

with a look-alike, would not also have taken the precaution of as-
signing men to cover the chancellery, just to ensure the plan's success. It would also be illogical to assume that Page was not being
followed, or that when whoever it was that planned this terrible deed
saw the two men together, they would not figure the plan had been
compromised. No, indeed. The police could not be called. Not yet,
anyway. Not until Carmen was safe with them.

"We won't go to the police until we've contacted the DEA personally," Rivero said. "Now Mr. Page, I want you to follow me, and say
nothing. If he's still asleep, I want you to see someone in the bishop's
room. And another thing," he said as he reached under his robe and
withdrew the .9MM, "can you use one of these things?"

Page stepped back suddenly. "Who are you?" he asked.

"Let's just say I'm a guardian angel," Rivero answered dryly. "I have
something else I'd rather carry."

18
Getting Lucky

Both Dawson and Rivero viewed the imposter resting in Bishop Michelsen's bed. Satisfied he was sleeping soundly, Rivero asked Page to accompany him to his room.

Rivero whispered, "I'm sorry for the rush, Mr. Page, but your education is going to have to be done quickly. I hope you are a fast learner."

Page nodded, still bewildered by the events following Saturday's sighting. "We all have to start sometime."

"Yes," Rivero replied mechanically. "According to Carlos' diary — he was the man the police found in the grave, Rivero explained, "*That* man's name. . ." he said, pointing in the direction of the bishop's room, ". . .is Pablo Ernesto Madrid — an assassin hired by the. . .," he would not say the name *Voluntad de Dios*, ". . .Los Grandes Mafiosos, a drug cartel more powerful than your own mafia, and more sinister, I might add."

Standing in his quarter's now, Rivero continued with his incredible story. "He was sent here to replace the real Bishop Michelsen prior to his trip to Rome later this week. They must have figured that the time element — the closeness of the trip — plus a severe case of the flu would prevent anyone from getting too close or discovering that a 'switch' had been made."

"Then the real Bishop Michelsen is dead?" Page asked, although he knew the answer.

"I'm afraid so, Mr. Page," Rivero said as he paced back and forth. "Two things the mafiosos didn't plan on: First, Carlos' defection. He must have caught them by surprise, otherwise he never would have escaped the country alive. Maybe they were just caught up in their revolutionary zeal, actually believing that Carlos would buy into what they planned. They were sloppy in their research, and erred in their judgement. That was their biggest mistake. Carlos never did accept any of their revolutionary bullshit. He said so many times in his correspondence with me — and in the diary."

"And the second reason?" Dawson pressed.

"Ah, yes. The second reason. They didn't understand Carlos. You see, Mr. Page, I was one of Carlos' must trusted friends. He was like a son to me, actually. When Enrique was sent to America in 1968, Carlos asked that I attend a Catholic school — by special arrangement of course — to become a Brother in the church. My training was shorter, and with proper connections, and two years of condensed study, I was assigned to work along with Bishop Michelsen in America."

"Didn't Bishop Michelsen recognize you?"

Rivero smiled. "No, Mr. Page. You see, Carlos loved Enrique as a brother. Carlos had us watch over Enrique many times. We live in dangerous times, Mr. Page. Especially in my country. So, it was important to Carlos that Enrique not know who I was right from the very beginning. Although we did meet once, but that was over thirty years ago. He couldn't have remembered that far back. . ."

"I hope you don't mind my forwardness, but how could you just give up your life as. . ."

"His bodyguard?" Dominic offered.

"Yes. And enter a religious order to boot. It seems like an awful lot to ask of a friend — even a close friend."

Rivero laughed. "Yes, it is Mr. Page. At first I found it difficult to give up the ways of my previous life — especially the freedom to travel around. And on numerous occasions I had to lie to convince my superiors that my long walks in the courtyard were for spiritual fulfillment. . ."

"Meaning?" Page asked.

"Meaning, Mr. Page, that I broke many a young girl's heart during my stay in the Order. So, in fact, I lost nothing. I gave up nothing. And in many ways my life actually became less complicated. Carlos visited regularly, and just as regularly I got laid."

Page's mouth dropped open with that admission. "I must admit you're not the kind of Brother I'm accustomed to meeting, Brother Dominic," Page said.

As he continued with the story of his life and trip to America, Brother Dominic removed his robe. Underneath he was wearing black slacks and a tee shirt. Page made a mental note that Brother Dominic was a man of sturdy build — no lightweight. "We are not always what we seem to be," Brother Dominic continued, folding his clothing and placing it neatly on his bed. "You would be surprised how many people lead double lives, Mr. Page," he said as walked over to the closet and removed a black turtleneck jersey from the one shelf running across its length, and drew it down over his head in one swift motion. "Just look at our friend in the other room. . ."

"You mean Madrid?"

"Yes," Rivero said as he reached into the closet again, only this time high above the door. After a moment's struggle, he removed from its rack . . . the Israeli UZI.

"What the fuck?" Page said as he stepped back.

"Believe me, Mr. Page," Rivero said as he strapped on a shoulder harness, "when I tell you that the people who are behind this switch are ruthless. They wield absolute power. Why do you think they wanted to replace Bishop Michelsen?" he said as he continued dressing. He waited for an answer. "On Thursday our time, Bishop Michelsen will have the first in a series of meetings with the Holy Father."

"They want to murder the Pope?" Page asked incredulously. "Brother Dominic," he continued, feeling suddenly extremely uncomfortable, "this entire situation is incredible. I just don't know what to say."

"You don't have to say anything, Mr. Page," he said as he continued to dress. "Even the Vatican has leaks, Mr. Page," he said as he removed his shoes, replacing them with jogging sneakers. "The Pope is planning a tour of South and Central America in the near future. Then a similar tour of America. His itinerary is drug abuse. He'll be making a call to the faithful to turn against drugs. He will offer absolution from all past sins to anyone who turns in information on dealers. He will forgive the sins of those who renounce drugs and those who traffic in them. That's a strong inducement in my country, Mr. Page. Very strong. And it has the revolutionaries worried. His Holiness' trip to the United States will echo the same theme. Every bishop, every priest, every sister, brother and lay person who believes in Jesus Christ — and they number in the hundreds-of-millions, Mr. Page — will be asked to take the pledge. Accept absolution."

"But do the people behind this scheme really believe the Pope has that much influence over his people?"

"They tried to murder the Pope once before, Mr. Page," Rivero said referring to the most recent threat on the Pope's life. "They fear him more than any other man in the world right now. It would be a great symbolic victory if he were assassinated."

"Brother Dominic. . ."

"Please, Mr. Page, call me Rivero."

"Dawson," Page said returning the favor. "Shouldn't we go to the police with all this? I mean, I want to help, and all that, but this is unbelievable. It's beyond you and me..."

"I have no difficulty going to the police, Dawson. But first we must ensure that Carmen is safe."

"Carmen?"

"I will explain who she is as we drive to her place," Rivero said as he strapped the UZI to his shoulder. "Come, lets go," he said as he slipped into a lightweight blue windbreaker, fully opened at the front so as to allow immediate access to the firepower he carried beneath. "The three of us will contact the DEA after we are safely together."

"That's fine with me," Page said.

"Your coming here today was a chance visit, Dawson. Carmen's visit this morning was unexpected. If I were assigned to watch over the chancellery," he said, referring to the contract killers he suspected were watching over the imposter, "I'd be getting mighty suspicious about these visits. Let's just hope they haven't had enough time to figure out what's going on."

"I don't know that we have to worry about that yet, Rivero. I can't figure it out myself."

"If we're lucky, Dawson, we will all be together this evening — you, me and Carmen. And the police will have enough information to prevent this tragedy from going any further."

"And if we're not lucky?" Page asked dryly.

"We'll be dead, my friend."

19
The Tap

Something's wrong, Rivero thought as he and Page walked along the path leading from the chancellery to the street where Dawson parked his car. It's too quiet. It was 3:00 P.M.. With the discovery of Carlos' body, the drug syndicate was certain to be cautious. They'd be watching the chancellery — closely. Yet, as Rivero exited the compound, traffic on the street was light. There were no signs of surveillance or suspicious movements anywhere. And as for Dawson, Why hadn't they taken him out yet? The organization would not go through all this planning only to leave loose ends in the final stages — and Dawson was definitely a loose end. What were they waiting for? Indeed, there was every reason to be suspicious. All was not as it appeared. Rivero was certain of that.

He walked guardedly, keeping his hands in his jacket pockets, holding the sides of his windbreaker in place so as not to expose the dark blue steel under his arm. Page walked cautiously beside him, his .9MM snuggled at the small of his back, handle barely protruding above the belt line.

"How far down the street is the car parked?" Rivero asked.

They stopped by the front gate and Page pointed to his right. "Rivero, see that car over there?" he said as he nodded in the direction of Gomez' car, "It's a police escort. I just thought you should know. It'll be with us wherever we go."

Rivero cast a cautious glance at the car, then scanned the street in both directions before continuing. Where the subject of drugs was concerned, Rivero trusted few people — including the police. Yet, Gomez' presence did explain the absence of other vehicles. Maybe.

"You don't know the drug syndicate, Dawson. A police escort won't prevent them from getting to us, if that's what they want." He paused a moment to organize his thoughts before continuing. "I just don't like it, Dawson. It's too quiet. The people you saw in Vermont, they must know who you are by now. They wouldn't be this complacent about you and me walking together, unless they felt certain we were being watched."

"Well if we are being watched, at least we have a police escort. If there's any trouble Gomez will call in, and we'll have every police car in the city here in a matter of minutes."

Rivero raised an eyebrow in doubt, and said as he headed for Dawson's car: "If they want us, Dawson, they'll take us, regardless of the number of police who respond."

"I don't know, Rivero," Dawson offered.

Rivero stopped, and reaching for Dawson's arm, said: "But I *do* know, my friend. This is America. You are an American. You don't understand our ways. If the organization decides to kill someone in this country, they will dispatch fifty men to do the job. Fifty eager men. Fifty men so strung out on cocaine, so dependent on their next fix to survive they'll kill anyone who gets in their way. Cops, Catholic brothers, yes, even newspapermen. No one is safe from their reach."

Dawson nodded. "I understand, Rivero," he said as he reached over and unlocked the passenger's door. "I understand." And Rivero slid in.

"Before heading for Carmen's place," Rivero said when both men were safe in the car, "I think we should take a long ride. Go through the city," he said with a flip of his hand. "Maybe even drive south. If we are being followed I want to make it impossible for our tail to keep up with us."

"Any suggestions," Page asked.

"Some place that will buy us a few hours."

Page nodded, then suggested they drive to the Cape, figuring the trip would last a good four.

"Good," Rivero said, stretching his legs in front, "we can use the time to get to know one another better as you drive."

"Fine by me," Dawson said as he pulled away from the curb, glancing in his rear view mirror to reaffirm Gomez' presence.

As they drove south Rivero talked freely, hoping to keep Dawson's mind free to watch the road and concentrate on the flow of traffic. There was little sense in keeping secrets at this point, anyway, he figured. With Carlos and Bishop Michelsen dead, and Dawson being the only person alive able to identify their killers, he had to trust him.

He told Dawson of his friendship with Carlos and Bishop Michelsen, and of the organized crime society known as *The Will of God*. He told of his participation in the formation of the drug syndicate years ago, or Los Grandes Mafiosos as it was referred to today, and of Carlos' disenchantment with the recent politicalization of the trade.

For his part, Page drove in silence, like a good newspaperman. Indeed, as Rivero spoke Dawson reflected on how he had learned a long time ago the value of listening instead of talking, and how on more than one occasion he advised new reporters fresh out of journalism school, eager to cut their teeth with a weekly paper, that if they would use their ears twice as much as their mouths, they'd surely win a Nobel prize one day. And he smiled as he thought of it, causing Rivero to wonder what *he* was smiling about.

But Page listened for another reason: he was literally overwhelmed by the nature of Rivero's admissions. Anything he could offer would pale next to what he was hearing.

"I'm telling you these things, Dawson, because I have to trust you. I'm getting too old for this type of life," Rivero said, more thinking out loud than conversing. "Our meeting by chance, your witnessing the burial of Enrique — and then getting shot for your efforts. You can't be one of them."

Dawson responded pointedly to the assertion. "Goddamned right I'm not one of them," he said, staring directly at Rivero, ignoring the road in front of him as he spoke. "Let's get that right out of the way, first. I want you to understand something, Rivero, this isn't my idea of fun, I. . ."

"I'm sorry, Dawson," Rivero interrupted, "I didn't mean it the way it sounded. I assure you I trust you. I wouldn't have said what I just did, if I doubted your honesty."

Dawson relaxed somewhat, and directed his attention to the road again. "What you just told me would make a great book, though. Pulitzer material." Then he added quickly when he observed the frown on Rivero's face, "But you asked that I not repeat anything. And I won't. My word is good, Rivero."

Rivero exhaled deeply and nodded. "I believe it is, my friend."

Although it had taken most of the afternoon to travel to the Cape, the time was well spent: Rivero spoke and Page listened. On the return trip Page reciprocated the exchange of personal information and told Rivero of his own background. It couldn't hurt, he figured. Indeed, the long conversation brought the two closer together, and bonded a friendship which would one day save their lives.

For his part, Rivero breathed more easily when he learned that Dawson was a combat veteran — even though that was twenty years ago. "You have killed before," he said with satisfaction over the admission, and smiled contentedly when Dawson acknowledged his combat experience.

"Nothing that I'm real proud of, Rivero."

"Yes but combat firms up one's character."

"War sucks!"

Rivero chuckled, "Sometimes."

As the miles turned into hours, their respect for each other grew, and each began to feel more confident their meeting was still a private affair. And even if it were not, they trusted their journey was sufficient in length to disrupt any tail that might have been assigned them. As for their police escort, Gomez — he remained about three car lengths behind, careful not to lose sight of them even for a minute. Dawson breathed easier each time he gazed in the rear view mirror and observed Gomez, reflecting on the very real possibility that he and Rivero might need Gomez' added firepower later if the people who murdered Carlos and Enrique decided to turn a small drug army loose on them — something Rivero felt certain would happen once the mafia learned the switch had been discovered.

As they approach Boston again on the return trip, Rivero grew more tense and ill-at ease with surroundings. He looked at his watch every five minutes timing their approach to Carmen's apartment. The daylight bothered him. It afforded no protection, no concealment. "If they're going to make a move on us, Dawson, they'll make it when we establish contact with Carmen. They'll want to get the three of us together if possible. That's when we must be on our greatest alert. We must be prepared for anything."

Dawson nodded in agreement.

As Rivero continued outlining his plan, Page's mind drifted to Bob O'Neil. "Rivero," he interrupted, "My best friend is a lieutenant with the drug unit of the Boston Police. I trust him with my life. . ."

Rivero cast a doubtful glance in Page's direction. "Yes. . ."

"Earlier this afternoon, before I met with you, I spoke with Bob and a DEA agent named John Geary. If there's going to be any shooting or violence, I'd feel better if we called Bob on his private line and asked him to be available."

Rivero hesitated before answering, then agreed to the call. "Maybe that would be a good idea, Dawson. But if he joins us, he must come alone. You and me, Gomez and O'Neil. . . no more cops than that. The wider the net, the greater the chance a few extra fish might slip through. We can't afford that. You just have to trust me, Dawson, until we are safe with Carmen, the fewer people know where we are, or what we're doing the better. Besides," he said as he exposed the long knife under his belt, "I want to personally deal with that cocksucker lying in Enrique's bed. And I'd rather not have a lot of people around when I do."

As Rivero spoke Dawson pulled his car onto Allston Street, where Carmen was staying. It was 8:05 P.M.. Both men were alert and cautious, and suspicious of any unnecessary traffic in the area. But as before, the street was exceptionally quiet.

Rivero reached in his pocket and removed the piece of paper on which Carmen had scribbled her address. "Here," he said as they approached number twenty-one, "she's in room 2B." As Dawson pulled over to the curb, Rivero closed his eyes, drew a deep breath and exhaled slowly. Page glanced across the seat and wondered just what they were getting themselves into.

Not taking any chances, Dawson removed the weapon from his back and tucked it snugly just to the right of his belt buckle. "We've got to move quickly, Rivero," he said as he rubbed his hands together, taking note of the steady increase in his heart beat. "Once she's in our custody, we'll take her directly to the police. When we get to the station I'll call for Bob."

"Very well, Dawson. But please understand," he said, emphasizing the point, "I will guarantee Carmen's safety with my life. There must be no question from the police or anyone that she will be my ward, under my care. You must guarantee me that your friend will not interfere. . ."

"I guarantee it," Dawson said as he removed the gun from his belt one more time, checked it's safety and slide action. "I'm ready when you are."

"Let's get her, then," Rivero said as he slapped a loaded magazine into his shoulder weapon and surveyed the area one last time for any signs of suspicious activity.

The apartment in which Carmen was staying was situated in the middle of a row of wood and brick structures which housed college kids and some elderly residents. The buildings were old, and there were no elevators. Fire escapes located at the rear of the building provided the only other egress, next to the front doors.

"Rivero," Page said, clutching Rivero's arm as he prepared to leave the car. "Be careful. These old buildings have very narrow hallways, lots of stairs, and very little in the way of security. I'll be behind you, covering your exit. Grab the girl and let's get the hell out of here."

Rivero smiled and squeezed Page's arm. And in an instant he was out of the car, moving quickly around the front hood. Instead of walking directly into Carmen's building, he walked briskly to the apartment building next door — just in case they were being watched. No need to telegraph her location. After five minutes, Rivero ran from that building to the one next door. Page looked at his watch. The clock was now ticking. They had to get in and get out — quickly.

Rivero's hasty exit from the first building was Page's cue to move. He took a deep breath, still wondering what the hell he had gotten himself into, and stepped out of his own car, approaching Gomez' at a fast gallop. "Let's go Sergeant," he said in practiced military fashion, "she's in twenty-one."

Gomez opened the door and jumped out, holding the butt of his revolver as he did.

"In there," Page said as he moved toward the building, prepared to act as back-up for Rivero. "I'll stand watch downstairs, you head up to 2B for the girl. . ."

"Fine," Gomez said as he began to follow. "Oh, shit," he said sharply, stopping abruptly as if he forgot something, "Let me get my radio, just in case."

Page continued to move toward the building. He approached the front stairs, took another deep breath and reached for the butt of his revolver just to assure himself that he could get to it quickly in the event it was needed. He walked up the stairs, stopped and turned to see what was taking Gomez' so long. "Shit!" he exclaimed, as he raced down the stairs, observing that Gomez was talking into his radio. I forgot to tell him not to call in our location.

As Page approached the car, he noticed that Gomez had two walkie-talkies. "Two radios?" Page asked suspiciously.

"Just a precaution," Gomez said as he threw the second radio onto the back seat. "I'll take this one," he said as he placed the receiver in the pocket of his blazer. "Come on, let's get going," he said, urging Dawson back into the building.

Something is all wrong here, Dawson thought to himself as he followed Gomez into the building. "Why don't you go up first, Sergeant," he said as he glanced behind them one last time before committing himself to the climb, "Head up to room 2B. Brother Dominic's in there now. I'll cover the hall until you come out."

Gomez didn't like that plan. He hesitated momentarily, then decided to move forward as asked. He moved up the stairs slowly, his hand resting lightly on the butt of his revolver.

Page studied the detective as he climbed the interior stairwell, and thought that maybe he was being too cautious. For chrissake, he said to himself, Gomez is a cop. Trust him. "Maybe, I'll join you, Sergeant," he said as he followed Gomez upward.

It came to Page in a flashback. He saw himself lying in the mud. What did he notice that was different? Out of the ordinary. He stopped on the stairs, and stared at the tap on the bottom of Gomez' shoe. It was broken. The stupid prick didn't even think to fix it. Probably noticed it was loose a few days ago, gave it a good bang against the curbstone, locking it back on the rubber heel temporarily, then forgot to have it fixed later. Its positioning on the heel of the shoe made it appear as a bright silver object on the bottom of Gomez' shoe.

"I saw that before," Page mumbled to himself, "on the shoe of the man who shot me. On the shoe of the man who killed Ortega and Bishop Michelsen."

Gomez froze where he stood. He heard Dawson's last remarks.

Then, the sound of doors closing. Car doors, lots of doors. Page turned and faced the entrance to the building. His face went ashen, and his heart pounded furiously against his chest. There were several men entering the building, all with automatic weapons drawn. And they weren't the police. Page stared in disbelief, then turned and faced a smiling Gomez.

"It is *The Will of God*, Mr. Page," Gomez said mockingly as he reached for his revolver.

"You mutherfucker," Page said coldly, piecing it all together almost instantly. No wonder there was no other surveillance. Gomez was on the other side.

Adrenaline raced through Page's veins as the thought of betrayal and death jolted his senses, numbing his initial fear. He had to act quickly. He had to create a diversion.

"Turn around and face me, Page. And raise your hands, now!" Gomez said, stepping toward him slightly. His voice was cold and sharp.

Page turned away, instead of toward Gomez, and faced the men downstairs. This obscured the movement of his hand. In an instant, he withdrew his .9MM, turned again, and to Gomez' total surprise, shot him in the chest. A glob of blood spurted from Gomez' mouth as the bullet severed his aorta artery. Gomez was slammed against the wall with such fury that its surface splattered instantly with blood and parts of bone and intestines. He remained standing, although dead — his eyes moving wildly back and forth, almost as if his brain was in shock — which it was — trying desperately to figure it all out. It was the look of a dead man. A frantic, confused look. Page saw it often in Vietnam, and wondered then as he did now, what a man's brain process was when life slipped away faster than his brain could comprehend.

"Rivero!" Page shouted loudly, simultaneously turning his attention on the men downstairs. All hell broke loose when *they* realized what had occurred.

Plaster began flying all over the hallway as bullets ricocheted about, thumping into walls, tearing violently through wood and into metal beams. Page knelt behind a wooden banister and began shooting in the general direction of the men at the bottom of the stairs. The noise in the hallway was deafening as Pandemonium erupted in the quiet building. The intruders were spraying the hallway randomly, shooting at anything and everything in view. Page fired and fired again, but found himself blinded by the think cloud of smoke and dust kicked up around him. Three men fell in his relentless volley. But more entered.

"Rivero" he shouted again in desperation.

A voice, louder than the stream of bullets flying past him, commanded: "Get down!" It was Rivero.

Instantly Page crouched lower, pressing himself into the wooden support against which he leaned.

From under his jacket Rivero let loose a deadly burst of automatic fire. Four more men fell instantly. And for just a moment there was silence from gun fire.

The hallway was filled with gray smoke and dust from discombobulated pieces of dry, brittle plaster. And people throughout the building could be heard screaming and crying, terrified by the sudden explosion of violence in their building. Page looked up at Rivero and said nothing. His face was covered with tears and dots of blood from Gomez' chest, and plaster from the walls.

"You look like shit," Page said, half jokingly.

"Are you okay?" Rivero asked calmly as he loaded another clip of bullets into his weapon.

"Yeah. And you?"

River shrugged. "It's not over, Dawson. There are more of them out there. I saw them arrive from Carmen's apartment. We're going to have to leave Carmen here. They don't know anything about her yet," he said as he kicked the feet out from underneath a very dead Gomez. The corpse dropped to the floor and separated at the waist. "Stupid bastards must have thought he was me," Rivero said as the front half of the body tumbled down the stairs coming to rest upside down in the lower hallway.

Page felt himself gag as the body glided past him on its gruesome journey.

"It's our lucky day, my friend," Rivero said as he reached down and assisted Dawson to his feet. "We bought some time."

"Oh, yeah. I can feel it all over. Think I'll go out and play megabucks tonight."

Rivero chuckled.

"I'm almost out of ammunition, Rivero," Page said as he checked the number of bullets in his weapon. He was high. Just like the old days. And scared to death, just like the old days.

"Take your pick from one of them," Rivero said, pointing to the bodies piled at the bottom of the stairs. "I'll cover you."

Page moved cautiously down the stairs. Rivero followed, hesitating only long enough to shout: "Carmen. Stay in your room. Do not leave until this is all over. They don't know where you are. When it's safe to leave, take the diary. Wait until you hear from me." He didn't know if she heard him amidst the wailing of the building's tenants. He prayed she did.

"Let's hope someone is calling the police," Page said as he sifted through the carnage under Rivero's watchful eyes. "Jesus," he said, jumping back slightly when one of the bodies he turned over spurted blood all over his pant leg. The man was still alive but in shock and paralyzed, his heart pumping what little life remained all over the marble floor. Page had recovered two automatic weapons. He was ready.

The sun was setting, now, and an uneasy calm seemed to envelope the neighborhood. Almost as if everyone were holding their breath, too afraid to move, to speak, to run.

Page and Rivero positioned themselves by the front entrance, leaning against the two concrete columns for cover. They stared outside, sizing up their situation. not liking what they saw. Over a dozen automobiles were parked zigzagged in the middle of the street, blocking traffic and creating an impenetrable wall of man and machine. Maybe thirty men, all Latinos — all armed with automatic weapons, were crouched over the fenders of cars awaiting further instructions.

"You must understand by now, Dawson, that the drugs do it to them. Half of them probably don't even know where they are."

"This doesn't look good, Rivero. Not good at all. We can't hold them off much longer, you know."

"If the police don't get here soon," Rivero said coolly, "they'll tear this building apart — and kill everyone in it just to cover themselves. But first they'll come for us."

The air was charged with emotion. Violence! The leader of the men, hidden somewhere behind one of the cars, was shouting instructions to his men. As he shouted, a young woman ran from one of the buildings. She was holding the hand of a child who followed obediently behind. The woman was crying, panicked, terrified. The child smiled an innocent smile as he raised his hand to his small face, brushing his fingers through his sandy blonde hair. A volley of automatic weapon fire cut them both down.

It was then that the first police car arrived on the scene. Foolishly, it came to a halt at the location near the end of the street where the last in the long line of cars was parked. The driver was, no doubt, young and inexperienced with this type of situation. Before one foot was out of the cruiser the officer started yelling at the men who were looking on in total disbelief. "What the hell is going on here?" the voice demanded, though unconvincingly. The police officer probably realized at the very moment of her death what a mistake she had made. It ended quickly as hundreds of rounds tore into tender pink flesh and slammed and threw metal chards and pieces of glass over the street where she stood.

When they were done with their fun the attackers turned their attention on the men in number twenty-one.

"Take them!" the leader shouted. And with that the armed men let loose more frenzied fire, this time at the entire line of buildings. Glass and chunks of brick and concrete fell to the ground as the street erupted in a volcano of smoke and noise. Residents were screaming and running for cover — others fell dead in their apartments as bullets tore through glass openings and plaster walls. It was the most horrible sight Page had ever witnessed — and this was Boston.

"We've got to divert their attention," Rivero shouted over the noise as he stepped from behind his cover, and to the surprise of the seven men rushing the steps, let loose a burst of fire which stopped the seven dead in their tracks. Page crouched low and following Rivero's lead did likewise. The noise was deafening as the bloody assault on the building continued.

Rivero ran out of ammunition first as the second human wave of men stormed the building. They were firing in a mad and haphazard manner, almost as if they wanted to capture, not kill the targets of their attention.

Page was low on ammunition and returned fire a single shot at a time. Not enough to stop the human wave rushing toward them, though. The shooting from outside subsided as the first man through the door met Rivero's knife at throat level. Blood gushed as the first man turned to face his comrades for assistance. They finished him off in a hail of bullets. The second man to reach the front entrance grabbed the muzzle of Page's gun and lost his face for that misjudgment. But it was Page's last bullet. And now both men were unarmed. The third and forth man through the door lunged for Rivero, who was growing tired. Page lunged for one of the men, grabbed him by the head, and with a quick snap, broke the man's neck. Then a fifth attacker burst through the door and grabbed Page, placing a muscular arm around his neck, pulling him backward onto the floor, crushing his windpipe. Page jerked his body violently and thrashed his arms about madly in an attempt to free himself, but it was useless. He could feel himself loosing consciousness. Then a sixth attacker rushed into the hall, and grabbing Page's ankles, prevented him from moving at all. A needle pierced Rivero's neck and his knees buckled. A needle was jabbed into Pages arm and the lights went out entirely.

As quickly and as violently as it began. It ended. For some reason the two were not killed. If they died in the assault, the attackers were told, fine. But if they could be taken alive the reward for their capture would be doubled. The reward was just too alluring to pass up.

Police sirens echoed through busy streets as dozens of officers raced to the scene of unbelievable destruction. From every section of the city police cars responded to the call "officer in trouble." But it was too late for that officer.

The first units on the scene arrived precisely seven and a half minutes after the call for help went out. They were shocked by what they observed. The scene was chaotic. Dead bodies were everywhere.

The men who raided the area were ruthlessly efficient. They killed every one of their wounded who could not walk. No one would be alive to break the silence.

And as if matters were not bad enough, there was a new danger: sporadic fires in several apartments began to burn through old roofs, lighting the evening sky, casting an eerie, orange pall above the street, hinting an ominous tragedy was about to follow. What had started as a wild shootout in the streets turned into a holocaust as the tenements burned all too quickly. It was a firefighter's nightmare as loose electrical wires and hot lead easily ignited the dry wood of century old buildings.

And there was an even graver danger brewing for residents gathered at the scene. The smell of gas was growing stronger with each passing moment. The series of small gas leaks actually threatened everyone in the area. Anticipating calamity, and without being ordered or directed from their superiors, dozens of heroic police officers dashed into smoke filled buildings and ushered frightened residents to safety. For many, it would be their last act of humanity.

Lieutenant O'Neil was one of those who responded first. His shift was just ending when the call from the dispatcher described the shooting on Allston Street. As others ran from building to building, warning residents of impending disaster, O'Neil walked amidst the rubble of the street, looking for clues which might explain what happened. When he approached number twenty-one, he stopped in amazement, and studied what appeared to be Sergeant Gomez' car. It troubled him that Gomez, and hence, Page might be involved in this incident.

People were assembling on the streets now, many of them were weeping openly, shouting for loved ones. Fire trucks, police cruisers and TV vans all pressed onto the small street near twenty-one, each busy with activity, each desperately attempting to find answers. And the sky grew darker as black clouds rose from roofs and gushed through windows.

"Everybody, out of here," Captain Jordan of the fire department ordered. Years of experience and intuition told him what was about to happen. He moved frantically through the crowd of people pushing them further and further away. "Move away from these buildings," he shouted as he directed other firefighters and police to move the crowd back, away from twenty-one.

Yet, more people arrived on the scene — some onlookers, others, residents of the buildings, searching for loved ones lost in the confusion. Most were just dazed and walked aimlessly about. This kind of violence never happens in America.

The police had their hands full as they pushed against the wave of spectators which gathered to help the victims still pouring out of buildings. And all the while the smell of gas grew. His face covered with sweat and loose ash, Captain Jordan continued to try to bring some order to the scene. "Lieutenant," he shouted to O'Neil, "get your men off the street and out of those buildings now. They're about ready to go," he shouted, referring to the buildings.

The morning papers would describe it as the worst example of urban violence and disaster in modern American history. One entire city block of Boston simply vanished in fire and explosion. Of the seventy-six residents who occupied the buildings, only nineteen had made their way to safety when the first thunderous eruption occurred. Toll: Five police officers, three firefighters and fifty-seven civilians — mostly elderly, Gone! And no one could figure out why.

The media reported that Bishop Michelsen, as ill as he was, actually wept when he heard of the tragic incident.

And Carmen Velasco Terry Ortega was alone once again.

20
Aftermath

Tuesday, May 21

8:00 A.M. Throughout the long evening reporters badgered police for more details — for information which no one had.

"Can you explain, Lieutenant, what this is all about? Does it have something to do with the drug violence occurring in the city?" a young female reporter shouted as she jammed a microphone at O'Neil's face.

"Please," O'Neil said, brushing the microphone aside. "We haven't even had time to separate bodies from the rubble. I can't comment one way or the other until we have more to go on. We're still trying to piece it all together for chrissake."

"It's rumored this has something to do with the Ortega murder in Vermont," the reporter persisted. "Can you confirm that for us?"

O'Neil glared at the young woman and wanted very much to elaborate. He wanted to vent his rage and bang table tops and turn the clock back — but he couldn't. Neither could he elaborate as the reporter asked. "I'm really sorry," he said considerately, "I have no comment to make at this time."

"But Lieutenant. . ."

"Look, it's just too early to tell what happened," he said as he pushed his way through the crowd of cameras and newspaper reporters, and headed for the quiet of his office.

O'Neil was weary and puzzled. After noticing Gomez' car at the scene, he felt personally involved in the shootout and fire which followed. What happened to Dawson and Gomez? he wondered. They were apparently on Allston Street for a reason. But what reason? Indeed, as he sat alone in his office, he realized that he had enough questions to answer on his own without interrogatories from the press, which persisted and annoyed him. The press wanted answers. And he didn't have any. Damn it! Can't they understand English? he kept asking himself. I don't know what happened, or why.

By the time the fire department and gas company arrived last night, the buildings were reduced to just so much debris. The gas explosion shook windows loose in every structure within a mile radius, and could be heard reverberating off buildings as far away as Boylston Street. It was a real disaster. A terrible night.

Activity in the police station during the early morning hours was at a feverish pitch as reporters turned their attention to the commissioner and members of the command staff. O'Neil sat alone in his office, now, thankful attention had been focused elsewhere. It was really the first opportunity he had to relax since last night. He welcomed the solitude and quiet. He needed the time to organize his thoughts and unwind. Because he had not returned home at the end of his regular shift to shower and cleanse himself of the dirt and smell of smoke, he felt especially tired and beaten this Tuesday morning.

He leaned forward in his chair, and placing his elbows on the desk, rested his head in his hands. He rubbed his forehead, hoping the gentle massaging motion of his hands would alleviate the tension he felt building. It worked for a while. But he was restless and uncomfortable. He leaned back in his chair and ran his hands through his hair, then swiveled and gazed out the window. As hard as he tried to explain last night, he kept drawing blanks. Maybe he was just too tired to think clearly... yet, he was alert enough to recognize that his thoughts were fuzzy, lacking the kind of detail he was accustomed to summoning during such emergencies.

As he leaned back, hands propped behind his head, fingers locked at the bottom of his hairline, a picture, hanging on the far wall caught his attention. His eyes grew misty as he stared at the images behind the glass. He paused, then rose slowly and walked across his office, eyes still fixed on the images in the picture, staring alternately between his own tired reflection in the glass and the image of two friends, arms around each other, laughing... What were they laughing at? he wondered as his mind filled with recollections of their childhood. He was barely able to restrain his tears.

"Dawson," he said as he reached toward the smiling face — again noticing his own haggard reflection in the glass frame. He looked so gaunt. So fucking tired of the same old shit. Every day having to deal with losers, assholes, mixed-up teenagers, violence, druggies. How many times in better days had Dawson and Joyce prodded Bob and his wife Susan to "Leave the rat race. Set up a small store in Vermont. Become mountain men..." Maybe that's what they were laughing at, he thought as a smile passed over his face. Dawson was a funny guy. Loved the outdoors, but hated bugs. Loved the wilderness, but enjoyed his home. He'll sleep in a tent, but want breakfast served hot and fresh at the pancake house. Christ, what an appetite that guy had... Had? It jarred his consciousness when it occurred to him that his best friend, Dawson, might actually be dead.

I've got to take a break from this place, O'Neil said to himself as he returned to his desk, determined to get some rest before tying all the pieces of the puzzle together. First order of business was to get some sleep. He was both physically and emotionally drained. "I'm leaving for the day," he told an astonished staff as he walked from his office, oblivious to the activity occurring around him.

"Lieutenant, I think the commissioner wants to talk with you about this thing before you head home. You were the first person to arrive on the scene," his assistant Jim Davis said. O'Neil continued to walk.

"Lieutenant?" Davis called again.

"It's in my report," O'Neil answered mechanically, then thought better of just walking out without an explanation. "Look," he said as he turned and faced his staff which consisted of four other officers and two secretaries, "I'll be back later. I'm tired. I need a rest," he said, realizing he couldn't just walk out and leave eveyone without any explanation. "...I don't want any calls at the house, either. None of you know where I am. Is that clear?"

Heads nodded as the staff acknowledged his message. It was evident from his appearance that he was exhausted. They'd cover for him.

As O'Neil walked from the building he paused on the front steps to study the morning sky once again. More rain is on the way, he thought. He walked slowly down the concrete steps, stopping on the sidewalk, his mind filled with conflicting emotions about his job. Is it really worth it? he asked himself as he studied the headquarters building. What have I accomplished in all my years on the force? Sure, I've put some people away. But most of them are back out on the street again. And there's more crime today — more violent, drug-related crime, than ever. And then there was last night. Five police officers and three firefighters, and dozens of civilians dead — for what? And the people who planned this violence, Where are they? Where did they come from? Why did they pick Boston? And if we do catch them, How soon will it be before they are out on the street again?

All in all, O'Neil thought as he walked to his car, he'd seen better days. Yet there was *one* thought which brought a brief smile to his face: The commissioner would have to answer to the press all by himself. And the commissioner detested members of the press. No question about it O'Neil thought as he turned the key in the ignition, the commissioner is going to hold me personally responsible for leaving the building at such an inopportune time. This drew a mild chuckle from O'Neil who found himself caring less and less about how anybody else felt, including the commissioner.

With the engine idling smoothly, O'Neil sat and mulled over his options. He tapped the wheel lightly with his finger as his mind churned furiously through the abundance of unrelated, incomplete data evolving around this case. He kept seeing Gomez' car parked outside number twenty-one. And he wondered why. Maybe one last visit to the scene prior to heading home would help him solve that mystery. If nothing else, a closer examination of Gomez' car might help him calm the uneasy feeling he had rolling around in the pit of his stomach. A feeling which told him something was not right. Maybe if he took that closer look, he might uncover something he missed in the confusion of last night. Anything at all, no matter how insignificant could be important. There had to be a reason for the violence — yet. . .

As he pulled away from the curb into the traffic of Berkeley Street, his mind pondered question after baffling question. Could the events be tied together? Was Dawson involved in the shootout? That would explain the presence of Gomez' car. Gomez was assigned to stay with Dawson. There had to be a connection.

The traffic was exceptionally light, considering the abundance of media vehicles parked all over the street. O'Neil headed toward Commonwealth Avenue, past Boylston and Newbury Street. With any luck he would be on Allston Street in a matter of minutes. He re-hearsed his plan as he headed west on Commonwealth. First, get a list of every tenant in the affected apartment buildings.

Second, find Gomez' car. For what? He couldn't figure out why, yet. But there had to be something.

Third, Ortega must be the key. O'Neil was convinced of that now. The shootout had to be related to the incident in Vermont. Not enough for a D.A. to go on, but enough for a good cop. Piece it all together, he prompted himself, as he grew more excited with the prospect that he might just find what he was looking for — a clue — whatever it might be.

Fact: Page went to Allston Street, and was in one of those buildings for a reason. What reason? Information on Ortega. Had to be!

Fact: Page was either alone, with Gomez, or with Gomez and someone else. Had to be one of the three. Which one of the three? Fit the pieces, he told himself. His mind raced.

And what of the body Dawson was referring to? The one with white hair. Dawson may have been a dreamer, but he didn't hallucinate. Sonofabitch, if Dawson said he saw a man with white hair being buried, he saw a man with white hair being buried. But who is the mysterious man with white hair? Where is that body? Another missing piece.

O'Neil depressed the accelerator and sounded his siren for the first time as he raced through Kenmore Square. He was tired, yes, but the questions this case presented stimulated his curiosity and caused his body to come alive again, like a runner's second wind. "No major crime ever occurs," O'Neil remembered instructing new recruits at the police academy, "without evidence being left behind. If two people are at the same location at the same time, and one does something violent to the other, evidence of that crime will exist. Has to!" And the recruits would look up from their note pads and nod — and understand nothing of what he was saying.

"A good cop is like an archaeologist," he would tell them. "We know that dinosaurs roamed the earth at one time. But we haven't seen any lately. We piece bits of evidence together which points to their existence, and come to some pretty astounding conclusions about their lifestyles. If we can dig into the past and construct from evidence, specific conclusions about events occurring over a million years ago, how much easier must it be to dig into the recent past and solve crimes?"

And the recruits would nod.

"Experience teaches that men are thinking animals," he would say. "The fact that we can think also means that we can forget. Correct?" And they'd nod. "And what is it that we sometimes forget?" And they'd stare. "Details. Evidence left at the scene of the crime which the perpetrator never expected would be uncovered. A piece of lint might tell us what color clothing the individual was wearing. We can learn a person's favorite cologne from the smallest trace of clothing. We all know fingerprints can be lifted, but do you know how many murders have been resolved because of the discovery of a shoe print? The point I am making," he would say, "is this: A good cop looks for these deceptively obvious clues..." And the students would nod. Indeed, he thought as he sped past Boston University on the right,

What new evidence will we uncover today, which was overlooked last night, because we were preoccupied with other details?

Two very non-scientific conclusions occupied O'Neil's mind as he approached the police barricades surrounding the Allston Street area. First, the list containing the names of building tenants was of critical importance. Second, Gomez' car would yield a clue as to his presence in the area.

As he eased up to the police barricade at the end of Allston street he was greeted by Sergeant Keough, a veteran cop of thirty years. "You look like shit, Lieutenant," Keough said as he rested his hand on the window frame. "I thought you were going home to get some rest."

"Thanks for the compliment, Dave," O'Neil said dryly, inching the car along the curb. "How's everything going here?"

Keough stepped back as O'Neil got out of the car, and pointing to the bulldozers said, "They came in about six hours ago, cleared the street first and are now working on the buildings. As for 'how' everything's going, we'll leave that up to you guys."

O'Neil smiled as he surveyed the area from the police line. "Have they found any more bodies?"

"Anything they find from this point on will be in pieces. And talking about pieces," he said gloomily, "we found part of Gomez."

"I thought we would," O'Neil said evenly.

"What the hell was he doing here?" Keough asked

"Working."

"But he wasn't even on duty, Lieutenant. First thing we did was check the duty roster. Unless he came over with you. The other four cops all responded over their radios."

"He was on an assignment with the drug unit."

"Oh shit," Keough responded after a moment's hesitation.

O'Neil's face reflected uncertainty. "What do you mean by that?"

Keough shrugged. "I don't know. I mean, Oh shit. Nothing special." Then he thought about his answer for a moment and offered more. "I don't like all this drug shit, Lieutenant. That's what I mean. You know, J. Edgar was right keeping his agents away from all this shit. He knew what it could do."

O'Neil exhaled deeply. "You mean keeping them out of organized crime investigations?"

"Yeah. Don't get me wrong, Lieutenant, I'm not saying Gomez was connected with any of this — but, ah. . ."

"Yeah, I know, Dave," O'Neil said.

"Anyway, Lieutenant, it's a real mess here."

"Dave," O'Neil said as he walked toward the activity further down the street. Keough walked alongside. "There were cars parked along the curb last night. Where are they now?"

"Hell, most of them, Lieutenant, are over there," he said, pointing to a pile of debris pushed off the road onto a vacant lot at the end of the street. "The bulldozers and tow trucks had to move everything off the street just so we could get to the buildings. You saw what it was like last night."

"Yeah, I know," O'Neil said as he increased his pace, putting distance between himself and the crusty sergeant.

"Nice talking to you Lieutenant," Keough said as he dropped behind and assumed his position at the barricade once again.

O'Neil walked briskly toward the rubble. There *were* automobiles amidst all the dirt and wood. He walked around the pile careful not to stumble over chunks of wood, since many of the loose boards contained nails, and some still simmered from the intense heat of the blast. He searched the debris for one car in particular, though, moving boards and broken doors, and parts of trees which once dotted the sidewalks. What a mess, he thought as he sifted through the mess before finding what he was searching for. "That's it," he said, congratulating himself. He brushed a pile of dirt from the car closest him. The intense heat caused most of the paint to burn off. But it was unmistakably, Gomez' car. There were bullet holes in the door.

Carefully, O'Neil moved tree limbs and pieces of wood from the frame. When the car was sufficiently clear of debris, he poked his head inside the window to take a closer look — and gagged when the smell of burnt rubber and vinyl assaulted his nostrils. "Jesus," he protested as he stepped back and placed a hankie over his face. But he was determined to press on with his search. He was extra cautious now as he lifted pieces of metal, still warm from the fire, and then entire pieces of vinyl from the seats.

Given the extraordinary circumstances, there didn't appear to be anything you would not normally find in a burnt out car. Yet, he searched thoroughly, leaving no area uninspected.

Just as he was prepared to call it quits, for no evidence could have survived the heat and flames once the car caught fire, he noticed, wrenched between the springs of the rear seat, a walkie-talkie. It didn't look like a departmental issue. But then, neither did the car. Stretching into the rear section of the car he grabbed the antenna and jarred the unit loose. It was crusty and hot to handle.

With the unit in his hand he stepped away from the wreck and examined the radio more closely. It could be a toy, he thought.

Something for the kids or nephews. But to be certain, he would take it back to the station and have the lab go over it in greater detail.

Since there was evidently nothing else worth taking from the wreck, he walked back to his own car and called into the station. On channels reserved for the drug unit there was very little need or desire for formality. So O'Neil just squeezed the button on his mobile microphone and said what he wanted. "Jim, are you there? It's O'Neil." Jim Davis was his second in command.

"Bob, where are you? I thought you were taking a few hours off. The commissioner's pissed about you walking out as you did. He's been raising hell all morning because he had to deal with the press over this thing."

O'Neil coughed as he inhaled some of the fumes from the burned walkie-talkie. Ignoring Davis' warning to make his presence officially known, he said only what he wanted. Fuck the commissioner. "I'm on Allston Street. Look, Jim, I need two things: A run down on the tenants in those buildings." There was no need to say what buildings he was referring to, since it was the big news of the day — made all three networks; "And I want you to meet me across from the bus station on the Stuart Street side. On the QT, Jim. I have something I want you to run by the lab. Will you do that for me?"

"The commissioner's pissed. . ." Davis said, raising his voice tauntingly. "But I'll be there. When?"

"Fifteen minutes," he said, ending the conversation.

O'Neil tapped the roof of his car and thought for a moment before leaving the scene. Was there anything else he forgot? He glanced one last time at the scene of devastation, shaking his head in despair. There were radio, TV and newspaper crews all over the place, and hundreds of civilian onlookers trying to get a glimpse of bodies and whatever else fascinated people who flocked to incidents such as this.

Satisfied he could do no more, he left Allston Street and headed for the bus station. Once that chore was completed, he would head home, clean up, and get some sleep.

21
The Puzzle

Lieutenant O'Neil slept soundly because his body demanded rest. It was 3:00 P.M. His mind, however, was preoccupied with details of the previous evening's events.

He was trying to arrange pieces of the puzzle while he showered earlier in the morning, prior to collapsing on his bed; he was trying to fit the pieces together now, as he was awakened by the ringing of the phone. Except for the fact that he slept for five and one-half hours, the continuity of his thoughts was uninterrupted — or so it seemed.

He propped himself on his pillow while his wife made small talk with the caller on the other end of the line. It was the office.

When Susan was satisfied he was fully awake, she passed him the portable phone — then walked to each of the three windows in the bedroom and slowly lifted the shades. Her eyes were still swollen and red from the tears she shed when her husband told her of Dawson's apparent death. And she was distressed now, as she sat on the edge of the bed listening to his conversation.

He rubbed his eyes and yawned. "Go ahead, give it to me, Jim." It was his assistant, Jim Davis.

"Sorry for bothering you Bob, but I got the list of names from those buildings. Also got some information on the walkie-talkie," he said as he shuffled through papers. "Which do you want first?"

O'Neil thought for a moment, resisting the urge to discover what the lab report said about the walkie-talkie. "What's on the list?" he asked lazily.

"Just the names of occupants. . ."

"Give 'em to me. . ."

"Sure, hold on," he said as he rifled through the stack of papers on his desk until he found what he was looking for. "OK, here goes. . . Alden, Adler, Abrahams, Buckley, Bennet, Bennoit, Brown, Doris, Dennahey, Delany, Hallet, Hennigan, Horace. . ." He read the list mechanically, not knowing who lived or died in the hail of bullets and firestorm which followed. The department hadn't drafted that list yet. ". . .Norris, Ngyun, Nee, Nesbitt, Riley, O'Brien, O'Mally, Ortega, Pauley, Pepper. . ."

"Jesus," O'Neil said, throwing the covers off his body. His movements started Susan. "First names, Jim. Give me the first name of the one — Ortega," he said as he rose and stood by the night table by the side of the bed.

"There is no first name, Lieutenant. Just an initial: 'C'"

"Bingo," O'Neil said excitedly as he leaned over and pressed the lever on the amplifier, placing the phone back on its receiver. "Can you hear me, okay, Jim?" he asked as he walked over to his closet and removed a clean pair of pants.

"Yeah, no problem," Davis replied, adding, "It sounds like you're in a tunnel, though."

"I'm on the amplifier," he said as he yanked his pants up. "Jim, I'm going to shave then head in. This is important, I want every one of those cars we towed from Allston Street checked immediately for a similar walkie-talkie."

"Yeah, I wanted to talk to you about that, Bob. The walkie-talkie you gave us is real. It's not a toy. Neither is it a departmental issue."

"That's why I want the other cars checked."

Davis paused before responding, weighing what O'Neil was implying. Davis knew from past experience that if no one else in the city could make any sense out of what happened last night, Lieutenant O'Neil could.

"Can you tell me what's up, Bob?" Davis asked.

"I'll tell you when I get in, Jim. Look, it's important that those cars be checked immediately, before anyone has a chance to vandalize or strip them more than they already are. If you find another walkie-talkie, I want the frequencies checked against the one I passed on to you. The one I found in Gomez' car."

Davis was shocked. The implication caused him to stand from his chair and peer out the window of his office, just to make certain his conversation was not being monitored. "You suspect a set up from one of us?" he asked in a whisper. "You think that Gomez was connected to the guys who shot up the neighborhood? The commissioner's going to be pissed when he hears about this," he said, his voice rising as he spoke.

O'Neil stared into Susan's eyes as he spoke, "You think he'll be pissed? I may have just assigned a crooked cop — Goddamn, I hate to even say it — to protect my best friend. . ." O'Neil's voice trailed off as he struggled to control his emotions. "I want every available man we have on the unit, not already on a priority assignment, to be available this afternoon. If my hunch is right, Jim, we may just be on top of the biggest drug case in the country."

"You want anyone else briefed?"

O'Neil walked back to the phone and lifted the receiver, disconnecting the amplifier, "Contact John Geary of the DEA. His number's in my file on the desk. Ask him to drop by headquarters in about an hour. I'll make arrangements to call the commissioner and everyone else when I get in."

"Anything else?"

"No, that's all," O'Neil said. "I'll see you then," he said, terminating the conversation.

He stood motionless for a moment, and rubbed his hands through his hair. He took a deep breath and glanced at Susan, who was sitting on the edge of the bed, her hands pressed gently over her lips, forming a steeple effect. Her face reflected her anticipation, her fear, her sadness.

O'Neil reached down and cupped her chin with his hands. "We don't know for certain that he was in that fire, Susan," he said, answering the question she hadn't yet asked. "Some of the bodies were burnt. . ." and his voice trailed off to a whisper.

"Oh, Bob," she cried as she stood and embraced him warmly.

"I know," he said, fighting to hold back his own tears. "I've got to get ready," he said as he made his way across the room to the bedroom.

As her husband shaved, Susan stepped behind him and placed her arms around his waist, resting her head on the back of his shoulders in a comforting gesture. "It's not your fault, Bob. You couldn't have known." Tears welled in her eyes again, but this time she refused to cry.

At 4:30 P.M. word came from the lab that a second walkie-talkie was, indeed, found — and the frequencies matched. The commissioner, himself, addressed the hastily convened task force assembled to hear the evidence O'Neil said he had. In attendance were agents from the FBI, the DEA, the U.S. Attorney's office, Justice and Immigration. The Vermont State Police dispatched Lieutenant Dowling to Boston earlier to lend whatever assistance he could.

"I don't want any grandstanding on this thing," the commissioner said reprimanding O'Neil mildly for not volunteering what information he had earlier. "From this point on we work as a team. The incident last night has attracted national attention, and questions are going to be asked. I don't think it's in anyone's best interest to speculate publicly, or fight for turf on this thing until we know for certain exactly what we're dealing with. As of this moment, it's a local affair, under investigation by the Boston Police Department. Does anyone have any problem with that?"

Silence.

The commissioner nodded to O'Neil who was sitting at the rear of the briefing room. "Lieutenant," he said, pointedly, "it's all yours."

O'Neil walked slowly to the front of the gathering. The room was quiet. The air was charged with anticipation, though. "Last night," he began, "an entire city block of Boston was destroyed. Police officers, firefighters, and fifty-seven civilians lost their lives in the single largest incident of premeditated drug-related violence in this country. . ."

At the breach of the subject "drug-related" everyone shifted uncomfortably in their seats.

"This man," he said, pointing to a picture of Carlos Ortega, supplied by the DEA, "is responsible for it all."

O'Neil paused, and walking over to a window, drew one of the shades back and glanced outside. "What I am about to tell you," he said as he turned and faced the gathering once again, "is part conjecture and part fact. I believe enough of it is on target for us to be concerned that something very big is going down. Something affecting more than the residents of the City of Boston." He paused again, and walked over to the desk at the front of the room, sat on one edge, took a deep breath, then released it in a long sigh.

"Carlos Ortega was planning to break from Los Grandes Mafiosos, the South American Mafia. He came to Boston sometime within the last three weeks and lived in a small rented flat on Allston Street. Last Friday, I believe, he was abducted at knife point from a small variety store — obviously trying to call someone. Saturday afternoon he shows up dead in Vermont. Interestingly, it was a sloppy burial, indicating to me at least that whoever killed him didn't care if the body was found or not. Everything is apparently going fine, except the burial has a witness, Dawson Page — a Boston newspaper publisher." O'Neil stood and started to pace back and forth as he outlined his case, emphasizing selected parts by stopping and making eye contact with the various agents.

"Then something closer to home happens. I assign a Boston cop to cover the witness, and this cop does a very stupid thing. He exposes himself as an operative in the drug syndicate. . ."

The room literally erupted with cynical comment with that admission. But O'Neil forged on with his case.

"I believe he was attempting to interfere with either a meeting between Page and another person — maybe a friend of C. Ortega, or prevent Page from finding something left behind by Carlos. In any event, a whole lot of people die in the shooting and explosion that follows. That was last night."

"And what evidence do you have that one of our boys was involved?" the commissioner asked.

"I base this conclusion on the only piece of evidence we have. A set of walkie-talkies. One in a cop's car, the other in a burned wreck abandoned on the street. *That* car is identified as a stolen vehicle, registered out of Rhode Island. The frequencies match. We all know the rules where that is concerned."

The commissioner rubbed his chin and said: "It's pretty weak, Bob."

O'Neil was not discouraged by the lack of enthusiasm for his hypothesis. He wasn't finished. "Now there's one other detail which I should mention," O'Neil said as he walked amidst the assembled officers. "Page indicated that he saw a different man being buried on Saturday. He swore both to Lieutenant Dowling and me that Ortega's body was not the body he saw going under. We both believe him," he said, pausing, allowing his statements to settle. "Gentlemen, you're all trained professionals, and you know as well as I that that doesn't make sense. That if there were two bodies being buried, the one Page said he saw going under is much more important to our understanding of this case than the one we found. Even though the discovery of Ortega's body is no small-time event. That other body, the body of the man with white hair. *That's* the story here. And that shootout last night had something to do with it. I'm certain of it."

"You're stretching things aren't you, O'Neil? Making an awful lot of assumptions with very little in the way of hard evidence," the D.A. said, adding sarcastically, "And I never thought I'd hear one cop accuse another of being a murderer. For chrissake, Gomez' body, what we found of it, was riddled with holes. If this guy, Dawson Page was in that building for a reason, what leads you to believe that Gomez was not just doing his job?"

"My intuition, for one thing. . ."

"Oh, for chrissake," the D.A. protested.

"My intuition," O'Neil insisted, raising his voice over the taunt of the D.A., "and the walkie-talkies, *and*," he added, "the way we operate on the DEU. We play it real close on the drug unit. Gomez was assigned to watch over Dawson, surveillance. If Gomez left his car and walked into a building, he would have called for a back up outside. That's just the way we do it. We don't go into hallways without someone outside — even those on special assignment, as Gomez was, don't take any chances when it comes to drug deals."

"I take it you're not expecting me to go to court with any of this, Lieutenant, because, quite frankly you don't have a case here."

O'Neil's jaw tightened. He and the D.A. had a history of conflict, and the D.A.'s taunting now did little to lessen the underlying conflict between the two. "Something very big is about to go down here, gentlemen. And I have a feeling that unless we can get a handle on it real soon, the drug syndicate of which Ortega was a member, will pull off a major crime in this city — and we will all be left looking pretty foolish. Just look at what happened last night," he said as he turned and faced the picture of Carlos Ortega. "Yeah, that's all I have to go on Mr. District Attorney. You want to ignore it, go ahead. But do me a favor, stay out of my way." The tone of O'Neil's' voice convinced the D.A. to drop the matter.

"Now gentlemen," the commissioner interrupted, "let's not forget that we're all on the same side in this thing. We, ah, have questions of jurisdiction, timing, coordination and appropriate legal action. Let's work as a team, here, if for no other reason we have to answer for last night. A lot of people died because of something. . . Granted, Lieutenant O'Neil's case is weak, but some of what he says also makes an awful lot of sense. And he is right: It may be weak for a D.A. to go to court on, but for old bloodhounds like us," he added, mimicking Humphrey Bogart, poorly, "It's the stuff dreams are made of. I say we go with it. . ."

"There are questions of interstate transportation of stolen weapons," Jack Pierce of the FBI said. "We're in."

"And the fact that two of the bodies we have been able to identify are illegals — and there are probably more," Murray Laurence of Immigration offered, "brings us in."

"At this point, drugs are only suspected of being involved," John Geary of DEA remarked, "We'll operate on the assumption they are."

When the meeting was concluded O'Neil breathed with satisfaction. He accomplished what he set out to do. He held their undivided attention as he carefully pieced the puzzle together. No one asked any questions. No one doubted that his hypothesis was entirely believable. But when the meeting was completed, neither did anyone have the final piece: Who was C. Ortega? And what information did that person possess that could have generated such violent reaction from the pushers in this city — and the South American drug syndicate?

22
C. Ortega

She was sixteen years old and alone.

Carmen stayed the previous night at the Red Cross center established to aid victims of the Allston Street tragedy. There, she received blankets, warm coffee and donuts, and the comradeship of others in the same predicament. Fortunately, there were few questions asked of those gathered, and this suited Carmen, since she was not familiar with American customs, nor did she feel comfortable communicating in English — even though she studied the language at Carlos' insistence for two years. Mostly, she just observed. And when the lights were finally dimmed at 11:30 P.M. Monday evening, Carmen Velasco Terry Ortega prayed to God for guidance and help.

Carmen was the only person alive, as best she knew, that possessed the knowledge of the terrible deed to be committed, and she trembled as she weighed her options in this new land.

If only Rivero were here, she thought, as she walked down Commonwealth Avenue toward the city. If only she had someone she could talk with. If she could just tell what she knew she would be able to explain everything. Instead, she trembled, and was frightened by the prospect of facing her destiny alone.

When she ran from the apartment last night she carried with her a small bag of clothes and thirty-one hundred dollars in fifty dollar bills. Until Rivero contacted her she would have to make do with what she had — while being as inconspicuous as possible. She also had to prepare herself emotionally in the event she had to prevent that imposter from stepping on the plane Wednesday evening. Will I be able to do *whatever* is required of me? she asked herself as she strolled along the wide avenue. Will the Americans shoot me for this? Will I be able to explain? Will they listen?

As she approached Kenmore Square, she paused and glanced inside her carrying bag to assure herself, once again, that she was carrying the diary. That she had not misplaced it. She hadn't. As she resumed her pace she remembered what Carlos had told her about being an American: "When you are in America, Carmen, act American. Do not stop to talk with people. And even if you are confused, it's important that you walk with your head high and always give the appearance that you know exactly where you are going. No one will question you if they think you have some place to go. You must remember this."

So today, Carmen walked tall and hid her innermost fears from those she passed.

A brisk, warm, humid wind swept intermittently along the broad avenue leading into the city, causing dirt and discarded debris to blow and swirl about her feet. She was fascinated by the sporadic gusts which created dozens of miniature cyclonic-like disturbances in the gutters. Another storm is coming, she thought, as she quickened her pace, staring straight ahead again, resolving not to allow herself to be distracted by events over which she had no control. The storm clouds pushing in from the ocean did reminded her of the violent weather a few days ago — and of her last passionate morning with Carlos. She would allow herself *that* one distraction as she walked, for her thoughts of Carlos comforted her and gave her strength. Indeed, Carlos taught her much about life. He renewed her passion to live after the horrible death of her parents. He taught her English. And assigned his closest friend to be her guardian — to watch over her. If Rivero lived through the bloody assault and fire, he would find her, of that much she was certain — for Carlos told her that Rivero would never abandon her. But was Rivero still alive? Now, even that was in doubt.

I am so... hungry, she thought as she passed a small fast food restaurant in the Square. Her breakfast, donated by the city, consisting of scrambled eggs, toast, orange juice and coffee, had long since been digested by her system. Her stomach now ached for more nourishment.

And something else... she was tired. For the better part of the day she walked alone along the busy streets, hoping to be noticed by Rivero. But as the morning passed to afternoon — and now the afternoon was passing into evening, she experienced a desperate need for rest, for a place to stop and organize her thoughts, a place to get off her feet, if only for an hour or so. She also needed a place to stay for the night. A place where she would be safe and secure. A place where she could rest and regain her strength.

She paused in her journey, turned and gazed back at the crowded restaurant, debating whether it would be too dangerous for her to be seen in public. She had to chance it, she told herself, otherwise she would surely die of starvation — or so it felt.

Carmen was born in 1969 in a small town in central Peru named Uchiza. Her parents, like most others in the region were poor, and for the most part lacking in formal education. They were subsistence farmers, primarily, who occasionally sold or traded their produce to others in the region. Carmen treasured the memories of her youth, and found strength in the dignity of her family's character. She fondly remembered how as a very young girl she would accompany her parents to the small field where they cultivated their produce. While her parents worked she would spend the day playing by herself, imagining that she was a lady of great wealth and good fortune — sought after by all the handsome men of her country. And she would twirl and swirl and jump ballet-like through the open fields as her parents watched and worked, and silently grieved, for they too, once dreamed of a better life. They would not deprive Carmen of those harmless thoughts.

Carmen's childhood was a happy one, though, despite the poverty. She knew no other life, anyway. And she was not always alone. Her father would often carry her on his back to and from the fields, and run with her until he became exhausted and they both fell gently to the ground. Her always pleading for more; him, gasping and laughing with his daughter, and at her wild innocence. "There is no more," he would say as he tickled her under her ribs, adding sternly, "The horse is too tired now. Go! Work with your mother, or go play."

"I love you father," she would say, hugging him firmly around the neck.

And he would smile and hug her gently. "And I you my little flower."

"Will I grow up to be beautiful?" she would ask, almost ritualistically after their play. And he would cup her face gently in his rough hands and brush back her long, dark hair, and looking deeply into her eyes and say, "God has made no lovelier a creature than my little Carmen. Yes, darling you will be the most beautiful woman in the world. You are my little flower today. But some day, handsome men will seek you out and bring you presents beyond your wildest dreams. And you will chose a man who can provide for you. And you will have beautiful clothes and children and a grand home with servants and a large garden. And you will travel all over the world and see such magnificent things."

And she would dance and swirl away into the field, lost in the magical world of beauty and grace which her father assured her would be hers one day.

Indeed, although Carmen worked the fields with her parents, she never lost those delicate feminine features which made her so alluring. And as the months passed into years, it became evident to all who knew her that Carmen Velasco Terry *would* one day be a beautiful young woman. By her twelfth birthday, for instance, she had three suitors in the village — each bringing her flowers, fruit and sugar candy at every opportunity. Almost daily they would appear at her front door, pushing and shoving each other hoping for the opportunity to have her accept their attention.

But her mother would not allow Carmen to be bought so easily. And she often lectured the boys when they were ill-mannered, telling them, "You must act like gentlemen if you want my daughter to pay any attention to you. Now, go, and come back when you have learned how to act in the presence of a lady." For their part, the boys often laughed at, and mimicked Carmen's mother when they were alone. But they always left when instructed, not daring to offend the woman who stood watch by the door of their sweet Carmen's home.

The years would pass quietly for the Terry family and the flower which was Carmen would blossom.

Carmen first met Carlos in the last few months of her fourteenth year. Both she and her parents had finished working the fields that day, and were on their way home along the dirt road which intersected a larger road that ran north from Tingo Maria past her small village of Uchiza. Carmen and her family were introduced to Carlos at that intersection in a most unlikely fashion. As Carlos' car raced by, a wheel splashed through a puddle, causing mud and water to jump from the hole, soaking the entire family.

"You ignorant person!" Carmen shouted, waving her fist in the air as the car sped past.

Carlos glanced out the rear window, and ordered the driver to stop.

This terrified Carmen's father who knew who the white Cadillac belonged to — and of his power and reputation for violence. Wanting to shield his daughter from the barrage of bullets sure to follow, he stepped in front of her and held her shoulders firmly in place behind him. "Say nothing!" he ordered firmly. And Carmen and her mother obeyed.

"I am sorry señor, for the inconvenience," he said, bowing as Carlos exited the car and began walking toward him. "My daughter meant you no disrespect. We were clearly in your way..."

And Carlos moved closer.

"As you can see señor, we are just poor farmers. We would never make an accusation against your good name. My daughter is young, she..."

"It is I who owe you the apology sir," Carlos interrupted. "My driver did not see you, nor did he see the puddle in the road. I will have the hole fixed tomorrow. And if you will give me your name and address I will see to it that you are provided with new clothes for the ones ruined by my carelessness."

Carmen's father stood speechless, his mouth drooping open, for Carlos was sincere in his offer. These people meant him no harm. Clearly, they could not afford to suffer the loss of even the wretched clothing they wore.

Carmen, apprehensive at first, glanced from behind her father, eager to see the polite stranger — the handsome, polite stranger she concluded when she saw him.

"I compliment you, señor, for having such a fine looking family," Carlos said, captivated immediately by the sheer physical beauty which radiated from this young girl.

"I am grateful for the kind compliment, Señor Ortega?"

Carlos was literally hypnotized by the young girl, his concentration broken only by the use of his name. "I compliment you again, señor, for you have me at a disadvantage. You know my name and I do not know yours." Carlos found it difficult to keep himself from staring at the young girl who stood protected under her father's arm.

"Forgive me, Señor Ortega, I am Juan Ramos Velasco Terry. This is my lovely wife Maria, and my beautiful, if somewhat impetuous daughter, Carmen."

Carlos bowed slightly and flashed a broad, friendly smile. His teeth were perfectly white. "If you will not allow me to deliver new clothing to your home, I insist that you take this small donation for the trouble I have caused." And as he spoke he reached into his pocket and handed Carmen's father what was surely the equivalent of a month's wages.

Juan was shocked with Carlos' generosity. "Señor," he said with all humility, "I cannot accept this gift. You are too generous." He was actually relieved he was not staring down the barrel of a gun — or worse. Yet, Carlos surprised him. He was not the brute people said he was. Not at all what he expected. Carlos was tall and thin. And he walked with grace and exuded confidence — and even appeared to be gentle.

As they spoke, another man exited the car. A big man, well dressed, but in casual attire. Carlos turned when he heard the door close behind him. "You will meet my driver, Manuel. Do not worry," Carlos said when he observed Carmen step behind her father. "He is a gentle man, as gentle as a lamb."

Manuel was an older man, and much bigger than Carlos. As he approached the family he tugged downward on the front of his shirt, ensuring that the butt of the .45 he was carrying was hidden from their view.

"Excuse me, Carlos, but we are late," Manuel said, whispering softly as he bent at the waist and spoke into Carlos' ear, all the while keeping a watchful eye on the three standing before him.

"Yes," Carlos answered. "We must be leaving," he said, addressing the Terry family. "If I might visit you when I am in the region again," Carlos said, hiding his infatuation with the young girl, "I would be honored to dine with you, sir. And your family. Perhaps we can even discuss business. . ."

Juan surprised himself by the abruptness of his answer. "I know of your business, señor, and neither I nor my family would care to discuss that in our home. But," he added quickly, "we would be honored if you would join us as our guests whenever you were in the area."

Carlos smiled. He understood Juan's answer. The coca business provided many of his countrymen with employment and extra money. It also wrecked as many lives. Therefore, Carlos did not pursue the subject. He simply nodded his head, then inquired respectfully if Monday evening would be a suitable time to visit.

That Monday visit, Carmen remembered, became a regular occurrence. And each time he visited, Carlos spent more hours talking with her. "What were you and Manuel talking about as you walked back to your car the day we met?" Carmen would inquire three months later as they lie in bed together, naked.

Carlos smiled and said nothing.

"Please tell me," she insisted in her girlish way as she rolled on top of him and gently swayed her breasts across his smooth chest.

Carlos arched his back and cupped her face with his hands. "If you must know, my beautiful flower. Manuel commented about your beauty. And I told him I would have you."

"And you both laughed over that?" She didn't understand.

"And what were you and your parents arguing about as I walked away on that same day?" Carlos asked, teasing her by moving his hands downward and grabbing the smooth cheeks of her round buttocks, and squeezing them gently.

Carmen blushed and smiled as she remembered. "My mother knew what I was thinking as I watched you walk away," she said coquettishly, "and told me that my impure thoughts would earn me a place in hell right beside you."

"Oh?" Carlos laughed.

"Carlos," Carmen said seriously, stroking his hair first, then kissing his eyes, "she must never know of our affair. She still believes you treat me as a kind uncle."

Carlos arched his back and groaned, sliding further into her, until they were both lifted off the bed where their bodies joined. "Your kindly uncle thinks you are great in bed," he said. And she laughed and slapped his face, calling him a pervert.

"You know they are working for the government and the Americans, Carlos," she said, her tone more somber now as she pressed herself closer to his body. "The Americans are having great difficulty with your business, Carlos. They pay the people well to cut the leaves before you can cultivate them."

"I know, Carmen."

"There is terrible violence between those who oppose what you do and those who support you," she said, her face reflecting the worry in her heart.

Carlos breathed deeply, lifting her body on his as he did. "I know of their jobs, Carmen. Your parents have nothing to fear from us ," he said as he ran his hands gently up and down the small of her back, adjusting himself within her as he spoke. "I also know of the violence. You must believe me, Carmen, the violence is not *our* doing. There are newer groups, younger men eager to make names for themselves. They respect no one... One day we may have to confront them... And teach them respect..."

"But not today," Carmen said as she brushed her lips against his, inviting his passionate kisses, signalling that she did not want talk of business to interfere with their lovemaking.

Carlos was aroused again, and moved with Carmen in gentle rhythm. She arched her neck backward, while still on top of him, and shook her head ever so gently back and forth. Her long hair brushed against her back and tickled — arousing her to even greater heights.

Carmen enjoyed her sexuality, thinking this was so much more pref-erable than playing those stupid kids games with the smelly boys of the village. What boy could provide her with such pleasure?

Carmen leaned forward on Carlos and pressed her breasts against his firm chest, and with her arms encircling his shoulders, cupped his head with the palms of her hands, and kissed him deeply, her body aching for the release she knew was eminent. "I love you, Carlos," she whispered. "I love you," she moaned as his hardness moved inside her and aroused her to even greater heights.

"And I also love you," Carlos said, licking, then nibbling her erect nipples.

"I'm. . . I'm. . ." she gasped. "I'm. . ." and her breath grew short and heavy. I'm. . .." she said sweetly, eyes closed tightly, head tilted back, body trembling uncontrollably. . .

And to the sounds of soft music playing in the background, Carmen and Carlos culminated their lovemaking together for the third time on the first day they made love.

It was exquisite: Carmen, totally spent, drained of energy. Her body glistened with a layer of fresh moisture, their lovemaking was that intense; Carlos, physically exhausted, relieved and content.

"I never knew it would be this good, Carlos," Carmen said as she nestled in his arms, secure and fulfilled as a woman.

Carlos embraced her lovingly, smoothing his hand over her arm and shoulder. "It will always be this way, Carmen. I will always love you."

"Always?" she taunted as she moved her hand down his chest and massaged her fingers playfully through his pubic hair.

"Oh, Carmen," he said as he reached for her hand and lifted it gently to his lips. "Do you wish to kill me so soon?"

A knock on the bedroom door interrupted their afterplay. "Carlos!" It was Manuel. "It is urgent. I must see you now."

Carlos propped himself against his pillows as he sat up in bed. Manuel would not interrupt 'this' unless he had important informa-tion. "I'll be right there, Manuel," Carlos said as he patted Carmen's head. "I'll be right back," Carlos said as he rose from bed, stepped into his pants and tucked his shirt in while walking across the room toward the door.

Carlos opened the door and stepped into the hallway, startled by the sight of Manuel covered with blood — not his own. "My God, what is it Manuel? What happened?"

"Come," Manuel said as he led Carlos down the long corridor toward the stairs, "Come to the garage."

Carlos hesitated in the hallway and reaching for Manuel's arm asked: "Who is it?"

Manuel shook his head as they walked briskly down the stairs leading to the garage. "I'm sorry, Carlos, for what I have to show you. I was visiting Uchiza when one of the local villagers told me of a raid on one of the American sponsored teams. I went as quickly as I could," Manuel said, "knowing that Carmen's parents were part of the team."

As they approached the garage where Manuel parked his car, Carlos understood *who* Manuel had brought for him to see. Laying in the back seat were Carmen's parents. Their throats cut. Both naked and mutilated.

Carlos approached the car, opened the door and stared. "My God, Manuel. Who is responsible for this?"

"It was a band of guerrillas, the Shining Path, I suspect."

"Why?"

"It's a message to the Americans and us, I suspect," Manuel said.

Still staring at the bodies, Carlos stood immobilized and in shock. "Goddamn it!" Carlos shouted, banging his hand against the fender. "They did this," he cried, "for their fucking revolution? What did these people ever do to them?"

Manuel stepped forward and placed his arm on Carlos' shoulder. "It's the newer breed, Carlos. They have no control."

"They'll pay for this, Manuel. They'll pay for this," Carlos said his voice choked, filled with emotion and sadness. "Carmen must not see her parents this way. Do you hear me?"

"I understand, Carlos."

"She must not see her parents this way," Carlos protested, and as he spoke he turned to face Manuel and saw Carmen standing there with tears running down her cheeks.

"Hey bitch, how 'ya doin?" Carmen was startled from her daydreaming by the voice of two young blacks sitting at the table next to hers. "Watcha crying bout, bitch. You gut no dude to do 'ya?"

And the other boy laughed. "Hey, sister," he drawled, "you look like you need a vile, baby. Cracko! Bang! White powda. Chill out bitch," he said, as he dropped a small vile on the table next to her arm. "You guts to go to heaven some day, bitch. Why not now?"

"Please leave me alone," Carmen pleaded as she grabbed her carrying bag and ran from the store, wondering what she was even doing in America.

23
Compromises

Shortly after the death of Carmen's parents in July, it became evident that the power of the old bosses was diminishing. The acts of violence committed against civilians ushered in the ascension to power of a new breed of mafiosos. More ideological in their beliefs. More spiteful in their retaliations. More passionate in their desire to change society so that it reflected their vision of the perfect order. More intent on destroying the most visible symbol of capitalism and free enterprise in the world — the United States.

Evident, not abrupt. That was the most accurate way to characterize change occurring in the organization. A gradual metamorphoses, not noticed until it was too late to stop. This latest act of violence against Carmen's parents, as well as the other people who were assisting the government in their anti-coca campaign, was totally uncalled for. The older bosses knew this, and would not have ordered such vicious retaliations. Like Ortega, they would have tried to persuade the civilian population to support them by sending poor children to school and paying their medical bills whenever the costs became too burdensome. This was the tried and tested method of winning the minds and hearts of the people. Violence was unacceptable — except against those who asked for it.

Now the younger leaders were blowing up embassies, assassinating cabinet ministers, murdering civilians, working closely with the communists in Nicaragua, Cuba and other Soviet block nations, and gaining support from some of the older bosses — if not so much out of respect for what they stood for, as much as fear that the movement couldn't be stopped. The money from the drug trade, estimated to be around one-hundred billion dollars a year could buy tremendous influence — and power. Carlos and Manuel understood this better than anyone, and for this reason feared the direction the business was moving more than anyone.

In January of '85 when Colombian drug king Carlos Lehder offered to help pay off Colombia's national debt of $13 billion if his government would agree not to extradite him to the United States, Ortega was furious and ordered such flamboyant statements from members of the organization stopped. "We must continue to work within the political divisions which exist in our countries," Carlos wrote to various leaders, "not flaunt our wealth in their faces. Our countrymen are poor people. We must be cognizant of our responsibilities as businessmen to stay within the boundaries of common sense."

Lehder responded to pleas for moderation by calling a press conference, brazenly portraying himself as a revolutionary with a vision. He called the enormous drug trade, appropriately enough, the "Latin American atom bomb," and vowed to use it to topple the government of the United States.

What disturbed Carlos and Manuel most, however, was Lehder's vague ideological threat to join forces with Colombia's Marxist M-19 guerilla movement. Another example of disunity and division among the leaders.

It was about that time that Carlos decided to call a meeting of all the drug kings throughout South and Central America. It was time to deal with the problems created by the newer members of the organization.

After months of preliminary bargaining and positioning for power, the established drug leaders, agreed that on April 3, 1985 they would meet at the *Campamento en el Bosque* to iron out their disagreements — and there were many.

On that day security was tightened around a ten square mile radius of the fortress. Over fifteen-hundred men from the various organizations in Colombia, Peru, Mexico, Ecuador and Bolivia were assembled and given security assignments on roads, highways and bridges leading to and from the main compound. The idea being that a mixed security force would be the best insurance that the leaders of today would not end up like the leaders of years ago, staring at the sunset from equal positions of power, impaled on poles outside Carlos' front window.

Within the fortress itself, however, only personal bodyguards were permitted. And women were forbidden — even house maids. Another concession made out of respect for the power of young women to distract one's attention. The camp's perimeter was guarded by Carlos' men. This, to ensure privacy and protect the owner's investment in security devices. As for the town lying outside the boundaries of the fortress, there were no limitations on personnel. The other leaders were free to bring as many men as they saw fit to protect their own self interests — and survival. And they did. That day, assembled outside, and throughout the small town of Tingo Maria was a drug army consisting of over four thousand armed men, prepared to respond to whatever emergency might occur.

The *Evil Empire* as Newsweek magazine would later refer to it was gathered once again, prepared to do business with one another — like the old days when it was *The Will of God* that no unnecessary blood be spilled within the organization. But times had changed.

In all there were only twenty men, each with one bodyguard, allowed into the conference chambers of the main building. The room, eighteen hundred square feet, was decorated modestly with expensive modern furniture. Original works of art dotted the walls, and beautiful green plants and small trees scattered at key locations throughout the room created an aura of serenity and peace.

The large, teak conference table situated at the center of the room, was like an oasis in the middle of a peaceful forest setting, its surface buffed to a glossy finish, reflecting the images of clouds and rays of sunlight shining through the oversized sun roof above. There was no need for air conditioning, even though the entire complex was centrally air-contitioned. In this room, six large windows, each over twelve feet high and four feet wide provided a cooling breeze on the warmest of days, as evidenced by the continuous movement of the sheer curtains hung from each.

The one *invited* exception to the nineteen recognized leaders of the drug trade, and their personal bodyguards, was a man known only by the name of Contero. In the interest of peace and compromise, Carlos was forced to accept the presence of a member of the leftist Shining Path movement. Contero was that person. Although he was not a recognized member of the drug cartel, his power and influence could not be minimized. The guerilla movement, along with its supporters from outside the country were a force to be reckoned with. Drug money funnelled into terrorist organizations worldwide gave groups such as Shining Path and M-19 power and influence where once they had none. This was the reality the old bosses refused to accept — until now.

Carlos brought the meeting to order shortly after a sumptuous meal was served and the dinner plates cleared. Carlos assumed his position at the head of the table, with the ever-present Manuel standing, arms folded, behind him. Each of the other leaders assumed their places, with their personal bodyguards in similar positions. The room was noisy with conversation when Carlos tapped an ashtray, signalling the beginning of business. And shortly thereafter, not a word was spoken.

Carlos stood and personally acknowledged each of his guests, beginning and ending each introduction with a gracious compliment. But when he got to the one named Contero, he just stopped and stared. Carlos did not like the idea that he was only able to see the man's eyes. But it was already agreed, after heated debate between coordinators, that the hooded man would remain hooded due to a facial disfigurement.

At the conclusion of introductions, Carlos lifted his glass of wine and toasted the gathering. "It is *The Will of God* that we are brought together today in unity and peace. It is my sincere desire that when we have completed our business today, we leave as brothers and associates. To your health, and our continued success."

When he was finished, Carlos placed his glass on the table and dabbed his lips with a clean cloth. "Gentlemen," he began slowly, deliberately, measuring his words as he looked directly into the eyes of each man. "When my father Simon Gabriel de San Martin, passed this business on to me years ago, many of you were not yet in the trade. When we *reorganized* years ago you replaced the older leaders and assumed the power and privilege of their office. And business has been good since."

"To business," Bedoya of Colombia said, lifting his glass in another toast. And the others followed.

Carlos paused, acknowledging the toast. "I have worked with each of you over the years," he said as he walked slowly over to one of the windows overlooking the compound. He stood silent in the sun's warm rays and took a deep breath of the fresh air, exhaling slowly through his nose as a refreshing breeze lifted the curtains about him. No one in the room said a word. "I have never wanted what was yours," he said pointedly. "I have never been greedy or unwilling to share the wealth — and it is considerable as all of you know."

Several members nodded in agreement. Others just stared.

"I have never asked you to do anything which would jeopardize. . ." and as he spoke he rotated his hand in a circular motion, ". . . a good thing."

Louis Bodge of Ecuador interrupted, motioning with his hand "Carlos, please, sit with us. Do not stand separate. Come. . . come. . ."

Carlos smiled and acknowledged his old friend's invitation. "You all know me. . ." he said as he walked back to the table and assumed his position at the head. "You know what I stand for. You know that within our organization we must have rules and guidelines for our own conduct. And these rules must be followed." He then sat, slouched back comfortably in his chair and resting his elbows on the arms, fingers pressed lightly under his chin, stared directly at Contero.

He took another deep breath through his nose and continued, in complete control. "Rules...," he paused, "...are not...," and he paused again, "...made ...," another pause, "...to be broken." This last phrase spoken with a scowl. He then leaned forward in his chair, and resting his arms on the shiny surface, smiled contentedly. He knew he was taking a gamble bringing the subject of Rules up so early, but it had to be done. It was a gamble, but if he could just separate the organization from the leftist movement talking hold, he could order Contero cut into little pieces and disposed of — this, in payment for the murder of Carmen's parents.

But that's not the way it turned out. An air of uneasiness settled over the room as Carlos continued. "But it seems of late, some of us have taken it upon ourselves to go outside the boundaries of good business." Several members grunted in agreement. Some remained silent. Others fidgeted. Contero was one of those who fidgeted, glaring through his black hood.

"The Organization," Carlos said forcibly, banging his fist on the table as he spoke, "which we have built must not fall victim to the same insane political manipulations as the governments within which we exist. We must resist the urge to become a political force, and be content with being rich. We must be stronger than any government. That is why we have survived and they have not. This is business," Carlos fumed, jabbing his index finger forward in the direction of the hooded man, "not some foolish political struggle. And those who say otherwise do not have the interests of business at heart. They will destroy this organization and everyone in it if they have their way."

The room grew noisy again as members argued openly over Carlos' admonition to separate the drug trade from the political process.

"What are you talking about, Carlos," Frederico Chevas of Nicaragua spat, arrogantly. "The revolutionary forces of the world provide billions of dollars to this very organization each year. What would you suggest we do? Deny them our markets? And then what? Compete with them? What you suggest is foolish, not the other way around. The revolutionary movement is the future of this hemisphere, not your old ideas..."

Carlos' skin tingled and adrenaline pumped through his veins at the challenge from the left. "Revolutionary bullshit, Chevas. Under Samoza you prospered and made millions, and your organization grew. Since when did you become a revolutionary?" he demanded.

"Since the Sandanistas threatened to cut his fucking throat if he did not capitulate," Bodge taunted.

"Liar! Filthy bastard, capitalist coward!" Chevas shouted.

And the frustration which had been building steadily for years suddenly came to a boil, as members argued viciously over the political future of their trade.

"Whether you like it or not, Carlos, cocaine has become a revolutionary weapon in the struggle against imperialism," Chevas fought.

"Can you hear yourself, Chevas?" Carlos shouted over the rising chorus of angry voices in the room. You sound like a broken record with this revolutionary bullshit. It is business we are interested in doing. Not revolution. Business! Can't you understand?"

"It is you that does not understand Ortega," Dominic Botero shouted contemptuously from the other end of the table. Of all the members assembled, Carlos despised Botero the most. He was the most arrogant, filthy, uncouth and unnecessarily vicious of all those assembled — or so Carlos thought. "You do not understand," he said as he stood and pointed toward Carlos, emphasizing the word you . "We are not living in the Sixties anymore, my tired, sleepy comrade. Where have you been sleeping? Do you not see what is happening in the bourgeois United States? They are falling apart. And we are responsible for it!"

"You are responsible for nothing," Carlos persisted. "If it were not for the fact that we operated throughout all the years as a business, we would not be here today. You, Botero," he said bitterly, "would still be sleeping with sheep if it were not for the fact that your mother introduced you to little boys."

Botero jumped from his seat, and appearing to move toward Carlos, was prudently restrained by his own bodyguard.

"It would be the biggest mistake you ever made, Botero," Carlos warned sternly, reasserting his authority over the organization. "Sit down all of you and listen. Now!" And the room grew quiet when Carlos commanded it so.

The session which began at 5 P.M. lasted long into the evening with tempers flaring repeatedly, and outbursts bordering on physical contact threatening to send the various leaders on their separate ways, more divided than ever before. By 11:30 P.M. on the evening of April 3rd, it was evident to Carlos and Manuel that the vote of the members would tilt in favor of a compromise offered by the Bolivian representative. The compromise was as follows: The South American drug trade would be continued as a business. But politics would be dictated by the Shining Path and its sister organizations, positioned for power among themselves as they saw fit. Although the political actions of these groups would be funded with drug money, their actions would not be permitted to interfere with the operation of the trade as a business. The corollary was also true.

That was the deal. Not everyone liked it. And even after it was settled tempers flared and veiled threats ensued. For his part, Contero remained silent throughout the debate, and rose to speak only after the compromise had been struck. And either out of exhaustion, frustration or anger, the room grew silent when he rose.

It is doubtful more than a few in the room realized the significance of the shift in the balance of power which just occurred. The revolutionary point of view would be heard for the first time. And from that day forward, it would be factored into every decision the organization made. Indeed, the revolutionary forces achieved a significant victory that evening. They succeeded in dividing a once powerful organization which served one purpose, one master. Now, through sheer force and threat of violence, and social disruption, and the apparent defection of several tired members, who foolishly believed that compromise with these devils was preferable to confrontation, the left would force the organization to serve another sinister, more devious and powerful master — worldwide communist revolution.

"American imperialism must and will suffer a devastating defeat at the hands of world socialism." Contero spoke slowly, contemptuously, sounding odd, as if his jaw were wired shut. "We will use drugs to corrupt the children of the West, exposing their bourgeois weaknesses and inability to come to grips with the reality of what we create. What we could not accomplish with armies we will accomplish with the white powder of our lands."

Carlos leaned back in his chair and listened intently, rubbing a closed fist against his jaw as Contero spoke.

"The first demonstration of the power of our new alliance shall be simple, but effective. It will deliver a message to the United States, and all those who oppress the working class of this world. A simple demonstration to demonstrate to the Americans what modern, revolutionary warfare is all about. We will eliminate a world leader who has spoken against us repeatedly — and who, I might add, is planning a worldwide campaign against us even now as we speak. The imperialist Pope!"

This latest admission caused yet another more physical and violent confrontation, and open split between those who supported the plan and those who threatened open warfare if such a plan were carried out.

"You," Carlos shouted furiously, as he stood and pointed directly at Contero, "are a fucking nut. Manuel," he ordered, having heard enough of Contero's grand plan, "get him the fuck out of here."

Contero pounded the table, displaying a violent side of his temper not revealed before. Leaning across the table he waved his hand at Carlos' face and shouted through his hood, "I am a fucking nut? I am a fucking nut? The revolutionary movement will not be stopped, Mr. Ortega. Not by the likes of you. That is what I have been sent here to tell you. That is what I have been sent here to tell all of you."

As Manuel moved toward the hooded man he was forcibly restrained by three other bodyguards who pleaded with him not to lose his temper, to withdraw.

"You should know by now that we have taken control in Cuba and Nicaragua, and we are taking control in El Salvadore and Panama, and Mexico and. . ." Contero, paused to regain his composure, breathing deeply, his chest heaving noticeably. "You will side with us because as strong as your organizations were in those countries, once the revolutionary zeal of the people was turned against you — your organizations disappeared."

Contero was taking liberties, now, even with those in the room who considered themselves aligned with what his goals. He wasn't offering compromise. He was laying down a new set of rules, irrespective of what they had just agreed to. He was saying, in effect, accept what I offer or be crushed by the new governments our groups create.

"Where are your drug organizations in those countries," he taunted, sensing the disunity about him. "I will tell you where they are!" he chided. "They are gone!" he shouted. "And where are those who led these organizations?" he asked. "I will tell you where they are. They were placed before firing squads and shot!"

Carlos stood in shock and silence. And waved Manuel back to his side.

Contero continued with his belligerent warnings. "Those who side with us will survive, and will be given special consideration, allowed to continue their operations and make money — but operating against the imperialists to destroy the social fabric of their corrupt societies. That is the only reality we have to deal with here today. That is the business we are interested in. And no other."

"Carlos, please. . ." one of the older men gathered pleaded. Carlos could see it was his old friend, Enrique Suarez, a close friend of his fathers, and one of the few survivors of the original leadership. "What Mr. Contero says is true. Our countries are undergoing social revolutions now. How much longer can we hold out? How much longer will the governments survive before they fall? And who in this room doubts they will be replaced by revolutionary councils? Who seriously believes the United States will sacrifice men or money to save this region. We must cooperate now while we can make a deal. . ."

"A deal with the likes of this low life, Enrique, is no deal," Carlos pleaded, "It is the kiss of death."

"Do you really believe you can replace an American bishop with a look-alike and send him off to Rome to murder the Pope? And get away with it?" Augustin Antonio of Panama pleaded weakly to Contero. "This plan will cost us all. It will backfire I tell you. It will destroy our business."

"Carlos," José Bedoya of Colombia spoke. "I am not in agreement with this plan, or the politicalization of the trade. But surely, Carlos, you must realize that we must deal with these people. I trust in you, Carlos. I believe in you. I only ask that we not go to war over this thing. And I fear, my friend, that unless we accept what Mr. Contero offers, we will have no choice."

Luis Bodge spoke next. "If our people discover that we are actually condoning this madness we will lose them — and our business. We need the people to cultivate the crop. If they refuse to work the fields, Who will pick the leaves?" he asked angrily, moving his arm in a semi-circular motion as he spoke, "which of you with your manicured fingernails will dirty your hands in the fields every day? I ask you." Turning toward Carlos, now he stood and pledged firmly, "If a war is what it takes to bring this matter to a head, I will commit my men to you, Carlos. And we will beat back this challenge."

"And you will be the first to die," Dominic Botero threatened.

"Not from the likes of you, Botero. . ."

"And where did we all of a sudden get our morals from?" Botero demanded, ignoring Bodge's remarks. "All of a sudden we give a shit about morality." He banged the table and shouted. "The guerilla campaign is the winning campaign. That is the only business I am interested in. Don't you see it? Survival! That is the name of my business. Survival! Mr. Contero is offering a compromise, and you are talking about morals. Who gives a fuck about the Pope? Is he on our side? Will he come to a dinner and speak on our behalf? When he comes to South America he will turn the people against us. That is what he will do. Why doesn't he mind his own fucking business? He's nothing to me. He should be nothing to you."

Carlos had had just about enough of this talk. He drew a deep breath and released it slowly before speaking. "Gentlemen, gentlemen. It is clear to me that we will make no additional progress this evening," he said, calling the members to order once again. "So you will have your way, Botero," Carlos conceded bitterly, suspecting that Botero was the driving force behind the revolutionary movement's influence in the organization. "I urge all of you to leave this compound as business associates, and to refrain from allowing the emotions expressed in this room to carry over into the countryside. It is clear that we must talk some more. That it is not over. . ."

"A vote was already taken," Contero interrupted pointedly, then added menacingly, "Will *you* abide by it or not?" He directed his remarks at Carlos.

Carlos' chest was heaving, his anger was that great. He never hated a man as much as this Mr. Contero. "All of you will now leave my estate," Carlos said calmly, coldly, refusing to answer Contero's taunt. "We will see what tomorrow brings," he said as members began filing out of the room. As Contero passed, Carlos grabbed his arm and said: "As for you, Mr. Contero, or whoever the fuck you are, you're lucky I don't cut your throat right now."

"Not twice," Contero said as he pulled away from Carlos' grasp, leaving Carlos bewildered as to what he meant.

24
Manuel

Manuel died on Thursday, April 11, 1985. His final actions, however, would alter the course of history in the United States. Indeed, throughout the world.

It was apparent, after the April 3rd meeting that the drug trade emanating from South and Central America, especially that part which flowed into the United States, would be taking a more violent and political turn in the future. The drug barons were convinced that the socialist revolution alluded to by Contero was gaining momentum in every country in the region, and they truly feared this movement. They were also convinced that the United States was powerless to interfere in the politics of those countries most affected and, therefore, was not to be relied upon to restore social order, once order broke down.

The Monroe Doctrine, which addressed foreign involvement in this hemisphere, said nothing of drug involvement or social revolution. Furthermore, the often-stated American commitment to the defense of the region was viewed as meaningless, since few nations, or drug barons, believed the United States had the inclination, understanding of the depth of the problem, or congressional support to intervene in the internal affairs of South or Central American governments, regardless of how distressed the political climate became. In short, South and Central America was ripe for the picking -and picked it would be.

Whether Los Grandes Mafiosos liked it or not, Mr. Contero and his revolutionary comrades were the wave of the future. And if the drug barons wanted to continue with business as usual they would have to adapt to the socio-political change which was clearly moving in the

direction of the socialist camp. And if this movement meant continued assassinations and civilian massacres, and outrageous acts of violence against the established order, so be it! Too much money and
power was at issue.

Carlos considered all this carefully and made his decision to withdraw from the business and to flee to America only after he wrestled
with his options for three days. "It has become clear to me," he wrote
in his diary on April 6, "that the options are more narrow than I, or
anyone else, cares to admit. We cannot control these revolutionaries
as we controlled the governments before them. These people clearly
intend to use whatever means they must to attain power — and once
they attain it, they will seize control of our enterprises and use them
for their own socio-political objectives. They are no better than us.
Indeed, they are far worse."

"I am not so much surprised by their intentions in that regard," he
wrote, "as I am by the complete lack of understanding displayed by
my colleagues with whom I have worked for so many years — and
who should know better than to trust these people. I am convinced
the revolutionaries will accomplish their objectives. And although I
couldn't care less about the plight of our American neighbors when
they finally wake up and find widespread revolution and terrorist
activity spilling over their borders, I am not willing to permit the
death of Carmen's parents to go unavenged. Nor will I permit my
dearest friend, Enrique Michelsen, to be murdered and replaced by
these fanatics. Drastic actions are called for; drastic actions must be
taken to prevent this from happening. I shall leave for the United
States as soon as I have completed what I now know I must do."

After Carlos made that entry into his personal diary he asked that
both Carmen and Manuel join him in his study.

It was a warm, clear evening. Carlos stood by the large, tinted
window which overlooked the compound. Everything looked so
calm, so tranquil and peaceful. How deceptive, he thought. Clearly,
powerful political and revolutionary alliances were being forged
throughout South and Central America, and these alliances were
being funded in large part by monies derived from the illicit sale of
drugs. Worse, the forces pushing hardest for change were exploiting
cultural differences, leading inevitably to violence and death.

It's all over, Carlos thought, as he gazed out over his private domain
-except for one last act. He walked to his desk and sat, resolved to do
what he knew had to be done. But first, he would discuss his plans
with his two closest friends — Carmen his wife, and Manuel.

Carmen arrived first, clad in her nightgown. Her face was gentle and sweet, but even her beauty could not hide the deep concern she felt inside. Carmen understood from her conversations with Carlos just how serious the divisions which infected the organization were. She was prepared to accept whatever plans he prepared.

"You look so tired, Carlos," she said as she walked behind his chair and massaged his shoulders. "I know you are disturbed by the events of the past few days," she said reassuringly and tenderly as she leaned forward and kissed his neck. Her warm breath caused his skin to tingle. "Whatever you decide, my darling, I want you to know that I will be by your side. I love you. I trust you."

Carlos smiled, buoyed by her support and warm words of encouragement. "I also love you, my little flower." he sighed as he embraced her soft arm and closed his eyes. How I will regret losing you so soon, he thought.

Manuel arrived shortly thereafter, fully dressed. He very rarely retired before Carlos and Carmen were safe in bed. "I think you have a lot on your mind, Carlos," he said after taking a seat at the front of Carlos' desk. "I also think it's time we spoke of the future."

Carlos kissed Carmen's arm, and asked her to sit beside Manuel.

"You are right my friend," Carlos said, smiling at both. "I guess I cannot hide my feelings from the two of you much longer."

"There is no need to hide anything from us, Carlos," Manuel offered.

"You are right, of course," Carlos answered, sensitively. Folding his hands on the desk, Carlos leaned forward and addressed his remarks to Carmen, first. "Carmen, very shortly, you and I will be leaving for the United States."

Carmen gasped, truly surprised by this decision, realizing, perhaps, for the first time just how deep the split in the organization had become.

"I have decided that you will accompany me to Boston," Carlos said evenly, "where you will be introduced through letter to my good friend, Rivero. It is time that you meet the man who, like Manuel, has sacrificed so much on my behalf. . ."

"But what of you?" Carmen interrupted. "You talk as if we will not be together," she said as she leaned forward, an expression of concern on her face.

Carlos struggled to conceal his true feelings. There would be no debating his decision. The choices were, indeed, narrow. He knew Contero and Botero would welcome the opportunity to kill him and have their way with her.

"I am convinced, Carmen," he said calmly, "that whether we stay or leave my fate is already determined."

"No," Carmen pleaded, bringing her delicate hands to her lips.

Manuel reached across the distance between their chairs and patted Carmen's shoulder gently, assuring her he would not allow anything to happen to Carlos.

"Please, Carmen," Carlos asked, "be strong for me. And for yourself. We are together now — and will be together for a long time. These are just precautions." Carlos knew this was not the truth, but couldn't bear seeing Carmen suffer more than she had. "You must believe me, Carmen, what I have planned is the only way out for us. You must not let me down. Agreed?"

"Yes. . .," she pouted.

"Besides, you will like America. Once there we will be very rich. We will live in a beautiful house."

Carmen sank in her chair and fought to hold her tears back. There would be plenty of time for crying later when she was alone in her room. "I will go with you anywhere, Carlos. And I will do whatever you ask," she said bravely.

"I love you," Carlos said tenderly, provoking Carmen to jump from her chair and rush behind his desk and embrace him fiercely — and passionately.

Carlos held her warmly, committed to following his plans through, regardless of the hurt he felt inside. "Over the next few days, I want you to pack one bag of your personal belongings. Pack only the clothing you will need for a brief journey — enough to last anywhere from a week to ten days. We will not be staying in hotels during these days, Carmen, and there will be times when our going will be rough. No dresses. Just pants, shoes, shirts and delicate things. Is that clear?"

"Yes," she answered.

"Good," Carlos said as he stood, faced his wife, holding her hands in his, and smiled. "Now there is something else you must do."

"I will do anything you ask of me, Carlos," she said bravely.

"During the next few days," he said, "I want you to act as naturally as you can. Let on to no one what I have just said. I want you to tell all our social and business acquaintances that you are planning a big party for the end of the month. Order cakes, beef and party supplies. Book the best bands and begin ordering decorations from the local stores. Our enemies are watching both of us closely, so we must be very convincing. No one must suspect that we will not be here to enjoy the festivities. It will be up to you to convince everyone that we are celebrating a very romantic occasion."

Carmen nodded,   fighting to hold back a torrent of tears.

"Good," Carlos said as he embraced her gently. "You and I will talk of these things later. I know that I can trust you, Carmen to be strong with me and to give me strength. Come," he said as he placed his arm around her shoulder and led her around the front of his desk. "Everything will work out as planned, Carmen," he said as he stopped and embraced her firmly. "Now," he said as he stepped back and kissed her forehead tenderly, "I ask that you allow me and Manuel to discuss other business. Business I'd rather you not hear."

"I understand," she said lowering her eyes, sobbing openly now for she could not bear the pain and sadness which tore at her heart any longer.

"There is much about my life, Carmen, you have yet to learn," Carlos said as he reached for the diary he kept. "This will be a good place for you to start."

Carmen looked into lovingly into Carlos' eyes as she took the book, honored that he displayed such trust in Manuel's presence. For the diary told everything — everything known only to Carlos and Manuel, and now her. Her eyes filled and her chin wrinkled as she struggled to hide her emotions. "I will hold the book for you, Carlos. But I will not read it," she said as she clutched it to her bosom. "This part of your life, Carlos, is a trust between you, Manuel and Rivero. I am your wife," she said holding her head high. "As we hold certain matters in trust between us as husband and wife, so too, I respect your right to hold matters in trust between you and your closest friends."

Now it was Carlos who fought to hold back his tears.

"Please look after him, Manuel. I do love him so, and don't want to lose him," she said as she extended her hand to Manuel.

"I will value his life above my own," Manuel pledged as he stood, and kissed her fingers.

Carmen then turned and left the room, walking briskly barely able to control the flood of emotion tearing at her insides.

When she had departed Manuel walked over to his friend and whispered, "You heard that Contero has been making overtures to the others to replace you?"

Carlos turned and faced Manuel, and reaching up, placed an arm around his friend's shoulder and smiled. "I heard it from Lopez, this morning. Come," Carlos added as he led his friend across the room toward the small bar in the corner, "let us have a drink together."

"I heard the same from one of Botero's men, of all places."

"From Botero's camp?" Carlos said surprised.

Manuel shrugged. "For a price, lesser men will sell out their mothers."

"Indeed," Carlos said as he motioned Manuel to sit at the bar.

"I should have cut the bastard's throat while I had the chance," Manuel reflected out loud, referring to his encounter with Contero at the recently-called meeting. "I guess age slows us all down," he said as he slid onto one of the leather chairs facing Carlos.

"It may slow us down, Manuel," Carlos said matter-of-factly as he filled their glasses with his finest wine, "but it doesn't dull our intelligence. In fact," he added almost triumphantly as he passed Manuel his drink, "one could argue that our experience gives us an edge in this little game." He raised his glass in a mock toast and said: "Here's betting our experience will give us the upper hand."

"You have a plan," Manuel said after he sipped his drink.

Carlos looked at his watch. "Oh, indeed, my friend. At this very hour our very good friend Botero is meeting with an unfortunate industrial accident. I believe," Carlos added, feigning genuine impartiality, "that Botero is having his balls sawed off at this very moment."

"What?" Manuel said, jolted by the revelation. "How did you plan that, Carlos?"

Carlos lowered his glass and with a look of satisfaction smiled, shrugged and said: "It is *The Will of God*!"

Manuel gulped the remainder of his glass and asked for a refill.

"Easy, my friend," Carlos chided. "Let it flow gently as molasses down your throat. Savor the taste at six hundred dollars a bottle."

"I congratulate you, Carlos," Manuel said as he held his glass out for more. "That is news worth toasting. But you hinted you had a plan for the bastard Contero. I can hardly wait for your answer."

"I'm clearly not going to allow Contero and the Revolutionaries to murder Enrique as they did Carmen's parents — and get away with it," Carlos said bitterly as he moved to the front of the bar, bottle in hand, and sat beside his friend. "More?" he asked.

Manuel sipped his wine, slowly this time, savoring the taste, swallowing slowly after swirling the sweet liquid over the surface of his tongue.

"There... Now isn't that better?" Carlos said urbanely.

"Oh, indeed, it is señor," Manuel mimicked a drunken peasant. "More... more."

Carlos laughed. "Manuel, where do we stand in the production and refining stages as of today?"

"We've processed over fifty tons to date, and have another eighty in the pipeline," Manuel said, his curiosity piqued.

"Yes, that's the figure I want," Carlos said as he did some quick mental arithmetic. "How much raw product is actually awaiting immediate processing? I mean, How much can we actually get our hands on? What is under our direct control?"

"Ours?"

"Yours and mine, if it has to be that way."

Manuel placed his glass on the counter and swiveled to face Carlos, a quizzical expression on his face. "What are you getting at, Carlos? Do you mean, How much can we actually. . ." and his words trailed off as he gestured by moving his hand, palm down, across his throat. "But how?"

"Do you remember that Russian scientist who defected a year ago? The one who was working on that toxic stuff — ah — TE1. That's what he called it." He was referring to Ivanovich Gorbachev, a chemical warfare expert attached with the Soviet Embassy in Nicaragua. His passport identified him as an expert in forestry, assigned ostensibly to assist the Sandanistas in exploiting the rich green forests of their homeland. In fact, Gorbachev was a nasty little sonofabitch of a scientist who experimented with the natural water supplies used by the contras deep in the jungles of Nicaragua. Killing was his game. Killing with extremely toxic, non-traceable poisonous substances, the most deadly of which was a clear liquid poison called, simply TE1.

Manuel thought for a moment, then remembered. A smile crossed his lips as he recounted the treasure they uncovered when they learned of Gorbachev's unquenchable passion for young boys and cocaine. "The little talking bird," Manuel commented as he reached for his wine glass again. "He went insane didn't he?"

"Very much so, my friend. Seems like he got a little too much of both vices when he came to us for safe transport out of the country," Carlos mused. It was an understatement to say that Gorbachev had vices. His lust for excess was insatiable. Indeed, once Gorbachev tasted the fruits of real freedom, he became a slave to his own weaknesses, and a willing pawn in the hands of Carlos Ortega and his organization. In the Soviet sphere, Gorbachev was always watched closely. Not that the Russians didn't know of his weaknesses. They just controlled the supply better. His actions were monitored in the Soviet system which suppressed, sometimes brutally suppressed, his more controversial sexual preferences. But as a free man, in the company of other free men who professed no false moral code or political ideals, Gorbachev wallowed and floundered helplessly. His loss!

"It was *The Will of God*," Manuel chided as he toasted Carlos again. Carlos placed his glass on the counter, stood and walked over to the large tinted window. There he stood for several moments, enjoying the affects of the wine on his system, gazing off into the stygian night, reminiscing. "You know, Manuel," he said, continuing to stare off into the night, "my father taught me never to trust outsiders. Never to place my complete confidence in anyone but you and Rivero." Carlos turned and faced Manuel. He placed his hands in his pockets and leaned gently against the glass. "In this business, Carlos," he would say to me, "never rely upon just one position. Never believe that today's friends could not turn out to be tomorrow's enemies. Always keep it to yourself, but always prepare a plan with that eventuality in mind."

"Your father was a wise man," Manuel said fondly.

"And Gorbachev was a fool," Carlos answered, as he walked to his desk, sat, opened a draw and removed a key which unlocked the basement safe. "The Soviets wanted Gorbachev to work on a chemical they could use against us — our business. Not traceable by know tests. Extremely toxic and deadly. What they got," Carlos laughed, "was one liberated Soviet citizen who thumbed his nose at the empire, and gave us a secret formula, which if it exists anywhere else, is kept under tight wraps — TE1."

Dangling the key in front of him, Carlos mused, "Here's to all the boys he loved, who gave so much that we might now be the only people in the world with Gorbachev's little discovery." Carlos dropped the key on his desk and leaning forward, motioned for Manuel to join him. "I now have a job for you, Manuel. A dangerous job, my friend. I hesitate even bringing it up, but if my plan is to succeed, what I propose must be done."

Manuel walked over to the front of the desk, leaned forward, hands clasping the edge, and looked Carlos squarely in the eyes. "When you arrive in Boston with Carmen, do what you must do. Don't worry about me or the danger I face, because I don't worry for myself." He then straightened and adjusted his shirt which had risen slightly, caught in his belt. "For over thirty years, Carlos, you've been as a son to me. Whatever I can do to give you and Carmen a fresh start is not my danger — it's my greatest honor."

"You're a rare breed, Manuel," Carlos said as he stood, walked over to Manuel and embraced the man who would discharge the final act of *The Will of God*. "You and your brother, Rivero, have given so much to me. What can I ever do to repay. . . ."

Manuel interrupted, "You go with Carmen, and let me deal with the likes of Contero and his supporters. That will make me very happy."

Through the remainder of the evening Carlos and Manuel planned what would be their final revenge on those who betrayed them.

Manuel would carry out that part of the plan. Carlos would make arrangements to leave for America, to inform Enrique of the plot against his life — and that of the Holy Father. And when that task was completed, Carlos would disappear and Carmen would be protected by Rivero until she was comfortable with her new country — able to fend for herself.

If Carlos lived he would communicate through correspondence under an assumed name, channelling all letters through separate boxes located at Boston's central post office. Carlos would make these arrangements during his last few weeks in Peru.

On April 11th, however, as Manuel was preparing to retire, exhausted from the strain and pressure of the last three days, three days in which his part of the plan was executed flawlessly, eight professional assassins, hired by Contero, made their way stealthily onto the compound of the Campamento en el Bosque.

Poison darts quickly disabled the first three guards they encountered. Their orders were to take no prisoners or hostages. Everyone, including guards were to be killed, since the guards who actually worked on the compound were the most trusted and loyal to Carlos.

The executions might have been carried out flawlessly — except for one small detail. Manuel did not like air conditioning, and therefore, slept with his terrace window open. After thirty years on this compound, Manuel was familiar with the sounds of the night. Perhaps it was just his cautious nature, but he listened even as he slept. And tonight as he prepared for bed he did not hear the occasional laughter, or the passing greetings from the three guards who walked this sector of the inner compound. Nor did he hear the chronic cough of the guard who regularly patrolled the helicopter port outside his window. And the absence of these sounds made him suspicious.

Still in his underwear, Manuel removed the .45 caliber semi-automatic, and two spare clips of ammunition from the drawer beside his bed. He moved cautiously toward the door which opened to the hallway, leading to Carlos' room. There, he paused and listened — to the sounds of footsteps outside his door.

The assassins worked unbelievably fast. Manuel opened the door slowly at first, then flung it wide at the sight of four heavily armed men walking toward Carlos' room, with their backs to him.

"Carlos!" Manuel shouted as the spacious estate exploded with gun fire. The four assassins were caught completely by surprise, and died in a hail of deadly accurate gun fire, discharging their own weapons into the ceiling and walls as they staggered and fell dead.

The sound of shooting jolted Carlos. "Get under the bed," Carlos ordered as he jumped reflexively to his feet, grabbing the .9MM from his drawer in one smooth motion.

"Carlos, please come here. . ." Carmen pleaded as she jumped out of bed and knelt on the floor by her side of the mattress, prepared to slide underneath at the least provocation.

"Shhh. . ." Carlos signalled as he moved stealthily toward the door leading to the front hall. He pressed himself against the wall, listened, took a deep breath, and stepping back with his weapon at the ready, flung the bedroom door open. "Manuel! Behind you," he shouted in desperation, watching helplessly as a fifth assassin approached Manuel from behind.

"Ayeee!" Manuel cried as he clutched his throat and wobbled unsteadily into the deadly embrace of his assailant. In the last few moments of his life Manuel's thoughts were of Carlos, though. With a violent jerking motion, he threw his upper torso backward, banging his head into the face of his murderer, causing the man to release his grasp and slump against the door frame, clutching his bloody, broken nose in pain.

In that instant, with only seconds left to live himself, hoping to buy Carlos the time he needed to save himself, Manuel turned, and fired one round point blank into his assailant's forehead. Blood from the fifth assassin's head splattered the face of yet a sixth assassin approaching behind him.

And Manuel fell dead to the floor.

Sensing the need to act decisively, Carlos raised his weapon and fired in the direction of the last man standing — or so he thought. Three of the six round nose projectiles slammed violently into the man's body, sending him reeling into the darkness of Manuel's bedroom.

Instinctively, Carlos ran to Manuel, forgetting that Carmen was still alone in the room. "Manuel, Manuel," he cried as he dropped to his knees and clutched the limp body of his trusted friend. "Please, God. Don't let this be happening," he pleaded, but to no avail. Nothing could change the reality of the moment. He sobbed uncontrollably over the loss he had suffered.

"Carmen," he called, still clutching his friend, weeping into Manuel's shoulder. "Carmen. . ." he cried, looking up this time only to observe Carmen standing in the doorway, weeping, terrified by the presence of the man with his arm clasped tightly around her neck.

"Oh my God," Carlos muttered.

"Move!" the man shouted to Carlos, motioning for him to step away from the corpse. "Drop your weapon!" he ordered, tightening his grasp around Carmen's neck, causing the young girl to rise on her toes to relieve the pressure.

"Please... Please...," Carlos begged as he rose and lifted his hands above his head. The weapons at his feet were useless to him now. With Carmen's life in jeopardy, all he could do was pray for mercy.

The last of the assassins stepped out of the darkness and around Carmen and her captor and grunted contemptibly, displaying a wicked smile as he glanced into her eyes. And it was clear to Carmen what he planned for her.

"So, you are the powerful Carlos Ortega, son of the infamous Simon Gabriel de San Martin," the assassin taunted as he stepped over dead bodies and approached Carlos, pumping a round into the chamber of the shotgun he carried by his side.

"And you...," Carlos said meekly, hoping not to offend the man in who's hands Carmen's life hung in the balance. One quick snap and she would be dead.

"I am the man who will kill you," the eighth assassin said menacingly.

With every ounce of strength in her body, Carmen plunger her elbow into the rib cage of the man standing behind her, causing him to yelp in pain, then gurgle blood. Carmen had broken two of his ribs, sending one jagged bone fragment into his right lung. And the seventh man fell awkwardly to the floor, fighting a desperate but losing battle for air.

This distracted the eighth assassin long enough for Carlos to grab one of the automatic weapons at his feet, and before the eighth man knew what was happening, spray one quick burst into the man's chest and stomach, killing the final assailant instantly.

During the brief gun battle, activity throughout the compound was frantic as guards ran to their assigned positions along the inner perimeters. Others sped toward the house, hoping for the best, knowing, though, they were too late to affect the outcome of the silence inside — an eerie silence which signalled the end of a violent life and death struggle just moments earlier.

In all, the entire assassination attempt lasted fewer than seven minutes. Toll: Twelve dead, including Carlos' dearest friend, brother, father, son -Manuel.

Although Carlos would feign surprise and complete shock over the next few days, and act thoroughly baffled when asked *who* would do this to him, he knew *who* planned it. And he would exact his revenge — from America.

Indeed, it was clear to both Carlos and Carmen that from that evening on they would be watched regularly, prisoners in their own home. It was also clear that the best time to leave would be during the brief period when confusion over the failed execution attempt caused their opponents to hesitate before making another, perhaps, bolder attempt on their lives. So, after a brief grieving period for Manuel, Carmen went about her business and talked cheerfully of her end-of-the-month party for Carlos, and had everyone convinced she was no more than an immature and self-centered child, exactly as she and Carlos planned it.

During the same period Carlos made painstakingly detailed arrangements for their escape. Supporters had to be enlisted. Supplies had to be purchased. Routes had to be cleared. New alliances had to be forged. And silence had to be assured, for it was a dangerous journey they would be undertaking. A journey filled with hardship and sacrifice for both. A journey which commenced simply enough during the early evening hours of April 19, 1985, when, with the assistance of several co-conspirators, they departed the *Campamento en el Bosque* for the last time. Hidden under the rear seat of a small van headed ostensibly to town for household supplies, the two prayed for salvation and their lives.

God must have been listening.

The incredible fifteen day exodus, which would carry the two at different times by small plane, automobile, boat and mule from Peru to the shores of the United States, was so meticulously executed it caught Contero and his men completely by surprise. Indeed, not until the next evening, following their hasty departure, did anyone even suspect the two were not in their room, foolishly loving the last few hours of their lives away.

As for the health and welfare of the *business*, God was less kind.

The organization, stung by Carlos' abrupt departure, experienced a brief but bloody struggle for power among the remaining drug kings. Yet in less than nine days it was Contero, the angry revolutionary, who emerged as the singularly most powerful and influential figure at the helm of the incredibly ruthless South American drug syndicate, Los Grandes Mafiosos.

Obsessed with Ortega's escape, Contero ordered every man, woman and child working or living near the compound rounded up. They were summoned before him on a bright and sunny Thursday afternoon, questioned briefly, assumed to have been co-conspirators in Carlos' escape, and summarily executed. Some were tortured slowly and died by mutilation. Some were burned alive. Some, hanged. Others were raped, or drawn and quartered. And some were simply strangled by Contero, himself.

"Carlos must not be permitted to interfere with our plans," Contero ordered from inside *his* new headquarters at the *Campamento en el Bosque*. "I want our people in every country between here and America to be alert for his presence. I want it made clear that anyone caught harboring this imperialist dog and his whore will be executed." And no one doubted his sincerity.

"Anyone who provides us with information as to his whereabouts will be handsomely rewarded," he said. "Two million American dollars to the man who kills this traitor, imperialist dog. But his death must be slow. I must have proof that his death was slow and agonizing. Is that understood?"

And the word from South America, found its way quickly onto the streets of Miami, Chicago, Los Angeles, New York, Boston, Washington, Dallas, Central Falls Rhode Island. Where there was large-scale drug use, there were contacts and pushers who heard of the offer: Find Carlos Ortega, bring him back. And if that cannot be arranged, kill him. Reward: Two million dollars dead, Three million alive.

Yet, Contero was still not satisfied that what he had ordered was enough. Burning inside his stomach was a hate more powerful than his zeal for the revolutionary cause. Contero wanted to deal with Carlos personally. He wanted Carlos to pay dearly for his past sins. The very thought that Carlos was within his grasp, and escaped, tortured him emotionally beyond any physical suffering he ever endured. He planned long and hard for the day when he could reveal his identity, then exact his brutal revenge. He would not be deprived of that moment.

On May 2, 1985 Contero ordered three separate hit teams, each comprised of over a dozen ruthlessly brutal men, representing the drug trade in Peru, Bolivia and Colombia, to leave for Boston, and await Carlos' next move. Contero was certain that Carlos' escape was somehow tied into the plan to replace the American bishop with an imposter. If Carlos intended to interfere with those plans, he would feel the wrath of Los Grandes Mafiosos and be crushed before he succeeded. Whatever the price, Carlos would not succeed.

"We will hold over here a few days," Carlos said as he looked at his watch, noting the time and day. "We've been in America for two days now, Carmen, and nothing extraordinary has happened," he said as he held his young wife gently by her shoulders, hoping to soothe her frayed nerves. "The journey was long but we made it. We are safe."

"Are we really safe, Carlos," she said softly, pressing her head against his chest. "We have not gone out or made any contact with Rivero since our arrival."

Carlos laughed. "Is that what is bothering you, my little flower?"

"You know the organization will be looking for us..."

"It's a big world, Carmen. This is America. We are in a little town, in a little motel in a place called..." and he gazed over her head and read the cover of the tourist map placed on their bureau, "...Falmouth Massachusetts. Who would think of looking for us here?"

"I don't know," she said as she squeezed her arms tighter around his waist.

"When we arrive in Boston we will wait a few days, just in case they are expecting us to contact the chancellery. We will wait and watch. See if there is any increased activity in the Boston area after our arrival."

"And if there is?" she sobbed lightly.

"We'll do what we must, my little flower. Time is on our side," he said, kissing her forehead gently. "The switch cannot be made for another week or so according to the plans I've seen. They are as much a captive of circumstances as are we. They must wait, the same as us. When I feel it is safe, I will contact Rivero and inform him of what is happening."

"I want to make love with you tonight, Carlos," Carmen moaned, sensing inside, although not expressing her deepest fears outwardly, that her days with Carlos were numbered.

"And what a grand night it shall be," he said as he lifted her in his arms and carried her to bed.

25
The Escape

Rivero blinked several times, trying to focus his vision. He was still groggy. It was 5:00 P.M.. He rubbed his hands in a circular motion over his forehead, then through his hair. As he sat and straightened himself against the wall of the cell, he had an uneasy sense of being in this place before. The cell was warm and moist. And the air smelled of lush green plants and tropical forest.

He looked at his watch. If was five o'clock — but the *day* window displayed Tuesday. His body ached and his bones hurt from the obvious beating he received... yesterday? Yesterday, Monday. He leaned forward slowly, placing his elbows on his knees, cupping his face in the palms of his hands, trying desperately to understand what happened. There was something very familiar about this place, he thought. He sat upright again and gazed around the cell, through the iron bars, down the hallway. He did know this place. He had, indeed, been here many times before.

"Page," he whispered across the cell. "Wake up!"

Dawson was just regaining his consciousness. "Oh shit," he said, rubbing the back of his neck, smoothing his hand over the lump behind his right ear. He, too, gazed around the strange surroundings, wondering where he was, before continuing. "Where are we?" he asked, thoroughly confused for the second time in three days. "Are you okay, Rivero?" he said, as he sat up and massaged his arms, chest and face.

Rivero stared blankly ahead.

"Rivero," Dawson prompted, "Are you hurt?"

Rivero flashed an *obviously I'm hurt* kind of smile across the cell. Dawson returned the smile. "Yeah, me too."

Rivero glanced through the bars of the cell into the hallway, then toward Dawson again, assured they were alone — temporarily. His mind was elsewhere, though, as he spoke. "Listen closely, my friend. We've been kidnapped. We're no longer in the United States. . ."

"What?" Dawson asked incredulously.

Rivero shook his head. "We're in South America — Peru, to be exact," he said as he leaned forward again, rubbing his sore wrists. He looked at his watch to confirm what he observed moments ago. His sentences were brief and factual. "It's Tuesday. They must have taken us here for a reason. Carmen is alone. We've got to get out of this place. This isn't good. Not good at all, Dawson."

Slowly, Page stood, inching his way up the wall gradually, allowing his legs to regain their strength. He glanced at Rivero, then through the bars at the dark hallway. "Peru?" he mumbled, as he limped over to the one window, and stretching painfully on his toes, tried to glimpse their surroundings.

The cell was quiet: Rivero, lost in the past, remembering; Dawson, planning an escape. "Rivero," Dawson said as he walked over to where Rivero was sitting, and joined him on the floor, "I thought we were dead for sure, yesterday. But I don't understand. What is this place? Are we prisoners? Why? Why didn't they kill us when they had the chance?"

River stared straight ahead as he spoke. "We're worse than prisoners, my friend," he said quietly as he rose slowly to his feet, Dawson following. "We're in hell." His words were cold and distant.

"Listen," Page said as the motor of an approaching helicopter whirred closer. As the sound grew louder Page moved toward the window again where he strained to take a closer look. His efforts were futile, though. The window was too high. He turned and faced Rivero, leaning against the wall and said: "Are you absolutely certain we're in Peru?"

Rivero limped over to the window and stood beside Page. "I grew up here, Dawson. Carlos grew up here," he said, adding: "They want something from us."

"What?" Dawson asked.

"Information."

"About Ortega?"

Rivero rubbed his hand against his face as he walked across the cell. "Whoever brought us here, believes we know something. They want to keep us alive because they want to know if we've talked with anyone else."

Page followed Rivero across the cell, and placing an arm on Rivero's shoulder said: "Rivero, listen to me. You know this place. You say you grew up here."

"Yes, my friend. This was my home."

Dawson shook his head, still confused. "How well do you know the surrounding terrain?"

Rivero turned and looked into Dawson eyes. "Why?"

"If we can get out of this place," Page said referring to the building, "will you be able get us out of the country?"

Rivero nodded. "I don't know. Maybe. Yes, I guess I could. But it is very dangerous, Dawson. We are isolated in the forest, miles from the nearest road. Dealing with people who are ruthless. We can't trust anyone."

"If we can get to that helicopter," Dawson motioned with his hand, "Maybe we'll stand a chance."

"Maybe," Rivero conceded, skeptically.

"Are we dead if we stay?" Page asked.

"Most certainly," Rivero answered. "But only after they've had their fun with us. Believe me, Dawson, this is the worst nightmare you can imagine. They will torture us for information which we may not even have, and then they will kill us — if we are lucky," he added parenthetically. "Listen to me, Dawson. The people who murdered Carlos and Bishop Michelsen want us alive for information and nothing else. Whatever it is they're hiding, they think we might know something about it."

Page turned and leaned against the wall. He drew his head back slightly and inhaled deeply the aroma of moist green forest outside. "If we stay here much longer my sinus are going to start acting up," he said seriously, then laughed when he realized the absurdity of his observation.

Rivero turned and rocked against the cell's bars and laughed with him. "Oh, most assuredly your sinuses will be acting up, my friend."

"Yeah," Page observed wryly, adding, "Rivero years ago before going to Vietnam we went through special training called *escape and evasion*. It left one hell of a lasting impression on my mind. We have to get out of here as quickly as possible. The longer we hesitate, the longer we'll end up staying. And if we're going to die anyway..."

"A miserably slow and painful death," Rivero assured him.

"However," Page acknowledged. "We have to move soon."

"Agreed."

"We can't be separated, Rivero. We've got to do this together, very first chance we get."

Rivero nodded.

Page massaged his hands across his face, then over his entire body to relieve the tenseness and soreness of his muscles. "Let me take the lead, Rivero. The moment I make a move to escape, follow me without a moment's hesitation. Even a two second delay can cost us our lives."

"Agreed," Rivero said. "Once we are outside, if we make it outside, follow me closely."

Page nodded.

The sound of approaching footsteps caused both men to brace themselves for whatever the future held. Their hearts raced and muscles tensed in anticipation of what would follow.

Four guards, each armed with an automatic weapon, approached the cell. They shouted orders in Spanish, motioning for the two prisoners to step away from the doors. Rivero translated: "They want us to go with them."

"Quiet!" one of the guards barked as he raced through the door and slapped Rivero's face, causing the tender area under Rivero's eye to turn deep scarlet. "Follow!" the biggest of the guards ordered as he pointed down the hallway.

As they walked along the length of the deserted basement passageway, Page observed that they were the only guests. "Up! Up!" one of the guards ordered, pointing to the stairs. Neither Page nor Rivero spoke a word from this point on. They just observed in cautious silence. But Page, especially, made an effort to commit his surroundings to memory. If anything happened to Rivero he would be entirely alone. Every detail was, therefore, important.

When they arrived at the top of the stairs, they were met by another guard who carried only a pistol on his hip, and a cynical, menacing sneer on his lips. Almost as if he recognized Rivero.

"This way," the house guard ordered in Spanish as he removed his pistol and waved it in Page's face. And Page realized, now, more than ever how important it would be for Rivero to survive. Page didn't understand a word of Spanish.

As they proceeded across the large reception hall, toward Carlos' study, Rivero glanced at familiar surroundings, and his mind filled with memories of days long gone. He remembered how this place once looked when Simon Gabriel ruled. He remembered the first day they brought young Carlos to his new home.

"Stop!" the guard said as they approached a set of doors. The guard knocked, softly, stood back, and the doors opened electronically.

"In," the guard ordered, and Rivero and Page proceeded in silence as they were told. As they entered Page noticed a large banner on the far wall of the room. It read, *Ayacucho: Guerra de Guerrillas*.

"Leftist bullshit?" Page whispered.

"Shh!" Rivero cautioned.

Standing alone at the far corner, beneath the banner was a man. Since his back was toward them, neither Page nor Rivero could explain the reason he sounded. . . odd.

"I have waited a long time for this day," the man said in English, without turning."Bring them closer," he ordered, and the guards shoved the two prisoners forward until they were about half way into the room.

"You the American," the man said slowly, intrigued with Page's involvement, "I don't yet know who you are. But I soon will." The last part sounded ominous. "But you, Rivero. I will never forget your face. When they brought you in earlier today I was overjoyed. I had no idea you were still alive."

This puzzled Rivero, since he didn't recognize the voice of the man speaking to him.

The man held up his hand, index finger waving slightly back and forth as he spoke. "It is not necessary that you know the names of these pigs, Carlos. It is only necessary that they know who you are. . ." The man's voice was filled with scorn. "Do you remember those words, Rivero?"

Rivero nodded. His breathing uneven, his heart pumping furiously. The man was quoting Manuel's words of some thirty years ago. Rivero would never forget that day of revenge.

Slowly, the man turned and faced his guests.

"What the fuck?" Page whispered when the man was fully turned.

His face was grotesque. It looked as if it was literally sewn together. On each side of his mouth were large, uneven scars which started at the corners of his mouth and extended to the base of his ears. When he spoke, only his lips moved, as if his jaws were fused together. "My name is Contero," he said as he swaggered slowly toward them. "You will remember that, Rivero," he said instructively.

As he drew closer, Page studied the man's face closely. Something happened between these two men thirty years ago, he figured — and it wasn't good.

Contero stood in front of Page and stared intently into his eyes. "I am beautiful, no?" he taunted, then raising his head spit into Page's face. Page recoiled when the vile liquid splashed against his forehead. But was restrained from moving when the guards grabbed his arms and held him in place. "I will personally fuck you in the ass later," Contero smiled evilly. "And you will tell me everything I want to know."

"Your mother's cunt!" Page answered sarcastically as he struggled to free himself. A rifle butt slammed into his back, causing him to drop to his knees, gasping.

"Quiet!" one of the guards ordered as he pulled Page to his feet again.

Contero then motioned for the biggest of the guards to hold Rivero's arms behind his back. "And as for you...," he said as he reached into his pocket and removed a set of pictures. One by one he held the photographs in front of Rivero's resentful eyes, his hand blocking the face of the victim in the photos. "Well?" he chided as he flicked through the pictures, laughing in a series of staccato grunts.

"Sick bastard," Dawson spat.

"Shut up!" Contero yelled as he slapped Dawson's face.

Rivero's anger grew more intense as he was forced to look at each gruesome picture. The guard's choke-hold, however, was just too tight. It was impossible for him to escape.

"And when I have the information I want from you," Contero said, as he prepared to turn over the last photograph, "You will live and live and live -and every day of your life you will wish you were dead. Now, I suppose you want to see who this person is..." he said as he held the card before Rivero's face. "Very well."

Rivero's jaw tightened as he fought to hold back the outrage he experienced when shown that it was Carlos who was being tortured.

"This — is justice," Contero laughed as he discarded the last photograph of Carlos being mutilated. "What is wrong," he asked insolently, "I would have thought you would enjoy these pictures. They cost me two million dollars, you know."

"What do you want from us?" Rivero gurgled as he tried to free himself from the grasp of the biggest guard.

"Wait... wait... Rivero," Contero teased, "I thought you would enjoy my little show. These are family photographs. They make me happy. Why do you grow so angry?"

Contero's mood changed abruptly when he saw neither Page nor Rivero cowering as he had hoped they would. "Take them downstairs and beat them to within an inch of their lives," he instructed the guards. "I want you to break a leg and an arm on each. I don't want them running away before I've had an opportunity to talk with them later."

"You're a real charmer, pal..." Page said as he was dragged away.

"Stop!" Contero said as he walked over to Page and thumped his finger against his prisoner's chest. "If you should kill them by mistake, or if you do not beat them sufficiently," Contero added menacingly to his guards, "I will skin you alive. Do you understand? I want these men to know pain." The guards nodded obediently, not doubting for an instant Contero would do just as he said.

"Soften them up so they will answer some questions for me later," he ordered, then turned and walked back into his study.

Page's heart was pounding wildly against his chest. No doubt about it, these people meant business. An escape would have to be made soon — very soon. But where? he thought as he was pushed and shoved toward the basement stairs again. In the basement, he concluded. That would be the place to begin. The walls would probably muffle the sounds of a struggle. Jesus, I hope Rivero is up to this, he thought. Hell, I hope I am.

Four guards, one on each arm, escorted the prisoners away from the study.

"Very soon," Page grunted as he struggled.

"Ah ha," Rivero said, his breathing short and uneven.

"Quiet!" the guard holding Page's right arm cursed as he twisted Page's wrist and jerked his arm up toward his neck.

Damn, Page thought, these guards are strong. Yet, one of them is going to have to release his grip long enough to open the cell door. That would be the time to act.

There is a period of time during the first few moments of capture Page recalled his escape and evasion instructor telling him years ago, *when extremely violent and specific aggression directed against your captors will give you the upper hand. One man can take down four men almost instantly if he directs his attack to kill instantly. Shit, Page thought, as he and Rivero were shoved down the stairs, this could be the last day of my life. His mind raced with conflicting thoughts. If we do nothing, he rationalized, we'll end up being beaten to death. Fuck that! he said to himself, resolving the inner conflict quickly.*

Once at the bottom of the stairs, the guards grabbed them again — in the same vice-like grip. Rivero waited for Page, but began to wonder as they moved down the passageway if Page would ever act. Yet, he had to trust Page, he reasoned, as he was almost lifted off his feet by the guards on each side. Age had taken its toll on this rusty warrior, and the guards were young and tough.

When they reached the cell door, one of the guards released his grip to open the door. Page had an awful feeling in the pit of his stomach — but it had to be done.

The moment the guard turned his back, Page clenched his fist as tightly as he could and drove it upward into the nose of the guard who held his other arm. The guard didn't say a word — just gasped and fell backward. Out cold on his way to dead. The bone from his nose had been driven with such force that it pierced a corner of his brain. Page then swung the same hand back in the direction of the guard to his immediate front, driving his knuckles a full quarter inch into the man's temple. The guard's eyes popped as his mouth opened in a silent scream. He was dead before he hit the ground. There was no time for checking details, wondering, thinking. Instinctively, one of the guards holding Rivero's arm released his grip to restrain Page. That gave Rivero sufficient time to drive his free hand into the face of the remaining guard. Bones cracked.

In combat situations such as this, an aggressive individual has two crucial elements on his side: surprise and clear intent. It was the intent of the guard who lunged for Page to restrain the prisoner. Big mistake! Page's intent was to kill the guard. No contest. It was over as quickly as it had begun. Similarly, it was the intent of the guard holding Rivero to restrain his prisoner. It was Rivero's intention to kill the guard. Check point. The entire deadly confrontation lasted approximately ten seconds. The escape had begun.

"Now what?" Page said as he stripped one of the guards of his weapons and watch.

Rivero thought for a moment. "We have to act quickly. What time is it now?"

"It's 5:45," Page answered mechanically.

"Damn," Rivero said. "The only way out of this place is by that helicopter out there, and I don't know how to fly one of those things."

"Neither do I," Page answered. "We'll have to make a deal for the pilot."

Rivero weighed other options, but none made any sense. Forget an escape by road. That would be too dangerous. There were too many people working around the compound to believe they would ever get out of the forest alive. If they were to prevent the *switch* from occurring, it was essential that they make contact with authorities they could trust, and convince them to stall the bishop's departure from Logan Airport tomorrow evening.

"Here," Dawson said, interrupting Rivero's thought. "Take these," he said, handing Rivero two small machine guns. "Dawson, we have to make a run by helicopter over the mountains to Lima. That's the only sure way out. Using the plane we can place some safe distance between us and them."

"Fine," Page said, his forehead dripping with sweat. "My fucking sinuses are starting to act up. Let's get out of here."

"Wait," Rivero gulped as he clutched his chest.

"What is it, Rivero? Are you okay?"

The physical strain was taking its toll on Rivero as his knees began to buckle and he fell backward against the wall.

"Jesus, Rivero," Page said as he rushed to his friend's side, preventing him from falling.

"We'll have to gamble that the phone lines will be clear at the airport," Rivero continued without commenting on his condition. "Listen, Dawson," he said as he clutched Dawson's shirt, "I'm not certain I can make this run with you. I'm getting too old for this shit. I'm not in as good as shape as I thought. You make a run for it. I'll cover you with these," he said, patting his weapons.

Page straightened and leaned into the wall, one arm on each side of Rivero. "Now you listen to me, Rivero," he said breathing heavily himself, sweating profusely. "If I have to carry you out of here on my back, I will. But I will not leave this place without you. You understand?" he said as he held his finger up to Rivero's face. "Let's be very clear about that, my friend, because I won't leave a friend behind. Ever again."

Rivero's face reflected his confusion. What did Page mean by "again".

"If you stop, I stop. If you fall, I wait. I don't have time to explain it all to you here, pal, but I will not leave you. Besides, I can't speak a word of Spanish, and I'm not going to lose a good interpreter. Settled?"

Rivero looked at Page and nodded his head. A remarkable man, he thought as he brought his hand to his face and wiped the beads of sweat from his brow. He may not have understood Page's reasoning, but he understood honor. And he remembered the old days when a man's word was his sacred bond. "One thing, Dawson. . ."

"Yeah?" Page said as he dragged the four bodies into the cell.

"I have a score to settle upstairs," Rivero said, pointing to the room above.

Page smiled. "Yeah, I understand," he said, adding, "Look, we've got to find a way to get the helicopter pilot into the house. Without him we're as good as dead."

As he spoke the sound of footsteps above signalled additional people entering the house. "With any luck, one of them will be the man we're looking for."

As Page and Rivero made their way down the dark passageway toward the stairs, Contero welcomed his guests into his private study. "Have the guards finish with their business downstairs," he instructed his aide. "I want one man posted outside this door and one at the front and back entrances. We are not to be disturbed," he said.

"As you wish, sir. May I get our guests something before attending to that detail?"

"No," Contero shot back. "I want our 'guests' downstairs attended to first."

"Very well, sir."

Page only glimpsed one of the visitors from behind as he was greeted by Contero and led into his private study. But it was clear from the uniforms they were wearing that the visitors were military men — Russian military men. Two of the men visiting with Contero were, in fact, high ranking military advisors on leave from Nicaragua. The third was their helicopter pilot. "Interesting," Page thought as he recalled reading about Soviet influence in the region. He never expected he would observe it this closely, though. Neither did he know that the State Department had recently issued a white paper detailing our government's suspicions about Soviet military advisors in the region, or their support of the burgeoning drug trade.

Very carefully, Page closed the door and motioned for Rivero to stand at the ready. Contero's aide was heading in their direction.

"Step back," Page cautioned as he withdrew a long knife from its sheath. "This is going to be messy if I miss."

Christ, I hate this shit, Page thought as the door opened.

"Ahh. . ." the guard gagged as Page pulled him forward violently and drove the knife into the man's solar plexus, twisting the blade to the left and right, once it was in, causing the guard to gasp: "Ah. . .Ah. . . Ah. . ." before he died. It was a tactical error on the guard's behalf. The moment he felt Page's hand on his shirt he should have stepped away and fought his way back into the foyer. Instead he went for his gun, using precious seconds on wasted motion. He never got to fire a round.

When the guard slumped and went limp, Page stepped away, withdrawing the knife, brushing the blade clean against the man's pants as he slid down three steps. Funny, Page thought, how in the movies men die with loud shrieks. Ayeeeee! In real life their eyes just seem to widen in shock and horror, and then they fall dead.

There was no turning back now. Five men were already dead. With weapons at the ready Rivero and Page glided across the wide expanse of exposed floor which led to the study now occupied by Contero and his friends. The doors were closed. Thank you God, Page thought as he whispered, "On the count of three, we go through."

Rivero slid the bolt back on his weapon, chambering a round in barrel. "Ready," he said.

"One, two three. . ."

They plunged directly into the crease where the tow doors joined, causing the door frame to crack under the weight of their assault. And the doors flung open, banging against the walls, startling Contero and his advisors.

Holding his automatic in a firing position, Rivero rushed immediately to where Contero was sitting. Page moved quickly, directing his attention to the Russians. "Not a word!" he warned in English. They understood.

Foolishly, Contero reached for the weapon he kept in his top desk drawer. Without a moment's hesitation, Rivero fired a short burst onto the top of the desk, causing wood chips and glass to fly about and Contero to fall off his chair, a five inch piece of wood protruding from the surface of the back of his hand. "Ayeeee. . ." he cried as he pulled the wooden projectile from the back of his hand, and stood to regain his composure.

"You will pay for this," he said in Spanish.

"Place your hands above your head," Rivero ordered as he stepped forward, jabbing the barrel of his weapon in front of Contero's face.

"Who flys the helicpoter?" he asked, also in Spanish, addressing his remarks to the Russians who were now lying on their stomachs on the floor. The one who looked to his superiors for guidance, that was the pilot, Rivero concluded. "Page, the one in the middle. He's the man we want."

"On your feet, pal," Page said, stepping between the two officers, barrel of his weapon pointing at the pilot's head. When the pilot refused to move, Page reached down and slapped the man's head hard, causing his face to bounce slightly off the hard wood floor. "I said on your feet."

"Good!" Rivero said as he pushed Contero toward the pilot. "You two stand together," he said in Spanish. "Page what do you want to do with them?" he said, referring to the military advisors.

"I'd like to shoot the fuckers right here and now, but I'll settle for tying them up and gagging them," Page said as he removed each of their belts and tied their hands securely behind their backs.

As Page worked on the Russians, Rivero ordered the pilot and Contero to kneel with their hands behind their heads. They were in no position to argue. "I'm going to offer you a deal, Contero," Rivero said as he walked behind Contero and tied his hands. "I don't want any more killing, if I can avoid it. You accompany us to the helicopter and take a little ride to ensure our safety, and when we arrive at our destination I'll leave you and Boris, here, alive and well. As much as I want to kill you right now for what you did to Carlos, I will spare your life. But if you try any tricks, I'll kill you instantly."

The senior Russian spoke while Contero weighed the offer. "You are making a big mistake, young man," he said, addressing Page. "I am an official representative of the Soviet Socialist Republic. What you are doing is an act of international terrorism. I will personally. . ."

Page shoved the muzzle of his gun against the Russian's head. "Now you listen to me you piece of shit. You're not sitting at the United Nations talking to a bunch of assholes. And I'm no diplomat. Now, you and your buddy, here, keep your mouths shut, or I'll be forced to cut your throats, something, given our present predicament, would not much matter to me one way or the other. . ."

"You do not frighten me. . ." the Russian blurted unwisely.

Without speaking a word, Page kicked the Russian's head as hard as he could, snapping the man's nose against the floor. Blood poured uncontrollably as the Russian jerked spasmodically, then passed out.

"You got any questions?" Page taunted the other Russian who looked on with concern at the blood pouring from his comrades face. "Say nothing!" Page ordered. And the Russian understood.

"Well, Contero," Rivero asked. "It's your move."

"I'll do as you ask," Contero said arrogantly. "If only because I will enjoy watching you and your friend die slow deaths. You and your friend will not escape Peru alive."

"Lets get out of here," Page said as he finished gagging the second Russian advisor. "We've got to move fast."

The four men moved from the study to the foyer, pausing at the front door before making their run for the helicopter. Page braced himself against the wall and chambered another round in his weapon while Rivero, speaking in Spanish advised the pilot and Contero what was expected of them. "Once we are safe, you will be safe," Rivero said. "If you or Contero try anything foolish you will be shot on the spot. You understand?"

The Russian nodded.

"How do you expect me to run with my hands tied behind my back?" Contero asked, turning his back to Rivero, waiting for his enemy to loosen the knot.

Rivero untied Contero's hands, then slipped the rope over Contero's head, drawing a noose which could be held at arm's length as they ran. "I wouldn't want to pull you all the way, Contero. I hope you can run fast."

"Okay, here goes," Page said as he opened the door. "Now," Rivero instructed. And all four raced from the main entrance. Page held the pilot's arm. Rivero clung tightly to the rope around Contero's neck. What little activity there was around the compound, no one took any notice of the wild dash for the helicopter. First, Page, then the helicopter pilot boarded the Vietnam-vintage Huey. And within minutes the engine whirred, and dirt and small pebbles were lifted off the ground by the down draft created by the spin of the helicopter's blades.

The noise created by the starting of the engine attracted some unwanted attention as perimeter guards peered to observe who was leaving so early. "Get on!" Rivero shouted as the blades turned faster and faster and the helicopter began a slow lift. "Get on!" he shouted louder to Contero who hesitated and began to back away.

The helicopter lifted. "Wait! Wait!" Rivero shouted over the rhythmic pat, pat, pat of the engine. He pulled against the rope holding Contero who resisted boarding.

"Shoot them! Shoot them! Shoot them!" Contero began yelling as he clutched the rope around his neck, trying to free himself from Rivero's grasp.

"Bastard!" Rivero shouted into the force of wind and dirt flying about.

"Up! Up!" Page signalled with his hand, realizing that Contero had tricked them. He had no intention of boarding the plane in the first place. "Up! Up!" Page yelled into the pilot's face, pressing his .45 against the pilot's cheek as a warning. And the helicopter lifted quickly off the ground.

"You broke your word", Rivero shouted as he pulled at the rope, still holding a kicking, cursing, raging Contero.

As the helicopter lifted into the air, with Rivero perched precariously by the open door and Contero kicking and flailing about outside, slowly choking to death under the weight of his own body, projectiles from guards' weapons below began snapping through the helicopter's thin metal frame. Their escape had been noticed, thanks to Contero.

"Watch out," Page shouted as he stepped around Rivero and fired his weapon in the direction of muzzle flashes below, hoping to scatter those sighting in on them.

Not wanting to lose Contero yet, Rivero secured his end of the rope around the frame of the helicopter which lifted them safely out of the range of those below. "I will enjoy watching you die," he shouted at Contero who was grabbing the rope with his hands in an attempt to relieve the pressure from his throat.

As the helicopter raced away toward Lima, Rivero stood in the door way and stared down into Contero's frantic, frightened, hate-filled eyes.

"Are you going to keep him swinging there for the whole flight?" Page shouted over the noise of the engine.

"As long as it takes for him to die," Rivero answered coldly.

Contero, meanwhile, was losing what little strength remained. The force of wind pushing him back and sideways and turning him around was just too much. He tried in vain to kick his legs up over the runners but failed at each attempt. His arms remained raised above his head, grasping at the rope in a futile attempt to relieve the suffocating pressure. His face was deep purple and his eyes were cloudy and bloodshot. And he gurgled and foamed at the mouth when he tried to curse his tormentor.

Rivero glanced across the countryside and over mountains of his beloved homeland, sensing in his heart that he would never be able to return after this. He glanced down at Contero, who even in his death, glared in defiance. "Pass me your knife," he said as he leaned toward Page. "It's time to say good bye to the past."

Rivero leaned out the door and grabbing Contero's hand tightly, proceeded to cut the rope which held the most powerful man in South America by its threads. Now, Contero's life hung in Rivero's strong grip. "It is *The Will of God*, Contero, that it ends this way."

"Bastard!" Contero shouted.

And Rivero let go.

When it had ended, Rivero stood staring from the doorway, the forward motion of the helicopter creating a rhythmic flap, flap, flap, sound as the fabric of his pants slapped wildly in the breeze.

Rivero," Page called as he reached and touched his friend on the shoulder. "It's over. We can't change anything."

But Rivero continued to stare blankly out the door. What was he thinking? Page wondered as he called again. "Rivero, please. we have to start planning our next move. Do you hear me? We can't bring any of them back, Rivero. Our only hope now is to save Carmen, prevent that man from boarding the plane before tomorrow evening."

Rivero turned slowly and slumped on the seat beside Page. With his legs outstretched and head back against the backrest Rivero closed his eyes, blocking the tears he felt building. "I understand, Dawson. I understand," he said, almost distantly.

As Page sat, tired, dirty, bloodied and near broken, he wondered what would happen next. He assumed word of their escape had been relayed ahead to other groups, that the syndicate would not allow them to leave Peru alive. And then there was Contero, — dangling, yelling obscenities from the runner of the helicopter as it pulled away from the compound. Christ, Page mused, even in death the man was defiant and filled with contempt.

It was Rivero who broke the silence. "We can't show ourselves to the authorities, Dawson. When we arrive in Lima, we'll have to check on plane flights to the United States. And even then, we have no passports, no money, no papers. . ."

"Or a pot to piss in," Page added. "If you check on the flights, I'll make contact with my friend in Boston. If I can get to him by phone I can convince him to have the authorities down here let us board."

Rivero nodded his approval.

"Americans," the pilot shouted over his shoulder as the engine began to sputter. "No more petrol," he said, pointing to the gauge which was bouncing on empty.

"Oh, great," Page complained, "What next?"

They decided the best course of action would be to set the helicopter down outside Lima, rather than try to make a precision landing in the middle of the airport. "We'll abandon it in the bush, with our Russian friend here tied to the steering column," Rivero said as the helicopter set down. "We'll sleep the night outside, then steal an automobile or some other means of transportation first thing in the morning."

"Wouldn't it be wiser for us to make a run for the American Embassy or the consulate's office?" Page asked.

"No Dawson, that wouldn't be a good idea. The moment our whereabouts is known our lives will be in danger. Believe me the people we are dealing with are tough. They'd think nothing of assaulting an American compound, killing a few Marines if they thought they could prevent us from interfering with their plans. Our strength is our anonymity."

"Fine," Page agreed reluctantly. "We sleep outdoors."

"Yes," Rivero said, "But first we have some business to attend to."

Indeed, that evening, after having stolen enough food to satisfy their hunger, they visited the airport, undetected, and confirmed that there was, indeed, a 10:15 morning flight bound for the United States, with only one stop-over in Panama City.

"Tomorrow morning, we make a run for it, Dawson. According to the flight plan the plane is scheduled to arrive in Boston at 6:30 P.M."

"Then I better make that call to O'Neil as close to departure time as possible."

"Yes. As news of our existence spreads, our chance to escape drops dramatically."

"It doesn't give us much time, Rivero."

"Will you be able to convince your friend to have the flight postponed?"

Dawson smiled. "I don't know what I'll tell him. But, yes, I think I'll be able to convince him to hold the flight."

"Then we have to make it."

"Yeah," Dawson said wryly. "It's *The Will of God.*"

26
A Woman's Intuition

Wednesday, May 22

8:00 A.M. Although they worked around the clock, the police learned very little about the reason behind Monday evening's shootout on Allston Street. The bodies which could be identified by autopsy offered precious few clues. Although, two of the men were identified as Colombians. But there were no papers on them. No evidence was found linking Dawson to the violence, either. And this troubled Lieutenant O'Neil, because Gomez' body — what they could make of it — was positively identified.

No, there were too many loose ends in this case. Page *had* to be in the building at the time of the shootout. And the evidence linking Gomez to the setup was sufficient to satisfy O'Neil that there was a connection. And then there was C. Ortega, whoever that was.

Although Wednesday was his day off, Lieutenant O'Neil found himself too preoccupied with the case to enjoy the break. And now, with the absence of Dawson's body, there was reason to hope that maybe he had survived. But where was he? Endless questions, precious few answers. It went on like this for hours.

There was one encouraging development out of all the confusion, however, the drug related violence in the city came to an abrupt halt after the disaster Monday evening. Every drug dealer and pusher went into hiding with all the DEA, FBI and local police assigned to the case. The city was literally transformed into a police stronghold.

The mayor was touring the ghetto every day promising funds and programs to help the disadvantaged. The Congressional Select Committee on Narcotics Abuse and Control called for public hearings in the Boston area, and prominent citizens, clergy and elected officials were calling for immediate action to halt the escalation of drug deal-ing and terrorist violence sweeping the predominantly black and Spanish areas of the city. "We will not shy away from the fight by waging a war of containment," the mayor of Boston testified, promis-ing to bring the battle to the pushers. It sounded tough, except the mayor refused to concede the scope of the problem. "...the increase in arrests represents increased enforcement and not an increase in the drug epidemic..." he insisted, trying to sound reassuring. The pushers chuckled over the incredulous admission.

For his part, the police commissioner announced the formation of a drug task force whose job it would be to "go into the community and root out, once and for all, the cause of this terrible plague on our city." That pronouncement disturbed the pushers a little more. But their attitude was one of wait and see. It had all been said before, and nothing ever came of it.

O'Neil was neither encouraged nor impressed by any of the tough talk. So what's new about pledges from elected officials? he thought as he lie in bed beside his wife.

"You're still troubled by that case aren't you, Bob," Susan said as she snuggled next to her husband, nestling her head comfortably on the side of his chest.

O'Neil breathed deeply, exasperated with his own inability to make sense of it all. "I'm sorry, honey, I didn't realize it was so obvious. I didn't mean to wake you," he said as he patted the side of her head, and massaged his fingers through her long auburn hair.

"You really believe Dawson might have survived that horrible fire?" she asked dolefully.

"I don't know," he replied problematically, drawing his arms up behind his head. "We've gone through most of the debris left over from the fire and explosion pretty carefully," he said in a relaxed, thoughtful manner. "I just don't think anybody is left that we haven't accounted for."

Susan snuggled closer, resting her head on her husband's chest, draping one of her legs between his.

Bob breathed deeply, closing his eyes as her smooth thigh brushed lightly against his penis. "I just don't know..." he said as he gently stroked her naked back and shoulders with his right hand. "If I could just piece this thing together in my own mind," he said as he pulled her warm body closer. Her breasts firm and round, pressed against his side. "I'm missing crucial explanations," he said. "I spoke with Lieu-tenant Dowling last night about the man with white hair..."

"The one Dawson says he saw them burying?" Susan interrupted softly.

"Yeah. I mean, Why would Dawson tell Dowling, then me, about this guy unless he really did see him? And if he did see him, then that means finding Ortega's body was only part of the mystery. Ortega may have held the secret to what is going on, but whoever buried him was certain his death wouldn't tell us anything. But the man with white hair, *he* must have known something also. Whoever buried him felt his identity would tell us something we shouldn't know. That's why his body hasn't been recovered yet."

"Bob, do you remember that story you told me about you and Dawson when were little kids. You stole some parts off the older boys' bicycles," she said softly as she stroked the soft hair on her husband's chest with her fingers. "You broke the original parts," she said as she smoothed her palm across his firm stomach, then lower. "When you thought they'd find out, you replaced what you stole with new parts. . ."

"What are you getting at, Susan?"

"Well, I was just remembering," she continued as she squeezed his erection teasingly, "what you told me about how you and Dawson worried that the older boys would discover the switch and beat you up. . ."

"Yeah. . .," he remembered fondly. "We were a couple tough kids."

"Well they never did notice the new parts because they never noticed the old parts missing."

He arched his neck back and moaned slightly as the massaging motion increased.

"Well, you can call it a woman's intuition," she said lovingly, "But what if the man with white hair was like the stolen part, being buried far away so that nobody would notice. . ."

"Jesus, Susan, you might have something there," he said as he raised his head off the pillow.

"Yes, I know," she said, smiling as she glanced below.

"No, not that. I mean your intuition," he said, arching himself lightly off the bed where her attention was fixed.

"Would you like me to stop what I'm doing while you think about it," she said teasingly.

"Stop what?" he smiled. She continued.

"Let's assume that what you've just said is true. Then it follows - Christ, Susan that feels good — that there may be two men — oh — with white hair. Don't stop — ah — one alive — Jesus Susan — one dead. . . That feels so good."

"Will you just be quite for a moment," she cooed. "I have some business to take care of down here," she said as she pressed closer and increased the friction and stroking action of her hand. His release was imminent. "I love you honey," she whispered tenderly as the contractions began, and lowering her head, provoked a powerful release with her lips.

And for the first time in three days Bob O'Neil forgot completely about murder, death and unanswered questions, and concentrated on pleasure.

When it was over Susan retired to the bathroom, soaked a towel in warm water and returned to bed where she lovingly attended to her husband.

"Do you feel more relaxed now?" she asked as she patted him down, sprinkling baby powder across his abdomen and genital area.

"I owe you one," he replied contentedly.

"Just relax, honey. Clear your mind of everything. Would you like me to fix you something to eat?"

"Sure," he said as he propped himself on the pillow, "but first come over here and let me hold you."

After several moments of silence, locked in tender embrace, Susan asked: "Well, what do you think of my scenario?"

Bob smiled. "It's a little far-fetched," he said, dismissing the premise as being "too James Bondish."

"Maybe," she said, unaffected by his doubt. "Maybe, not."

"We're dealing with the South American drug mafia. What interest do they have in mystery? They push drugs. . ."

"Yes, but they're also involved in a lot of other things."

Bob, kissed Susan's forehead and smiled lovingly. "I don't know Susan. If I had even the slightest inclination as to what to look for, I'd follow the lead. You know that."

"But Bob," she persisted, "You always said a good cop never dismisses anything. I mean, obviously they were trying to hide a couple bodies. Maybe they panicked when they discovered that Dawson saw the more important of the two. Maybe they tried to kill Dawson because he found out *who* that second body was."

"I've already arrived at that conclusion. . ."

"Then pursue it," Susan prompted.

Bob smiled again, his interest was piqued. Susan's hypothesis was an alluring one. "A man with white hair," he thought out loud. "A man with white hair. Discovered in Vermont. South American hit men. Assassination attempts. Carlos Ortega. Gomez. A man with white hair.

A man with white hair. Who? There must be ten thousand men in this city with white hair."

They rested in bed together for almost fifteen minutes trying to piece the puzzle together, each trying to answer the one unresolved question: Who was the man with white hair.

"Pass me the remote will you, honey," O'Neil said motioning for the remote control to the television set. "Let's see what the news says."

Susan reached for the control and clicked the set on as she passed the device to her husband. The television screen brightened just as the morning news, concerning a Mass and breakfast in honor of Bishop Michelsen's historic trip to Rome was concluding. O'Neil laughed. "See what I mean, Susan, even the bishop has..."

His sentence was cut short by the ringing of the phone. Propping himself against the backboard of his bed he reached for the receiver and lifted it to his ear. "This better not be the office," he said, placing his hand over the receiver. "Hello," he said cheerfully.

"Dawson! Is that you? Yes... Yes, operator I'll accept the call," he said excitedly.

"Oh my God, Bob. Is it really Dawson? He's alive?" Susan said as she jumped up, and resting on her knees, her hands pressed on her husband's chest, asked: "Where is he, Bob. Say something."

O'Neil waved her remarks away, covering the phone with one hand. "He told me not to say anything just listen... Yes, Dawson, I'm here. I was just telling Susan you were alive. Yes... Yes, go ahead," he said, his face reflecting disbelief. "What? Dawson.... Yes, I understand... Yes..." His brow wrinkled as he gazed past Susan into the television set. "I can't believe this, Dawson..."

"Bob, please... What is going on?" Susan implored.

"Dawson, how can you expect me to convince the commissioner and the mayor and the fucking press that this man is an imposter..."

"What?" Susan cried as she turned her attention to the television screen, her eyes filled with tears as she glimpsed the man with white hair.

"Dawson, he just celebrated Mass — and had breakfast with the mayor for chrissake. Yes... Yes... I understand..." As impossible as Dawson's story was, it fit. Damn, did it fit, O'Neil thought, as he acknowledged Dawson's directions. "I'll keep an eye out for her," Bob said, signalling for Susan to take a note. "What's her name? Carmen? Carmen Ortega." That was the C. Ortega on the resident list, he recalled. "Yes, I'll be at the airport. I'll make arrangements for you to be on the flight... What's his name? Rivero? Okay!... Him too. Yes... Trust me Dawson, I'll be there. I'll be there... See you then..."

When O'Neil finished, Susan collapsed into his arms and wept. "Oh, Bob... this can't be happening. Bishop Michelsen is the man with white hair?

"Yes," he answered distantly. "Yes."

"Where's Dawson, now?"

"You won't believe it. He's in Peru. But he's okay," he added quickly when Susan sobbed, "He escaped from the fire and shootout, and is on his way home. We don't have much time, Susan, I've got to get going. . ."

They rose from bed and dressed quickly. Bob explaining what Dawson told him; Susan, listening intently, concerned for her husband's safety.

"What if they're waiting at the airport for you — and Dawson?" she asked, referring to the people who shot up Allston Street Monday evening.

"I won't be alone, Susan," Bob said reassuringly, strapping his shoulder holster over his arm.

"Oh, damn," Susan said in exasperation when she couldn't reach a button on her dress.

"Here, let me help, you," Bob said as he walked behind and fastened the button for her. "Relax, honey. Everything will turn out just fine."

"I'll never know why they put buttons on the back of women's clothing," Susan humphed as she smoothed her hand over her pantyhose, exposing the full length of her leg as she pulled.

"Susan," Bob said as they completed dressing and prepared to leave. "After work tonight, I want you to go over to your mother's house. Don't come right home. I may be late. And I'll want to know that your somewhere safe."

"I don't understand," Susan said concerned, worried.

"Look, Sue, Just trust me, please. When you're finished work, do as I ask. I'll call you as soon as I know everything is okay. . ."

"Do you think that the people who are after Dawson, might come after you?"

"I know I may be a little paranoid about this whole thing. But I'd just feel better knowing you were not here alone tonight." he said as he led her to the front door. "It may be nothing, but these drug cases bother me. Christ," he said, shaking his head as he stopped and embraced his wife, before parting, "One of these days I'm going to transfer to an easy job like homicide."

"Hold me," Susan said as she drew her husband closer and kissed him passionately on the lips. "I'll be at my mother's. But call me as soon as you hear something. Promise?"

"I promise," he said as they kissed one more time, then went their separate ways.

For his part, O'Neil would not follow departmental procedure on this case. It was imperative that Dawson be on the 10:15 A.M. flight leaving Lima. It was already 9:10. He would approach John Geary, explain the situation briefly, then ask him to pull whatever federal strings had to be pulled to get Dawson on the morning flight.

"I know it's not easy, John," O'Neil said as he paced back and forth in Geary's office. "John, I don't have the time to run this thing through city channels. They'll laugh me right out of the station if I tell them that Bishop Michelsen is dead, after he just ate breakfast with the fucking mayor. You've got to help me on this thing. We've got to get Dawson out of Peru. He's the only one who can corroborate this incredible story."

"Jesus, Bob," O'Neil pleaded. "Do you have any idea what you're asking?"

"Time is cutting like a knife, Bob. You just have to trust me. I believe Dawson is correct. We can't allow that plane to leave until he arrives back in Boston this evening."

Geary, stood, then walked over to his window and gazed outside - unfocused. He drew a deep breath, then exhaled vigorously, turned and faced O'Neil again. "If you're wrong, Bob, we'll end up up shits creek."

O'Neil bit his lip and looked at his watch. "It's 9:25, John."

Geary reached for the phone and dialed Washington. "I want Bill Hamilton's office," he said, when the line was answered. "Margorie," he said, addressing his immediate supervisor's personal secretary, "I need to talk with Bill. An emergency has developed rather suddenly up here in Boston. It can't wait."

O'Neil stopped his pacing and sat nervously as Geary waited for his boss to pick up his line.

"Is he in?" O'Neil asked impatiently.

Geary signalled with his hand that he was. "Bill," he said, "as soon as the phone was answered. "It's John Geary. . ."

O'Neil listened anxiously as Geary ran through an abbreviated explanation of events of the past few days. There were two kidnapped Americans waiting to board a 10:15 flight from Lima, Peru, he told his superior. They have no passports, no money, no identification. Just names: Dawson Page and someone named Rivero. They have to be on that morning flight. It's a matter of national importance, he said.

Geary played his cards well. "There isn't enough time right now for me to go into more detail," Geary responded when confronted with

the bureaucratic answer that *it* couldn't be arranged in so short a
time. "I'll take full responsibility for this thing, Bill," he said as he
increased his pressure to act. "At exactly 10:00 A.M. this morning,
Peru time, two men will walk up to the ticket counter and identify
themselves as Page and Rivero. If they're not on that goddamned
plane, Bill, heads will roll — from there to here. . . No I'm not threatening you, Bill, for chrissake," he said after Hamilton protested the
implied warning that if *he* didn't pull the necessary strings, it would be
his head that rolled first.

O'Neil stood and began pacing once again. "Bureaucrats! Jesus!"

"Done!" Geary said pointedly, in response to his superior's insistence that he, John Geary, take full responsibility for the operation,
especially if anything went wrong. "It will all be in my report, Bill. I
assure you. . . Yes, I'll be at the airport personally to greet them.
Yes. . ." Geary said again, growing impatient with Hamilton's persis-
tent line of questioning. "Look, Bill, it's already 9:30. You've go to
make those calls. You've got to trust me on this one, Bill, That's all I
can say right now. I've got other things to do right now. . ."

It was only Geary's reputation as one of the best senior agents
which kept him from being terminated on the spot for giving orders
to *his* boss. This, and the fact that he was rumored to be in line for an
important promotion with a chair next to the director himself. Geary
was a man who played his hunches — and his hunches always paid off.
Therefore, as unorthodox as his request was, the two Americans
would be personally delivered into the hands of the American diplo-
matic community — and with torn and bloodied clothes, be permitted to board the flight from Lima to Boston as hoped.

"Thanks John," O'Neil said as he rushed to the door, prepared to
bring his men together for a special assignment at Logan Airport.

"Call me this afternoon," Geary said as Dawson turned to leave.

"I'll do better than, John. I'll call you from the station after I make a
pitch to the commissioner to let me follow my instincts on this thing."

"I'll be in my office, Bob," Geary said, patiently. "I'll be waiting for
that call."

O'Neil boarded the elevator, convinced he would succeed with his
plan.

As he gazed out the window, waiting to watch O'Neil leave from the
side exit, Geary noticed something peculiar. There were two cars
parked along the sidewalk across the street. Two beat up old cars.
Obviously, not government personnel. They were parked outside the
New Sudbury Street exit, their engines running, as evidenced by the
grayish exhaust emanating from their tail pipes. And it appeared there

were men sitting in both front and rear seats. Yet nobody was moving. And this, itself, was odd, since the JFK building was at a high level of alert, and neither automobiles nor pedestrians were encouraged to gather alongside the building for more than a few minutes. So why were those vehicles parked there?

Geary stepped back to his desk, reached for the phone and dialed building security. He continued to stare out the window, straining to see activity on the street below. "Yes, security," he said when the front desk answered, "This is John Geary at DEA. I want to report two automobiles park along the New Sudbury side of the building..."

The sound of automatic gunfire disrupted the routine of morning traffic below as half a dozen men, each armed with automatic weapons, opened fire on the exit immediately under Geary's window. The exit, O'Neil was leaving from.

"Sonofabitch!" Geary shouted as he threw the receiver on his desk, grabbed the gun from his drawer and ran for the stairs as quickly as he could. Racing from level to level, skipping whole blocks of stairs in his rush to reach the lobby, Geary prayed there were no visitors or staff near the front entrance when the shooting erupted.

The hit team struck quickly and vanished immediately after they accomplished what they set out to do.

Geary flew down the last several stairs, crashing through a side door leading directly to the lobby. The sound of screams and wailing filled the building as employees and visitors began to realize what happened: Boston had once again been struck by terrorist violence.

"Oh my God!" Geary murmured when he reached the entrance. The hall was filled with glass, and chunks of building and bloodied bodies, sprawled grotesquely along the floor. "This, can't be," he said softly as he lowered his weapon and walked, stunned, through the debris and dead. No one in the hallway had survived the initial volley.

Geary paused, and gazed around. Where's O'Neil?

A man's hand reached out and touched his shoulder, startling him momentarily. "Jesus, John. Are you okay?" It was O'Neil.

Geary turned and embraced his friend. "I thought they were after you, Bob. I thought you were down here. One of them," he said pointing to the bodies lying on the floor.

"Not this time, John," O'Neil said as he surveyed the cost in human lives of this latest attack. "What the hell's going on, John. How did it ever get this way? What do they want?"

"Let's give a hand," Geary said, as police and security, joined by other government employees, arrived and tended to the dead.

Within minutes ambulances from the Boston City and Mass General hospitals could be heard rushing to the scene. Police officers from District One head-quarters located almost directly across the street also joined the effort to restore order, and calm the crowd of curious, horrified onlookers, numbering now in the hundreds.

"I better continue down the station, John," O'Neil said as he removed a handkerchief from his pocket and dabbed the perspiration building on his forehead. "It looks like it's going to be one of those days."

"Everyone's going to be asking for answers, Bob," Geary said as he accompanied O'Neil outside past the crowd and police lines. "Since I placed the initial call about the cars, I better hang around for a while and see what assistance I can offer."

"Yeah," O'Neil said apprehensively. "Look, John, I'm having second thoughts about this thing. . ."

"Oh, shit, Bob. Not after I called. . ."

"No, not about that," O'Neil answered. "I'm having second thoughts about opening this thing up too far. With Gomez. . ." he said, shaking his head, not finishing his sentence, ". . .and then this. . ."

"What are you suggesting?" Geary asked.

"I'm thinking that maybe I'll run this by the commissioner. Ask him to let me cover the airport just in case. Tell him I'm following up a lead. No more."

"You really like to walk on the edge, don't you."

O'Neil laughed. "Not hardly. . ., " he said rubbing his face. "But this thing is getting out of hand. I just feel the less people who know the better."

"Okay, look Bob, I've got to get back inside," Geary said as an ambulance backed onto the sidewalk. "We've got to get this mess cleaned up. . ."

"I'll be at the airport tonight, John. Say, quarter till six. I expect I'll see you there."

Geary sighed. "Oh, you can count on it, Bob. This is one arrival and departure I wouldn't miss for the world."

27
The Confrontation

The time was 5:30 P.M. After scheduled stops in Panama City and Miami, Page and Rivero were finally on their way to Boston. They were joined on the 4:00 P.M. flight from Miami by two FBI, and one DEA agent. By special arrangement with the airline, the first class section of the plane was reserved for these five men — and for good reason.

During most of the flight Page and Rivero were questioned at length about their kidnapping, their eventual escape, and the plot alluded to by Agent John Geary. And in a broader sense, Rivero gave them startling information about -and insight into a drug syndicate they never knew: The *Voluntad de Dios*.

Rivero's narrative was compelling as he detailed a worldwide drug empire so vast and so powerful that few governments had the resources or manpower to deal with it independently. He spoke of an unholy alliance developing between narcotic dealers and terrorists, and of a new phenomenon, narco-terrorism. "You cannot stop us, gentlemen," he intoned gravely. "You have no idea what you are up against, or *who* the real enemy is. Do you want to know who your greatest enemy is? No, let me tell you: It is your very people. They have been our greatest allies all along. Don't you see it? Who do you think lies and steals and kills for us? Who do you think supports us? Who do you think pushes our poison? If it were not for you Americans we would all be poor farmers."

The agents sat in stunned silence, literally hypnotized by Rivero's boundless knowledge of the subject. "Los Grandes Mafiosos feeds cocaine to terrorist organizations worldwide. Just look at what we accomplished during your Vietnam War — both in your country and abroad. We used every useful idiot who wanted what we sold. But in those days it was different," he emphasized, forcefully, "In those days we operated as a business, with business interests in every capital. As dangerous as we were, we were nowhere near as dangerous as the threat imposed by the newer groups operating today. The new leaders *do* care about your political motivations. They feed drugs to your society not for profit, but for political destabalization. Your people want ecstasy: They want your people. It's that simple."

Rivero detailed how the drug empire trades drugs for money supporting terrorist organizations such as the IRA, the Spanish ETA, the Red Brigades, the PLO, and the Lebanese Hezbollah, "You don't think the man who drove that truck into the marine barracks in Lebanon was acting on his own do you?" he asked. "We provide drugs, you provide your own destruction."

It all seemed so incredible, yet somehow it all made sense. "But there is a matter of more immediate concern," Rivero concluded, "We must ensure the safety of the young girl, Carmen. She holds the key to unraveling what's been going on over the years. She has in her possession the names of contacts, drop points, routes, hidden jungle camps, corrupt police officials, prosecutors, judges and media people friendly to our cause. She must be protected."

The agents assured Rivero his wishes would be honored. Their instructions were to question the two men, then deliver them to John Geary in Boston. If Carmen Ortega had information on the drug syndicate, she would be extended the full protection of the United States Government.

"If what you have told us is true," one of the agents said, "We could have a break here bigger than when Joe Valachi came forward and informed on La Cosa Nostra. But if that is the case," he added ominously, "all your lives will be in jeopardy from this day forward. You understand that?" he asked as he leaned across the small cocktail table separating the men. "As long as these people wield such power, and have such influence, with all that money at their disposal, our guarantees — I want to be perfectly frank about all this—are not ironclad."

Page and Rivero nodded their understanding, then asked when the interviewing was completed, if they could eat, then rest for the remainder of their flight. They knew the confrontation at Logan Airport could be explosive and tragic if it was not contained. They slept — and would not be awakened until the stewardess tapped their shoulders and informed them they were on their descent into Boston.

For her part, Carmen Ortega spent most of the day preparing. She slept at the YWCA Tuesday evening, but left early Wednesday morning when she suspected authorities were being called to question her about her parents, and where she lived. So, once again, Carmen was alone.

Yet, as nervous as she was, she was also at peace with herself. Carmen had no more tears to shed. Her parents were killed by the same monsters who killed her husband. . . and Rivero. Now, she would exact her revenge by preventing the switch from taking place. It was all so mechanical. I will purchase a long knife, and I will be at the airport waiting for this false bishop. I will wave at him and smile — then plunge the knife into his stomach as hard as I can. And then, I too, will die.

Carmen practiced the trip to Logan Airport earlier in the day, and was amazed by the volume of traffic on American Streets. Indeed, sometime around 9:30 that morning the streets were filled with police cars and ambulances racing to and from one of the larger buildings situated on the Boston side of the Callahan Tunnel — an underwater connector which runs across and beneath Boston Harbor between East Boston, the airport, and Downtown.

"There was a shooting over there just a while ago," the cab driver informed her, pointing to the buildings along New Sudbury Street as he dodged around cars and through busy intersections. "It came over the radio this morning. They think it has something to do with the shootout the other night. I tell 'ya miss, this whole country's going to shit." He glanced over his shoulder and added, "Excuse the English."

Carmen smiled and nodded sheepishly, and said nothing for the remainder of the trip.

"You just want me to drop you off at the terminal, wait, and drive you back downtown again, right?" he asked as they arrived outside the main terminal.

"Yes, please," Carmen said softly. "My parents will be flying to Boston later this evening and I want to be certain I know where to greet them."

"Whatever you want, kid," the driver said as he parked in front of the TWA terminal. Normally he would question someone as young as Carmen, but she was dressed well and spoke with a certain air of authority.

Carlos' advice paid it's first dividend, she thought, as she stepped from the cab and entered the building. She acted self-assured, and was, therefore, believed to be doing exactly what she said she was doing. "And what time will the plane be leaving for Rome this evening?" she asked. "Will we have an opportunity to see the bishop off? Oh? There will be a press conference? Where?" Yes, Carmen planned her actions carefully. She would be at that press conference — waiting.

Waiting, that's the hardest part of an undercover cop's job. But waiting for tonight was especially difficult for Lieutenant O'Neil. Working quietly, and behind the scenes, O'Neil assembled a small, select undercover unit to accompany him to Logan Airport. His team consisted of five other Boston police officers and himself. Six altogether. And with John Geary and Lieutenant Dowling, who asked to accompany them, eight.

When conducting surveillance operations on airport property, local police are expected to notify airport security and the state police, since the airport is under state jurisdiction. When O'Neil informed Massport authorities of his operation, he was afforded complete cooperation. With assistance from Massport, O'Neil's force of eight officers was supplemented with an additional seven personnel — five plain clothes and three state policemen. In all, there would be fifteen police officers assigned to this one location.

For most of the afternoon, O'Neil briefed his men, explaining the facts as he understood them. "Why not just arrest the bishop, now?" one of his men asked. "And worry about the details later?" But even without answering, everyone knew that that option was impossible. Arrest him for what? For not sounding like the bishop. He had the flu! And what if they were wrong? What if Dawson was mistaken?

O'Neil let the question slide. "We have to respect their intelligence," he cautioned his men. "With everything that has been going on, they still have no reason to believe we know of their plans. And remember, we still don't have a body." He was referring to the real Bishop Michelsen.

"And one other thing," O'Neil intoned, gravely. "We cannot overlook the shootout on Allston Street, or this morning's attack at the Kennedy building, right across the street from our own station. There's no telling what these people will do if we come on like gangbusters. We can't jeopardize a hostage situation developing, or another gunfight occurring in the middle of a busy airport terminal. Caution will be the operative word. I want everyone to keep their guns holstered at all times. Is that clear?" he asked, surveying each of his men carefully as he spoke. "I want everyone in predesignated positions. No one is to make a move until we have concrete evidence

— either from Page, Rivero or Carmen Ortega, that a felony has occurred, and this man is not who he says he is. Understood?"

After each officer nodded his understanding, surveillance teams were designated. One man was assigned as a flight attendant working in the plane's doorway. One, as a ticket agent. One would sit as a lookout in an unmarked car at the front of the terminal. Two would be stationed in the lobby, between the gate and the car. Geary would be the central communications manager, and was positioned near where the press conference was to occur. He would apprise each member of the other's movements. If trouble developed, each man would respond immediately to the point of conflict. O'Neil and Dowling would pose as passengers, since they expected Page to arrive on time, and they knew what he looked like. Three uniformed state police officers were assigned ostensibly to provide security at the press conference. And four plain clothes officers would be posing as passengers in the boarding area.

With the exception of uniformed state police officers, who would normally patrol the airport, the bishop's arrival at the boarding gate would elicit no apparent additional presence of interest.

That was the first thing Pablo Ernesto Madrid, now Bishop Michelsen, noticed as he stepped from his privately chauffeured automobile and walked to the reservation desk at the TWA reception area. There was a sense of business as usual throughout the airport. He liked that. It reassured him. Despite the sudden absence of Brother Dominic, Monday evening, everything appeared to be going along as planned.

His actions would be those of a cautious and prudent man from this point onward. Once outside the United States it would be virtually impossible to prevent him from carrying out his plan. And, as he looked at his watch — it was 5:55 P.M. — he realized how soon that time would arrive.

After verifying his reservation and seating arrangements, he was asked to conduct one last official act before boarding the plane. Meet with members of the press, but only briefly, after all, even members of the media understood his need for rest. They had better understand, he thought, having asked Sister Margaret earlier to contact the media and inform them of his physical condition.

His demeanor was one of supreme confidence as he arrived in the passenger area, acknowledging the applause of well wishers — none of whom he recognized. Nevertheless, he blessed each and every one of them as if they were his closest friends. Can never be too cautious, he reminded himself as he stepped behind the podium provided for this very occasion.

He glanced around the crowd, meekly, and smiled humbly at his admirers. And he posed benevolently for the cameras as they clicked and churned, capturing the image he wanted to leave with his — victims.

"My dearest children in Christ," he began, slowly and deliberately, "Our Lord has truly blessed us with His love. . ."

As Madrid continued his hoax and addressed the two dozen people gathered directly before him, flight 817 from Miami was taxiing to its docking platform on the other side of the airport.

Page and Rivero sat patiently, waiting for the passenger canopy to reach the forward area of the plane. The strain and worry of the past few days reflected on their haggard faces. And although neither man spoke, each knew exactly what would be expected of him if anything went wrong.

"Mr. Page?" the co-pilot said as he exited the front cabin and walked to the middle of the first class section where they were seated. "Lieutenant O'Neil of the Boston Police Department has asked that you be escorted immediately over to the TWA terminal." Then directing his attention to the agents, he informed them that a Mr. John Geary would be waiting for them once they arrived.

The men rose, solemnly, and adjusted their clothing. "Well gentlemen," the DEA agent said, "If everything you say is true, this is where it all begins. I wish you both good luck," he said, extending his hand to Page, then Rivero. "For your security, gentlemen, please stay between the agent in front and to the rear. Let's go!" And the five men hurried through the portable walkway to the inside of the terminal.

Their escape from Peru went undetected. There were no armed men waiting for them in the lobby. No sticks of dynamite beneath chairs or in lockers. Indeed, although the terminal was busy with activity, few people even noticed their arrival. A good sign.

"It's good to be back in the United States," Page confided to Rivero, who looked straight ahead and nodded his agreement as they were whisked across the wet pavement between the two terminals.

As they approached the area where Madrid was concluding his conference, they observed the bright glare of television lights, and flashes of newspaper cameras. And their hearts raced as they drew closer and closer to the man who replaced Bishop Michelsen only six days ago. Remarkable, they thought as they closed in. The plan almost succeeded.

"It can't be permitted to happen here," Rivero said as he halted abruptly, observing the bishop slowly make his way through the crowd. "Too many people around. Make contact with your friend, Dawson, and ask him to wait until Madrid boards the plane."

Page agreed. "Bob! Bob O'Neil, Page said as he moved to greet his close friend. "It's so good seeing you here? You and the wife going away?" he asked loudly to divert attention or suspicion. O'Neil understood. "Not here, Bob," Page whispered as the men embraced. "Too many people. Wait until we have him isolated inside."

"Why, Dawson, you old son-of-a-gun. It's great to see you again," O'Neil responded, as the entourage of cameramen ignored the two friends and followed the bishop to the boarding area, where the receptionist was instructed to allow the bishop to enter quickly.

When the press had passed, O'Neil signalled his men to hold their positions. Once the bishop was on board they would seal the airplane and confront him directly. He then raised his walkie-talkie, and speaking barely above a whisper said: "Dowling, meet me at the refreshment stand." This was the code for all men to assemble at the ticket gate.

"Damn, it's good to see you alive, Dawson," O'Neil sighed as he gazed over Dawson's shoulder, and saw a young girl approach the bishop with a bouquet of roses in her hand.

"Thank God this whole thing will soon be over," he said, feeling relieved, paying no attention to the exchange about to take place in front of him.

"I have someone I want you to meet, Bob," Page said as he introduced Rivero.

"You're Brother Dominic?" O'Neil asked.

"Yes," Rivero answered calmly, straining to see the young girl standing with Madrid. Then, his expression changed from relief to horror when he realized 'who' the young girl was. "Oh my God. That's Carmen."

Madrid was taking no chances. As he walked through the boarding area he stopped and placed his arm around the shoulder of the young girl carrying the boquet of flowers. "Come my child," he said to the weeping girl, "Accompany me to my seat," he said, asking the flight attendant if it would be acceptable for him to walk with the youthful well-wisher.

Carmen squeezed under the rope and walked beside the man, his arm draped firmly on the back of her neck. All eyes were fixed intently on the two as they ambled leisurely toward the plan's door — talking, smiling. The media relished the image. A truly humble and loving man.

Amidst the glowing reports of television anchorpersons, and the favorably descriptive chatter of newspaper columnists, Page, Rivero, O'Neil and Dowling pushed their way to the front of the crowd. And their breathing quickened and their hearts raced — fearing something was terribly wrong.

Very slowly, Carmen reached into the roses she was carrying — and grabbed what appeared to be the handle of a long, silver object.

"No!" Rivero shouted, startling the people around him. "Carmen, don't!"

She turned and faced Rivero. Madrid turned, his face contorted. The flight attendant, who was a member of the Boston Police Department, turned, confused.

Madrid squinted in an attempt to get a better look at who had shouted. He clutched Carmen's shoulder. Then squeezed it. Then, when he suspected something was not right, he tightened his grip around her neck and began to choke her, stepping backward, sensing at first, then realizing the hoax was discovered. But how could this be? His eyes were wide and wild as he looked in disbelief at Brother Dominic standing with three other men.

As quickly as the police officer beside him lunged, Madrid grabbed the roses from Carmen's hands and jammed what he thought were the stems into the man's face and throat, wishing he had a knife, instead. Then, he noticed that that was exactly what he was holding. He laughed maniacally as he plunged the blade again and again into the man's face and throat.

The crowd grew deadly silent, and stood in shock and disbelief over what they were observing.

"This was planned for me?" Madrid shouted, his voice filled with rage and fury. Panic and fear ignited the crowd as police officers drew their guns and shouted for everyone to lie down. Women wept and men called for their families to stay together and do as they were told. The mortally wounded police officer's eyes were open and glazed. He sensed his imminent death as he felt his life blood spurting from his severed artery.

"It's over, Madrid. Step away from the girl and raise your hands," O'Neil ordered as he withdrew his weapon and stepped forward.

Madrid's head turned frantically from left to right, and sweat beaded on his brow as he considered his next actions. There were police officers everywhere, it seemed. Still kneeling over the dying police officer, and clutching the young girl for protection, Madrid grabbed the knife, then reaching into the officers belt, withdrew a .38 caliber service revolver. He laughed maniacally. "Well what do we have here?"'" he said as he stood, waving the gun about, pulling the girl closer to his body.

As he pulled her closer he could feel her firm, round buttocks against his pelvis — and he wiggled suggestively into her in a mocking, sexual manner. Carmen, cried out, but to no avail as he lowered his arm from her neck and squeezed her breasts.

"Let her go Madrid," Rivero shouted, as he stepped forward. "Take me in her place. I know as much as she does. If you need a hostage, I'll go willingly."

"Step forward!" Madrid shouted, his voice quivering with bridled emotion.

Rivero did as he was told.

Madrid raised his weapon and shot Rivero.

The crowd screamed as Rivero fell backward, knocked off his feet by the violent impact of the bullet.

"Hold your fire! Hold your fire!" O'Neil ordered, as he stepped in front of Dawson and Dowling. "I don't want any shooting," he motioned as he turned and faced his men who were kneeling with weapons poised. "Not if we can avoid it."

"You three step forward. Now!" Madrid ordered as he moved further back toward the canopy. His breathing was heavy and uneven. "I am warning you — all of you — don't try anything or the girl will be the first to die," he shouted above the cries of onlookers.

"Just hold your position men," O'Neil urged.

Page's eyes were fixed on Rivero who, although still breathing, was lying in a puddle of his own blood. Something's got to give, Page said to himself as he drew alongside his friend, O'Neil.

"You fucking Americans think you have it all figured out. You oppress the working people of the world with your capitalist money, thinking you can buy friendship. We will crush you!" Madrid spat. "We will annihilate you!" he babbled. Pushing Carmen in front, he changed direction and instead of pulling back, headed toward the three men standing before him. He waved his gun menacingly as he proceeded. "I want the television cameras turned on," he shouted, firing a shot into the roof of the building. "Did you hear what I said? I want the cameras turned on. Now! I will make a statement," he shouted bitterly, his face contorted in anger. "I want to be flown to Cuba If there are any tricks this young girl will die."

"Please. . ." Carmen begged,

"Shut up!" he ordered as he slapped the side of his gun against her cheek. Carmen cried and sobbed uncontrollably.

"You'll never pull this off," O'Neil said angrily, as he inched his way closer to Madrid.

Another shot rang out as O'Neil fell to the floor.

Again, people screamed and wept and sobbed and pleaded for the entire affair to end. "Jesus Christ," Dowling shouted as he turned left and right, lifting his badge for all the officers to see. "Hold your fire, men. Hold your fire."

Madrid was obviously crazy, and believed he stood nothing to lose. Page, meanwhile had knelt beside his fallen friend and embraced him, feeling O'Neil's warm blood soak into his shirt.

"You'll get what you want, Madrid. Just let the girl go and we will guarantee your transport out of the country. . ."

"What do you take me for?" Madrid shouted in a frenzy, now. Sweating profusely, he began to step back again, dragging Carmen with him.

The confusion had given Page sufficient time, with his back to Madrid, to remove O'Neil's weapon. He lowered O'Neil gently, checking his friend's strained breathing as he lie motionless. Dawson wiped O'Neil's brow, saying: "I'm sorry, Bob," then stood with the gun by his side and faced Madrid.

"You!" Madrid shouted at Page. "Step forward or you will be the next to die," he said as he inched his way back further down the hallway leading to the plane's front door. "Everyone else stay where you are."

Dawson and Dowling followed Madrid cautiously, Dawson staring into the frightened eyes of young Carmen. Yet, it wasn't Carmen he saw, it was the face of the young girl he shot twenty years ago. Tears welled in his eyes as he recalled how she died. Not again, Dawson sobbed to himself as he tightened his grip on the revolver.

As Madrid ordered, cameras were turned on, recording the entire occurrence before one hundred thousand stunned viewers. A live kidnapping and hijacking at Logan Airport.

"Lieutenant," Page said grabbing Dowling's arm gently by the elbow. "Get behind me right now."

"Dawson, don't do anything foolish. . ."

Dawson stepped in front of Dowling, and took a deep breath.

Madrid, meanwhile, was frothing with rage. His eyes were darting wildly back and forth. As he inched back further he taunted Carmen by squeezing and pinching her breasts. He was fully intending on raping the young girl and throwing her out the plane's door, first chance he had.

"What's going on?" Madrid shouted, waving his gun in Page's direction. He didn't understand the shift in position of the two men closest to him. "You, the man in back," Madrid cried, "step out front where I can see you. Right now!"

"Stay where you are Lieutenant. It's over." Page said.

"It's over Madrid," Page shouted as he raised his weapon. "There will be no flight to Cuba. No negotiating. No hostage taking. . ."

"What?" a newly arrived police officer from the state's crisis intervention team said as he stepped cautiously over the throng of people who were still lying on the floor along the walkway. "There will be no more shooting."

"I told you to get down. . ." Madrid shrieked in an ungodly voice as he fired another round over the head of the approaching officer. "Now, you two, get down," he said, addressing Dowling and Page. Dowling stretched out flat. Dawson remained standing.

"What is this," Madrid shouted as the cameras churned. "What the fuck is going on here? You think nothing of your life?" he shouted as he turned the gun to Carmen's head. "You will drop your gun or I will shoot the girl," he said, waving the revolver in front of the cameras.

"I couldn't care less what you do Madrid. Shoot her. Shoot me. I'm going to blow your fucking head off one way or the other."

"Jesus Christ, Page, get down," Dowling ordered.

For one excruciatingly long moment there was complete silence — except for the whir of cameras. "I'm not running, Madrid. I'm not getting down on my knees for you. I'm one American imperialist who says: Go fuck yourself. Now make your move."

Madrid cocked his revolver and smiled as he placed the tip of the barrel in Carmen's ear.

Page's jaw tightened as he lifted his revolver, cocking the hammer as his arm levelled at shoulder's height.

"And now you will die," Madrid whispered into Carmen's ear.

Carmen lunged forward, bending at the waist, exposing Madrid's upper torso. "Shoot him pleeease," she screamed in a high-pitched voice.

The words were no sooner out of her mouth when Page fired the first shot which smashed into Madrid's right collar bone, causing him to release the girl completely and scream in pain. He stumbled backward firing wildly, uncontrollably, reflexively. The second shot followed almost immediately, splattering a rib and piercing a lung, causing Madrid to gag spasmodically and spit up blood. Then everyone began firing. Windows shattered, walls exploded and people cried in terror during the brief eruption of gun fire. Carmen, who learned from Carlos what to do in situations such as this, dropped to the floor at the first volley. And Madrid, after being pummelled and bounced back and forth from the impact of .38 and .357 slugs finally fell dead.

"Jesus Christ," an excited reported blurted into his microphone. "They just shot Bishop Michelsen — or a man posing as him. It's not clear yet which. The scene here at Logan Airport, ladies and gentlemen, is one of unbelievable terror as what appears to be three Boston police officers and one man — named Madrid, lie dead in the walkway leading to TWA's flight 315 leaving for Rome, Italy. Men and women — apparently passengers and well wishers — are embracing and weeping openly as the ordeal has ended. And there is massive confusion all about the terminal as police officers rush to the man who brought it all to an end. We don't have his name yet, nor the name of the brave young girl who placed her own life in jeopardy so the police could get a clear shot at the man named Madrid. As soon as we have their names, we'll update you further on what has occurred."

28
The Will of God

June 30, Sunday.

2:30P.M. The wounds received during the confrontation at Logan Airport would eventually heal. And both Rivero and Lieutenant O'Neil were assured their recoveries would be complete. It was during the first few days of their stay in the hospital that unsettling events began occurring which accelerated after the first reporting, and snowballed thereafter, causing genuine panic throughout the United States — then the world.

When he was well enough to sit up in bed — which was Wednesday, the 29th of May, Rivero began asking if he could peruse the dozens of newspapers and national magazines which had accumulated beside his bed. He wanted to read them all, he said. And he did. The hospital staff thought his interest in local and national affairs was nothing more than a curious and quite normal preoccupation. After all, the confrontation at Logan Airport received international attention. His interest was much more than casual, though.

On May 24th, for instance, the first indication that the process had begun appeared in the newswire reports of the major dailies. United State's Senator Gary Rogers, a perfectly healthy specimen of a man, simply dropped dead on the floor of the United States Senate during a debate on the 23rd. Thirty-five minutes after that three members of the United States Congress similarly died.

By early Friday morning most dailies were holding their press runs as accounts of other mysterious deaths began pouring in through the wire services. Indeed, it was reported that on Friday alone, between Los Angeles and New York, sixty-two television actors similarly died. Three passed on during live broadcasts — in front of millions of viewers. Nineteen of the nation's most well-known movie stars, along with one-hundred and sixty-two lesser-known character actors were hospitalized and died within minutes of their emergency room visits.

In city after city thousands of deaths were reported. And there was no evident cause — or connection. The mysterious plague touched young and old alike. Affluent as well as poor. In Boston three hundred and seventy-five deaths were reported by Sunday. In Chicago, six hundred. In Rhode Island, over one thousand.

At first it was believed an extremely deadly form of Legionaires Disease was sweeping the nation. The National Center for Disease Control in Atlanta was placed on the highest level of alert. Sunday evening the President of the United States implored the nation's scientific community to find the cause of this "terrible and frightening epidemic sweeping our nation."

Then the rumor mills started. Based on an erroneous radio report originating in Philadelphia, half a dozen local television stations started reporting a national epidemic of AIDS. Word of this latest *finding* spread across the country, and in an unbelievably irresponsible fashion, onto each of the national networks faster than the rumor could be contained and proven false.

Riots in California between fanatics on both sides resulted in millions of dollars in damage, and over twenty-five deaths — mostly gay men.

Every ten minutes, it seemed, the nation's airways were filled with this single item: "We interrupt this program to bring you the latest news of the mysterious and sudden outbreak of deaths occurring among thousands of this nation's citizens."

On May 26th matters grew worse. The nationwide death toll rose to sixteen thousand. Then on the 27th, it was reported an additional nine thousand had been stricken and died, some sixty-five hundred of those, mostly minorities, under the age of sixteen.

It was an enterprising toxicologist in Colorado who first advanced the theory that the deaths did, in fact, have a common link. That was on Monday evening, May 27th, when it was reported an additional five thousand Americans died horrible deaths. "Each of the people I have examined — and there were twenty-six in all — every one of whom died —   he said, "used cocaine within twenty-four hours of their deaths. Whatever the substance is that is in the cocaine," he continued as he was interviewed by all three networks, "is, I believe, the culprit in these deaths. It is extremely lethal, and highly soluble once absorbed into the blood stream. That is why making a confirmation of this hypothesis is so difficult. We can only deduce this conclusion from the data we have gathered to date. But I am betting the cause is drug abuse."

And the death toll continued to mount. By press time early Tuesday morning, the 28th of May, the nationwide death toll touched forty-five thousand Americans from every walk of life, ranging in age from ten to sixty. The European account was somewhat lower, totalling seventeen thousand — mostly artists, professional people and young drifter types, which meant American students and visitors.

An answer had to be found. If the drug-related connection posed by Dr. Hubert Wall was valid, it had to be verified — and the flow of drugs stopped.

Rivero read, then reread each account daily since his release from the hospital. He would read until he grew too tired to read anymore. Then, he would close his eyes, sigh and place the pile of papers and magazines on the table beside his chair — and reflect. His actions confused Carmen, who thought he was feeling, somehow, personally responsible for what was occurring.

But Carmen was not the only one who suspected. Nor was she the first. "You know something about all this, don't you," Lieutenant O'Neil said one day as he looked across from his hospital bed. Rivero hadn't noticed O'Neil's interest in his daily ritual and fascination with the mounting death toll.

"I know nothing, Lieutenant, except what I read," Rivero answered quietly as he glanced across at O'Neil. Rivero liked Page's friend and didn't want to anger him, or arouse suspicion, after all, O'Neil was a pretty good cop. "Perhaps it's something they ate," Rivero observed dryly. "You know what they say about the water. . ."

O'Neil grimaced from a slight pain which shot through his body, then nodded and stared into Rivero's eyes. "You know something," he repeated, then closed his eyes and went to sleep. And never mentioned it again. Not even when they left the hospital.

I know something, Rivero repeated to himself as he rested on his easy chair with five weeks of paper clippings beside him. I know something, he thought, as he recounted the people he loved — and lost. He closed his eyes and thought of the close, fatherly friendship he knew with Carlos. He thought of his brother, Manuel. He thought of Bishop Michelsen — and of the decent and humble man he really was. His death was a tragic loss. And the body was never recovered. Yes, I know something, he said to himself as he thought of Carmen and

Dawson Page, the man who vowed to give his life to save a stranger named Rivero.

Rivero stretched, then groaned slightly, for his body ached and his mind was tired. He rested his head on the soft pillows placed behind him by Carmen and glanced at the magazine covers on his table. The picture which caught his attention was the one of Carmen, pleading with Page to shoot, captured that unforgettable day by a UPI photographer. Worldwide reproduction made her an instant celebrity. She symbolized so much to so many people. Her courage earned her a luncheon invitation to the White House, since the president's wife was actively involved with, and noted for her interest in publicizing the dangers of drug abuse. The First Lady was an eloquent spokeswoman for drug rehabilitation programs. But as each day passed there were fewer and fewer of the nation's youth willing to experiment with their lives.

And when the Vatican learned of her courage and humble background, and willingness to sacrifice her life that she might save the Holy Father, a personal invitation, signed by the Pontiff himself, soliciting a private audience was delivered.

Carmen's possession of the diary and her cooperation with the FBI and DEA earned her the respect and admiration of everyone with whom she worked. She was a remarkable young girl. Indeed, the diary provided such a wealth of information that the drug routes, the pushers — the big ones — who before seemed immune from prosecution, and literally hundreds of officials in six countries, including the United States, were rounded up and placed behind bars. There was simply no refuting what Carlos had written.

And when the pushers were arrested, and their refining plants located and destroyed, the few thousand of addicts who were wealthy enough to horde a sufficient quantity of the old supply of cocaine, but were now desperately in need of a new fix, began to talk up a storm. Hell hath no fury like a drug addict scorned, Rivero laughed.

The sound of a door bell ringing interrupted Rivero's concentration. "I'll get it, Rivero," Carmen said as she raced from her bedroom. And as she passed him, she squeezed his shoulder. Both she and Rivero knew who was calling this sunny afternoon. It was Dawson.

Since their meeting a few weeks ago, and the harrowing ordeal experienced by both at Logan Airport, the bond of friendship between Page and Rivero had matured and flourished.

"So, you have come to court my little girl," Rivero teased as Dawson and Carmen embraced at the door. "I am happy for both of you," he said with genuine affection as they entered.

"I guess you saw this morning's paper," Dawson said as he approached.

"I saw it, and approve wholeheartedly," Rivero said. They were referring to the arrests of forty-three mafia bosses, and seventy-five Latin-American drug mafiosos across the United States. The U.S. Attorney General's office indicated they would prosecute the American dealers and pushers as mass murderers, and accordingly set bail at over five-million for small time pushers and no bail for drug kings. The evidence was that strong! Indeed, public sentiment was running so heavily against these people, the national media likened the expected trials to those of Nazi war criminals.

And there was one other factor: Carlos' notes were so extensive, and his reference to people and places so thorough, and his attention to detail so excruciatingly accurate, the trials were more to meet the requirements of due process, rather than to establish guilt or innocence. Through legal wire taps, undercover surveillance, daring raids, and where the evidence was so compelling, outright arrests, the FBI and DEA, working with the full cooperation of local police departments across the United States, were able to effectively bring the drug trade to a virtual halt. The death toll was that staggering.

With the unexpected deaths of over fifty-five thousand Americans, the conscience of the country was jolted, and elected officials were required to take firm and decisive action against users, pushers and growers.

Pointing to a stack of clippings on the table, Rivero commented that he read everything about the change in American attitude toward the use of drugs. "Carlos, predicted this would happen," Rivero said as he reached for the letter Carmen was never to see.

"You don't mean that Carlos was responsible for all those deaths, do you?" Carmen asked in horror. She believed Carlos was a powerful force behind the business. She never suspected he would go to such an extreme as this.

"No, of course not," Rivero assured her as he patted her hand. "What I mean is that Carlos knew when he left Peru with you how dangerous the new bosses were — and he predicted they would not be as careful as he was. That's all."

Carmen smiled and hugged Rivero. "I am glad it's over — and we can all lead normal lives again."

"Of course," Rivero whispered in her ear.

"Dawson!" Rivero said, directing his attention to his friend. "Carmen is a young girl who will some day be very wealthy. She is beautiful now and desirable," he said. causing Carmen to blush. "I can see from the way you act toward one another that in time this caring and affectionate relationship will blossom into full love," he said, nodding his approval as he spoke. "And I wish you both all the happiness in the world. But. . ."

"Rivero, we're only going to a movie," Carmen interrupted. But Dawson knew what Rivero was saying.

"Everything you want for Carmen," Page said warmly, "I want too. I give you my word, Rivero, she will not be rushed or pushed — or forced to grow up faster than her years, even though she's been through a great deal already. I'm willing to let time heal all our wounds — and if by chance we are lucky enough to find love again," he said as he reached for Carmen and placed his arm around her waist, ". . . well, I don't want to walk away and lose her by default. . ."

"Well let me tell both of you something," Carmen said, "I know what I feel now, and I feel very lucky to have two men in my life who care for me. I like Dawson, Rivero — and I loved Carlos. I know the pleasures and responsibilities of married life. So. . ." she said as she patted Rivero's head and squeezed Dawson's waist, ". . .don't be too surprised if you both are doing exactly what I want you to do."

Rivero laughed. "I can see why Carlos was so beguiled by you," he said thoughtfully. "Be careful Dawson, she may be more dangerous than you think." Then he waved his hand and dismissed the two. "Now the two of you get out of here and let me read. I'll see you both later this evening."

"We'll be here," Page said as he escorted Carmen to the door.

When he was alone in the room, Rivero unfolded Carlos' letter and read it for the final time.

. . .Finally, my friend, I have taken measures to ensure that the Will of God, as I see it, is carried out. I have managed to deal with over fifty tons of refined cocaine headed for the United States. Carmen does not know of this, and I trust she never will know it was done by my hand. Because of the growth of our business operation we found in necessary to diversify operations. We can process and ship more refined cocaine when we operate this way, rather than compete for limited and extreme difficult to obtain materials. For our part we handle the acquisition of materials, primarily either, acetone and hydrochloric acid necessary to refine the paste. That was Manuel's suggestion. He calculated, correctly, that by controlling production at the first step, the refining stage, we could exert more control throughout the system. And he was right.

Shortly before his tragic death, Manuel managed to disperse sufficient quantities of a highly toxic chemical substance known only as

TE1 into the acetone supply. TE1 was discovered by the Russian scientist mentioned in the diary, and has proven to be effective in tests we ran. When the refined product is shipped to the United States and filtered into the population, the results will be dramatic and deadly.

Only an event as tragic as this will prevent it from ever happening again. Only by such a national tragedy will the American people wake up to the danger they face from groups such as ours. . .

Indeed, Rivero thought to himself as he folded the letter. He rose from his chair and carried the paper to the fireplace. He stood motionless for several moments, reflecting, remembering, then took a deep breath, and with a match burned the last remaining evidence which linked the actions of Carlos Ortega with the wholesale slaughter — and salvation of the American people.

As he watched the paper burn, he reflected on O'Neil's words. "You know something about all this, don't you."

I know nothing, Rivero whispered to himself as he watched the paper disintegrate in the flames. Why did it have to turn out this way? he thought, then shrugging, walked back to his easy chair and read.

Why, indeed, did it have to turn out this way, he thought, as he thumbed through the stack of magazines. Maybe it really was *The Will of God*, he smiled. Maybe it was.

The End

Of the first Dawson Page Mystery Adventure novel. Dawson Page will return next in *The Miller Expedition*, an archaeological thriller.

Dawson Page will return next in:

The Miller Expedition

On April 27, 1983, Professor Jonathan P. Miller and his entire archaeological expedition, consisting of seven university students and two Mexican guides, disappeared while on a *dig* in an obscure, isolated area of the Palenque region of southern Mexico. Dr. Miller was known to be working on a major research project involving the equally strange disappearance of the Mayan civilization which existed some one thousand years ago.

Until recently, it was believed Dr. Miller's non-published writings, which provided the only insight into his work on the project, would also provide investigators with tangible clues as to what might actually happened to cause the mysterious loss of the ten-person team.

Since no one had ever been able to decipher his notes which were coded and cryptic, and since it was his policy to enforce a strict informational blackout on all his students when they accompanied him on any of his digs, and this policy was carried out by opening their mail and screening phone calls among other things, what he was searching for, as well as what he might have actually discovered during the last three years of his Palenque project, had remained a complete mystery — both to the scientific world and the international police community. It remained a mystery, that is until my quite accidental involvement in the entire affair just a few months ago.

It started when a note arrived at the home of Professor Irwin and Jeanne Lewis, whose daughter, Karen, was a member of the ill-fated team. The note read, simply: "Please help me. I'm alive. Start at Palenque. Love Karen..."